Mr. Jory

By WILBUR HALL

WILDSIDE PRESS

This book is for
Mary and Radford and Ruth
and for their Lovely Mother.

*"Once I passed through a populous city,
imprinting my brain, for future use,
with its shows, architecture, creations,
and traditions . . . ."*
From *Leaves of Grass*

CHAPTER ONE

———◆———

```
┌─────────────────────────────────┐
│                                 │
│            THIS LOT             │
│          F O R   S A L E        │
│     ROWLAND — REAL  ESTATE      │
│             ———◆———             │
│                                 │
│        POPULATION OF L. A.      │
│          Now . . . . . 52,000   │
│          1900 . . . . 100,000   │
│                                 │
└─────────────────────────────────┘
```

IN THE LATE afternoon on Sundays the tall consumptive youth would leave the Luke farm in the San Fernando Valley with his two-horse load of fruit and vegetables and drive over the Pass and down through Hollywood village and thence on dusty roads between the fields to Los Angeles. His name was Adam Jory, and he had come west only a few weeks before.

He had made a good dicker, he told Simeon Luke, with the man who ran the Tally-Ho Stables. A dollar to tie Mr. Luke's team in, another dollar for two old plugs to pull the wagon about the streets all day Monday and, in exchange for his breakfasts and for supper, what oranges, figs, apples, potatoes or other garden sass Mrs. Thrasher needed. He would be back at the farm by ten or eleven Tuesday mornings and start off for town again Wednesday and Friday evenings. Back in Urbana Doc Musgrove had said he wouldn't live a year if he tried to lift a hand to work, but Doc had been wrong. Adam picked up steadily, was soon free of the daily fever, was developing a lusty appetite and putting on weight.

Alex Thrasher bought and sold horses and mules and pretty soon he found out that this Jory boy knew stock and was a brisk trader. So Adam branched out, bringing in animals from the Valley for the liveryman to dispose of.

With his first hundred dollars he bought a corner lot out on Vermont Avenue and a year or so later when a carline began to build that way he sold for a thousand. He hadn't been surprised at this development, because, on his rounds, he had noticed a surveying crew working along Sixteenth, Union, over to Vermont, and he had put this and that together. Old Mr. Luke, chuckling, said Adam would make out — he kept his eye peeled for the main chance.

Still doing just that, Jory put his thousand dollars back into Los Angeles real estate.

In the fall of 1892 he answered a want ad in the *Daily Sun*. The newspaper wanted a solicitor to hustle advertisements and subscriptions. The monthly pay would be forty dollars and commissions. Something about his quiet assurance interested the manager and, even though Adam had had no experience, he got the job.

He sold his fruit-peddling business to a man from Keokuk, said good-bye to Simeon Luke and his wife and moved his meager possessions into a room on West Fourth Street, at the edge of the growing business district. At The People's Store he bought a suit, three shirts, half a dozen celluloid collars, a ready-tied cravat and a pair of lace shoes.

In his first month he cleared sixty dollars. He made the down payment on another lot.

One hot afternoon that summer he noticed a new sign

2

being painted on a window in the open lobby of the Y.M.C.A. Building at Second and Broadway, so he walked in. There he found a young man about his own age and something of his own tall, thin build.

"Are you Mr. Rowland?"

"That's me."

"I notice you're a real Los Angeles booster."

"You mean my sign?" The stranger grinned in friendly fashion. "What do you think of it?"

"It's a smart notion — guessing on the population."

"Maybe you think I'm shooting pretty high saying we'll double in ten years."

"You'll get a lot of fun poked at you. But I think you're right."

"I don't care if they make fun. They'll talk about me."

"That's what advertising is supposed to do. I dropped in to talk to you about it. My name's Jory. I'm rustling ads for the *Daily Sun*."

Rowland offered his hand. "Glad to know you, Mr. Jory. I wish I could afford a *Sun* ad. But opening up here has about strapped me."

"Maybe you've got a lot or two you'd swap."

"You mean you'd give me an ad for a lot?"

"I'd dicker."

Presently Adam Jory had a memorandum of sale for a lot out on Pico Street in a tract that the agent said was staked out in a barley field, and William Rowland had a receipt for ten insertions of a 4-inch, 2-column display advertisement, one to run on a Sunday.

The agent put his paper in a file. "I'm sort of surprised Major Oddie is taking lots in trade. I thought — "

"The *Sun* isn't taking your lot. I am. I'll pay cash for your ads and get my commission back."

Rowland laughed. "So that's it?"

"That's it. And I'll tell you something else. You say you've got twenty-odd lots in that tract of yours?"

3

"Twenty-six left."

"I'd raise the price on them."

"How's that?"

"I'm not spreading it around, but those two new men, Sherman and Clark are planning to run an electric line to Santa Monica Beach. The line will have to go somewhere along where your tract is."

"No!" Rowland slapped his thigh. "That's why you were so ready to make a trade, eh?"

Adam Jory didn't smile. "One of the reasons." He put his papers into an inner pocket and walked to the door. "Los Angeles has got something no place in America has, Rowland — and it's something a whole lot of people are going to hurry out here to buy a piece of when the word really gets around."

"What's that?"

"This sunshine. The climate. Don't worry about your guess on the population being too high. Good-bye. Maybe we can do some more business together as time goes along."

He went out into the hot street, down which the regular afternoon sea breeze from the southwest was just beginning to stir refreshingly. He took a deep breath — and he did not cough after it.

A profitable adjunct to the *Daily Sun* was its job-printing department, and part of Adam Jory's work as a solicitor came to include picking up business for this shop. So, to consult the foreman or pick up a proof or get a sample layout, he was in and out here several times a week.

It seemed to him that the employees were about as silent and colorless as any he'd ever seen; they looked as though they were parts of the machines they operated and as though the boss might shut them off at five o'clock, cover them with dust cloths and leave them with their presses and cutters and stitchers, to start them all up together the next morning.

But after a time, coming and going in the plant, Adam began to be conscious of one of the workers who was different.

Under a row of grimy windows in the rear wall of the shop were long benches at which women worked, stuffing covers, folding, stitching, binding catalogues and so on. Among them was a handsome girl, taller than the average; presently he was carrying away with him an impression of her dark beauty, her clear skin, her deft hands and especially of her eyes, that were large, gray, well-set and framed in long curling lashes. He began to think of her sometimes when he was on his way to the place. That's right — there was that woman. Clean looking. With a fine breadth of shoulders, a deep chest and shapely hips, that her big work apron could not conceal. He began making excuses to go back to the bindery tables, remembering that she always looked at him straight with her beautiful gray eyes and that she seemed always about to break into a smile of welcome.

He knew nothing of women. He remembered his mother only vaguely as a thin shadow, dying of consumption; his step-mother had proved cold, resentful of his father's inability to get ahead and callous to his own timid efforts to conciliate her. He had grown into a fragile, shy boy, then he had contracted the lung fever that had killed Judith Jory. Thereafter he had been compelled to put what energy he could muster into the fight to live. As a street peddler in Los Angeles he had encountered two or three women who were friendly and even cordial to him. He had cultivated their interest to make them better customers; it had never occurred to him that they might have had something more in mind.

But this girl in the print-shop impressed her image on him and he commenced to exchange greetings with her. Then he asked her a question about a job. She was quick and knew her business — seemed to know it better than old Whitten, the bindery foreman, did. He learned that her name was Beulah. Presently she was calling him Ad. No one had called him Ad since his mother's death.

One spring evening he found her alone in the rear of the shop. Except for the foreman and the bookkeeper, who were

5

in the front office wrestling with some tangle in the accounts, she was the last of the force to leave. She turned from the stained wash-bowl with a towel in her hands as he came up.

"Hello, Ad. I thought you might be in. It's about that Chamber of Commerce bulletin, isn't it?"

"That's right. But how did you know?"

She laughed. "Maybe I keep track of your jobs."

"Is it going to be ready tomorrow?"

"No. Whitten couldn't get the cover board. You'll have it Monday night, though."

"Thanks." He hesitated. "You going home?"

"Sure am."

"Which way?"

"Why don't you come along and find out?"

"Maybe I will."

He walked with her up the hill to Temple Street and they boarded a cable-car, westbound, finding seats on the gripman's dummy, facing out. Beulah took off her big, flower-laden hat, brushed back her thick, chestnut-colored hair and breathed deeply.

"This ride gets some of the smell of printers' ink out of my system," she said, smiling at him.

"How about that glue you use in the bindery?"

"Oh, that! I'll smell it all my life, most likely."

The little car jerked and rolled, was stopped and jolted into motion again, up and down the low hills of West Temple Street. Passengers alighted and went hurrying off, following the cross-streets, or turning in at the more pretentious homes along the carline. Farther out shabbier men and a few tired women plodded away towards mean little shoeboxes that were almost shacks. But even the humblest of these were brightened by beds and borders of early flowers and many had lawns, fresh and green after the rains. There were many trees: the ever-present palms, a few oranges and lemons, groups of eucalyptus, tall, impressive, with their cinnamon-colored bark stripping loose; there were rows of weeping pepper trees with

6

their fernlike leaves and the sharp smell of their oil that gave them name. And, in the hills, the air was fresh and warm, with a faint tang of sea-salt in it, carried inland by the gentle southwesterly breeze.

A different, heavy smell cut through to them. On both sides of the carline, here and there, rose ugly, stark frameworks of timbers, carrying cables on giant pulleys, supporting long lengths of piping, and these and the ground, the nearby houses and trees were stained with thick black smears.

"That man Doheny!" Beulah said, with a sniff. "Him and his oil! He's going to ruin this part of town."

"I hear a good deal of talk about oil. I'm wondering if there'll be money in it."

"Dad Kerner thinks so."

"Who's he?"

"I live with them. You'll meet him at the house."

"Is he in the oil business?"

"He's an inventor. Dirt poor now, but he thinks he has some kind of oil dingus that will make a fortune."

When they left the car Beulah led the way northward along a street of weather-worn old houses in need of paint and repairs. She turned in at the middle of the block to a house seedy like the rest but with the yard kept up and the windows shining and neatly curtained. In the rear was a barn surrounded by miscellaneous heaps and piles of rusty iron, pipes, rods, chains, boilers and such mongery; from a lean-to a smoke-stack protruded and from it a thin wisp of smoke rose lazily. Machinery whirred and clanked and pounded in the building.

"Mr. Kerner works there at his inventions," Beulah explained. "His wife has a time getting him to quit for meals."

A motherly, plain woman came to the door of the house. She was taking off a white apron and this she rolled into a neat bundle as she met Adam Jory.

"Mr. Jory works for the *Sun*. He's going to have supper with me," Beulah said.

"Oh, I couldn't do that," Adam broke in, flustered.

7

"Of course you can. Sit down and visit with Mrs. Kerner while I get something stirred up."

"Maybe I could help some way."

"If I need you I'll yell."

Mrs. Kerner sat down in a creaking rocker on the front porch. "That stool is pretty wobbly, Mr. Jory. You better try the hammock." She began to fan herself with a folded newspaper, rocking back and forth contentedly. She was kind, matter-of-fact, friendly.

Jory said: "Beulah didn't say anything about me eating with you folks. I thought I was just coming out for the car ride. I don't want to put you out."

"You won't be putting anybody out. I guess Mrs. Rountree didn't explain things. You see, she uses our kitchen and fixes her own meals. We eat at different times. So if anybody's put out it'll be her — and I don't think she's much put out, do you?"

Adam laughed with her. "No. She seemed to want me to stay."

Mrs. Rountree. Jory had never heard her name before. Married, eh? Then there would likely be a Mr. Rountree showing up pretty quick. He felt a little disappointed. But not surprised, really. He might have known that a woman as handsome and jolly as Beulah wouldn't be allowed to stay single very long.

When she appeared again she was wearing a fresh white shirtwaist and a full, long tan skirt, with a bright-colored gingham apron tied on. She had let her hair down and it hung in two heavy braids, one over her shoulder, one down her back. She looked younger; she was prettier than ever.

"Are you hungry, Ad?"

"I certainly am."

"Come and get it, then."

He followed her through a long, dark hall to the kitchen.

"I could have set the table in the dining room. But I like it better here. It's homier."

8

It was a large, old-fashioned room, spotlessly clean, with gay curtains at the windows, a worn linoleum underfoot, a small deal table set in the middle under a hanging coal-oil lamp. There was a gleaming range in one corner, and cupboards and shelves displayed china and glassware or shining pots and pans. A cabinet clock ticked cozily away on a bracket above the sink. The place was filled with appetizing smells. Beulah handed Adam a fresh towel and he washed up at a basin on the back porch.

"You're a wonder," he said, as he pulled up his chair. "How did you manage to get all this ready so quick?"

"I didn't dawdle; I guess that's it. Help yourself, Ad."

He saw there was no third place set.

"Mrs. Kerner told me your name," he said, bluntly. "I never knew you were married."

"No? Well, really I'm not. I was. There's gravy in that covered boat. Do you like parsnips?"

It was the first home meal he had eaten since leaving Simeon Luke's farm. It seemed delicious to him. And he found Beulah a joy — relaxed, full of fun, alert to make him comfortable and to stuff him with food. She had evaded talk about that husband, and Adam Jory was not curious. His spirits rose. She wasn't married any longer, at any rate.

He insisted on helping her do up the dishes. They frolicked like children — as he never had, child or man. In one tussle Jory dropped a plate and broke it.

She gave him a hand-brush and he got down on his knees to sweep up the pieces. She brought a dustpan and knelt to hold it for him. With the last fragment whisked on to the pan he looked up. Beulah's face was close to his. She was laughing, her lips parted, red, moist, tempting.

He kissed her, a hard, square smack.

"I wondered when you were going to get around to that," she said, in a low voice.

When the kitchen was tidy they went out to the front

porch again. Night had fallen and the moon was coming up, big and pumpkin-yellow over the mountains, where some fields of snow still clung. Houses and trees were silhouetted in the foreground and a glamorous glow transformed the drabness of the neighborhood. A gnarled, shabby, quick-moving little old man sat on a top step, pulling spasmodically at an unlighted pipe.

"Mr. Kerner, this is Ad Jory," Beulah Rountree said.

"Pleased to meet you, Jory. Myra tells me you work at Beulah's place."

"That's right."

"What do you do there?"

"Now, pa," Mrs. Kerner warned, from her rocking chair.

"What's the matter? Is it some sort of secret, young man?"

"Of course not. I rustle ads for the *Sun*. Ads and printing jobs — that sort of thing."

"Make pretty good at it?"

"Why, Gus Kerner!"

"It's all right, Mrs. Kerner," Jory said. "I'm doing pretty good — for now."

"For now, eh? Figuring on getting something better pretty quick?"

"I don't say that. Maybe I'll stay with the *Sun*. It's a good place to pick up pointers. And I'm looking for places to put my money to work, when I get some."

"Maybe you think Los Angeles is going to be quite a town."

"Nothing to stop it. And fortunes are going to be made here."

Beulah Rountree had been listening attentively; she was watching Adam Jory. Now she said: "I've been telling Mr. Jory you expect a lot of money to be made in oil some day, Dad."

The old man twisted around to face Adam. "You interested in oil?"

"I've heard a good deal of talk about it. Seems like nobody has found any way to use the stuff much."

10

Mr. Kerner jumped up. He did nothing quietly, deliberately; he jerked, fussed, pulled at his pipe, knocked it against the step, filled and lighted it, then forgot to draw until it would go out. He was a bundle of nervous energy.

Now he said sharply: "Want to take a look at something I've got out back?"

"Look, pa," his wife protested once more, "maybe the young folks —"

"I'd like to see, Mrs. Kerner," Jory interrupted. He was interested in this fidgety old man. He saw that inner force — drive — that would not let him rest, sit, relax. "Excuse me, Beulah."

"Oh, she'll come along," Kerner said. "She's up to snuff, Beulah is."

There was no smoke coming from the lean-to now and the machinery in the barn was still. It was a cluttered and disorderly work-shop, littered and crowded with all sorts of machines, intact or half-dismantled, with tools, pipes, coils of wire, bars and plates of iron; there was a smith's forge in one corner and lathes, punches, presses lined up under a pulley-shaft that ran overhead, with blackened loops of belting hanging limply down. There were odors of grease, coal gas, metals and that heavy smell of crude oil that Jory had noticed coming out through the well field. Kerner turned up a hanging lamp near the door and lighted another in the middle of the floor.

"That's my wool-carding machine over there," he explained, waving a hand. "And a new deep-well pump I'm trying to figure out. But they're put by for now. I've got something better here."

He led them to where a small horizontal boiler sat on a brick firebox in the middle of the dirt floor. Nearby was a drum of crude oil; from it a small pipe ran to the front of the furnace, where was a clumsy device of valves and tubes with a sort of snout poking into the firebox. Kerner squatted here.

"You know anything about engines and such, Jory? Do you see what I'm up to?"

11

"It looks like you're going to heat your boiler with oil. But that don't mean I know anything about machines."

"You'll learn. Look here." He turned a valve and oil began to drip from the fan-shaped snout into the firebox opening. He took out a block of California sulphur matches, broke one off, struck it and held the flame under the dropping oil. The match went out.

"Doheny's oil is too heavy to burn," he explained. "If I heat the pipe that brings the oil to the furnace it makes a gas that will burn, but I can't get enough of that gas to make a hot flame." He reached for a crank at his elbow. "Now watch."

The crank rotated a fan, creating a draft of air; when the drops of oil were caught by this blast they turned to a sort of spray and this spray caught fire from another match. The flame was blown into the firebox and presently the interior began to glow with a rosy heat.

"I'm on my way to the answer now," Kerner said, rising and shutting off the oil. He wiped his hands on his grease-smeared pants, knocked out his pipe, refilled it. "The trick is to break up the oil drops. When I find the right way to do that I'll have a burner that will use all the oil Doheny and the rest of them can pump." His eyes sparkled. His pipe went out and he lighted it impatiently. "Damn the thing!" he said, irritably. But he forgot it at once. "There's no coal out here on the Coast; every ton we burn has to come from back east — to heat with, to run factories and locomotives. And here's this oil! I'm going to put it to work."

Jory was studying the burner. "Yes, you've got an idea here, all right. But it looks to me like your burner is too complicated."

"Yep, that's the hitch." Dad Kerner was suddenly depressed. "The oil has to be broke up, but my fan isn't the right way to do it."

"Broken up?"

"It's called atomizing it. To make the oil into a fine spray. Crude oil is too heavy, you see — runs too thick and slow."

12

"You mean your fan here isn't just to make a draft?"

"Oh, it makes a draft, but that ain't the idea. The idea is to atomize the oil. And it's got me stumped."

He went off into a brown study, muttering to himself.

Beulah Rountree squeezed Adam Jory's arm. "Come on," she whispered. "He's in one of his trances. You won't get another word out of him." She led him away.

On the front porch Mrs. Kerner gave a start. She sat up straight with an apologetic laugh.

"I must've dropped off to sleep. Well, Mr. Jory, did you get all the inventions you can stand for one evening."

Jory replied quietly: "It was mighty interesting, Mrs. Kerner. But I guess I'd better be getting along now."

Beulah Rountree didn't try to keep him. "Good night, Ad. You'll be out again, won't you, soon?"

"I will if I'm invited."

"You'll be invited, all right. Dad Kerner will invite you, even if I should forget."

He was soon going to the Kerner's frequently — and not only to be with Beulah Rountree.

He had made up his mind that Gus Kerner was on the track of big proposition with that fuel oil burner notion. It was a fact that the crude petroleum producers were finding their oil a drug on the market only because there was no known way to put it to work as a substitute for expensively imported coal. The man who discovered that way would become a powerful factor in an industry that, Jory realized, might grow to enormous proportions. The old inventor would never be that man; he probably wouldn't care to be. His interest was in ideas — methods. He would be content with enough money to enable him to get on with his other notions. All right; that could be seen to.

Jory was a reserved young man; no one would ever describe him as a hail-fellow-well-met. But he had solid qualities that gave others confidence in him — in his judgment, his balance, his capacities. He wasted no time or strength in drinking, sociability, amusements. Older men said of him that he had his head screwed on the right way. They could do business with him. Moreover, now that he had got the upper hand over his disease, he was beginning to fill out and to put on weight that gave his big-boned frame an increasing look of strength and power. There was no doubt that he was a comer.

He was having good success as solicitor for the *Sun*. He was making more money and meantime his eye was always peeled for the main chance. Pretty soon his mind was made up that the oil industry was that chance.

Some weeks after his first introduction to the Kerners, Jory inserted a want ad of his own in the *Sun*, without mentioning that it was his.

> Fine opening for Mechanic. Experienced man who understands engines wanted to develop mechanical device. Wages and an interest to right man. Box 35, Sun.

He had plenty of answers. Times were hard all over the country; the Republicans blamed conditions on Cleveland; the farmers were in a revolt against "Wall Street" and many of them were joining the Populist Party. In Los Angeles there were many men out of work, although conditions were not as bad here as elsewhere.

Jory studied the letters he received — interviewed two or three applicants. None suited; finally he went to look up the writer of a letter he liked. He found that Jernigan, in a poor shell of a house out south of Jefferson Street, was a straightforward Yankee, very hard up. Jernigan was no talker and he didn't complain. But he had a sick wife and three small children and he made it plain that he was desperately anxious for a job.

Jory questioned him closely; he was soon satisfied that this was his man.

"It looks like you haven't any money to invest in this proposition, Jernigan."

The mechanic's face fell. "If it takes money, I'm the wrong fellow for you, Mr. Jory."

"I can find the money. But if you come with me you'll have to show the same interest as if your cash was in the business. For instance, you'll have to keep a close mouth."

"Look at me!" Jernigan cried, strongly moved. "Look at this shack we're living in. You've seen my three little girls. Them and my wife are beginning to get hungry. Do you think I'd talk about your business if you gave me a chance to earn wages again?"

Adam Jory wrote out an address. "I'll meet you there tomorrow morning at seven-thirty." Not on impulse, for he was rarely impulsive, he handed Jernigan a five-dollar gold piece. "That's not an advance," he said; "it's to bind the bargain."

He hurried away. He disliked being thanked.

Keeping his own counsel Jory had rented a dilapidated, abandoned blacksmith shop on Aliso Street, near the river, and had moved to it one of Dad Kerner's burners and a second-hand boiler he had picked up cheaply. Jernigan was waiting for him at this place the next morning — had been there for an hour, afraid of being late.

He was quick at understanding the problem his new employer put to him. Adam had a vague notion of his own about perfecting the burner; Jernigan thought it might work out.

"We'll figure it through, Mr. Jory. And don't you ever worry about me not keeping it to myself." He added awkwardly, "My woman wanted I should thank you again for that five dollars. We had beef last night, and this morning there was plenty of milk for the girls."

"All right. You get at this burner." Adam left him.

He had entered into a loose partnership with Gus Kerner, paying two hundred dollars for "an interest" in the project and undertaking to put up what cash was needed for further experiments. He hadn't told the old man about putting someone else at work on the burner — had explained that he had found a man who would install it for a practical test. What he did not

15

know was that Dad Kerner had been just as reticent — hadn't mentioned that he had applied for a basic patent on the idea.

In a few weeks Jernigan had gone far enough to give a demonstration of the burner he had tinkered up, using steam — a modification of Jory's own idea — to atomize the heavy oil. The nozzle he had contrived was not perfect, but an important step had been taken.

"All right, Jernigan," Adam said, "tear it down and start over. But first you'd better make me some sort of drawing of the contraption. I'm going to get it protected."

A few days later he took Jernigan's sketch and description to a lawyer he had met in his work for the *Sun*. Judge Valentine asked for a retainer of a hundred dollars, explaining that half of that would have to be sent to the Washington patent expert whom he would engage to make the necessary showing there.

Jory drew out this amount. "Thanks, Mr. Valentine. Push the business along, will you? I don't want to let any grass grow under my feet."

That payment ate into Jory's savings, though he did not let that be known. From the beginning he had put everything he could spare into vacant lots; renting and fitting up the shop and hiring Jernigan had used most of his ready cash. He needed more capital — he knew that well. Right at the time, though, real estate was not moving. And he would not sacrifice anything, though he was full of the new idea of perfecting the burner, marketing it and getting into the oil business itself, so that he could take advantage of the opportunities he was sure the Kerner notion would open up. He meant to own oil land, drill wells, become a producer.

Meantime, while he was pondering this, Lawyer Valentine sent for him.

"Ingersoll has hit a snag in that oil-burner proposition, Jory."

"There must be ways to pull snags."

"There are ways. But the patent is going to cost you more

16

than I figured. Do you know of a man named Kerner?"

"Yes. What about him?"

"It seems that last year he applied for a basic patent on an atomizing oil burner nozzle. He's a Los Angeles man."

"That's right. Did he get the patent?"

"On his burner, yes. Ingersoll — that's my Washington associate — will have to make a showing that your device is different and new. This will cost at least three hundred dollars."

"Have him go ahead. When will you want the money?"

"No great hurry. A week or so will do."

"I'll have it here."

Unruffled Adam left the lawyer's office. Now he would certainly have to get rid of something to keep the burner project going. And he would have to put off, perhaps, another venture to which he was committed.

Pursuing his plan to get actively into oil production he had been canvassing property owners in the vaguely-defined oil-bearing area in the northwestern section of Los Angeles to find any who could be interested in his scheme. He had located two — a retired grocer and a woman, a school teacher, who were half persuaded to go in with him, on a share basis, they to provide the ground and he to finance drilling. He was determined not to let this program fall through. But now his immediate problem was to secure the oil-burner patent.

He was surprised to learn that old Gus Kerner had got ahead of him; he was more surprised that the inventor had been secretive about it. But he was honest enough with himself not to criticise: he and Kerner had both been sly. And he was not disturbed over the outcome. Two patents would be better than one and he was confident he could always handle the abstracted old genius. In any case he decided to let sleeping dogs lie. No use stirring Kerner up at this stage.

Adam's friendship with Beulah Rountree had ripened fast. In the print shop they spoke casually, and no one there could have guessed at their meetings at the Kerner home.

Busy though he was, Adam Jory had given some thought to that friendship, intimacy — had speculated on how far it might go and on whether he wanted it to deepen. His instinct was to be cautious. At times he regretted that impulsive first kiss, and he had not kissed Beulah again for some time. But in the end he had acquired the habit of bidding her good night that way. He could not make out whether she was particularly interested in his caresses or not. She was frank and easy — almost like another man in most of their relations, yet he had a feeling that she held strong emotions in leash, sometimes with an effort. She liked to be with him and he with her. They did not talk of this, but each knew that the other knew.

By gradual degrees Adam had fallen into another habit in his friendship — one that was surprising, when he thought of it, to himself. He had begun talking to her about his business plans and projects. Beulah never showed any surprise at his revelations, never asked probing questions, never brought the subject up. This tact of hers made him feel easier, on the rare occasions when he scolded himself for being so gabby. And it was a relief and a comfort to have somebody with whom he could talk.

One evening when they were sitting on the Kerner front porch, after another of Beulah's good little dinners, Adam told her that he was applying for a patent on the burner. Dad Kerner was hammering and clattering away in his barn workshop and Myra Kerner had gone to a church meeting.

"I thought you were up to something, Ad," she observed. "You're sort of worried about it, too — about that or something else."

"Worried? That's foolish."

"All right. Have it your own way." She laughed at him gently. "But don't try to fool me, Ad. You can't, you know."

He had to smile back at her. "Maybe you're right about that, Beulah. And maybe I've been worrying some, too."

"It's about money, isn't it? This patent business costs a good deal."

18

"Well, not a great deal, yet. But I'll admit I'm a little short."

"Would a thousand dollars help any?"

Adam turned to her. "Why?"

"I can let you have that much."

"You? Where would you get a thousand dollars?"

She laughed. "Oh, I haven't been robbing the *Sun*. It's mine. I've saved part of it. I screwed a little out of Jeff Rountree when we split up, if you've got to know. You can have it tomorrow if you want it."

He didn't waste time or words thanking her; it did not occur to him to ask her if she knew what she was doing.

"I can use it. It would get me over this hump. I'll give you security enough to — "

"If you talk like that I won't give it to you, Ad!"

He apologized.

"All right." She sat back. "No use letting the shop know anything. I'll draw it out at noon, then you can drop by for it any time."

He did not kiss her good night when, shortly, it was time for him to leave. Instead, he shook hands with her — for the first time, as he remembered later. In the faint glow from a street light he saw that she turned red as a peony.

Striding off toward Temple Street and the carline he wondered at that. But soon he was thinking of something else.

It was of his next step in the climb upwards in Los Angeles. The next step — and the next. In fact he thought that he could see several steps in the long, slow, ascent — long, slow, but now sure.

When one of his staff spies reported to Major Oddie that the mechanical force of the *Daily Sun* was organizing a union that winter he flew into a rage, firing the ringleaders summarily and defying the rest, not through his subordinates inside the office but in a screaming editorial on the front page of the paper, for the whole town to read.

Angry at this, where they had been peaceable before, the crew struck, except for a few old fellows and a handful of the timid or cowed. For a day or so the situation was tense. But Oddie and his foremen managed to get together a skeleton crew and presently a complete force was at work, made up of more or less experienced printers and pressmen from the ranks of the unemployed or those weaned away from the two other struggling Los Angeles papers.

There was much bitterness and a few fights, but Major Oddie broke the strike. Later, some of the men came back asking to be forgiven and put to work again. Major Oddie turned them away in a fury. They were on his black list. Never would one of them have employment on the *Sun* again. And, still raging, the editor declared open war on all labor unions, a few of which were just beginning to get a foothold in the Southland. He raged that Los Angeles should never be shackled by the agitators and strong-arm thugs of the labor-union movement: it was to be an "open-shop" city.

This was the beginning of a long, turbulent and costly war, merciless and exhausting on both sides. And, as long as he lived Major Oddie led the forces of the employers.

In the middle of the *Sun* strike the owner sent for Adam Jory.

"Whitten and Young have walked out of the job department," he said, in his harsh, angry fashion. "I've made Tellet foreman. But he's no manager. I'm giving you the print shop."

"I don't know anything about printing, Major."

"Learn, then. I've been watching you. Take hold." He turned his back. "That's all."

"That isn't quite all. What do you mean to pay me?"

The owner bristled. "Huh! Looking out for Number One, eh? All right. A hundred and twenty-five a month."

"I'll take it for three months. If you want me to stay on after that you'll have to double it."

The Major snorted again. It was a habit of his. "Huh! Well, see that you're worth it. Now get out."

20

This unexpected promotion put a new pressure on Adam. He had been devoting all his spare time to his other interests; now he would have to work longer days.

Attorney Valentine at length had an encouraging report from Washington: it was certain that the atomizing nozzle Jernigan had perfected would be granted a patent. At once Jory put the mechanic at making burners and presently had induced three small manufacturers to install the devices for a practical test. The results were encouraging; two burners sold outright and other orders began to trickle in.

Meantime Jory had signed up with old Mr. Coleman and with the school teacher, Eliza Winter, to sink test wells on their lots on a share basis. He found a pair of husky youths with experience in boring water wells and talked them into gambling their skills with his capital, which he invested in machinery and tools. He had little difficulty in obtaining the latter from the Paynter Iron Foundry with a small cash payment down because, as he saw at once, Josiah Paynter assumed that Major Oddie and the *Sun* were behind the project. He did not correct the founder's impression. He had known before that his connection with the newspaper and its owner was a definite asset to him and he had no scruples about taking advantage of the fact.

These private activities required more capital, however, and although he had an ingrained horror of debt he finally borrowed two thousand dollars at his bank, giving his real estate as security. The loan was so easily negotiated that he began to realize that his early prejudice was groundless. It was not many years before he was borrowing tens of thousands, casually and without a thought.

He was increasingly crowded for time. It was true that he knew nothing of the printing business; now he not only had to keep orders coming in but he was confronted with the tasks of obtaining and holding skilled workmen, buying materials and supplies, figuring costs and fixing prices, learning something of the mysteries of type-faces and make-up, of style and the suitability of typography and format to the job involved —of the fine art of printing. Driven by necessity he learned fast. And not even the veterans in the shop ever guessed how rough the going was for him; characteristically he put on a bold and confident front and never showed any uncertainty or doubt of himself.

The office end of the business was simpler for him. At the first he found that the accounts were a confused jumble, having been kept after a system of her own invention by a middle-aged and ineffectual woman who had taken them in charge when the job-office was opened. Adam Jory discharged her immediately and borrowed a gangling youth from the *Sun's* business office to fill in until a competent hand could be found.

At about this time Jory was told that he was wanted at the counter and went out to find Walter Young, who had been shop foreman up to the time of the strike. Young was a man only a little older than Adam but he had been a printer since he was fourteen and, besides being a first-rate workman, had developed natural capacities as a leader. He was patient and he was kindly; though most of the shopmen were his seniors they had approved of his steady promotions and had backed him loyally. At the same time his qualities had made him influential with them when the organization of a union came up and, in the end, he had been one of the leaders in the movement and had been among those discharged by Oddie for that reason.

Adam Jory faced Young sternly. "You're wasting your time coming to me, Young. There's no place for you in a *Daily Sun* plant."

Walter Young colored but he did not falter. "I'm not asking for myself, Mr. Jory, though I could use a job. I heard that Miss Stebbins had left you."

"The bookkeeper. Yes."

"Well, the young woman who kept the want-ad accounts in the *Sun* office is still out of work. She supports her father and mother; she's having a hard time. I thought maybe you'd

22

be willing to give her a chance."

"How did she lose her place with the *Sun?*"

"She — she went out when the rest of us did. She felt that she ought to be loyal to the —"

"Now she's found that loyalty to the *Sun* would have paid better, eh? No, Young; you know Major Oddie's rule. People who aren't satisfied to do their work and mind their own affairs aren't wanted here. The *Sun* treats its people fair and pays well. But Major Oddie runs the business."

Young said, patiently: "You don't think, then, Mr. Jory, that workers have certain rights —"

"They have just one right, to do what they're told. But when they try to tell the owner how to manage his plants they're out. The *Sun* will have nothing to do with trouble-makers and anarchists."

Young sighed. "I hope the time will come, Mr. Jory, when you'll begin to think a little about other rights — human rights. Because if you and the other bosses don't see into things a little deeper the poor devils you call anarchists and trouble-makers will be driven to throwing bombs and making trouble that will turn Los Angeles into a battlefield." Abruptly his face became gentler. "There, now, I didn't mean to say so much, Mr. Jory. These times are hard and I'm pretty worried, just being married and all, the way I am."

"You won't help yourself by going around preaching violence and talking about throwing bombs, Young; remember that."

Walter Young's shoulders sagged. "I don't preach violence, Mr. Jory — I'm just afraid of it. And if that sort of war ever comes, then God help Los Angeles."

He turned away.

Adam Jory put the incident out of his mind, but he was to remember it many times, in the long years ahead.

A few nights later, while Adam Jory was engaged in taking an inventory of stock, he heard someone rattling the locked

front door of the shop. Through the heavy glass he saw Beulah
Rountree.

"What are you doing here?" he asked, when he had admitted her. In these crowded weeks he had not had much time
for her.

"I came back to see if I could help you some way."

"Well, you might. Sure, you can."

She was already taking off her light coat. She went for her
work-apron and came back to the stock shelves tying the
strings.

"What's first, boss?" she asked, smiling.

Thereafter she returned every night. Two or three times
they worked for a while after the printers had left, went out
for a quick supper together, then hurried back to drudge away
until a late hour. There was no rollicking now. Jory was en-
grossed in the task and Beulah took her cue from him.

On the third Saturday evening she came in from the shop to
his desk in the littered front office with her broad-brimmed and
flower-bedecked hat in her hand.

"You're not going to work tonight, Ad," she said, briskly.

"Of course I am."

"I say you're not. You're tuckered out. You don't know it,
maybe, but I've been watching you. First thing you know you'll
be sick again."

Jory pushed away from his desk. His hands fell to his
knees.

"I am tired," he admitted. "But a few nights more will
finish things up. You go on, Beulah. There's nothing for you
to do anyway."

She reached over and pulled down his roll-top desk cover.
"You're not going to work either. Not tonight nor tomorrow
all day. We're going to the beach."

"Wait a minute. I never heard such nonsense. What would
we do at the beach?"

"Tonight we'll listen to the band concert and take a walk
in the moonlight. Tomorrow we'll rent suits and go swimming

24

and lie in the sun and talk and maybe hunt for clams or hire some poles and fish off the pier." She spoke in a matter-of-fact tone, brightly and without hesitation. She took his acquiescence for granted.

"I'll admit it sounds good," he said, slowly. "I believe I'd like to go down tomorrow morning. I guess I could spare a day without everything falling to pieces."

She was adjusting her hat, facing a little fly-specked mirror Miss Stebbins had put up — the gray-haired bookkeeper's single concession to vanity. Beulah placed her long hat-pins expertly. She adjusted the lace fichu of her shirtwaist.

"Oh, come on, Ad," she said, in a softened tone. "Don't be so damned prissy. Get a wiggle on you. We're going down tonight."

CHAPTER TWO

WHEN SAN FRANCISCANS heard of the prophetic real estate signs of Will Rowland they scoffed and jeered. It was like that bumptious village of sleepy greasers, Iowa yokels and coughing invalids to vaunt itself. A population of 100,000 by 1900! It was not only nonsense but it was stupid impertinence.

For San Francisco was the metropolis of the whole Pacific slope and so destined by the Almighty. It was the financial hub of the West, one of the first seaports of the world, the "Door to the Orient," the appointed center of the arts and sciences, the home city of the millionaires of The Gold Rush of '49, the Comstock Lode and the Central Pacific Railroad grab, whose stately mansions crowned Nob Hill. It was the temple of industry, commerce and culture and certainly the very Holy of Holies of Society.

What was *El Pueblo de Nuestra Senora la Reina de Los Angeles de la Porciuncula* — the Town of Our Lady, the Queen of the Angels of "the Little Portion?" Snf-snf! It was merely an agglomeration of adobe huts, unplastered frame "bungalows," two-story wooden business blocks, a few with false fronts of brick, a superfluity of ugly churches, a "University" with a faculty of a dozen superannuated Methodist preachers and a large barn where cattle-fairs, prize-fights and the exhibitions of Gentry, the horse-tamer, alternated (still redolent of those earthy entertainments) with lectures on foreign climes, rare, second-rate concerts and the occasional appearance of a traveling opera company with its tawdry little repertóire. San Francisco called it LA, slightingly. Stung, Major Oddie, of the *Daily Sun,* spelled out the name phonetically — Loce Anghhai-lais — and entreated his readers to conform; most of them balked, continued to speak of their home-town variously as Lahs Angaluss, Luss Anglise, Lass Anjelus, La Sangluss, 'S Anjluss, and, in the end, as easiest and least Spanish, simply Loss. San Francisco chuckled — and made aggressive and embittered war on those aliens and outcasts who referred to their city as 'Frisco.

Meantime they admitted that Los Angeles had a climate salubrious for the sick, who had gone there — and welcome! They knew that the railroads, starving for business, had launched a campaign to tempt tourists southward; by dint of spending a fortune and blanketing the Middle West with dubious whoop-la they had aroused a good deal of curiosity and some passengers; finally, in a punishing cut-rate war culminating in 1886 with a fare as low as one dollar each way, they had filled their trains and precipitated a boom of considerable proportions. But now the boom had collapsed — the bubble had burst. And yet some bumptious vendor of vacant lots was predicting a 1900 population almost a third as great as that of the metropolis! Ridiculous!

Los Angeles took these sneers with bad grace, even though the most optimistic could scarcely share Rowland's roseate views. The wave of hard times had at last washed west and business and real estate values sank to sickening levels. Even under the most favorable conditions 100,000 seemed a large guess. And the thin-skinned were put out of patience with the prophet for furnishing such handy ammunition to northern traducers.

Rowland went his way unruffled. He had unbounded faith in the city of his adoption. Energetic and resourceful, he whipped up trades, deals, sales, and leases enough so that his business prospered and he expanded his office. He employed a clerk and an outside salesman; there was a rug on his floor; he had acquired a large flat-top desk and installed a telephone. On one wall he hung the biggest map of Los Angeles and its environs obtainable and to this map he affixed little colored tags to indicate his listings. The map was a smart selling device. Above it was a framed illumination:

```
┌─────────────────────────────────┐
│                                 │
│       POPULATION OF L. A.       │
│       1900 . . . . 100,000      │
│                                 │
└─────────────────────────────────┘
```

Into this headquarters of optimism one day came Adam Jory. Rowland saw that he was filled out, well-dressed, looked healthy and prosperous. He had a manner impressive and assured.

"Why, Mr. Jory, I'm glad to see you. Have a chair."

Instead Jory crossed to the wall map. He put a large hand on an area in the northwestern part of town. "What have you got up here north of Westlake Park, Rowland?"

"Let's see. Right now, not a thing. That's a backward section. Another carline, of course — "

"I know." Jory turned from the map. "I'd be interested in something out that way, if the price is right. Twenty or thirty lots, maybe."

Rowland looked sharp. "Maybe you've got some inside information — "

"If I have it's my own, Rowland." This big young man stood solidly on his feet, his eyes revealing nothing, his face unreadable. The real estate agent began to feel a little awe of him, though he was not easily awed.

"Sorry. I didn't mean to pry. You want me to see what I can locate for you?"

"If it's worth your while."

"Of course. I'll get right at it."

"I've come here, Rowland, because I think you can keep your own counsel. Most real estate agents are too gabby. They run to the papers with every little sale they make. I suppose the idea is to advertise the growth of Los Angeles. I'm not interested in helping them that way."

"I understand. Certainly."

Jory turned to leave. "Don't let any grass grow under your feet, Rowland," he said.

Jory had come quite a way in the two years that he had been managing the *Sun* print-shop.

The business there had doubled and then doubled again under his hand. Major Oddie, who was notorious for talking brusquely and being hard to get on with, had grumbled and growled his satisfaction two or three times; what was more important he had raised his manager's salary as the profits increased. Finally Jory recommended enlarging the plant.

"What are you telling me for?"

"Because you'll have to sign the lease, Major." The ghost of a smile played around the big young man's mouth. "I've already told the owners that we'd take over that small building to the south of the plant on Broadway."

Major Oddie exploded. "You had a hell of a nerve! What rent do they ask?"

"A hundred and forty a month."

"I won't pay that."

Jory shrugged his square shoulders. "If you start haggling you'll end by paying more."

"Get out of here! No young upstart can tell me what to do."

Jory left.

Major Oddie opened his mouth to recall him. The editor was obdurate as a mule and Jory was the only man in his employ who ever stood up and talked straight to him. He didn't like the young man's independence — or thought he didn't.

He telephoned for his real estate agent and sent him to negotiate with the Widney family for the lease. In a day or so Mr. Marsh came back.

"They want a hundred and a half a month, Major."

"What?" Oddie's roar was heard in the editorial offices one floor up. "I won't pay a cent more than a hundred and a quarter. Tell Widney he'll take that or he can go to Tophet!"

The real estate agent said, weakly: "It's no use, Major. Somebody has already offered a hundred and forty."

"Go back and tell Widney's office I'll pay that, but not a penny more."

In the end he signed a five-year lease on the property at $160 a month with a proviso that the rate for a second term would be $175.

A week later when young Owens, Major Oddie's secretary, said that Adam Jory wanted to see him the Major let out one of his outraged roars.

"Tell him I'm not in — to him! The last time he was in here it cost me around a thousand dollars."

The scared young clerk stammered: "He said you would be mad, Major. But he wants you to approve the purchase of twenty-eight hundred dollars' worth of new machinery for the job department."

"Go out and tell Jory to leave me alone. If he can't run his plant without being wet-nursed I'll put somebody else there." The Major paused, frowned, added, on an impulse that was partly malicious: "Tell him I'll give the job to you!"

Little Ferdie Owens backed out.

Adam Jory was leaving. From the door he called back: "All right. I heard him."

In the next six months he was successful in securing the job of printing the Los Angeles Directory, a book for the Chamber of Commerce and a history of Southern California; the three contracts netted a few dollars more than enough to pay for the bindery machinery he had ordered and the first year's rental on the leased building.

Jim Jernigan had perfected the oil-burner, and a dozen of them had been sold, with orders beginning to come in for more.

30

One or two users had trouble with clogging feed-pipes; Jernigan studied that problem and then worked out a filter for the fuel oil that Lawyer Valentine had no difficulty in patenting for Adam Jory. Two workmen were put on and the Aliso Street blacksmith shop was torn down and a new, compact, up-to-date plant was erected in its place.

Then somehow Dad Kerner learned of all this. He came to see Jory, considerably exercised.

"Looks a lot to me like you're aiming to steal my burner away from me, Jory," he cried. "If you try anything like that I'll law you, sure's you're a foot high."

Jory waited till the old man had finished. Then he said: "Keep your shirt on, Dad. Nobody's going to steal anything from you. I've advanced you money from the first and that money has come out of my own pockets. The burner hasn't begun to pay its way yet; when it does you'll be taken care of."

"Damnation, I don't want to be took care of!" He pulled at his pipe; knocked it out impatiently against the counter. "All I want is my rights and I'm going to have 'em."

"You are. You'll have to take my word for that. The burner is protected and you'll get your share of the profits." Adam added, carefully: "I've taken out some patents and everything is tied up tight."

The old inventor stared. "But — well, I guess I've never mentioned it, but I got a patent on the burner myself."

"So I heard. That's double protection, then."

"See here, though, Adam. Patents cost money. I know that much. What are they going to cost us?"

"They're paid for."

"You paid for them? Hm-m! Plague gone it, Adam, I'm sorry I busted out that way. But I'm so bothered about my new typesetting machine — one thing an' t'other — that I reckon I'm touchy. I always did say you had your feet on the ground." He loaded his pipe hurriedly and lighted it. "I feel better about things now." The pipe went out. "Dang the infernal dang thing!" he fumed, and went away at a half-trot.

After that first week end at the beach, Adam had rented a cottage there, and he and Beulah had made it a regular rendezvous all during the summer. At Santa Monica a few near neighbors knew them as Mr. and Mrs. Adams — a mere accidental bestowal — an easy solution for them. They were so quiet and homey that no one seemed to give them a thought or a doubt. Apparently they were quite free of suspicion — of gossip.

Now they were back in the city for the winter; Adam had come out for one of Beulah's suppers, and Dad Kerner welcomed him heartily.

"Want you should see a new idea of mine," he said.

He led the way into the kitchen, that was heated to suffocation. Mrs. Kerner, flushed and perspiring, wiped her face with her apron.

"Hello, Adam. This dratted contraption of Gus's is going to run me out of here yet," she grumbled. "I wish it was him had to cook over it."

The contraption was an oil burner for the cook-stove. Kerner moved a pot back and lifted a lid. "Never can satisfy a woman. Take a peek, Adam."

The firebox roared and swirled under orange-purple flames that took their fuel from a saucer-shaped casting set on the lower grates. A feed-pipe entered the stove and brought oil from a can set against the kitchen wall; the heat was so intense that the black fluid was changed to gas as soon as it hit the burner.

"Yes," Jory said, "it's a good idea. But it needs working on. You'll have to find a way to cut down the oil-feed."

Kerner sighed. "Sure! Sure, I know that. But I can't seem to figure out how. Wish you'd take the thing over, Adam. Let's see what you can do with it."

"All right, if you say so, Kerner."

Outside on the porch Adam said: "Is your wife put out with Beulah at all, Dad? About this beach business?"

"Myra? Not as I know of. 'Tain't our affair, I'd say."

"You don't object to having her stay here when she's in town?"

"Not a mite. Leastwise, not's far's I know."

"I see. All right."

When he left, swinging his arms, walking with long strides, later that evening, Dad Kerner thought he wasn't much like the slim, pale, puny bag-o'-bones he'd been when they first knew him. Los Angeles had done a lot for the young man, no doubt of that.

Then he had another thought. He turned it over in his mind slowly. After a minute or two he said to himself: "Los Angeles — and Beulah Rountree, mebbe."

Major Oddie sent for Jory one day.

"Max Meyberg has some kind of a meeting on, Jory. I'm damned if I'll go to meetings, but Max thinks this one is important. I want you to represent the *Sun*."

"What's the meeting about, Major?"

"I gather it's about the state of the Union. It's at the Saddlerock at noon."

"I don't eat at the Saddlerock. The prices are too high."

"Huh! Put the lunch on your expense account, then. Now get out."

Max Meyberg was a dealer in lamps and gas fixtures; he was an industrious and imaginative merchant who stood high in the community. Adam Jory had never met him; at John Brink's restaurant that day he found, in fact, that he had met only a few of those assembled. But one glance told him that here were the very top figures in the city — the ones he wanted most to know. They were the citizens who ran Los Angeles. And when they found that he represented Major Oddie and the *Sun* they welcomed him in friendly fashion — accepted him as one of themselves.

It was a handsome lunch, with the best of everything, and Meyberg insisted that he be permitted to act as host — pay the bill. He wouldn't talk business till after they had eaten.

33

Tiny glasses of port poured and fat cigars passed, Meyberg opened the proceedings.

"Los Angeles is in the dumps, gentlemen. Some people
think we'll never come out of them. If any of you feel that
way you'd better get your hats, because I don't want to waste
your time."

Grant Paynter, son of the iron founder, and a stolid, conservative young man, said morosely: "There's no use talking,
Meyberg, we've taken a setback. That damned boom the real
estate agents pumped up has burst and we'll be twenty years
recovering."

Thin, cool, dry little Charley Walton, himself a real estate
operator, said: "Somebody reach Grant his hat."

They laughed at that. Paynter colored, then said, sheepishly:
"Oh, I'm not going. But let's not start another boom."

Koepfli, the manufacturer, prompted: "Go on, Max."

"I'm afraid what I have in mind is just what Paynter is op-
posed to. I *want* to start another boom. I'm not afraid of booms.
Right now Los Angeles is suffering from a bad case of nerves.
I propose to give the patient a stimulant."

Several nodded. "What do you prescribe, doctor?" Leon
Loeb inquired.

"You folks know that Mama and I — Mrs. Meyberg —
well, we like to get around and see the world. We've gone
to every world's fair and that sort of thing we could reach.
We've taken in carnivals and celebrations — Oberammergau
and Rome and Paris; the Mardi Gras in New Orleans and
others.

"Those festivals attract thousands of visitors. They come to
see the fun, then they go home again. People that come to
Los Angeles don't go home, unless it's to pack up so they can
come out to stay."

"Are you proposing that we put on some kind of a fair
or show here?" Paynter interposed. "Why, damnation, man,
most of us are having a hard time paying our taxes. And
those shows cost a lot of money."

34

"Sure, they cost money," Meyberg agreed. "But they pay dividends, too." And, perfectly coolly, he proposed that those present contribute a fund of $25,000 to stage a great floral festival in Los Angeles during the next spring. Every man, woman and child was to be put to work on the preparations. The papers would fall in line and the news of this novel means by which the city was to lift itself by its own boot-straps would go all over the country. Outsiders would begin to believe that things were all right in the Southland; more important still, the local population would be imbued with the same optimistic idea.

Paynter and one or two others argued feebly against the project but they were soon silenced. The subscription list was passed around and in no time these "boosters" had pledged three-fourths of the sum suggested, with the balance to be secured from men who had been unable to attend the meeting. Meantime they were agreeing to constitute themselves an Executive Committee on arrangements and to meet in a fortnight to select sub-committees and plunge into details.

All this they did briskly and in businesslike fashion. If they had been organizing a close corporation for the launching of a big private venture they could not have been more diligent. They discussed the risks involved and set those over against the possible benefits to be gained. They were putting up their money and pledging their time and hard work for the cold-blooded reason that anything which profited the city profited them individually. It was a point of view that was to become universal in Los Angeles thereafter — that was to shape the whole future of the city.

Before they adjourned the chairman gave each of them a department to take care of; to his surprise Adam Jory, who had had little to say but that little strongly approving, was appointed head of the division of advertising and publicity.

That evening he went to Major Oddie's office to report.

"*Fiesta de las Flores* — huh! Where do they figure to get the money for this damned foolishness?" Oddie snorted.

Jory explained.

"Huh! Well, we'll give them all the space they want in the *Sun*. Might even do their printing at cost. That'll be our contribution."

"Oh, no, it won't, Major," Jory said. "I put the *Sun* down for a thousand dollars cash." Seeing the editor beginning to swell up and turn faintly purple he rose, walked to the door and there turned to add: "And I told them we'd raise the ante if they ran short."

Then he went out, closing the door quickly and hurrying off, the sounds of the publisher's bellowing and wailing pursuing him to the street.

As he expected, all that bellowing and wailing died away in a few days and before the week was up Major Oddie was saying in the *Daily Sun* (and believing in his heart) that, as a matter of fact, he had as good as thought up the Fiesta project himself and positively that it was one of the world's noblest ideas and should be carried through to a triumphant conclusion, under the aegis of Los Angeles' great family newspaper.

His inclusion on the Fiesta Committee, that had come about through the mere chance of Major Oddie's aversion to attending meetings, was a turning point in Adam Jory's career.

His job as solicitor for advertising had brought him into contact with a few important men but in no way that would make them remember him. He had done some business with the Paynter Iron Foundry in connection with his oil ventures and had met Grant, son of the head of that firm. But now, suddenly, he was associated with the real leadership of Los Angeles in a common cause; he handled himself well and soon they were all treating him as an equal, consulting with him and gradually giving him their friendship.

Characteristically he made these circumstances work for him. He had, for instance, tried unsuccessfully to get the two transcontinental railroads serving Los Angeles to give the *Daily Sun* printing plant a share of their business. But he had never been able to get past the clerks and assistants — had been turned aside with the brief explanation that all printing was contracted for by the head offices of the roads in the East. Now, as a Fiesta committeeman, he brushed by secretaries and went direct to the executives themselves.

They welcomed him as a friend and co-worker, since they were even more anxious than he to bring crowds of visitors to the Southland. They subscribed generously for their companies to the underwriting fund of the festival; they cooperated with Adam in his plan to flood their respective territories with advertising and publicity; they promised cut-rate excursions. Presently some of the higher officials of the roads began to appear in Los Angeles, attracted by the possibilities of this plucky venture; these men Jory contrived to meet.

The Fiesta project benefited from all this. And Adam Jory negotiated printing orders that eventually grew to considerable proportions. More important to him, he established connections which he was already planning to capitalize on when the proper time came — for his own personal and private account.

Yes, all was grist that came to Jory's mill. He was keeping his eye on the main chance.

There are still some hale and hearty Angelenos who remember well the thrill of those Fiestas of the '90's — recall them occasionally, and with pleasure.

There were day parades and night parades, culminating in the great "Festival of the Flowers" on Friday of Fiesta Week. Never any anticipation quite so deliciously painful as that with which, as youngsters, they waited with the throngs lining the downtown streets for the first distant sounds of a band, now heard, now lost, now certainly coming straight up Spring Street. Never any display of power quite so impressive as that made when, with Chief of Police Glass at their head, the sixteen mounted officers moved toward them, the pairs at either end of the platoon forcing the crowds back to the sidewalks and leaving the pavement looking suddenly clean-swept and awesomely wide.

Never was any single figure in history more elegant and heroic than that of Don Nicholas Covarrubias, born in the shadow of the Plaza Church sometime around 1835 and now, ramrod-straight, sitting his 90-pound, silver-encrusted saddle on his tall white horse, which pranced and pirouetted and minced and danced sidewise and even backwards till the tads thought they would choke before they really regained breath, driven out of them by admiration, worship and awe. Afterwards they were vaguely conscious of a double rank of vice-marshals who followed the stately old Don; these suffered somewhat by comparison, though, even while one knew that they were all famous and locally important citizens.

None so enviable as the wheelmen, on flower-decorated "bikes," high-wheeled and "safety," who formed a division immediately following The Native Sons' Silver Cornet Band. Why, each school-child wondered, wasn't he one of those who marched for the Department of Education, wreath-draped and blossom-bedecked, who tramped proudly by, *part* of them *sometimes* in step? After them another band and a long line of carriages containing the city's bigwigs — Tom Rowan, the Mayor, some Councilmen, a Judge or two, members of the Fiesta Committee and, in a *barouche,* several of the ladies of the Committee on Arrangements for the Queen's Ball. All these equipages more or less decorated, though nothing to compare with what was to come. But the eyes of the youngsters lighted up when they did recognize a familiar father. Gee! it's Mr. Rule, lives on Washin'ton, an' his kids is Roy and Ray, that go to Seventeenth Street. A real, live Committeeman, Mr. Rule! "Hey, Mr. Rule!"

"Hush up, Ernie! People are looking at you!"

Then the decorated carriages, dog-carts, victorias, broughams, brakes, drags and tally-hos, transporting the town's fairest daughters and a few stalwart sons (according to current newspaper accounts); more bands; more horsemen and their ladies; the entries of local lodges, fraternities and clubs — and another band. Then the floats! Dream-world fantasies, with such

38

titles as Star of the Sea, Harvest Time, The Battle of The Roses, The Old Oaken Bucket, The Ice King's Palace — ah, who could remember more than a few or describe any adequately? And the apparatus of the Fire Department! Golly whiz!

As for the Chinese Division, that transported young and old into another world (the world which had been brought from the Orient and set down along Marchessault and Commercial Streets, Nigger and China Alleys) with marchers, carriages and floats of their own, a band — Mercy on us, what squeals! — and, to cap it all, a dragon 150 feet long, carried by forty muscular, pigtailed men, with a head so gigantic that relays of bearers were required, each taking the prodigious task for a few hundred feet and then, panting, giving it over to a refreshed co-bearer. Brilliantly dressed youths ran back and forth before the monster, teasing it with flashing goads of silver, gold, tinsel and silk, and the horrifying head darted, weaved, reared high and swooped low in pursuit of the baubles, breathing fire and belching forth smoke like a story-book dragon!

Those Fiesta parades!

But there were other joys in that thrill-packed week of festival. The whole town was decked in Fiesta colors: gold for oranges, green for olives and red for wine; each child had at least one flag in a window at home and carried one or wore the tricolor as a sash or across the chest. There were "Fiesta" whistles, shaped like a shot-gun shell with one end crushed in and containing a wheel so that the force of the breath set the wheel spinning, and the harder one blew the higher the whistle sounded, so that a fellow was a sort of boy-sized siren all by himself and if he didn't have a Fiesta whistle he'd just as soon be dead — *and* buried. No school, of course, but picnics and parties at home and a box-lunch to take along so that the family could go early and secure a good place on the line of march.

If a boy was good and promised to hold on and not get lost

he might be taken down for the Saturday night street carnival, wearing a costume contrived from some cast-off finery and with a mask, and a horn to toot or a "tickler" that rolled up tight and, when blown into forcibly, would fly out into a paper wand tipped with a feather to titillate passersby, especially squealing girls — and peanuts or popcorn or a bag of gen-u-wine "Fiesta taffy" to eat on the horse-car or the cable-car or the trolley going home — if a little fellow could keep awake that long!

Perhaps the grown-ups enjoyed Fiesta Week in their own dull, stiff, complacent fashion. The children didn't fret much about that. But they might have heard Father say that the celebration had been a boss idea; it had certainly fetched in a power of tourists. And what would Ma think of selling that Wesley Avenue lot now? Prices were up again and maybe better times were ahead for everybody.

Yes, Max Meyberg had been right and Los Angeles had given a good heave at its own boot-straps!

La Fiesta de las Flores was so successful that it was repeated in the two succeeding years.

Adam Jory, forging steadily ahead now, was on the Executive Committees, of course. His affairs were prospering. His lots were going up in value and he sold and bought again and sold again. But he always hung on to the pieces most strategically placed, against the time when the increasing influx of population from elsewhere — more and more from the Middle West — should crowd prices to the ultimate top. He was pumping his own oil and the Kerner-Jernigan burners were paying handsome dividends. His salary from the *Daily Sun* was higher than that of any other man on Major Oddie's payroll; the owner squealed like a pig under a gate but he couldn't let Jory go. In fact he was putting additional responsibility on the younger man's shoulders; he was grooming him for the position of general manager of the *Daily Sun* — wondering if Jory wouldn't make him a pretty good son-in-law, everything considered.

40

Some weeks after the second Fiesta celebration he had something disquieting to talk to Adam Jory about. The interview was held behind locked doors.

"You're making a damned fool of yourself, young man," the Major began.

Jory looked at him with mild surprise. It had been a long time since the publisher had chosen to address him as he was in the habit of addressing most people.

"Maybe we won't agree on that, Major. What's the trouble?"

"This young woman. I'm told she is in the job-press department."

Jory's face revealed nothing. "Go on."

"See here, Jory," Major Oddie growled, impatiently, "don't try to pretend you don't understand me."

"I understand you as far as you've gone. Some busy-body has brought you a piece of gossip." Jory spoke quietly, and without rancor. He faced his employer squarely. "I wouldn't expect you, Major, to take an interest in the morals of other people."

The Major snorted. "Huh! I don't give a double-coupled damn about your morals, Adam. I'm thinking about your future."

A faint smile crossed Jory's face. "I've done some thinking about that myself. If that's what you have in mind, I'll be glad to listen."

"Now you're showing sense. Adam, are you planning to marry this young woman?"

It was a question Adam had asked himself. But, unready to answer it, he had put it out of his mind, as he was able to do with problems he didn't want to face or incidents he preferred to forget. Now, confronted with this direct challenge, he said, after a moment: "No, Major."

"Huh! I gave you credit for having good sense and I'm glad I was right." All the acerbity had gone from his tone; the publisher spoke almost mildly. "You're getting to be well thought of in Los Angeles, Jory. You're going to the top

of the heap. The time must come pretty soon when you will
have to make a home and find a wife to head it. When that
time comes you'll be in a position to pick and choose. You can
have a girl of position — money; most any girl you make up
your mind to have."

"I'm in no hurry, Major. But, in a general way, that's what
I've been figuring on myself."

"Good! Then drop this affair. Los Angeles isn't big enough
yet so but what talk gets around. People notice things. And
Los Angeles is a little particular about husbands for its daughters. We don't like to see pitch on a bridegroom's wedding
boots. That's all I've got to say." He picked up a paper from
his desk. "About that contract for the telephone company book,
now. If you get it we'll need a new press, won't we? . . . . "

Adam Jory had been seen but seldom in the city with Beulah;
at the beach they had taken care to be very inconspicuous and
to hold themselves aloof.

Jory knew that one of the foremen in the *Daily Sun* composing room had a cottage a few blocks from Beulah's in
Santa Monica, where he and his family spent the summers and
occasional week-ends in the wintertime. All *Sun* employes
were encouraged to carry to the editor any items that they
thought might interest him and some of them were down-
right spies for the newspaper. Moriarity was a possible source
of the story that had come to the Major's ears.

There was another possibility. During this second Fiesta
week Beulah had had the use of an office on Spring Street,
where . a friend worked, as a vantage-point from which to
view the parades. Adam Jory had accompanied her there
for the Thursday night parade; it was dark in the room and they
had sat close together, holding hands and thoroughly enjoying
this privacy and the brilliantly lighted spectacle below them
in the street. Afterwards they had gone out to the Kerners'
for a midnight snack. They might have been seen going or
coming or in the Sandstrum office by some watchful vassal of
Oddie's.

He was not yet ready to give up his intimacy with this com-
panionable, tolerant, laughing, vital woman. But Major Oddie's knowledge of his secret and the common-sense attitude
his employer had taken brought Jory up sharply. Without
giving a reason he obtained an isolated cottage well outside
of Santa Monica, furnished it comfortably — presented it to
Beulah Rountree on her birthday, that occurred in the Fall. She
was extravagantly pleased; Adam Jory had never before made
her any substantial present. And she preferred the new loca-
tion, here they found almost complete isolation; also they
were only a few hundred feet from a section of the beach that
very few others ever visited. Beulah called the cottage "Heav-
en"; in a few days she had turned it into a comfortable, completely homey retreat.

She and Jory were happier together, she said, than they
had ever been before.

Almost before they knew it the third year's Fiesta Week
rolled round again.

Busier than ever, Adam Jory excused himself from going
with Beulah to the Sandstrum Company office for the night
parade. She was perfectly understanding — went with her
friend, Alice Bolton, instead, and enjoyed herself.

But on Friday afternoon, when they were washing up
early in the rear room of the print shop, she said: "I've never
seen the street carnival, Ad. I'd sort of like to go tomorrow
night."

"You wouldn't enjoy it. Just a mob of kids and drunks
wearing costumes and raising hob."

"It's fun to raise hob for a change. But of course if you're
'fraid somebody might see you — "

He wasn't listening. He was in a quandary.

In the course of his Fiesta committee work that spring he
had been thrown a good deal with one of the biggest real
estate owners in the Southland, Julius Nostrander, and the
Jewish capitalist had shown an interest in him. Had gone so

43

far, in fact, as to invite Jory to his home to meet his family, including his daughter, Irene. Just how it had come about Adam was never quite sure, but the upshot of the new acquaintanceship was that he was committed to taking Irene Nosstrander to the Fiesta Queen's Ball.

Nothing had ever happened to him that caused him so much ill-ease as contemplation of this ordeal. The Nostranders were socially in the top circle, Irene one of the city's most prominent and most sought-after young ladies. She was not actually a beauty but she wore stunning toilettes and splendid jewels and she made not only a handsome appearance but a commanding one. Almost any of the young blades of local Society would have been glad of the chance to squire her to the ball, and Adam Jory couldn't quite understand why he had been so favored.

It was not his habit to show surprise or to be flustered by anything, but now he felt both. He had to buy a dress suit, of course, with all the fittings; he had certainly never expected that anything would lead him to that extravagance — indulgence in any such tomfoolery. Except for romping clumsily about now and then with Beulah Rountree at a beach pavilion he had never danced a step in his life; certainly he didn't know how a fellow went at performing in a polka or a waltz, and anything like a cotillion such as the papers reported as a feature of these balls was as alien to him as the routine of a Choctaw war dance.

But he was not one to be floored by difficulties. He had gone to Harris & Frank's for the necessary clothes; he had gone to the Public Library to read up what he could find on social procedure and, his face grim, had visited Prof. Kramer's locally famous dancing academy where, on paying what seemed to him a pretty stiff price, had been initiated into the most rudimentary of the mysteries surrounding the art of Terpsichore. Half a dozen lessons, in private of course, caused him to sweat profusely but resulted in his acquiring enough skill to pass muster. His will and his self-assurance would have to take care of the rest of it. He was prepared to make his bow in Society.

Now, here was Beulah proposing that, on the night after the ball, the two of them should join the riff-raff and hood-lums — and thousands of others, too — in the carnival that would make bedlam of the downtown streets. Not only was the project risky but it was, he thought, entirely out of keeping. He was breaking into the inner circles through his Fiesta committee work and through meeting the Nostranders. He had already been introduced to Irene's set. He was definitely beginning a new phase in his career in Los Angeles.

In the months following Major Oddie's talk with him on the subject he had, in fact, seen a good deal less of Beulah Rountree. He had kept her in a secret compartment of his life, so to speak, finding it pleasant to know she was there, and enjoyable to visit her there. But imperceptibly there had come over his feelings about her the deepening conviction that she held a lower station than the one he himself must now occupy. The truth was that he was beginning to be a little embarrassed by her earthy, sensuous, uninhibited nature.

And Major Oddie had merely focussed for him his own vague persuasion that nothing must stand between him and his future as a leading citizen of Los Angeles. He was fond of Beulah; he would miss her exuberance, her jollity, her understanding of him and his needs and moods. She made no secret of her love for him. Its weakness was that it was an undemanding and unquestioning love. It was exactly like that "charity" he remembered from dim Sunday School days that they told him might be translated "Love": it did not vaunt itself, envied not, was not puffed up; it was never provoked, thought no evil, bore all things, believed all things (of him) — it hoped all things and endured all.

As he was habituated in doing, he put such reproachful meditations out of his mind vigorously.

He had Adam Jory to think of.

"I'm sorry, Beulah," he said, now, as she hung up the towel in the back room of the print shop. "I hate to disappoint you but I don't think I want to go out for the carnival Saturday night."

She looked at him steadily for a moment, without reproach — rather with selfless resignation. "All right, Ad. I understand."

"What do you mean by that?" he asked, not sharply, but quickly. "You sound as if something was wrong or that I wasn't doing the proper thing."

"Oh, you're doing exactly right," she said, quietly. "You always do, don't you, Ad?"

He didn't quite know what to make of her attitude.

He went to the Fiesta Grand Ball with Irene Nostrander and pleased himself by getting through the ordeal, not with enjoyment, because he thought all this society folderol was a foolish waste of time, money and energy, but with relative ease and without embarrassment. He danced very little, but no one commented on that fact.

He spent some time, in the course of the evening, in the company of Julius Nostrander and a group of his rich and influential friends, in the gentlemen's smoking room or lounging in the Nostrander private box watching the colorful throng on the dancing floor. Mr. Nostrander paid him particular attention. He asked a good many questions. He urged Adam Jory to come to his offices soon, in the Nostrander Block.

"I think maybe I might put something in your way, Jory," the capitalist said.

"Thank you, Mr. Nostrander. I'll come."

"I've been seeing something of a man you ought to know, lately. He's a railroader — nephew of Collis P. Huntington, of the Espee. If things continue to look favorable to him he plans to put twenty or thirty million dollars into street-car and interurban lines here. In that case — "

"Yes, in that case, he certainly would be a good man to know," Adam said.

"All right; come up and see me. Don't put it off, now."

What Adam Jory had never once thought of was that the

Sunday papers, in their fulsome accounts of the Queen's Grand Ball, invariably printed the names of the more prominent guests. His own was mentioned more than once, as he found by glancing at the sheets Sunday morning. The society reporters had made all they could — especially the one of the *Daily Sun* — of the fact that he had squired Irene Nostrander to the event.

Beulah Rountree dropped one of these papers on Adam Jory's desk Monday morning. She had encircled his name with a red pencil mark wherever it occurred.

"You were right, Ad," she said, in her quiet tone, without rancor or reproach. "You would have felt foolish to be seen out with me on Carnival Night."

That was all.

He was impatient with himself for feeling uncomfortable and even ashamed.

But apparently Beulah did not notice this. She had gone on to the high desk she now occupied as bookkeeper and auditor for the *Daily Sun* printing office.

CHAPTER THREE

```
┌─────────────────────────────────┐
│                                 │
│     THIS CHOICE CORNER          │
│      F O R   S A L E            │
│     William A. Rowland          │
│     ───────────────             │
│                                 │
│     POPULATION OF L. A.         │
│       Now      103,000          │
│       1910     250,000          │
│                                 │
└─────────────────────────────────┘
```

ON A BRILLIANT morning in the early autumn of 1900 Adam Jory was being driven to his downtown office by Pickett, the coachman. It had taken Jory some time to get used to this service. He would have preferred to take the street car as he had always done. He hated to be fussed over. It had been his wife who insisted. She had given orders that the trap or the light carriage was to be at the *porte cochere* door every morning, rain or shine, for him. He gave in to save a long argument. To save argument he had accepted a good many changes Irene Nostrander had made in his way of living.

They had been married for a little over two years.

Although he was not conscious of it, he had given this important step much the same consideration he would give any business transaction; he had concluded that it would be an advantageous arrangement for both of them, mutually beneficial, and definitely advancing his own interests and promising desirable returns. If he had been asked or had asked himself whether love entered into the consideration he would have been puzzled to reply. He appreciated Irene's good qualities and was comfortable in her company. On her part, the estimable young woman admired Adam for his good looks, his ability to impress people favorably and his clear promise of developing into one of the big figures of Los Angeles. In the two years, if neither had awakened the other to ecstasy neither had caused the other pain or unhappiness. Society looked on them as a well-matched and fortunate couple.

Julius Nostrander, inheritor of a round sum and growing rich from his prime real estate investments, had given the lucky pair a two-acre lot on Figueroa Street as a wedding present and there Jory had built for his bride a residence that was substantial and worthy of her station, though it was a definitely ugly piece of architecture. He would have preferred going out to the foothill suburb of Hollywood, where he owned a close-in piece of land, but Irene put her foot down. She had no intention, she said, of living in the country — of becoming a farmer's wife. She did not mention the fact that her grandfather had been an Alsatian peasant nor that her mother's family had herded sheep in Montana. She simply vetoed Adam's suggestion. The gift of the Figueroa Street lot had settled the matter.

On this particular October morning the coachman was turning on Pico Street when Adam Jory, his eye always out for the main chance, saw a painter re-lettering a big signboard. It was one offering the corner lot for sale and was put there by William Rowland. The workman was changing the figures in the agent's now-famous population prediction, raising the guess to 250,000 for 1910.

"Pull up a minute, Pickett."

Jory's rare faint smile touched his lips. The reinsman was

encouraged by it to say:

"It was a hundred thousand, sir. Did we make it?"

"Yes. The *Sun* got the census figures from Washington Saturday. Rowland was right."

"Ain't he setting his sights pretty high this time?"

"Maybe. I don't think so." Jory remembered that his wife discouraged familiarity with the servants. "You can take me to the Nostrander Block, Pickett."

He was thinking of that corner lot. If the price was right, now —

Yes, Los Angeles had doubled its population in the decade of the 1890's. Max Meyberg's Fiestas had proved the tonic the young city needed. Its stimulation had given the people faith; they had taken over their water system and voted bonds for extensions; two or three up-to-date hotels and a number of substantial business blocks had been put up; a few crazy enthusiasts had launched a half-mad scheme for making a harbor at San Pedro out of some sand-dunes and a mud slough barely adequate to float a dozen fishing boats — and those zealots had plagued Congress until they had won an appropriation for the building of a breakwater and the dredging of a narrow channel. Now, at the end of the decade, the project was beginning to look a little less insane: it appeared that two steamship companies had actually leased docking space, and Senator Stephen White had been promised another two million for the port.

The outstanding fact of the decade had been the coming of Huntington, the railroad man. He had bought up the job-lot of street-car lines, built new ones, extended, spread out his network of modern electric railways in every direction. He had invested ten million dollars and they said he had another ten or twenty to put into interurban roads, tying into Los Angeles a dozen outlying towns and suburbs.

Of course home-seekers and real estate promoters put up houses on new tracks along these lines, built and promised, which caused real estate values to rise and which gave work to thousands of artisans and business to everyone. The Chamber of Commerce and the newspapers, never prone to hide the light of their city under a bushel, spread this glad story abroad and tourists began to pour in once more, most of them to stay. There were so many of them that the carlines and the city's streets had to be stretched farther and farther into the hills, into the barley-fields, into the cow-pastures, which gave work to more carpenters and painters and plumbers, which made business boom, which facts were advertised ever more widely, which brought more settlers.

It was a wondrous circus-ring in which to perform. And Adam Jory was one of the most alert and active, if one of the more taciturn, of the ring-masters.

This was highly satisfactory to his father-in-law. Julius Nostrander was well pleased with the young man. His connections were good, he had excellent business judgment, he shared the older man's abounding faith in the future of Los Angeles and, most important of all, he had a remarkable faculty for getting in with the right people and ferreting out invaluable information on coming projects and developments. In the four years they had been friendly, Jory had let Nostrander in on several very good things, including some investments, before the news got around, at the harbor.

After the marriage he had fitted up a fine corner office for the use of Irene's young husband on the top floor of the Nostrander Block, on Spring Street, where his own enterprises were centered. This was a definite advantage to Jory; he now had so many irons in the fire that he thought it just as well to heat some of them out of range of the sharp eyes and keen ears of Major Oddie of the *Daily Sun.* In charge here he installed a confidential man, Herbert Kinney.

As usual, this morning, Adam Jory was at his desk before anyone in the Nostrander offices appeared. He liked the quiet of this period; he could get more done; he was more keen and he relished his work as at no other time. He had long

51

since thrown off his illness — was now strong, hearty, full of energy. He might go to bed well tired but in the morning he awoke refreshed, renewed, keen and avid.

His hat on the back of his head, he sat down now and began ripping open envelopes. Swiftly he glanced at the letters, quickly made decisions, briefly noted on each epistle a penciled memorandum as to the disposition Kinney was to make of it. Very few letters were filed; all the rest were burned. Nothing was thrown into the waste-basket in a Jory office; that was one of his fixed rules and his employes soon learned it. Such personal documents as he cherished he himself put away in a secret compartment he had ordered built into his roll-top desk. He had an instinctive dread of prying eyes.

An office boy brought in the morning papers and presently, the mail gone through, Jory took them up. His association with the *Daily Sun* had put him in the way of perusing the news; he found that it paid him well, for the most insignificant item might contain a grain or two of information valuable to a rising young man. He did not read to inform himself of what people were thinking, hoping, planning for themselves, nor of their troubles, struggles, aspirations. He had no interest in such matters except as they offered hints of needs or concerns to which business could contribute. Foreign news he skipped, and national items got only a glance. His field was the Southland.

Presently Kinney came in. He was a thin-lipped, neat man, of indeterminate age and undistinguished appearance. Dry and capable, he was an ideal confidential agent, adept at making himself useful, running errands, gathering information, worming out the secrets of others while revealing nothing of himself or his employer. At attending to dreary details he was invaluable. And Jory found him a marvel at keeping his mouth shut. He was even secretive about himself; Jory believed he had a family but he could not be sure why he thought so or of what this putative household consisted. The man was, in brief, a bright and shining piece of human machinery, without a flaw, always well-oiled and moving silently and efficiently.

Adam Jory put his newspaper aside. "I came by Pico and Figueroa this morning," he said, without greeting. "It looks to me as though Pico is going to be a main cross street some day. If you can get that Rowland corner for three thousand I'll put it away and forget I have it."

"Is that your top offer?"

"Pretty close to it."

Kinney understood perfectly. Jory would pay up to three thousand and a half, probably — would be glad to pay thirty-two hundred.

"Yes, Mr. Jory."

His employer picked up a letter from his desk.

"Gus Kerner is raising hell again," he said. "He's been to see some blackleg lawyer." He glanced at the sheet. "Brian Wall. Do you know him?"

"Yes. He's a shyster. But a clever one."

"I don't want to be bothered with a lawsuit. Have you got any ideas?"

"Why don't you put Kerner on an allowance? So much a month for the rest of his life."

"I'd rather buy him off outright. A lump sum for whatever he thinks the burner is worth — his interest in it. Get rid of him."

"That's what he thinks you're up to — to get rid of him. He's suspicious of a swindle. I can handle him better my way."

"Well, try it. He's getting to be a nuisance. He wants a hand in running the business and he doesn't know anything about that sort of thing."

"I may have to offer him and his wife a little persuader — say a trip some place or a house. I'll see to it."

Jory turned to his desk and Kinney went out, quietly, as he did everything.

Jory took up the papers again, but presently he found that he was not reading them. Against his will he was thinking again of the old inventor and his comfortable wife. Reason told him that he was doing the best thing for the couple, but his heart — as some people, he supposed, would call it — told him they would be hurt and unhappy. Determinedly he shook off that train of thought.

But it brought on another, not less disquieting.

He had first met the Kerners through Beulah Rountree.

He had not seen her for more than two years now. One afternoon, without a word to him, she had gone to the cashier of the *Daily Sun,* informed him that she was quitting, drawn her pay. Afterwards Jory had remembered that this was at about the time the society columns had reported his engagement to Irene Nostrander.

Months later still he had received a letter from her, mailed in a small town in San Diego County, saying that she had news for him. He had put the note away; now he opened his hidden drawer and took it out. The girlish handwriting, so precisely formed, brought her back to him with painful vividness.

> *I have a baby, Ad, a little girl. She is well and pretty too and you bet I'm very happy.*
> *I will write you once in a while but please don't try to find us. You see Ad youre going to be such a big man in L. A. that I'll always know what youre doing and how youre getting ahead.*
> *If you want our baby to have some extras I can't afford you can pay it in to Mr. Noll in the Security. He will always know where I am.*
> *I have named the baby Judith.*

Yes, she had given the child his mother's name. He couldn't remember having told her what it was. Perhaps she had asked him, in one of those tender and melting moments they had known together when, lying close, their arms embracing, they had exchanged little confidences — whispered revelations, secrets, trifles hidden in their memories or their hearts. Repeating the baby's name to himself now he was choked with emotion as he had been on that first reading. It was an emotion foreign to the Adam Jory others knew.

Every month after getting the note he had sent Kinney to the bank with an envelope containing some money, in currency. As he had prospered the amounts had been increased. Once or twice he had wondered how much the trust officer at the bank knew of the story. Perhaps nothing. Beulah could keep secrets, too.

Now he was recalling her with strange clearness. Her voice, her smile, her full, red mouth, her even white teeth, the way she walked, moved, gestured. He remembered her in bedrooms lighted only by moonlight or by one of the candles she fancied: the whiteness of her skin, the modeling of her shoulders and breasts, the flowing lines that narrowed at her hips, then tapered down to make her lovely thighs, like those of precious statues he had seen pictured, her dimpled knees and her slim girlish ankles.

He remembered, strangely enough, the intoxicatingly sweet, clean smell of her body and of her crown of lustrous hair, the sounds of her sighs, her quick intake of breath, her whispers in his ear — then her clothes, rustling faintly as she lowered them over her head and the susurration of her silk stockings as, with slender white hands, she pulled them on; remembered how, laughing low, she would come to him wherever he sat watching her and make him fasten her garters, saying that they wouldn't stay up if she fixed them.

Out of one of those hours, somewhere toward the very end of their intimacy, had come her baby. She had told him long before, making a little fun of his innocence, that he needn't worry about any such happenstance, since she knew what she was doing. It occurred to him now, suddenly, that she had known what she was doing to the last. Sensing that they were coming to a parting, hadn't she let the preventable occur? Had she, in this, made sure of extending into her future the bond that had so long held them together? He couldn't decide. He knew so little of women. He would never know much about them.

Now, what of this little girl of his? She would look like
Beulah, surely, and he was glad to feel that. Would she look
at all like him? Would she have any of his characteristics?
This query brought him to a full stop. What was there in his
nature, character, that he could wish her to have? He had never
been introspective and he made hard work of this examina-
tion. He was simply a practical man, driving, calculating,
forging ahead. He allowed nothing to turn him aside. Once a
labor leader had called him ruthless. Had he nothing to give
a child but these qualities? He was ignorant of the scientific
theories. Judith's heredity must include a good deal from
him. Maybe nothing could save her. The thought shocked
him.

A clerk knocked.

"Mr. Nostrander has just come in, Mr. Jory. He'd like to
see you about that Palms syndicate before you leave."

Adam Jory locked away in the secret drawer Judith, Beulah,
his memories, his discomforting cogitation.

He went into his father-in-law's office, taking with him the
papers in the real estate deal they were pushing through.

Those irons Adam had in the fire multiplied so rapidly that
in the following summer he told Major Oddie that he must
leave the *Daily Sun.*

Oddie snorted. "You want more money, eh? All right. I'll
make you general manager of the *Sun.* You can name your
own salary."

"Sorry, Major. I'm striking out for myself."

"Huh! You've gotten too big for your boots, my boy.
You'll soon learn that you're mighty small potatoes and few to
the hill without the paper behind you. Drop this nonsense."

"I've made up my mind."

The choleric editor struck his desk. "By God, Jory, get
this through your head: if you desert me now you and I part
company for good."

Adam Jory smiled his thin, cold smile. "I'd rather be

friends with you, Major. But if you can't see it that way I guess I can make out."

The editor turned away. "Huh! There's the door!"

Jory was not disturbed. He was resolved to be free — to be his own man. And immediately he knew that he had followed the right course. It was a relief to be independent. And he was plunged into such a press of business that he soon forgot Major Oddie's angry dismissal. But he had made an enemy who forgot nothing.

Kinney had succeeded in getting the inventor, Dad Kerner, to accept a monthly allowance of three hundred dollars, though the old man had stubbornly refused to sign any papers covering a settlement. That was all right: Jory held the patents on the burner nozzle Jim Jernigan had long since perfected and also those covering the Jernigan oil-filter and the kitchen-stove burner Kerner had turned over and Jernigan had developed and was now marketing. The Aliso Street shop had been expanded and now had a sizable payroll and adequate equipment.

Three wells had been brought in on the Coleman and Eliza Winter lots and now the two young drillers, Capper and Hub Finn, were foremen, each of them with a tower of men, the former drilling a new hole on the Coleman property and Finn boring the first prospect hole on the tract north of Westlake Park that Rowland had bought for Jory. Adam pushed these enterprises without fanfare, but the other oilmen in Los Angeles knew him and what he was up to. They knew, too, that he held an advantage over them, since his burner business opened for his oil a market they did not have and badly needed.

They were to learn soon of another project Jory had afoot.

He had put Jernigan at developing a special burner for use in locomotives. When this was ready Adam took his idea to two of the railroad officials he had worked with in the Fiesta campaigns and they agreed to give the device a practical test in a yard-engine. The road's Master Mechanic was enthusiastic and he and Jernigan ironed out some difficulties with the nozzle until it was perfected. Thereafter it was not hard to induce the officials to equip a light road locomotive for an outside test and the day came when Jory and a group of company executives boarded a special train and were pulled out, at midnight, by the oil-burning engine for a test run.

It was highly successful. Conversion of six freight moguls and two high-speed passenger locomotives was ordered and the engineering department began to prepare designs to make the change-over from coal to oil in every engine operating on western divisions. Jory refused to sell the burners; they were to be leased and each one Jernigan built or that the company itself fabricated would bring in a yearly royalty.

Then Adam made his next move. At a gathering of all the railroad chiefs who had had a hand in the development, he spread out a big map of southern California that had been prepared on his orders.

"I don't have to tell you folks what your change-over is going to mean to the oil industry of Los Angeles" he said. "Oil will replace coal on every locomotive operated west of the Mississippi inside of a year or so. I'm going to put burners into coastwise ships next. I've got some figures to show you what this is going to do to increase consumption.

"And here's another thing. Some of us are still making fun of the horseless carriage. But it's coming in, as sure as taxes. Then oil *refining* will become one of the big industries of the country."

"You're dreaming dreams!" an older man growled.

But others disagreed. "Go on, Jory. Where do we come into all this?"

"Take a flier in oil with me. Not your roads—you, personally. I've been buying up options on promising land for some time now and I'm ready to organize a five-million-dollar corporation to start developing pumping wells."

Someone laughed. "Five million! You must think we're plutocrats, Jory."

MacAdam, a vice-president, broke in. "I like your proposition, Mr. Jory. And my guess is that you've figured out how to swing it."

"That's correct. You give me your names and I'll raise the money."

A Chicago director whistled. "So that's it. Well, trot out your subscription list, Jory. I'll sign up."

A week later the papers for the incorporation of the Golconda Oil Company were on their way to the Secretary of State in Sacramento. They had been prepared by Valentine some time before. Adam Jory, with his eye to the main chance, had been as confident as that.

Major Wellington Oddie's *Daily Sun* had a rival in the morning field, though scarcely a competitor, in the *Messenger,* actually the first newspaper to be established in the *pueblo* after the *gringo* invasion. The *Messenger* had been founded with monies supplied by Henry Sturdevant, one of that handful of early comers who, mostly through marriage, had attained to considerable properties and interests in the "Golden Forties" of Alta California. Sturdevant, a ship's master, had married into the great de Sola family, his bride bringing him a rich dowry and that elevation to the aristocracy of the Southland, the honorary title of *Don.* Don Enrico Sturdevant, more lucky than able, had soon found himself in possession of increasing herds and flocks, profitable vineyards and grain fields, valuable lands in the best possible locations in the country round about and many *varas* of street frontage in the *pueblo* itself. In a fumbling, hit-or-miss fashion he had backed innumerable businesses, many of which had prospered in spite of themselves as Los Angeles emerged from its sleepy beginnings into its wide-awake and bustling boom-times.

But his descendants and heirs, a large and easy-going clan, proved unequal to the task of holding their patrimony together under the onslaughts of the vigorous, pushing, unscrupulous hordes of newcomers. Much they lost through sheer inertia, much they sacrificed in times of need, more was taken from them by guile and trickery; little by little and piece by piece the Sturdevant properties melted away. If the *Messenger* had been worth grabbing, probably it would have gone with the rest. As it was, the paper, shifting policies, changing staffs, falling behind the times, had gone steadily downhill until it was, at last, eking out a miserable existence by grace of contracts it managed to hang on to for doing the city and county legal printing.

One day Julius Nostrander sent for Adam Jory and somewhat shamefacedly confessed that he was a substantial creditor of the Sturdevant family and that its payments were so much in arrears that he was going to have to foreclose.

"Foreclose on what, J. N.? I wouldn't suppose they had anything left to lose."

"*Ach,* that's how it is, Adam! I should have taken that San Gabriel land two years ago, but Peter Sturdevant and that no-account Grannis that married one of the girls — they begged me I should let them off because they could get cash for it from the Wellmans. Now all is left is the home and the *Messenger.*"

"Your mortgage covers the home place?"

"Yes. But actually, I couldn't take that, my boy."

"Why couldn't you take it? It's a double city block between Spring and Main and right in the path of developments. In ten years — "

The old man sighed. "Don't tell me. I know. But Dona Rosaria is — how old? — over ninety, and her sister and that brood of children — and their children — oh, no, Adam. Los Angeles wouldn't like that — to see the old lady put out in the street after all these years. I wouldn't like to see it myself!"

That was true, Adam Jory thought — Los Angeles wouldn't approve of evicting the venerable matriarch, almost a legend already and still a potent figure in society, though she had for so many years been poverty-poor. *Casa Felicidad* was a landmark; it must come down in time, overrun by progress and grown too valuable to be preserved for reasons of sentiment, but that day had not come. It would be bad business now.

"All right," he said. "That leaves the paper. And that is a liability you don't want."

"You say so, too, Adam? I thought you could find some way to help me with it. Look, now, you have been in the newspaper business — you know the tricks. You could talk it up to somebody, couldn't you? You I am counting on, or else I lose everything on this bad loan, eh?"

Jory's thin smile touched his lips. "Hustling ads for the *Sun* didn't make me a newspaper editor, J.N. And it would take a lot of money to build up the *Messenger*. But I'll think about it. I'll see if I can do anything to help you out."

Even while listening to his father-in-law's dolorous tale he had been visited by an idea and that idea had begun to take shape. Suppose that he acquired the *Messenger* himself.

It was true enough, as he had told Mr. Nostrander, that his experience on the *Daily Sun* had not made a newspaperman of him, but newspapermen could be hired. And newspaper owners were in a position to exert great influence in Los Angeles — to profit in many ways from occupying that strategic position. He could easily find men with money to share in such a venture, once they were shown the advantages. The city was already well able to support another first-class daily. The *Daily Sun* had numerous enemies; the belligerent Major Oddie was forever antagonizing people of importance who, if for that reason alone, could be counted on to patronize a rival sheet. And the local editors were on the inside of good things that others missed until too late. They were often able to push their private enterprises and personal business ventures through adroit use of their columns. Adam had no doubt that he could find advertisers the present owners couldn't reach; if the paper were improved it would gain circulation and circulation brought advertising in.

The more he mulled over the project the wider the prospect opened before him. He gave it his entire attention, pondering it from every angle. He made a list of the men who might be interested in going into the speculation with him and who would also have prestige enough to make them of value as his co-owners. But, checking available names and so finding growing doubts of this or that man as a desirable partner in an enterprise of such varied facets, he began at last to wonder how he might gain control of the paper for himself alone. He had warned Nostrander that it would take a lot of money, which was true; he did not have a lot of money in cash and he had no intention of sacrificing any of his numerous interests which were sure things for this project which might prove a costly gamble. But the venture appealed to him strongly. His ideas began to take definite form.

A few days later he took his agent, Kinney, off everything else and set him to investigating the business, resources and possibilities of the *Messenger*. Kinney's report, though conservative, heightened Adam Jory's interest. He made an appointment with the biggest banker in Los Angeles and with that shrewd, silent, mousy, razor-sharp little Midas spent two hours in confidential conference.

Then he went back to Julius Nostrander.

"I can take the *Messenger* off your hands, J.N.," he said, abruptly. "You will get back every penny you put out, but you'll have to wait for it."

The old man was jubilant. "Sure! Why not, Adam? Of course I wait. I leave it all to you. Whatever you say, that is with me perfect!" He lowered his voice. "Tell me, now, just between us boys — who is the sucker?"

For once Adam Jory almost laughed aloud. "Why, J.N.," he said, "I am."

It was some days, Adam learned afterward, before his father-in-law ceased shaking his head and muttering broken phrases of doubt as to the younger man's sanity.

That efficient fact-finding machine, Herbert Kinney, had reported to Adam Jory that among its assets the *Messenger* was reputed to have a first-class city editor. His name was John

Shelley and Jory took him over with his entire staff in making the deal.

Shelley was a nervous, quick-thinking, hard-driving young man with thin, sandy hair, piercing, pale-blue eyes and a complete disregard for sartorial elegance. His clothes looked as though he slept in them; rival city editors, jealously viewing his achievements in turning out a newsy paper with a skeleton staff, averred that he probably had to. He did contrive to get the news into the office and, by dint of cajolery, bullying, nagging, threats or flattery, to get it written in sprightly fashion by his overworked reporters. Unhappily for the success of the *Messenger* the copy that crossed Shelley's desk was badly printed, on the cheapest newsprint, and much of it was crowded out because the business office was hard put to get an adequate supply of paper and ink — often scraped the bottom of the barrel to pay the compositers, stereotypers and pressmen.

The mechanical end of the business Jory did understand; this he immediately straightened out. The composing room staff was enlarged; overdue material and supply bills were paid up; presently Adam bought, on favorable terms, a second-hand but useful press capable of turning out larger editions of much better copies of the paper than had ever been possible before. A new make-up man, brought down from San Francisco, gave the *Messenger* a fresh and much brighter appearance. And there was room for Shelley's news, now; the paper went to 16 pages, with 64 — by stretching things — on Sundays.

As for the editorial department, Adam Jory moved more slowly. He liked John Shelley and believed in him, and at first proposed to make him managing editor, with authority to publish the paper. Shelley demurred.

"I'm a city-desk man, Mr. Jory. I have no ambition to mess with editorials or policy-making and I couldn't deal with helpful subscribers or roof-raising advertisers or citizens whose names we spell wrong."

"Any suggestions, then?"

"No. But we might ask Billy Wing."

"Never heard of him."

"He's on the payroll as our fish-and-game editor. Somebody else has to write his column for him, because Billy can't spell, but the local sportsmen buy the *Messenger* just for his dope."

"What makes you think he'd know anything about finding me an editor?"

"Because Billy Wing knows everybody in Los Angeles and everything about everybody. Reporters say that he can almost tell what our leading citizens are thinking about while they're being shaved. They claim that Billy dropped up to the Court House once while the grand jury was in session and that seven or eight men left town that night on the Overland."

"If he's around, have him in."

The individual who presently appeared was a genial, lounging, easy-going man of middle age, wearing good clothes casually, smoking an expensive pipe casually, greeting the new owner of the paper casually and, by his casualness, giving evidence that he found the world a pretty good place and proposed to make the most of living in it.

"Yes, I know quite a bit about Mr. Jory," Wing said, offering a hand.

Jory's thin smile flickered. "Shelley said you had a way of posting up on the rest of us."

"It's perfectly simple in your case. I happen to do a lot of fishing with Elbridge Brinton. And with Joe Mennary, too."

Brinton was one of the top railroad officials in Golconda Oil; Mennary, on the other hand, was a carpenter Jory had often employed. If Billy Wing were chummy with many such ill-sorted pairs his intimate knowledge of the inside of things in Los Angeles was partially explained.

"I don't fish, myself," Adam said. "Never had time for it."

"You can't have everything," Wing replied, drily. "Me, now, I never could find time to make money."

"Let's have your philosophy of life some other time, Billy," the editor interjected. "Mr. Jory is looking for someone to write editorials and run the front office."

"I see!" Wing looked at the owner curiously. "If it's any of my business, Jory, what's the policy of the *Messenger* going to be from now on?"

"Policy? Why, to print the news, I suppose."

The other shrugged. "That won't build circulation in Los Angeles. If you want to make the rag go you'll have to pick a good lively fight with somebody — and win the fight."

That smile of Jory's appeared faintly again. "Whom do you suggest that I pick this fight with?"

"It doesn't matter. Major Oddie and the *Sun*. The Band of Hope." Shelley laughed and Wing explained: "That's my name for the inside clique that runs affairs in Los Angeles. Come to think of it, part of the time you're one of them, aren't you?"

"The Band of Hope, eh? Well, go on with your list."

"All right. There's the Industrial Association, that is beginning to need a trimming. Those tramps who are operating crooked dog races out at Agricultural Park. Then there's Tom Wild and the redlight district or the grafters in the police department — hell, Jory, you could draw names out of a hat and get yourself a worthy cause to take up, in this town of pious hypocrites."

Jory grew a little red. "You don't seem to like Los Angeles, my friend."

"Me? I love it. I was born here and you couldn't give me a home anywhere else. It's because I love Los Angeles that I want to start doing something about it."

"Is any of this true, Shelley — this farrago about graft and crookedness?"

The editor nodded. "Billy's only touching the high spots, Mr. Jory. But the important thing is what he says about the paper. Major Oddie has built up the *Daily Sun* mostly by his fight on labor. And yet two-thirds of the people here are workingmen and women. There's a fight, if you want one — the fight for the closed shop."

"I don't want a fight," Jory said, shortly. "Certainly not that one. All I ask for is a paper that prints the news and that tries to make friends instead of going out of its way to make enemies. Let's have that clear."

Not in the least disturbed the lounging Billy Wing said: "From what Mr. Jory say, John, you'll be your own managing editor. If he'll give you two or three more good reporters I'll back you against the field to win in a walk. That leaves the editorial page. And for that I'd suggest old Professor Morehouse, over at the Normal School. He can out-write any editor in town and he never had an unkind thought in his life."

Adam Jory knew of Dr. Morehouse and the suggestion appealed to him. He told Shelley to handle the matter and Shelley asked that it be left to Wing. The latter promised to see what he could do and lounged toward the door.

"Sorry if I gave you too much of a jolt just now, Mr. Jory," he said, in his easy-going drawl. "I've got an idea that once you get your feet really wet in this business you may turn out to be quite a swimmer." He sauntered away.

"I suppose," John Shelley said, unhappily, "that you'll want me to take Wing off the payroll, Mr. Jory."

"Take him off? Why, certainly not. I asked him a question and he answered it." And Adam added, slowly: "Come to think of it, he may be right."

The *Messenger* became an improved paper immediately. Its new editorial writer gave his page dignity and information and a scholarly tone, but avoided controversy. John Shelley's augmented reportorial staff turned out more news and, sure enough, circulation picked up.

Advertising, however, was slow to follow. There was a prejudice against the paper, born of a decade of gradual decay, that the mere change of management did not dissipate. For several reasons Adam Jory had not announced himself publicly as the new owner, and the few leading merchants who heard that he was, did not feel called on to venture cash on *Messenger* space either to encourage him in the venture or to curry favor with him.

The net result was that the sheet lost money. But Jory could stand the drain, for his other affairs were prospering.

The leading railroad was changing over to oil, using Kerner burners as perfected by Jernigan, and competing lines were being compelled to follow suit. The household burner was on the market and selling well. This device required a special grade of oil and Adam ordered two tank wagons and started a fuel-oil delivery service to cater to them. One coastwise steamship company had proved out and adopted the new system, and oil was replacing coal in the heating plants of a growing number of factories, hotels, business blocks and in two big local churches. And all of these bought or leased Jory burners. Of course, as he had foreseen, this development measurably increased the demand for fuel oil and sales fattened Golconda's treasury.

Looking ahead, as he was able to do, Jory had engaged a bright young chemistry student newly graduated from the University, provided him with a laboratory and set him to experimenting. Soon Wade was finding and coming forward with valuable and practical suggestions of new uses for it. This Southland oil, it appeared, was different from eastern oil, having a heavy asphaltic base with a wide range of by-product possibilities. Golconda gambled on these and a number of additions were made to its refinery. The result was that the company was soon offering lubricating oils of half a dozen grades and purposes and was also distilling a high-grade gasoline to meet the needs of the new market created by stationary engines and the new horseless carriages beginning to appear on the streets. At the other end of the production line Wade offered the residue from the refinery — a thick, black substance which, used with gravel and sand, proved satisfactory for "macadamizing" streets and busy country roads. Again on his own hook Adam Jory organized a small contracting company and began to take contracts for paving.

67

His real estate interests always thrived. Though Los Angeles had its ups and downs the general trend of values was steadily higher. The business section was reaching out and both Jory and his father-in-law contrived to buy just ahead of the march of building. Julius Nostrander had long dabbled in country properties, which were in increasing demand for truck farms and citrus growing; Jory made a few cautious investments in that way and also bought, here and there, lots and tracts in the numerous suburban towns toward which the railway magnate, Huntington, was steadily extending his lines. Adam had the inside track here, through his railroad associates in Golconda, and he usually knew before the public did where new interurban services were to go.

It should be clear that many who went into the Los Angeles real estate market lost money. But they were speculators, whether knowing it or not, and Jory never speculated. He bought for cash, he paid the taxes and kept his properties up, he was generally willing to take a fair profit and he never permitted himself to be caught in a falling market when prices, as sometimes occurred, were temporarily depressed. He had inside information, he had sound judgment, he had faith in the future of the city in the sun. He could not lose — and he did not.

The ownership of the *Messenger,* as he had surmised, brought him indirect benefits, even though the paper's books continued to be spattered with red ink. Shelley's staff, and particularly Billy Wing, had a most amazing knack of worming out secrets and coming up with information about projected developments and changes in the region that gave the owner many advantages. And because he could, through the newspaper, give them helpful support, the ring of civic leaders — the men Wing had called the Band of Hope — gradually included him in more and more of their schemes. The latter were all quasi-public, in the sense that they were primarily designed to benefit Los Angeles. It was only incidentally that they benefited also the business men who promoted them.

The Carstairs factory project was an example.

At his desk in the Nostrander Block office one day, hard at work with Herbert Kinney on plans for a new Golconda refinery, Adam was called to the telephone, which hung on the wall behind his desk. On the line was Grant Paynter, the iron founder.

"We've got a proposition on the fire, Jory, and you're down on the list for five thousand. Is that all right with you?"

"Is this something new?"

"Yep. Can't tell you now. But it means rushing a private car and some of the boys to meet a train at Reno to prevent our prospects from going into San Francisco. And we've only got a couple of hours if we're going to hook on to the evening train."

"Put me down, then, Grant."

He hung up the awkward ear-piece and returned to his desk.

"Now, what was that about an oil service line, Kinney?" he asked, briskly.

A few evenings later a dinner was given in a plushy private dining room at the Southwestern Club where Paynter, Bledsoe, Grannis, the influential little banker, Sussmann — the rest of the insiders of Wing's Band of Hope — entertained two Illinois men named Carstairs. After the excellent meal was finished two of Grannis' young engineers appeared and hung several charts, maps and drawings on the wall.

"Mr. Elliott will explain, gentlemen," the banker said.

Pointer in hand the engineer proceeded to give a brisk 10-minute talk on the advantages of building and operating a factory in Los Angeles and particularly on those advantages as applying to the erection and operation of a furniture factory. His diagrams and sketches showed such a plant, located on two railroad spur-tracks, supplied with water, gas and fuel-oil piped to the door, with an assured working year comprising a minimum of 320 sunshiny days, and manned by hands free of labor union shackles and made happy and contented in a neighboring model village of neat bungalows surrounded by

69

gardens. All this, the engineer concluded, in the very heart of a market clamoring for furniture to equip from ten to twenty thousand new homes and offices a year, as shown by Chart Number Three.

There were other brief talks made, while the brandies and the coffee circulated; the two guests asked questions and their questions were fully answered — fully and frankly and, it must be added, truthfully.

Finally the older brother asked: "Could you give any idea of what such a site as Mr. Elliott suggests would cost us?"

"I can answer that, Carstairs," the banker interjected. "Los Angeles wants your firm to locate here. We like you and your brother and we believe in your enterprise. We're offering you the site free of any cost whatever."

The visitors stared. "Do you mean that?"

Isaac Sussmann took from an inner pocket a folded paper. "Here is the deed, sir."

"By golly," the younger Carstairs cried, "this beats anything I've ever heard of in twenty years of business. We'll start building as soon as we can find a contractor."

Job Grannis spoke up. "Don't let a little thing like that bother you, Mr. Carstairs. My estimators are working now on a bid that we can have in your hands by tomorrow night. You'll have plenty of time to get other prices, of course — "

"Thunderation, Mr. Grannis," the other brother interrupted, "we don't care to do that. We want to get started on the plant."

Later Adam Jory and Paynter were cornered by the younger of the two newcomers.

"What I can't understand is how you folks got that special car of your's up to Reno to kidnap us. We were heading for San Francisco."

Adam said: "That's the way we do business in Los Angeles, Carstairs. We don't let the grass grow under our feet."

"But we didn't know ourselves that we were coming to the Coast for a look around till about three weeks ago."

Grant Paynter laughed. "Don't know as I ought to tell you

70

this, but we got the information from a brother-in-law of yours."

"A brother-in-law? Oh, you mean Andrews — married my wife's sister?"

"I guess that's it. She mentioned to Frank that you folks were headed this way and thinking of a move and Frank Andrews told Ralph Harris, the wholesaler where he works. So we did a little telegraphing and hustling around and got to Reno just two hours before your train pulled in."

Carstairs stared, then laughed. "I guess that accounts, then, for that pair of fast-talking young fellows who scraped an acquaintance with us on the train after we left Salt Lake. But I understood them to say they were in the fruit business."

Adam Jory nodded. "Rinehart and Wesley Smith. They *are* in the fruit business. We knew they were headed home and our telegram caught them on the train at Ogden. What's more, if you don't watch them they'll sell you and your brother some orange land before you've been here sixty days, too."

It was the Golconda Company that presently got the contract to supply, for a long term of years, the fuel oil the new factory required. At a good price per barrel, it may be added.

Yes, Adam Jory was prospering. He kept his eye peeled for the main chance. He had no other concern nor interest. He had no hobbies, played no games, went out into society only for Irene's sake and not for his own pleasure, enjoyment or relaxation. His only contact with his fellow man that counted with him was through his trading, dickering, promotions, enterprises. If, in some rare idle moment, he thought of Beulah or of their child he put the thought aside — out of mind. He had but a single purpose in life and he wasted no time speculating as to what lay behind that purpose, if anything. He was not greedy, he was not conscious of being ambitious or of wanting power. He was driven by a need to succeed and that urge carried him forward — in all material things.

Even his marriage, that venture into which he had gone

as a business project, Jory found prospering — satisfactory. He could not give it much time, for it was a matter consummated, finished, laid away like any sound permanent investment. It was mutually profitable to the two people involved and it returned such dividends as he had counted on from it. He was far too busy with more complex affairs which were being actively developed, improved, extended — which presented day-by-day problems and opportunities — to give thought to this static one.

He was not a neglectful husband; he gave Irene no cause for complaint. Her position in society was stronger than ever and it contented her. Adam's steady rise in the local world gratified her and reinforced her status as an important figure. She had money of her own, but that her father handled for her and she spent none of it. The husband was the provider; Adam understood this rule and approved of it. Early in their marriage he had assumed that they would have children but Irene was afraid of the natural process of childbirth and had no maternal instincts. Adam soon ceased to refer to it — seemed to have forgotten it. Irene sometimes said, carelessly: "Adam's business interests are his children." Later she decided that, for some unaccountable reason, that wretched little morning paper was his favorite baby.

Mrs. Jory was not far wrong. Adam was becoming steadily more interested in the *Messenger*. He had begun to like the smell of printers' ink and hot metal. He relished reading the news in galley proofs, hours ahead of the subscribers; often he would appear at the office and read the copy that came hot from the typewriters of the city staff. He began to feel a new sense of power in being able to prescribe how that news should be handled and what editorial slant should be given it. His increasing participation pleased him. And the excuse it gave him to spend many of his evenings down town was not unwelcome, for he was bored at home almost as much as he was by his enforced incursions into society.

He was looked upon universally as a rising young man, as

72

sure to become big and strong and rich as was this city in the sun that had adopted him and that, as far as he was capable of loving anything, he sincerely loved.

CHAPTER FOUR

THE SOUTHWESTERN CLUB, housed in a handsome gray-stone building just at the edge of the business district, was exclusive, proud and respected. While most of its members were well-to-do men, by no means all the rich Angelenos were on its roster, for The Southwestern had certain social and cultural standards which were jealously guarded. It had a slightly provincial prejudice against newcomers to the city and a man, no matter what his background or financial standing, could scarcely aspire to the club until he had been a resident for some time. Generally speaking this meant a score of years at least — counted a long term in Los Angeles.

It was a tribute to his capacities and his achievements (perhaps including his marriage to Julius Nostrander's daughter) that, in the middle of the first decade of the new century, Adam Jory was told that some of his business associates were proposing his name.

His first impulse was to decline the honor. He was not a social being and certainly not a convivial one. He had no patience with men who dawdled over expensive lunches, devoted long noon hours to games or highballs, or mixed business with pleasure. As an occasional guest in the Southwestern's club-house he had been oppressed by the opulent atmosphere of the lounge, irritated by the heartiness manifested in the bar and game-rooms and rasped by the patronizing tone with which certain of the older members greeted him. To this extent he looked on membership as a waste of time and money.

74

On the other hand he knew that it carried with it certain prestige and opened the door to certain contacts that might be very valuable. And Irene, who, to his surprise, knew of the proffer almost as soon as he did, was elated. She attached the greatest importance to the invitation (one her father might have had except for his race). She brushed aside Adam's objections. When he temporized she stormed. Being at best only half-hearted in his resistance, he gave in.

He was soon glad he had joined. Although a few venerable tories and a handful of snobs ignored him, the majority welcomed him pleasantly and made his first weeks as a member comfortable. He was surprised to discover how many of his business associates belonged. As a matter of fact he soon found that practically all of the inside clique of business leaders were members and also that they made The Southwestern their stamping ground, meeting there for conferences, bringing new problems or projects there for hastily organized confabs and more often than not launching their promotions there, perhaps as the result of some chance suggestion or some random bit of information dropped in casual talk. Now that he was immediately available these men got into the habit of calling Jory in more frequently, admitting him increasingly to their confidence and asking his ideas and opinions on their plans.

One of the results was his early inclusion in the very small group that was projecting a bold twenty-million dollar water supply project for Los Angeles.

Separated from the city by three mountain ranges, a forbidding desert and a semi-arid basin and located in another county, lay a long, narrow valley into which flowed the run-off from the almost perpetual snows of the Sierra Nevada. To bring this water to Los Angeles would require an aqueduct 250 miles in length and incredibly difficult to build. But it would furnish a domestic water supply adequate, they said, for all time to come. And the inside clique of civic leaders had decided to undertake the launching of the grandiose enterprise.

The most elaborate precautions were taken to keep the whole matter secret, since it was known that a big power company was casting glances that way, that the valley had been appraised by the United States Reclamation Service and furthermore since it was imperative to prevent speculators from rushing in to skim the cream by forestalling the city's right-of-way and water-rights agents. The secret had been kept. To make a start the men Billy Wing had called The Band of Hope had advanced a substantial sum; now they had let the City Treasurer in on the plans, they told Jory, and had prevailed on him to advance $100,000 for preliminary expenses from the city's general fund.

"That's against the law, of course," Adam said. "Suppose the people turn the whole thing down — refuse to vote the bond issue."

Sussmann, the banker, chuckled. "The Treasurer's bondsmen would have to make good, likely."

"Who's on his bond?"

"Well, I am, for one — and two or three of the rest of us."

The Band of Hope! Beginning in the days of the Fiesta these incurable boosters had gone on staking their money on the future of Los Angeles.

"Count me in from now on," Jory said. "But I must say that this scheme sounds like a tough one to put over. Will the voters back a twenty-million bond issue? Everybody knows that we have plenty of water for several years to come. How are we going to get them to look so far into the future?"

Job Grannis grinned. "We've figured on that, Jory. This summer there's going to be a water shortage. By next spring they'll fall over each other to vote the bonds."

"A water shortage! Where do you get that information, Job?"

Grannis let one eyelid fall, significantly. "Oh, I've heard it around."

Los Angeles did have a water shortage that summer. The

76

irrigation of lawns was limited, sprinklers were forbidden except for two hours in the evening and in a few districts in the hills there were actual brief periods of complete drought. In the following spring the newspapers broke the story of the plans for the Los Angeles Aqueduct and the City Council passed a resolution directing the City Attorney to draw up the call for a special election on a bond issue of $20,000,000.

At about this time one of the insiders proposed that Jory lunch with him. "We're going to cut a little melon on the Aqueduct proposition, Adam," he said.

"What melon is that?"

"The engineers have been worrying about providing sufficient reservoir capacity near the city. Now they've come up with a great idea. They've found that the San Fernando Valley is a big bowl of gravel, under the surface; the new scheme is to run the Aqueduct water into it and pick it up with pumps at the lower end as it's needed."

"I don't see where the melon-cutting comes in."

"I didn't either till the boys explained it. They plan to deliver the water to Valley land owners to use for irrigation."

Jory frowned. "Do you mean we're going to ask the voters to build a water line to supply a lot of vegetable growers? Why, they'd run us out of town on rails, and I wouldn't blame them."

"Keep your shirt on, Jory. The engineers say that the water will stay underground after it's been used and that the loss won't be as great as it would be from evaporation in surface reservoirs. What's more, reservoir dams are one of the big items of expense in the project."

"Maybe they know what they're talking about," Jory said, slowly. He digested the information. "There's another hitch, though. Our water rights and the rights-of-way across public lands are to be granted by the government only to bring a domestic water supply to the city — inside the city limits."

"That's correct. And the answer is to annex the San Fernando Valley."

Jory seldom laughed but he laughed at this. "Well, of all the nervy enterprises, that one takes the cake! Then our north city limits will be somewhere up in the sagebrush."

"What's the difference, Adam, if you and I and the rest of us have picked up a few hundred acres apiece inside them?"

The proposal left a bad taste in Jory's mouth. He prided himself on being scrupulously honest and he had always had a strong aversion to jobbery and graft. He had been shocked when ·the ubiquitous Billy Wing had told him some weeks earlier, that the water shortage of the summer before had been caused by the secret wasting of millions of gallons into the city's storm drains. He recalled a visit made him, as publisher of the *Messenger,* by a committee of farmers from the Owens River Valley and their bitter complaint that their water rights had been stolen from them and that the city's project would turn their 75-year-old colony of industrious and thriving agriculturists into a desert. He had dismissed both charges as preposterous — had put them out of his mind. Now he was less sure.

This San Fernando Valley business had the same shady aspect. And yet the men involved in the Aqueduct project were the most respectable and decent in the community; not one of them could be accused of sharp practice in his personal affairs. True, they had to adapt available means to their ends, just as Adam himself had made Golconda possible by showing his railroad friends how they could sell their own oil to their companies at a good private profit. If a business man were to boggle at such customary and entirely lawful methods he would not stay long in business.

As usual he put his scruples out of his mind and sent Herbert Kinney into the Valley to buy land for him and Julius Nostrander. The owners were glad to sell, at prices ranging from ten to twenty dollars an acre. Most of them had bought at less than five — a few had practically stolen their holdings from impoverished and improvident owners of old Mexican grants. They had planned to sink wells, finding the soil rich and easily tilled, but only the first comers got adequate water and these went to the courts and stopped further developments when the underground water-level began to fall. Now the bare land was a white elephant; they were glad to be rid of it and were secretly a little sorry for the buyers.

Among the pieces Kinney found, as it chanced, was the old Simeon Luke place where Adam Jory had made his start in the Southland. The Lukes were dead and the little farm had deteriorated in the hands of a succession of shiftless renters. Jory went out there, one day, while he was making an inspection of his new properties. On the spur of the moment he said.

"Get out the deed to this place, Kinney, and give it to me. I think I'll keep the farm."

That summer the $20,000,000 Aqueduct bond issue was approved enthusiastically and without question, by a vote of 7 to 1.

The circulation of the *Messenger* made a slow, steady growth, but the paper continued to operate at a loss.

John Shelley was turning out a sharp, lively newspaper, with particular emphasis laid on a feature new in those days — what he called human interest stories. Mostly these involved animals and children, unfortunates, hard luck cases, the poor, outcast and wronged; they were written to arouse the interest and the sympathies of the reader and were frequently followed up until something was done to give the episodes a happy ending. *Messenger* reporters soon learned that a fire that burned out some struggling little family was given ten times as much space as a 3-alarm fire that demolished a factory or a rich man's residence. The eviction of a poor spinster dressmaker by the agent of the owner of her cottage, scarcely mentioned by the other papers, ran half a column in the *Messenger* and was followed, to make a nine-day wonder, when Shelley's courthouse reporter, digging deeper, found that the hard-hearted landlord was the Methodist University, which had been left Miss Canby's rented home by a pious old church member. The burned-out family was provided with a comfortable cottage at low rent by one *Messenger* reader and others fairly flooded the unfortunates with odds and ends of furniture. Poor little Miss Canby was provided with new quarters and found more work than she could do. And the *Messenger* got itself talked about and picked up a hundred or two new subcribers.

But advertising income did not increase enough to show a profit. Jory was irked. He was in the habit of making his enterprises pay and he was stubbornly determined to turn the corner with this one, particularly because of the sneers and jibes of Major Oddie in the *Daily Sun*. There the Jory paper was referred to as "our panhandling contemporary," "a bankrupt journal" or "that expensive plaything of an oil-driller who makes good its payroll out of greasy profits that come from padded contracts with his dupes."

"Of course that's libel, Jory," Attorney Valentine said, indignantly. "It's high time somebody gave Oddie a lesson in common decency."

Adam Jory shook his head. "Not me. If I sued I'd have to admit that I read the *Sun,* and I wouldn't give Oddie that much satisfaction."

But such coarse digs increased his grim determination to get the *Messenger* out of the red.

John Shelley and Billy Wing made so bold as to declare that the trouble lay in the wishy-washy character of the paper. They urged a vigorous, militant, aggressive policy looking to the improvement of conditions in Los Angeles. Jory snorted that conditions in Los Angeles were good — but he refused to listen when Wing offered to bring him some later and more exact information.

"I didn't buy the *Messenger* to expose a few small-time gamblers or to tell the world that we have a redlight district. We want to bring people here, not drive them away."

The fact was that all his interest and preferences ran with the established order of things in the city. He was an em-

ployer and opposed to coddling labor. He prospered under
the existing political machine, openly controlled by the railroads and a few ward bosses, some of them admittedly of
unsavory repute; if the politicians had their little arrangements and advantages he didn't want to hear about them. And,
finally, he was, himself, one of the group Billy Wing scoffed
at as The Band of Hope; no matter how the quirky Wing
felt about it Adam Jory had no intention of attacking those
stalwarts and jeopardizing the future of Los Angeles which
they so sedulously guarded.

"You're probably right, Mr. Jory," the unabashed Billy
Wing said, once. "If you kicked over the traces you'd be
branded an outlaw by the Chamber of Commerce and at your
club. As for the city's blue-stockings, they'd crucify you socially."

"I don't like that remark, Wing," Adam snapped, stung.
"It sounds as though you thought I was either a lickspittle or
a coward."

"Hell, no," Wing said, with a straight face. "Whatever
gives you that idea?"

Adam was so wroth that for a few days he considered
having Shelley fire the cynic. But his sense of fairness prevented. His thin smile passed across his face. The fact was that
he and Billy Wing had a lot in common in their scant regard for social position and for the complacence of some
of the city's aristocracy. And the fellow did have an uncanny
knowledge of what went on in Los Angeles — a knowledge
that was worth much more to the paper than Wing's salary.
Better and more convenient to forget the matter. He could
do that and he did. But sometimes he wondered just how
nearly right Wing was about an editorial policy.

Jory was surprised one day to be told by a clerk that he
was being waited on by a committee of union labor people. He
was learning that, as a newspaper publisher, he lost nothing
by listening, and he had the visitors shown in. One of them
he recognized as Walter Young, once a foreman in the *Daily*

Sun print shop — the man who had sued for the forgiveness
of a woman bookkeeper at the time of the strike. The second
introduced himself as secretary of the local iron-workers'
union; the third was a visiting organizer from San Francisco.

"What is it now, Young?" Adam asked, on his guard.

"We've been watching the *Messenger* since you took it
over, Mr. Jory," Young said — "I mean the union people
have — and we think you're inclined to give us a square deal
in the fight we're making in Los Angeles."

"The *Messenger* prints the news, Young. My orders are
to treat everybody fairly."

"Even those who are in the wrong, Jory?" the San Francisco leader asked, sharply. He was a big bruiser of a man,
with a scarred face and gentle, sad eyes. "Even this Industrial
Association of yours, that hires spies to worm their way
into our unions, that puts the police out to beat up workingmen,
that blackmails little employers who want to sign up with
their union hands?"

"Those are loose charges, Erickson."

"Will you print them if we bring you the proof?"

"I can't answer that till I see what you have. And I'm not
sure I would, even if I were convinced. We want peace in
Los Angeles and we don't want the closed shop."

Walter Young broke in smiling. "You're going too fast,
Olaf. Mr. Jory, you're not opposed to organized labor, are
you?"

"I'm opposed to dictation from organized labor. I wouldn't
let you men tell me who to hire and fire."

"But you run a union shop at the *Messenger*."

"I do not. I — that is, I never signed any contract."

The three callers laughed. "Didn't you know that your
composing and pressroom are one hundred per cent organized?"

Adam's thin smile flickered. "I didn't know it. Probably
McAndrews thought it was better not to mention it. Well,
what do you folks want?"

They told him in sharp sentences of the growing strength of the unions in Los Angeles, of the bitter underground war being waged against them by Secretary Zaar, of the Industrial Association, of the elaborate spy system of the employers, of the importation of strike-breakers and non-union men whenever trouble impended over wages or working conditions. And they told him of union men slugged, beaten up or run out of the city, secretly, and with the police department turning its back, under orders from above.

Olaf Erickson was angry and bitter, but after a while, changing his tone, he said: "Mr. Jory, Los Angeles ought to be a poor man's Paradise. Workingmen are helping to build it up and they're going to keep on coming here. They have as much interest in making the city big and rich as the employers have. Some day the labor unions are going to lick the Industrial Association and establish the closed-shop rule. You have a chance to put the *Messenger* on the right side — on the winning side. You're a fair man and you love this town. Give us a hand."

These men nettled him, but Adam Jory recognized in them something of his own hardness, determination, singleness of purpose. He had never come face to face with them before — never given their cause a thought. Erickson's reasoning impressed him.

"I'll think it over," he said. "I can't promise anything."

"It would make me a proud man if our paper came out strong for labor," Walter Young said, as they rose to leave.

"Our paper?"

"I'm night foreman in the *Messenger* composing room."

Jory actually laughed. "The hell you are! It looks like I'd have to get downstairs some time soon and see what else I don't know about my own plant."

Adam Jory was deep in plans for the expansion of Golconda Oil a few weeks later when a lean, hard-bitten young man called, saying that City Editor Shelley had sent him.

"My name is Shively. I'm your day police reporter. Mr. Shelley thought you ought to pass on a story I've been working up."

"Why doesn't he pass on it?"

"It's pretty hot, Mr. Jory."

"Hot? Well, let's have it."

"A little two-bit gambler named Quayle was booked a while back here and he squawked so loud I looked him up. He was mad because he said somebody had double-crossed him and he talked. I put some time on the lead and now it looks like we've got hold of a story that would blow the lid off the City Hall."

"What do you mean?"

"I mean that money is being paid for protection — and its not chicken-feed money."

"What has the City Hall to do with it?"

"Some of the loot is going there."

"Wait a minute," Jory said, sharply. "I'm acquainted with both the Police Commissioners and I've known Mayor Archer for fifteen years or more. You're talking nonsense, Shively."

The reporter was unabashed. "Then it ought to be a good idea to take the story to the mayor and ask for a statement."

"I didn't say that. It would be an insult to him."

"Not if Quayle's squawk doesn't involve him, Mr. Jory."

"Damnation, Shively, you seem to be able to believe some little ratty gambler but not to believe me."

"That's right, sir. Because I think Mouse Quayle knows what's going on in Los Angeles and I don't think you do."

"I'm too rushed to go into this now," Jory said, impatiently. "Tell Shelley that I'll come to the *Messenger* office at eleven tomorrow morning."

The matter kept stirring in his mind. This was the sort of newspaper enterprise he most deplored — sniffing for scandal, for a sensation, without regard for what the results might be on the city. He had adopted for the *Messenger* the policy of printing constructive news and playing down every other sort.

And the gutter-sweepings the new police reporter had brought in revolted him. He decided, offhandedly, that he would have no truck with it.

He worked late that night and when he went to the editorial rooms the next morning he was curt and irritable. He found Billy Wing with Shelley.

"Where did you pick up this new police reporter of yours, Shelley?" he demanded, as an opener.

"Shively? He's from Chicago."

"This graft story of his sounds like it. I suppose such things could happen there."

"But not here, Mr. Jory?"

"Certainly not. I'll grant that a few dollars might be passed to a policeman now and then. But organized boodling — fiddle-sticks!"

Billy Wing, slouching deep in his chair, took out his pipe. "Maybe you wouldn't hear of it at The Southwestern or at a directors' meeting, Jory, but, in the low circles where I disgrace my family by moving, its been common talk for a long time. In fact, if you'll remember, I mentioned it to you when you bought the *Messenger.*"

"You like to poke fun at business men, Wing," Adam snapped. "But they're not all fools."

"Oh, fools? I haven't said they are. But I will say this much: You business men in Los Angeles know to a penny what our bank deposits are and just how many tourists come in every week, but you don't know who rents the back rooms in some of your downtown office buildings or how many girls are peddled every night along Commerical Street and in the Marchessault cribs. You have postal receipts and building permit totals on the tip of your tongue, but how many hopheads or shady bookies there are working the streets doesn't concern you. I'll go farther and say that, as long as business is good and the 'bloody Eighth Ward' is quiet, you don't care. Be fair, now; isn't that the truth?"

Adam Jory stiffened; scowled. Then he said: "Perhaps

85

it is, generally. What of it?"

"Nothing to be ashamed of. Because the same thing is
true of your kind of citizen in Chicago or San Francisco or
St. Louis — in any big town. The point is that your not
knowing about rotten conditions here doesn't prove they
don't exist."

"But I happen to know the Mayor — most of our city officials. I was on the citizens' committee that approved the
slate in the last campaign, in fact."

"Sure; the Band of Hope. Sorry! I mean, the civic leaders
of Los Angeles."

"It doesn't matter what you call them, Wing; they recommended the ticket to the voters because they believed every
man on it was a high-grade, respectable, honest citizen."

"And yet Shively comes in now," the city editor broke in,
"and tells us that Poker Harris is sending a thousand a month
to the City Hall for protection — and getting his money's
worth. A thousand a month isn't pin-money, Mr. Jory — and
we've found indications that it's only part of the story."

Jory rose abruptly. "It's just as I thought, Shelley — your
Chicago man has dug up some rumors and hints and gossip
and you fellows want to go to bat. If you'll bring me some
proof of serious grafting in the city I'll listen to you. But that's
going to be impossible, in my opinion."

Billy Wing chuckled. "Keep your fingers crossed, then,
Jory. Because I've got a notion that if John turns this Shively
bear-dog loose he'll tree some game that it'll take an elephant-
gun to bring down. And then — stand from under!"

The truth was, Adam Jory admitted to himself, that the
conference had disturbed him. He had cut it short partly
because he hadn't wanted to hear anything more. Childish
perhaps, but there it was. At least he had gained time in which
to prepare himself for whatever was to come.

That it would be something unpleasant he was inclined to
fear. John Shelley and Billy Wing were not actually scandal-

mongers, nor were they men to be taken in by tall tales. They suspected that there was some fire behind the smoke the new reporter had sniffed, and obviously they wished the *Messenger* to do something about it.

In the next few days Adam made inquiries on his own account among business associates and club acquaintances. The concensus was that Mayor Archer and Commissioner Canfield were upright and conscientious officials — that the city administration as a whole had been capable and satisfactory, if not especially brilliant. No one knew of anything against the police department, and crime and vice conditions seemed to be normal and Los Angeles an exceptionally clean city. This last boast, Jory noted wryly, was based only on the evidence that there were almost no arrests for gambling, dope-peddling, prostitution and the other seamy activities of night-life. Earlier he would have accepted that sort of proof without a question; now he found himself remembering what Shelley and the others had said about protection — paid for and delivered.

One man about whom he asked was mentioned doubtfully, he observed. Police Commissioner Luther Hayward, a contractor, had been well-thought of at the time of his appointment, four or five years back; now it appeared he was earning something of a reputation as a sport and a free-spending patron of lively cafes, the races, prize fights and like activities. Lawyer Valentine recalled that Hayward had been sued for divorce some time before; he said that the wife had talked of sensational disclosures but, in the end, the decree had been granted her after a very quiet hearing, during which none of the spicy matter promised had come out. That was the sum of the evidence against the police commissioner; clearly it was not enough to justify loose talk about receiving bribes.

Jory breathed more freely — began to hope that Shively's graft story had proved to be baseless. Then City Editor Shelley telephoned to ask for another confab — indicated that it was urgent. In grim mood Jory went to the editorial rooms. Shelly, Wing and Shively were awaiting him.

"You wanted facts, Mr. Jory," the editor said, tersely. "It looks like Shively has found you some. Will you take a look at this?"

He passed over a typewritten document of half a dozen pages that Adam recognized as a signed affidavit, acknowledged impressively by a notary public. He glanced at the signature.

"Antoine Gastineau. That name seems familiar."

"Down in the Eighth Ward," Billy Wing volunteered, "Tony is known as 'the king of the macs.' He operates the two biggest parlor houses on Commercial Street and controls probably half of the girls in the crib district. You've heard of him, I suppose, as one of Waldo Harker's ward-heelers — and a very useful one, too."

This Harker was ostensibly chief of the local claims division of a transcontinental railroad; actually, as a subrosa employe of the other railroads, the street car lines and the gas, telephone and electric companies, he was acknowledged boss of the Los Angeles political machine. Jory winced at Billy Wing's cynical bracketing of the two names — snorted.

"Do you expect me to believe anything a brothel owner says?" he asked, angrily.

The irrepressible Billy Wing shrugged. "When you come to statements about his own line of business Tony's testimony would mean more than an affidavit by the pastor of the First Methodist Church, Jory, wouldn't it? Especially to a grand jury."

Adam's thin smile passed across his face. "Maybe you have me there. Well, let's see what you fellows have cooked up."

He was still unprepared for the dish.

In considerable detail the Gastineau statement disclosed an arrangement by which the underworld was assured a practically unlimited license to operate in Los Angeles without interference from the police or the City Hall. For this protection $400,000 was named as the annual fee, the money being raised by fixed levies on the beneficiaries and distributed, Gastineau averred, by two pay-off agents, Abe Frankel and one "Guaymas" Gomez. Jory winced again. He knew Abe Frankel, a dapper, cocky little character who had for some years gone back and forth between Boss Harker's office and the head-quarters of the civic leaders who, with Adam himself, directed the destinies of the city, as far as its industry, business, development and exploitation were concerned. If this affidavit were to be credited, here was something very close to proof of a tie-in between business, the local political organization and the whole vice and underworld system of Los Angeles. And Adam Jory, feeling a little sick, found himself unable to deny the document that credit.

Angry and perplexed, he waded on.

Contributors to the slush fund, Gastineau asserted, included not only three gambling syndicates and the men who controlled prostitution but also bookmakers, a club of race-track touts, the operators of certain all-night saloons and dancehalls, both illicit under city ordinances, a gang of narcotic dealers and a lottery and fantan ring in Chinatown. In some cases Gastineau detailed the amounts subscribed; others were approximated. The total purse ran to $30,000 a month. The split-up as between officials the paper was vague about, but not about the recipients. Named were the Police Commission, the Mayor's office (through the Mayor's secretary), three police captains, four detectives, a deputy in the criminal division of the office of the District Attorney, and a job-lot of policemen and deputies sheriff; blandly it was alleged that a school of smaller fry were taken care of through Mayor Archer's office.

With a wry face Jory tossed the document to a desk. "How did you get this from Gastineau, Shelley — buy it?"

The city editor grinned. "My budget doesn't carry that kind of money, Mr. Jory. Shively screwed it out of him."

"Well, Mr. Shively?"

"It was partly luck, Mr. Jory. The first thing I did after our last talk here was to dig a little deeper into Mouse Quayle's squawk — the gambler I told you about. It checked both ways and I turned up a few more angles working on it. When

I finally went to Gastineau I told him enough so that he was convinced we weren't just out on a fishing expedition. The first break came when he asked me where I got my information.

"I knew he wouldn't be worried over the squealing of a two-bit bookie's tout like Quayle so I hedged with some pretty vague hints about a leak in Harker's office. What I didn't know was that a few weeks back Abe Frankel had stolen one of Gastineau's women from him and the two had been swapping insults and threats. Tony jumped to the conclusion that Frankel had turned him in and he blew up and talked."

"You didn't get this affidavit then?"

"That came just yesterday," Shelley interjected. "We had decided to stock up with a little more ammunition after Gastineau's first oratorio, so I put Shively and Wing and a couple of good legmen on the trail of the graft payments. They gophered out one policeman who lost his head, and that helped. A number of nice leads developed and pretty soon we had a fairly complete picture of where at least part of the boodle had been spent."

"For instance?"

"Well, for instance," Wing said, "His Honor, the Mayor, has paid off a twelve thousand dollar mortgage on his business in the past year. Police Commissioner Canfield seems to have kept his hands pretty clean, but Hayward is in up to his neck. His contracting business has gone to pot, and yet he's been able in the last three years to put a nice piece of change into the Vernon Sporting Club, which is only another name for a juicy gambling and prize-fight-ring enterprise. Also Lute has a stable of nags at Ascot Park and an orange grove nearly paid for."

Shively offered: "Detective Captain Polland hasn't done so badly. He's building a summer home at Arrowhead that even his French wife couldn't squeeze out of a policeman's salary. And some of the other boys are getting ready to retire and enter business. I can give you details — "

Jory interrupted sharply. "All this left-handed evidence

would be worthless in court. You people know that!"

Wing said, dreamily, "But it would make mighty persuasive reading in the *Messenger*, Jory."

"What about libel suits — and half a million dollars in damages?"

"We're in the clear there," Shelley answered. "I had a lawyer friend of mine, Earl Tomblin, check on everything we've done and it's judgment-proof."

Jory sat a moment thinking. Then he said: "I wonder if Gastineau and his shady friends have been getting their money's worth."

"That's Shively's department," Shelley said.

"They can't kick, Mr. Jory. Just for appearance's sake the Chinatown squad brings in a girl or a fantan dealer or a hophead once in a blue moon and they're fined a few dollars. But that's the extent of it."

"Do you mean that all these illegal businesses run scot-free?"

"That's right. And practically wide open."

Adam Jory rose and began to pace the floor. He was not in the habit of pacing floors — of vacillating or fumbling over decisions. But this revelation slowed him down. He would have found satisfaction in helping to jail the whole miscellany of venal policemen — gamblers, touts, narcotic peddlers and bawds involved; he would not lift a hand to save a double-dealer like Commissioner Hayward. But if the *Messenger* made the exposé Shelley had in preparation it would involve the city administration he and his business associates had backed; it might hobble Boss Harker, on whom they relied to operate the complex political machine that safeguarded their interests and, most important of all, it would be a catastrophic blow to the good reputation of Los Angeles. That consideration decided him.

He came back to his desk. "It's no use, Shelley. I can't turn you loose on this crusade. If you can suggest any way to put a stop to boodling without turning the city upside down,

I'll listen. But the *Messenger* isn't going to indulge in a mud-slinging campaign — that's final."

The reporter was rolling a brown-paper cigarette and looking bored. City Editor Shelley reached for the affidavit and began folding it up methodically. He was licked, and knew it.

Billy Wing took a long pull at his pipe. Then he drawled: "How about turning Gastineau's memoirs over to the City League, Jory?"

"That crowd of half-baked radicals? No, thanks! I understand some of them are talking about putting up a reform ticket and attacking Harker and the organization. This business might be just enough to give them a send-off."

Then Wing said something that Adam Jory didn't quite understand until long afterward.

The lounging observer knocked out his pipe and rose.

"There goes your big exclusive, John. It looks like it's got to be a poultice instead of a major operation."

Shelley smiled wryly. "At any rate I'm going to put this affidavit in the safe. It may come in handy some day."

Several weeks had gone by and Jory, absorbed in his multiplex business enterprises, had forgotten politics when, without warning, Mayor Frank Archer suddenly resigned, pleading pressure of personal affairs. Several of his appointees went with him, including the Chief of Police and the two Commissioners.

There was a buzz of speculation over the matter and plenty of gossip, but no scandal. Jory knew immediately that the *Messenger* investigation must have some connection, but he could get nothing out of either Shelley or Wing, and his friends were mystified. The inside clique of civic leaders was summoned to a conference, Jory among them, and they were asked to pass on the mayoralty candidate proposed by Boss Harker to fill out the unexpired term.

The man nominated was a politician of no importance and

with some bad associations. For the first time since he had been training with this group, and almost to his own surprise, Adam Jory unequivocally opposed them all. He said flatly that the candidate must be a high-class business man, with a sterling reputation and with no political background. Challenged, he proposed Hamilton Stewart, a successful wholesale merchant and active in church and charitable enterprises. A few die-hards protested feebly, virtually admitting that this would be encroaching on Waldo Harker's preserves and might offend the powerful boss. Jory bluntly damned Harker and stuck to his guns. Stewart was chosen. Surprisingly enough, Harker acquiesced cheerfully and on the following day Stewart was elected by the City Council. Within a week the new Mayor had appointed a dull but honest police lieutenant Chief of the department and had filled the numerous appointive offices vacated by Archer's men.

Some time later Adam Jory met Billy Wing in the hallway of the *Messenger* building.

"Well, Wing, it looks as though we've got an honest city administration in control now," he observed.

Wing showed the face of a wise old owl. "You're an incurable optimist, Jory. But you're not the only one. Optimism is a sort of epidemic among our best people in Los Angeles — they all suffer from it."

"What's the matter with the City Hall?" Jory demanded, a trifle testily.

"Oh, nothing that a clean sweep wouldn't cure. Maybe you don't know it, but the fact is that every Stewart appointee is a Waldo Harker satellite. What you've got now is the same old organization puppet show — in new suits of clothes."

"I'm beginning to wonder, Wing, if you're not a City Leaguer yourself — or maybe a member of the red Citizens' Party. If I thought you were — "

"I'm not, Jory. I'm a mugwump, and I consider that the only good politician is either a brand-new amateur or dead." He started on — turned back. "By the way, have you heard the news about our talkative friend, Tony Gastineau?"

"No."

"His body was found floating in the Inner Harbor turning basin this morning. There was a bullet hole in his head."

Billy Wing slouched away, reloading his pipe and whistling softly.

The City League Adam Jory looked on with so little favor had begun a few years before as a solemn, rather dull organization more concerned with the theory of good government than with practical efforts to attain it. It assembled for *table d'hote* dinners, listened to dry papers on municipal problems, studied measures pending before the City Council and occasionally recommended to the voters the names of candidates it approved for public office. Nobody paid much attention, not even League members.

But toward the end of the first decade of the century the League, like many similar bodies elsewhere, was caught up in a wave of practical political reform then sweeping the country and, transformed by new blood and galvanized by new contributions, it bourgeoned suddenly into a militant and effective force. One of its recruits was a smart, realistic young lawyer who had learned machine methods under the boss system and who proceeded to cross-index the Great Register, choose ward and precinct captains and preach the doctrine of getting out the vote. The rapidly growing party was vociferous for turning the rascals out and starting the city over with a clean slate. They had, as yet, no vigorous newspaper support, but the leaders were elated when Major Oddie, in a fit of temper, deigned to notice them in a vituperative editorial blast in the *Sun*. The immediate result was that a few thousand Oddie-haters, including many union men, who had scarcely heard of the movement before, hurried to join it.

Most of the business leaders of the city were aligned against the League because it proposed to oust them from power with the machine bosses — "to turn the control of the city back to the plain people." Adam Jory, as a business man, agreed with his associates. He had prospered under the rule of the railroads and the gas company, Los Angeles had grown big and lusty through the unstinted work and contributions of that clique of insiders whose first promotion had been the Fiesta, and, finally, Adam mistrusted the ability of the mill-run of voters to handle public affairs. That was how he felt *as a business man.*

But the corrupt conditions Clare Shively had revealed had given Adam, *as the owner of the Messenger,* a serious shock. He had no smug theories of God-given stewardship, nor had he spent much time worrying about social obligations. But he did have a deep-seated affection for Los Angeles and jealousy of her good name. Therefore he was appalled to find that grafters, gamblers, brothel-keepers and such rapscallions appeared to be joined in an unholy partnership with what he thought of as the best citizens in controlling the city's public affairs. He had been unwilling to believe, with Wing, that the time had come for a clean sweep in government, even at the cost of a scandal.

Two unrelated incidents gave him a new shock.

He had grown to like Billy Wing, and occasionally, if both were at the editorial offices late in the evening, dropped in with him at a neighboring bar for a nightcap. In Rol King's place in the Hollenbeck on one such night Wing jogged Jory's elbow — pointed a thumb toward the back-bar mirror. Reflected there Adam saw two men, concealed from direct view by a partitioning screen, seated at a small table and absorbed in conference, with their heads together.

One he recognized immediately as Luther Hayward, the Police Commissioner whose resignation had come with the Mayor's. A second glance identified the other.

"Isn't it Abe Frankel, that runner for Harker's office?"

"It's Abe. The man Gastineau named as paymaster for the boodlers."

"What does this mean, then. They certainly don't look like

they're dawdling over a casual drink."

"Jory, the leopard doesn't change his spots and Hayward wasn't made over when we pinned that graft charge on him. I knew the rats wouldn't stay in their holes long. Well, it looks like they're out hunting for crumbs again."

The incident was still in Jory's mind when a second occurrence pointed it.

After two years of considering the project he had decided to erect a business block of his own on a valuable lot he had long held on South Spring Street. The work was well started when his architect suggested to Jory that he might avoid the expense of a costly heating plant by buying steam from the new Hotel Victoria, recently completed across the street.

"Good," Jory said. "Can you attend to it?"

"I can do everything but get the permit to run a tunnel under the street," Allison said. "That takes more influence than I happen to have at the City Hall."

"Influence? I don't think influence enters into it. I'll have Kinney attend to it."

The colorless business agent was given the necessary drawings and map, and took them to the City Hall. Several days passed, then Dave Allison called to know what progress had been made. Jory summoned Kinney.

"I'm not sure I can swing it, Mr. Jory. I find that the gas company doesn't want steam or hot water sold in Los Angeles; naturally they'd prefer to have each owner install his own unit. So Sam Gunn's office has sent orders to the Hall to block applications."

Jory glowered. "You made it clear that I'm the man who's asking for this, did you?"

"Naturally. But the Engineer's office says the City Attorney is ready to rule that such a tunnel as you want would have to be covered by a franchise. And to tell you the truth, Mr. Jory, the present Council is in Sam Gunn's pocket. Of course, if you want to see Mr. Gunn or Waldo Harker — "

Adam Jory's frown became a black scowl. He thumped

his desk. "No, by God! Do you think I'm going to go to Gunn and Harker with my hat in my hand to get the right to equip a new business building in this city? Tell Dave Allison to cancel his arrangements for buying steam. We'll install a boiler as he first planned. Get out, now, and don't ever bring me any such a proposition again!"

It was while he was still boiling over this indignity and while the recollection of seeing Frankel and the discredited ex-Police Commissioner together was still rankling in his mind that Adam Jory arranged a conference with the leaders of the City League. Jory as business man and Jory as owner of the *Messenger* were coming closer together — were beginning to merge, for the sake of Los Angeles, into one man, with a single, new purpose.

A week later the *Messenger* carried a three-column story on the political program of the City League and in a box on the front page an editorial announcement that the paper was committing itself to wholehearted and unequivocal support of the League's campaign for the defeat of the machine's boss system and a wholesale house-cleaning in the municipal government. The editorial had been written by John Shelley, with the vitriol of indignation and the sting of a wry humor supplied by Billy Wing.

But it was signed: Adam Jory, Publisher.

Adam Jory was not a man to spend much time thinking about himself. He was concerned with externals — with the main chance; with the promotion and management of his affairs; with the upbuilding and development of this city which had adopted him and had treated him so kindly.

But on the day when his offices were moved to the handsome new Jory Block, simple yet elegant behind its severe greystone front in the heart of the expanding business section, he did permit himself a moment of gratification. He had come a long way, in a few years, from the peddler's wagon with which he had made his start. The cough-racked, cadaverous boy had become a healthy, strapping man; he was married to one of the social arbiters of the city and they lived in a big house on the best residential street; his businesses were far-flung and prospering; his newspaper was suddenly becoming a political factor which must be reckoned with. The Jory Block was sign and symbol of the whole. In other parts of the state, as he sometimes heard, he was known as Jory of Los Angeles.

A moment: then he was absorbed once more in his work.

He had reserved the top floor of the new structure for his own offices, which had long since outgrown the suite in the Nostrander Building. The fourth floor he rented to the Golconda Oil Company. The lower three floors he had instructed Herbert Kinney to find tenants for and they were fast filling up. Adam had paid little attention, though he was presently struck by the fact that several offices were being taken over by men active in the City League or the Good Government organization. Then Clarence Showalter, treasurer of the movement, began to move his big cut-rate shoe store into the ground floor.

A few days later the secretary of the League said: "The Board signed that lease this morning, Mr. Jory. They wanted me to tell you that they appreciate the rental you fixed."

"Eh? Oh, yes. All right, Dwight."

That afternoon he summoned Kinney. "What's this about a low rent for the City League? They're thanking me for it."

Kinney, imperturbable, replied in his colorless voice: "You wanted the space rented. I've figured to make the Block return you a little better than eleven and a half per cent. Do you want more than that?"

"No. But it begins to look as though the building is filling up with City League people. Is that an accident, or did you plan it that way?"

"I figured that all you would care about was that I got tenants who would pay their rent. Was I wrong?"

Jory dismissed him with a shrug. Certainly he couldn't quarrel with his agent's business logic. And it was plain that the man was volunteering no information on his own. Adam could scarcely credit Kinney with a sense of humor, but could he have a sense of irony?

He mentioned his agent one day to Billy Wing.

"Bert is a cross between a weasel and a fox," Wing said. "I've known him since we were kids together at Sixteenth Street school. A weasel and a fox — with a strain of wolf."

Adam said curtly: "He's very useful to me. Are you suggesting that he's dangerous — or crooked?"

"Hell, I'm not suggesting anything, Jory. Of course he's useful to you. Only don't forget that the weasel and the fox and the wolf are all predatory animals."

Adam changed the subject. Billy had a way of nettling and mystifying him that was exasperating at times. But the fellow was — well, stimulating. And his knowledge of men and motives and their doings was certainly amazing.

The City League had leased the entire second floor of the Jory Block for ten years and was installing there the political campaign headquarters of the Good Government Campaign Committee. Jory was mildly uncomfortable about this development, but still he could find no fault with Kinney.

Then the *Daily Sun* pinned the coincidence down, in an editorial sneer.

> Our news columns report this morning that the anarchistic City League has taken a floor in the new building put up out of his fat profits by the former farm-boy who likes to think of himself as one of our Messiahs.
>
> Huh! Now honest citizens know who is financing the radical element in its impudent bid for political control in Los Angeles.
>
> Wake up. Voters! Beware of Jumbo Jory and his trained seals, the Goo-goos.

Adam tried to laugh off this smear, but he did not make much of a fist at it. He had to admit that Major Oddie had jumped to a logical conclusion. And again he was troubled by vague doubts about Herbert Kinney. But they passed away.

The man continued faithful, industrious, smart — and invaluable.

At the Southwestern Club members began to draw away from Jory. One choleric veteran, coming face to face with him unexpectedly in the barber shop, muttered venomously something about "a traitor to his class," wheeled and slammed out of the room, his face purple and his neck swelling.

Irene Jory was first incredulous, then furious.

"But surely this doesn't mean that you're going to support Alexander for mayor, Adam!"

"That's the present plan."

"What has come over you! Are you losing your mind? Don't you realize how that will affect your future — hurt my standing?"

Jory's half smile played around his lips. "I imagine we'll both live just as long and go on eating three meals a day."

"How can you joke about it? Everybody will turn on you — and I shan't blame them. You must know already that none of our friends will allow that wretched little newspaper of yours in their houses — not even in the servants' quarters. And now — "

"I wouldn't let it upset me, Irene. Your friends won't turn on you. And what they do to me doesn't disturb me one whit. I've always stood on my own feet; I think I can go on doing it."

"Oh, my God! That I should live to see this day! Thank heaven we haven't any children for you to disgrace!"

Adam's face changed. Some of the color left it and his mouth hardened. He stood up.

"I'd be willing to risk what my children would think of me, if you hadn't refused to bear any," he said, almost harshly.

And he left her, for the first time since their marriage, in anger.

Led by the Industrial Association and egged on by the *Daily Sun,* Los Angeles employers had become increasingly belliger-

ent in the fight against union labor. Victor Zaar, the obese
and arrogant little secretary-manager of the I.A., had promul-
gated a code of principles governing relations between employers and employed which the directors adopted and which
Zaar got them into the way of referring to as "the Los Angeles
Plan." It made a polite bow to "honest and loyal workers"
but chiefly concerned itself with a defiant affirmation of "the
open shop" theory.

> We declare that every man has a right to work and that
> it is un-American for any group or organization to deny
> that right unless or until the worker becomes a member.
> We further declare that every American has the right
> to employ whoever he wishes irregardless of whether they
> belong to a union or not.
> Finally we declare that, as members of this Association,
> we will oppose the closed union shop with every means
> at our disposal and will shut up our business before we will
> ever allow labor bosses to dictate to us.

With grammar and syntax considerably improved, the code
was later published in the annual report of the I.A. But neither
polish nor scholarship was requisite to an understanding of
the fact that here was a blunt and open declaration of war.
And the challenge was soon taken up.

There had been increasing bad blood between the workmen
and the owners of the big Paynter Iron Works for a long
time; conditions there were bad, no adequate safety precautions
were taken, and Grant Paynter, oldest son of the founder and
boss of the plant, was intolerant and ruthless. Spies put into
the foundry by the I. A. presently reported that a union was
being secretly formed, and seven alleged ring leaders were
fired and their names posted as a warning to the rest. In the
middle of the next morning the whole force walked out.

Industrial Association huskies, hastily sworn in as deputies
sheriff, were thrown around the works and the Chief of Police
sent a riot squad out the next morning. Striking employes assembled, more out of curiosity than anything, and though
there were some verbal arguments and names were called no

101

open break occurred until the third day, when the I.A. had a special train shunted on to the foundry spur-track and began unloading strike breakers. Then the workmen and their sympathizers closed in and a fight started.

In it twenty or thirty men were badly hurt and two were killed. Los Angeles was aghast. This was the first time blood had been shed in the long war; the timid were frightened, the sentimental were grief-stricken, the civic leaders, always almost morbidly jealous of the good name of their city, were appalled. These groups, each for its own reason, began to put pressure on the City Hall to withdraw the police and drive off the I.A. strong-arm gang. While the Mayor and the Chief of Police, bullied by the Industrial Association and deafened by the clamorous protests of the peacemakers, vacillated and temporized, two days of minor clashes led up to a second riot at the Paynter Works. A dozen more men were hospitalized and a well-known and well-liked policeman, long a friend of Los Angeles school children and on the eve of retirement after thirty-seven years' service, was killed.

Clare Shively, the *Messenger* police reporter, taken from headquarters by Shelley and assigned to cover the strike, brought in the story of old Mike Mannon's death.

"Strikers?" Shelley asked, immediately.

"No. An I.A. guard. They had a Paynter man down and Mannon went in to rescue him. There were four or five of the guards in a tight knot and I don't believe they knew he was an officer — didn't stop to see. One of them caught the old man across the temple with a loaded billy."

"You're sure of that, Clare?"

"I took time to *make* sure. The guard's name is Svenson and he told me he came here from Butte with five other thugs on the payroll of the Kearns Detective Agency to work for the I.A."

"Write the story. Let it run."

"O.K. But will the boss print it?"

Shelley's jaw jutted. "This is a good time to find out."

Adam Jory had given Shelley no orders on the strike story, thus far. The city editor thought Jory avoided the subject. But he and Billy Wing had talked the situation over and Wing had urged that the *Messenger* take a strong stand, with the municipal elections coming on and a sharper line being daily drawn between the reactionary organization and the good government forces. Shelley, cautious and inclined to let Jory make up his own mind, had confined himself to the news of the Iron Works trouble. But he had set two reporters at work interviewing strikers and their womenfolk and getting facts regarding working conditions in the foundry. Their reports were written and ready for the linotype.

Now Shelley had them headed up and sent to the composing room. He pulled proofs and gave these to Doctor Morehouse to read.

"Shameful! Barbarous!" the old gentlemen grumbled. "A blot on Los Angeles."

"Why don't you write an editorial saying so, Doctor?"

"I doubt that Mr. Jory would approve, Shelley."

"So do I. But I'd like to be ready if he does."

Around ten that night Adam came into the office. Without comment Shelley laid before him Clare Shively's blunt, uncolored account of the killing of Policeman Mike Mannon, the three-column story of conditions in the Paynter Iron Works that had led to the strike and Dr. Morehouse's moving editorial of protest and condemnation. Jory read them through without comment or sign. Shelley, back at his own desk, glanced across the office now and then, expecting an outburst. He had no prejudice either way. It was asking a great deal to expect Adam Jory, with his background and associations, to sponsor such a blast against the established order in Los Angeles; its publication might not only ruin the *Messenger* but it might fail to accomplish any good purpose. To Shelley it was simply a great news break and, more than that, the human interest story of the year.

Adam Jory finished his reading, gathered the long, smudged

galley proofs into a sheaf and rose. He kicked his chair back
and crossed the room.

"You're usually certain of your facts, Shelley. Are you certain here?"

"Yes, Mr. Jory."

"Then put this on the front page."

"All of it?"

"All of it." Jory's thin smile played around his mouth.
"I believe you and Billy Wing think the owner of the *Messenger* lacks guts, Shelley. You're wrong. Good night."

The municipal election campaign came on in due course.
The old-line organization, that for a quarter of a century had
manipulated city politics in Los Angeles with an almost careless ease, showed signs now of being worried. It whipped its
machine into high-pressure activity and levied on industry and
business, on the saloons and the underworld, an assessment
double that ever before exacted. The party bosses spoke con-
fidently of success. But there were storm clouds on their
horizon.

The "treachery" of Adam Jory, with his despised *Messenger*
rapidly gaining circulation and influence, especially among the
midwesterners who made up so large a part of the city's population, was a serious threat. There was the fact, too, that the
City League and its Good Government party were attracting
the active support of a number of well-to-do men, mostly newcomers but nonetheless voters and, more important, as willing
to spend money to give Los Angeles better administration as
the Band of Hope civic leaders had always been to boost its
population and importance. Word began to get around, too,
that Minor Lister, the machine-trained lawyer who was managing the campaign, was doing a thorough and workmanlike
job and leaving nothing to chance. Sam Gunn and Waldo
Harker, the railroad and gas company bosses, were hearing
constantly of Goo-goo precinct workers invading homes and
shops, lining up voters, passing out literature and, so it ap-

peared, making deals with ward-heelers who showed themselves willing to transfer their allegiance in return for favors
or future petty offices.

"Goddam it all!" Harker squalled one day, "how can we
fight those holy bastards if they're going to promise our workers street-department jobs? Call *that* Good Government!"

This story was brought to Adam Jory by the ubiquitous
Billy Wing.

"How did you come to hear it?" Adam asked, always amazed
at the man's stock of information.

"Let's see. I think that one came from Ed Rourke, the
bartender over at the Virginia, where Harker hangs out some."

"A friend of yours, this bartender?"

"Oh, sure. Ed and I hunt ducks together." And he added,
thoughtfully: "Sometimes Sam Gunn goes along, too."

"You don't mean the gas company boss?"

"Why, sure. Why not? Sam's one of the finest fellows I
ever knew. A good shot, what's more."

With the election less than three weeks off John Shelley and
Billy Wing came to the publisher of the *Messenger* with long
faces one evening.

"How much do you care about winning this fight, Jory?"
Wing asked, abruptly.

"I certainly didn't go into it to lose."

"Then you're going to have to throw away the kid gloves,
Mr. Jory," the city editor said. "The machine has made a deal
with the Citizens' Party — Harker has promised them one
councilman in return for their support of the organization
ticket."

"The Citizens! That radical crowd? Why, they haven't
votes enough to wad a gun."

"Not over the whole city," Wing agreed. "But their strength
in concentrated in the Second and Ninth, where we need them.
If the reds throw their weight to the machine we'll lose two
councilmen and may lose the mayoralty. It's that close."

"What do you want to do about it?"

"There's one big element in this town that could be swung if we get them mad enough — the church people."

"But surely they'll vote for good government — "

"Oh, some of them, sure. Not enough, Jory. Churchgoers are conservative by nature. Most of the local churches are run with the contributions of your business friends. And the ministers are probably ten to one backing Harker's ticket."

Jory had no church of his own — knew little about them. What Billy Wing said surprised him, but usually Billy knew what he was talking about.

"Granting that you're right, what's next?"

The city editor answered. "Trot out the Gastineau affidavit and tell the whole story of the reasons behind the Archer resignation, to begin with."

Jory looked from one to the other of them. "I don't know that story, if you'll remember."

Billy Wing chuckled. "Don't look at John, Jory. I killed cock robin."

"How?"

"I'm afraid the law would call it blackmail. I dropped a few hints in the right places and then I sat in on an all-night conference in a back room of the Richelieu with Sam Gunn and Frank Archer's campaign manager. A few days later the mayor found that his business needed him."

"You'll get a knife in your back yet, Wing," Jory said, with his faint rare smile. "All right, now what's this new move?"

"I've had the staff on the alert since Archer's resignation," Shelley said, "and they've found plenty. The cold fact is that Los Angeles is right back where it was, including a paid-protection system. But what will really blow off the lid is that we know now who killed Antoine Gastineau — and with that handle we can find out who ordered him killed."

"Good God! Do you mean that the murder ties into the rest of this mess?"

"That's what I mean. And our broadside will kick Harker's machine out with the boodlers and the underworld gang. Los Angeles will have what the City League wants — a clean slate."

"All right. Then go ahead."

Shelley held the blast up for five days until the last loose end was secured. Then the *Messenger* blazed forth.

The explosion rocked Los Angeles. Angry, horrified, shamed or indignant, the citizens made it their one topic of conversation and debate. There were those who cursed Jory for spreading the shame of the city abroad, but they were in the minority. The City Hall and the Police Department squealed, squirmed and blustered. Two libel suits were filed against the paper and its owner. The *Daily Sun* was almost as purple in its columns as was Major Wellington Oddie in his face. The organization laughed loudly — too loudly to be convincing. Privately, as Billy Wing soon reported, Waldo Harker and Sam Gunn admitted that the Goo-goos actually had a chance to win.

Meantime the Los Angeles Ministerial Association met and, after a stormy session, voted by 28 to 7 to make the exposé the subject of their Sunday sermons and to come out boldly for Alexander and the whole Good Government slate. Pledges of money poured into headquarters. Volunteer workers signed up. The women of the city held a mass meeting and persuasive speakers, hastily recruited by Charley Dwight and Minor Lister, told these sheltered and unsophisticated ladies as much as they could of conditions in the redlight district, the bawdy saloons and the gambling hells hidden away in back rooms in Los Angeles, the fair and lovely city in the sun.

At twelve o'clock on election night the regular machine ticket of the bosses had established a substantial lead in the returns and was holding it. In the *Messenger* office Adam Jory, his hat on the back of his head, watched the tabulations that a dozen reporters were bringing in or taking by telephone and that girls from the business office were computing and totaling, a few of them at adding machines. The place was a litter of early editions, discarded sheets of figures and crumpled copy paper; it was hot and stuffy and blue with smoke. The din was constant and deafening.

Reports, fragmentary and unofficial, poured in faster as plodding officials in the hundreds of polling places droned through the count. At a little past one the scale tipped in favor of the City League ticket, but a flash from the City Clerk's office quoted Boss Gunn as claiming victory for the machine by a comfortable margin. Adam Jory lighted another cigar, chewed at it abstractedly, threw it away.

At two- fifteen John Shelley pulled up to his desk a battered old typewriter and began pecking at it with two stiff, jabbing fingers. He ripped the sheet from the machine, edited it with a big soft pencil, bawled: "Boy!"

A red-eyed youngster, his shirt out of his pants and his hair in his eyes, ran across the room to the desk they had set aside for the publisher. Jory read the smudged copy hastily.

> Los Angeles yesterday elected a good government Mayor and five, possibly six, councilmen of his ticket by a majority of at least 7000.
> The Second and Eighth Wards and the blue-stocking districts went, as expected, for the machine candidates.
> But as the returns began to come in from other residence sections where workingmen and plain citizens live, the machine lead was overcome and at two o'clock this morning it was plain that the fight which has been made by the *Morning Messenger* and the forces of good government had been won.

Adam looked up to find the city editor beside him. on his coat.

"We'd look pretty foolish if you were wrong, Shelley."

"Sure. But I'm not. We can go to press with that. I'm going out to get drunk."

The official count gave Alexander better than 8,000 plurality and confirmed the election of six Good Government councilmen, with a seventh so close that a recount later brought him in. Save for the City Treasurer, a respectable old gentleman with a long tenure of office, the other administrative posts all went to the reform party — it was practically a clean slate.

John Shelley's lawyer friend, Earl Tomblin, was retained by Adam Jory to fight the libel suits which the pre-election exposé by the *Messenger* had brought on. Tomblin laughed at them.

"Broderick and Moss are bluffing, Mr. Jory. Neither one of them can afford to go on any witness stand, anywhere, any time."

Sure enough, the Broderick complaint was withdrawn within a few days. Dan Broderick, an owner of property in the lower end of town, gave Oddie's *Daily Sun* a long interview, protesting his own purity and uprightness and assailing Adam Jory; it was reported that he had engaged the town's biggest law firm to prosecute his damage suit. But after a month or two of postponements and delays McKenzie, Thoburn and Crist asked for a dismissal. Their client, they said, was in poor health — had been ordered to Arizona by his physician for a long rest.

Gossip had it that several members of the Southwestern Club were organizing to have the directors ask for Adam Jory's resignation. Jory, who had never found the Club indispensable, put his back up at this news. Bill Rowland, the real estate man, was greatly incensed — proposed to make Jory's fight for him.

"No, thanks, Rowland," Adam replied. "I doubt that the Board will take any action. But if they want to try it I'll give them a row they'll remember."

In his mail a few weeks later Jory found an envelope addressed in a woman's hand. Beulah's!

I always knew, Ad.
I said you would be the Big Man in Los Angeles and
I knew you would be on the right side, too.
   Judith begins to look like you. And she's stubborn
like you about going through with anything she starts out
to do.
   Good luck, Ad.

The days, weeks, months, swept on. Los Angeles prospered and Adam Jory with it.

The election of the Good Government ticket had angered the business leaders, the industrialists, the big employers. Perhaps because they were irritated, perhaps because they were afraid that this victory over the vested interests of the city might seem to offer encouragement to the workers, the Industrial Association forces stepped up their war on union labor.

There were several lockouts, organizers were kicked out of plants, two or three leaders were badly beaten up; the whole battle line tightened.

Adam Jory watched this development with a rising wrath. It was not that he loved the cause of the workingman so much as it was that this industrial struggle hurt Los Angeles. That, to him, was inexcusable. So the *Messenger* became increasingly a defender of the unions — an aggressive critic of the I.A.

A crisis was approaching, plain to be seen by all.

*   *   *   *

The insistent clangor of the telephone bell awakened Jory. He switched on a light; as he reached for the receiver on the stand beside his bed he saw that it was almost two o'clock.

"It's Shelley, Mr. Jory."

"Yes?"

"The *Daily Sun* building has been bombed. Several men have been killed and a lot hurt. The whole block is afire."

Jory took a minute to comprehend this news.

"It wasn't an accident?"

"I don't think so."

"Any arrests?"

"Not yet. We got Major Oddie on the phone. He says the unions did it."

"Did they?"

"I'm afraid so, Mr. Jory."

"Get statements from Young and Zalinsky — as many of the union heads as you can reach. Print what they say with whatever the *Sun* has to say. It's hard to believe that any workingmen in their right minds would do such a thing — take that line, Shelley."

He hung up.

For some time he sat, his whole body drooping, his head lowered, his eyes somber.

He was thinking, not of the newspaper that had gone down in the ruins of its building, nor of the union men who, beyond a doubt, would be blamed for this horror, innocent or guilty — he was thinking of Los Angeles — and for the moment he was in a rage against both the contending forces because, through their stupid wrangling, they had dealt her this foul and scarring blow.

CHAPTER FIVE

```
┌─────────────────────────────┐
│         THIS PROPERTY        │
│       For Sale or Lease      │
│           ROWLAND            │
│     REALTY BOARD BLDG.       │
│       ─────────────          │
│      POPULATION OF L. A.     │
│      Now      319,000        │
│      1920     600,000        │
└─────────────────────────────┘
```

WILL ROWLAND SENT one of his outside men to Jory in the following spring.

"We have a client who wants to rent your barn out in Hollywood, Mr. Jory."

"Barn? Oh, you mean that tumble-down old building on the Gower Street property?"

"That's it."

"But what for? A good wind would blow it over."

"They'll shore it up, I suppose. They're going to make moving pictures in it."

Adam Jory had heard talk about this new picture-making

business. Half a dozen groups of strange-looking individuals had appeared in and around Los Angeles, who set up clumsy cameras, hired some cowboys, rented a stage coach or two, dressed a gang of loafers up in the paint and war-bonnets of Indians and proceeded to photograph scenes of carnage acted out in the foothills or on flat grasslands in the vicinity. The men in charge of these antics were easily distinguished from the rest and from normal citizens by their dress — they all wore riding pants and boots and they all put their caps on backwards.

With his fellow businessmen Jory looked on this new activity with suspicion and some distaste. They thought that it made Los Angeles look ridiculous and what they saw of the people engaged in it was not heartening. Nevertheless they were told by the few who investigated that the climate and natural beauties of the region were ideal for the infant "art" and that it might grow into an important asset, given a little encouragement. They were skeptical. An "art," eh? Maybe. Of course, if it were an industry, now — !

Now Jory said to the real estate agent: "I haven't much use for this folderol, Waring. To begin with, I don't think these fly-by-nights pay their bills."

"Our man has offered to put down the first six months' rent cash in advance."

"Has, eh? And probably he'll set the barn on fire for me."

"We'll stipulate that he's to insure you. How much rent would you have to ask?"

"I don't know. The barn is just a shell. But I wouldn't bother with them for less than fifty dollars."

"Mr. Rowland told them a hundred and a half."

"A month?"

"That's right."

"And they didn't faint? Well, go ahead. But tell Rowland that I think we'll be buncoed somehow in such a deal."

A few months later young Waring came back with an offer from the picture people to buy the Hollywood lot. Jory wasn't

113

selling. Would he lease for five years? Yes, Jory said, if the
rental was sharply stepped up each year. Agreed.

One day he had his new chauffeur take him out that way
in the Pope-Toledo his wife had recently acquired. At first
they had difficulty finding the tract — Hollywood was growing
so fast. Then Adam wouldn't believe the lot was his.

What he was looking out on was a sunny Southern village
street shaded by big trees that had never grown there and
lined with quaint old shops and stores. In the distance was
the pillared porch of a plantation mansion beyond a smooth
lawn bordered with blooming rose bushes. Nearby was a courthouse — the façade of a courthouse, really, propped up behind
by heavy timbers and with both wings raw and unfinished.
Courtly gentlemen in tight pantaloons, long-tailed coats,
flowered waistcoats and either high silk or broad-brimmed
white hats, strolled in and out or lounged on the porticoes
watching a group of darky singers and jig-dancers on the sidewalk. A few elegant ladies, in hoop skirts and carrying tiny
sunshades, minced about, their children dressed in Eton
jackets and long trousers or in starchy gay ginghams and
looking generally bored and sweaty.

A gangling young man (with his cap on backward) ran
out in the village street blowing a whistle and shouting
through a megaphone. A bugle sounded, shots were heard
and suddenly the villagers began to flee, just in time to escape
being run down by a charging troop of blue-coated cavalry-
men. The whistle sounded once more and a tight knot of
townsmen appeared in the open doorway of a livery stable
and opened fire on the bluecoats, several of whom pitched
from their horses, writhed in the dust, then lay still.

Whistle once more. The dead got up and, dusting themselves off, went looking for their horses, one of which was
eating a rose bush in front of the plantation house. The elegant ladies hurried off or sat down wherever it was convenient,
two or three of them taking off their shoes. The grave citizens
rolled cigarettes or began a card game on the courthouse side-

walk. A push cart man appeared and opened a thriving business in bottled drinks. The lanky youth with the whistle sat
down on an up-ended keg, turned his cap around and began
writing on a pad of paper, occasionally pausing to suck his
pencil and looking thoughtfully at the peaceful scene before
him.

Jory leaned from the car and addressed a freckled kid who
watched all this with a bored air.

"What's going on over there, son?"

"You joshing?"

"No."

"Huh! They're filmin' Robert Edeson in 'The Rose of Dixie.'
An' Bessie Barriscale is in it, too. That's her puttin' on another
dress over behind the courthouse."

"I see. They're waiting for her, now, I suppose."

The boy looked at him pityingly. "You don't know much
about pikshers, do you? See that feller sittin' down on that
barrel? That's the dee-recter. He got to think up the next
shot, don't he?"

"Is that the way it's done?"

"How else would you do it, mister?"

"I don't know, son." He gave the youngster a quarter,
estimating that this disillusioned mentor had earned it. He
was thoughtful as Lind drove him back toward the city.

Two or three weeks passed before he found time to pursue
his new studies, then he stole an hour and groped his way
into Tally's Moving Picture Theater on Spring Street. Posters
outside announced Robert Edeson in "The Outlaw's Revenge."
The little hall was hot and stuffy, but it was crowded and the
audience was breathless and intent, breaking out occasionally
in applause or in shouts of encouragement or warning to the
stalwart figure of the star on the flickering screen.

That night Jory said to his city editor, "John, I think we'd
better look into this moving picture business a little. Get up
some good, lively stories about it. Play it up."

"I wouldn't be surprised if something came of it, one of

these days," he told his father-in-law.

Julius Nostrander stared at him. "Really, Adam. Hm! You don't mean you'd put money into it?"

"I have, J.N. There's a new outfit starting up — the Picta-graph Company. I don't usually buy stocks, but I'm taking a little flyer in this one."

*　　　　*　　　　*　　　　*

The *Daily Sun* disaster was a sudden and violent shock to the exuberant, bouncing, boastful young city of Los Angeles. The thoughtful saw in it a lesson, perhaps a warning, but they were few. The majority looked on it as a tragic incident in the long war between capital and labor and they took sides according to their natures, their interests, their prejudices, their fears. The violence and horror of the affair made calm judg-ment impossible to the average, and generally the reaction was unfavorable to labor, guilty or innocent.

While the flames were still roaring through the demolished building, Major Wellington Oddie had come out with the flat charge that the unions had dynamited the plant, as the result of a plot, undoubtedly carefully laid after months, perhaps years of planning, to ruin the *Sun* and to kill its employees. He never once retreated from that stand. He began rebuilding within a few days. The *Sun* did not miss an issue of publica-tion. Moreover it came through in a stronger position than before.

Almost to a man the business leaders of the city, practically all of whom belonged to the Industrial Association, took Oddie's view. A score of men had lost their lives and most of those on duty at that late hour were injured, some dreadfully. The indignation in Los Angeles was shared by the employing class throughout the country. And public opinion abroad, like that at home, arrived at a verdict of guilty without wait-ing to hear the evidence. The *Daily Sun* had been fighting Labor for years; the *Daily Sun* building had been blown up by dynamite. There could be only one conclusion as to who was to blame.

Labor vigorously and universally denied the charge. They asserted that the plant had been wrecked by an explosion of gas that had been seeping all day from a leaking main and that had been smelled and commented on by scores both in and out of the building. What possible gain could anyone seek from such a stupid plot? What laboring man would jeopardize the lives of other workmen, union or not? And they pointed out, too, that while the *Sun* was an open shop, at least twenty of its composing and pressroom staffs were actually holders of union cards. Would Labor kill its own? As for the Oddie charge, they asserted that the belligerent publisher was privately gloating over the disaster as a heaven-sent excuse for this hideous libel on the working class.

There was plenty of money available to back Oddie; within a few hours telegrams were pouring in pledging unlimited financial and moral support from industrialists, capitalists, business organizations all over America. The potent Kearns Detective Agency, long under contract to employer groups, had a swarm of investigators in Los Angeles within three or four days. Presently it was announced that a heavy charge of dynamite had been discovered at Major Oddie's home and another near the Paynter Iron Foundry, where the strike had been lost by the workers, who were bitter and angry and said so openly. Neither of these two lethal bombs had been set off and Labor instantly charged that they had been placed there by Kearns detectives. Whatever the truth, the reputed plot against the iron foundry brought into the case one of the strongest of American employer's groups, The Amalgamated Structural Steel Council; from that time on the A.S.S.C. took an active part in the case.

Adam Jory was one of the few Angelenos who tried to withhold judgment until there were more facts to go on. He was not converted to the cause of organized labor but he had begun to learn that there were good and able men on that

117

side and to recognize that they were as sincere as their powerful opponents. As always, his first concern was the welfare of Los Angeles, and that he knew could not be advanced by internal war. But on the other hand, the great majority of residents in the city worked at jobs — were dependent for their prosperity and happiness on fair wages and decent treatment. If it would take a war to win these aims, as the labor leaders declared, who was he to say that all the right was on one side — the side of the bosses? Finally, he was not willing to believe that Labor had blown up the plant of the *Daily Sun.*

His orders to Shelley and Dr. Morehouse were to print the news in the *Messenger* and to avoid pre-judgment. Nevertheless something of his open-mindedness in the situation crept into the columns of the paper; it began to be said that Jory was friendly to labor. Oddie, in the *Sun,* sneered at his competitor as a rich man toadying to agitators and dynamiters; union men rallied to Jory's support and subscribed to the *Messenger.* John Shelley put two or three of his best men on the *Sun* case, trying to dig up facts that would disprove the Oddie charges. Clare Shively worked night and day on the case; he it was who came up with a gas company employe who admitted that he had been sent to the *Sun* office on the day before the explosion to look for a leak and that, while he hadn't traced it, he had found gas fumes in the pressroom and in places on upper floors. This supported the claims of the union officials. Unfortunately the gas company employe, in fear of his job and perhaps even of his life, refused to allow his name to be used. However, this and other random bits of information were gradually accumulating to support labor's accident theory when a bombshell was dropped by the employers.

John Shelley telephoned the news to Adam Jory.

"The Kearns Agency has made two arrests in the dynamite case."

"Two? Union men?"

"One of them is an official of the iron-workers' national — Carrigan. Picked up in Pittsburgh. The other one is Walter Young."

"Young? Not the foreman in our composing room?"

"That's the man. It turns out that he's head of the local printers' union."

"What's the charge — dynamiting?"

"It's murder. And Scheaff, at the courthouse, says the District Attorney is going before the grand jury to ask for twenty-one counts — one for each *Sun* man killed."

Adam Jory went to the County Jail and asked to see Young. At first he was refused, the jailer citing orders from the D.A.'s office, but Jory's quietly voiced insistence scared the man and he sent for the prisoner.

Sitting in a bare, white-painted room into which the California sun came only thinly through the barred and glazed windows, Jory watched his foreman as he was admitted by a guard.

He saw a frail man, smaller than he had remembered him, neatly dressed in well-worn clothes, his hair thinning, his face tired but serene and smiling now. Adam Jory thought: That man a murderer? Impossible! and put out a hand. The printer grasped it.

"Thanks, Mr. Jory. Thanks for coming. But thanks most for — offering me your hand."

Jory was not at ease. The sounds and smells of the jail oppressed him; it was his first experience with the world behind bars and he found it disturbing and a little frightening. But Walter Young was completely himself. He asked about the *Messenger* and Shelley; joked about the composing room doing better under a new foreman.

"You're my first visitor, Mr. Jory. They won't let even Mrs. Young and my boy come."

"But they can't do that," Jory said, angrily. "That's against the law."

"I know. It's like the case of the darky whose friends said

they couldn't put him in the calaboose for burning down his own house. 'Mebbe not,' he said, 'but hyar I is.' "

Jory's occasional smile lifted the corners of his mouth. He said: "Young, I want you to know that I don't believe this charge against you."

"Thanks, Mr. Jory."

"How can I help you? Do you want me to send you a lawyer? I — the *Messenger* would see to the — "

"No, Labor is taking care of us." Young spoke with a sort of quiet pride. "I've got to ask something else, Mr. Jory. Don't defend me in the paper. If you can, defend Labor. That's the real thing that's on trial."

"I don't see that, Young. This case looks bad for Labor. For the unions, anyway. The Kearns Agency claims to have found pieces of the wrapping that came around dynamite sticks. Kearns himself says that they have located the place, up near San Francisco somewhere, where the dynamite was made — and the man who sold it. The *Sun* is saying that you sent the two men to buy the stuff and bring it down here."

Young's hands were clasped on his lap; he looked down at them and pointed the first fingers, that were gnarled and calloused with a lifetime of work at a printer's case.

"I wasn't thinking about evidence — the testimony they will find and bring against us. In this fight, Mr. Jory, the District Attorney can prove just about anything he wants to. It's that kind of a fight." He paused, then added: "It's that important for the bosses to win."

"Nonsense, Young! If Labor is innocent, we'll say — "

The little printer's face lighted up. "Ah, that's it! Labor isn't innocent — not of fighting the employers. Labor is in the deadliest, dirtiest, most terrible war ever fought in America — fighting for life, for right, for a fair chance for themselves and their kids and their homes! And when you think about that war, Mr. Jory, just keep one thing in mind — the one important thing to remember."

"Well?"

120

"That in all this war Labor has not invented or been first to use a single, solitary weapon. Not one." He smiled. "Maybe we're not bright enough or something, but we've had to borrow every one of our tactics and all our ammunition from the employers." He shook his head. "Take dynamite, now. That's force—a terrible, destructive force. Who taught us to use force? The boss with his city police department behind him; the company with its imported strikebreakers armed with loaded billies and brass knuckles; the employer with thugs carrying sawed-off shotguns—and able to call out the militia if everything else fails; yes, and the company lawyers, with their judges in black gowns and their death-chambers and cell blocks." He took a long breath. "It's war, Mr. Jory—Labor's war. If you want to help, for God's sake explain that to Los Angeles."

A little impatiently Adam said: "But what about you, Young? Can't you see that you're in real danger?"

"Yes, I see that. Look, union leaders are always in danger —real danger. We expect that when we take the jobs. What happens to me in this business isn't important. The main thing is to get our story over to the people—make them think. I've given up my whole life to this fight and if dying will help I'm ready to die in it."

Adam Jory went away shaken, perplexed, still impatient. He tried to tell himself that Walter Young was dramatizing the situation. No use. The worn little printer was too simple to pose, too much in earnest to indulge in rhetoric. His consecration was complete. His cause could not be shrugged off.

He had evaded the question of his guilt or innocence and Jory had seen that it was not a question to be asked. That the man had planted dynamite in Ink Lane against the rear wall of the *Daily Sun* building he would not believe. That he had bought it or sent others to buy it for the purpose of wrecking property or killing men was incredible. That he knew it was to be bought, to be used in some sort of demonstration of protest, yes, that might have been. What a fool! What a crackbrained, futile gesture — and how hideously tragic in the result! And, as Young had shrewdly seen, the State would hang him as surely for having had a part in the futile gesture as for having abetted the hideous tragedy. Yes, that was what the printer had been telling him: whatever he had done had been enough to make his conviction inescapable.

Nothing could save him.

Could anything be salvaged out of the wretched business for Los Angeles?

Adam came to a decision with difficulty, not because he dreaded its implications or cared about the consequences to himself but because he had to be convinced that it was correct. Beyond argument this internal warfare between capital and labor was costly and dangerous. It was no better advertising for the city in the sun than was the reverse situation in San Francisco, where the unions ran roughshod over employers — the citizenry as a whole. And it had another aspect that Adam Jory, as an employer himself, had had reason to ponder.

A great population of workers was essential to the fullest development of Los Angeles — the employing class would always be coming on to create new jobs by tens of thousands. And, whatever the *Daily Sun* and the I.A. might say, Jory was convinced that workingmen who cared enough about their trades to organize, stabilize and protect them were vastly preferable, both as employes and as citizens, to the floaters, ineffectuals and migrants who made up the bulk of the non-union mass. He was strongly prejudiced in favor of the open shop — of the right of the employer "to hire and fire" and to run his own business without dictation. But suppose these union organizers were justified in asserting the worker's right to a job. If he had any such right he had a right to defend it against all comers. One form of defense was the strike. The strike, like the violence that stemmed from it, was war. And, for the first time, Walter Young had given him a picture of what war meant to Los Angeles — might mean to its future.

122

He sent for his city editor.

"Shelley, when you first called to tell me about the *Sun* disaster you said you were afraid the unions were responsible."

"Yes. I still think so. But that doesn't mean — "

"Let me talk. I've concluded you were right. I think now that it was planned as some sort of demonstration — and it misfired. Maybe the building was full of gas. Maybe the barrels of ink exploded. It doesn't matter."

"It matters to Walter Young and Carrigan."

"I mean that it doesn't matter in considering what attitude the *Messenger* takes. What matters is what was behind the dynamiting — the right and wrong of this labor fight. I think the paper has got to say so."

Shelley was sharpening a pencil, giving close attention to every steady, slow stroke of his knife-blade. Without looking up he said, "You know what that will cost you, don't you, Mr. Jory."

"I think I do." Adam's faint smile appeared. "You can send the bills to me. On my books I figure to charge the expenses to the good of Los Angeles." He turned to the galley proofs on his desk. "That's all, John. It's your baby now."

While Los Angeles raged or cheered, gasped or swore over the emergence of the *Messenger* as an advocate and champion of union labor and while advertisers fell away from that journal as leaves fall from the trees in autumn, all of Adam Jory's other irons were kept well-heated — continued to shape up satisfactorily.

The oil-burner business, operating under his name, was almost entirely in the hands of Jim Jernigan, who was now the manager as well as factory superintendent. He had proved invaluable — a lucky find. Not only was he a master of mechanics but he had developed into a shrewd and able business-getter and organizer. His ingenuity had perfected old Gus Kerner's nozzles and had developed new fields for their use. His practical experience had taught him to keep ahead of the numerous inventors and competitors who appeared, so that now the Jory burners held a virtual monopoly in the West. The railroads were all converting, under Jory licenses. As Adam had foreseen, the coastal steamship lines had been compelled to start changing over to this more economical fuel and Jernigan was negotiating with a trans-Pacific fleet operator and preparing to open offices in Honolulu and Hong Kong. A separate department had been created to handle the local household burner business and that, under the management of a smart young sales manager, was being extended to other cities in California and through Arizona to El Paso.

Adam considered increasing the monthly allowance he made Dad Kerner, but Herbert Kinney opposed the idea.

"The old folks are well taken care of. They have everything they want. Let sleeping dogs lie."

"Do you keep in touch with them?"

"I make it a point to," the secretive confidential man replied.

"Is Dad still working at his inventions?"

"Yes. He thinks he has a new principle for an automobile carburetor. But nothing will come of it."

"How do you know? He might have something."

"He might. But he'll never do anything with it. He carries his notions just so far, then he hits a snag and gives up."

It was true. Adam dropped the subject, thinking that he would come back to it. But in the press of his affairs he forgot it.

The backbone of his growing fortune was real estate. Will Rowland, the population prophet, had been proven right again; in fact, in the first decade of the century Los Angeles had exceeded his 1900 guess of 250,000 and he had raised it in 1908 to 300,000. Two years later the city's growth passed even this point.

The exuberant, booming, complacent, lusty young metropolis was spreading out, spreading wide. It began to take on a new aspect — not a homogeneous city, surrounding a sharply defined inner core — the retail business district — but an aggregation of great villages, each with its own trading center, perhaps at some busy intersection of important thoroughfares, perhaps flowering around some such focus as a group of factories or, in two cases at least, a college campus. There was a story told concerning a shrewd Iowan who, heeled with the money received for his farm, came to Los Angeles and began studying its opportunities. Pretty soon he was buying a corner lot or two at points where the rapidly expanding street car system established new transfer places. It was said that, following this system, the newcomer made half a million dollars in a few years. No one doubted the tale. It was too plausible.

These local trading areas sprang up in every direction and more and more distantly from the original center of town as one annexation after another brought large tracts within the city limits. As the inside clique had planned, most of the San Fernando Valley, three-quarters desert and small, scattered farms, was voted in presently and, when the Aqueduct water came, half a dozen towns within the city mushroomed. Trade followed convenience.

But meantime the old downtown section itself began to take on a shifting and unpredictable nature. In a few years the business center had shifted southwest by many blocks — came to a temporary rest around Seventh and Broadway, leaving Temple and Spring, First and Main to deteriorate — become shabby, then shoddy, then cheap-john. The shrewdest and smartest real estate operators were hard put to determine which way the cat would jump next, and how far. In some cases secretly organized syndicates craftily promoted business shifts, quietly buying up lots and then, suddenly, erecting two or three big stores or business blocks, and insuring plenty of newspaper enthusiasm for the new development, often by the simple device of letting the publishers in on the proposition. The final result of all these developments was to add an element of hazard to all real estate buying that had not been present in earlier years. For now there were sections of Los Angeles that began to retrograde — that would never come back. The neat trick was to guess where deterioration would set in and how soon.

Adam Jory and Julius Nostrander, his father-in-law, were well equipped to trade in this sort of market. They knew the city thoroughly, they were not moved by sentiment or given to wishful thinking, and they dealt swiftly and in cash. They seldom lost. Without compunction the older man sold the Nostrander Block, where he had kept his offices for a quarter century, and moved into a suite in the new Jory Building. The old structure was bought by an advertising doctor and became a shelter for all sorts of quacks, charlatans, herbalists and physical therapy cultists, who thrived there. Within a year property in the same block and northward generally fell off in value by as much as sixty and seventy per cent. And in the same period frontage in the vicinity of the new Jory Building and thence south and east for several blocks doubled and even trebled in price.

His oil interests alone were sufficient to make Adam Jory a very rich man some day.

The Golconda Company was expanding rapidly, and now Adam had Herbert Kinney working on the details of a bold new move — the absorption of several shoestring outfits in the field and amalgamation with two sizeable competitors, the whole to form a giant corporation capable of extending its business halfway around the world. Golconda was itself a large producer, operating in three Southland oil fields; it owned valuable lands not yet drilled in, it ran two refineries and a large asphalt plant and it leased a fleet of railroad tank-cars and chartered three coastwise tankers by sea. In addition Jory, with his instinct for getting a tight grip on the future, had fostered another Golconda enterprise — a laboratory and by-product plant, which he had turned over to the canny management of his young chemist, Sanborn Wade. Wade had built

126

up the only important scientific staff in the western industry; these pottering, abstracted mooners had popped up with all sorts of absurd uses for petroleum and Wade had contrived to give most of them commercial possibilities. It appeared that almost anything could be made from oil — perfumes and drugs, a base for cosmetics, candles, leather dressings, sprays for killing insect pests in house, garden, orchard and field, roofing materials — an endless list. Golconda Laboratories was growing to be a flourishing concern on its own. Finally, the automobile was established as an American necessity and Golconda Red Eagle gasoline was powering a quarter of the cars in the Southland, with its own supply stations scattered about the city and being pushed out into the suburbs to serve the farmers and the small-town drivers. Jory urged Kinney on in the plans for the consolidation that would at least double Golconda's power, control and business.

Adam Jory still went often to the Southwestern Club, in spite of the fact that he was now coldly received by many of the prominent members. Perhaps all would have turned on him had it not been for his growing importance in the financial life of the city. His ability forced them to respect him; his power compelled them to recognize him. Even the *Messenger,* through which he had betrayed them, was a factor they had to deal with and count on in any project touching the development of the city. The local revolt against the political domination so long maintained by the railroads and the public utility corporations had spread throughout the state and the old machine had been forcibly and dramatically ejected from control at Sacramento and in most of the county courthouses of California. This threw all the cogs of finance, commerce and industry out of gear and forced even the most hidebound reactionaries to make such peace as they could with the good government crowd, of which Jory was, naturally enough, considered a leader. What few smiles he indulged in during this crowded period of his career were caused by the antics of some of his business associates and Club acquain-

127

tances when trying to placate or appease him without relaxing their bilious hatred of his Goo-goo and Labor affiliations.

He saw less than ever of Irene, his wife. Her pride, her lingering admiration for his capacities and his good looks and her preoccupation with appearances kept her publicly loyal to him. They went out together socially, though Jory, as before, could not be counted on for any long stay anywhere, no matter what the occasion. After one act of opera, one symphony number, a greeting from his hostess and (rarely) a dance or two at one of the balls Irene deemed important, Adam would excuse himself — leave his wife to be taken home by her chauffeur.

Never lovers or in the least lost in one another Irene and Adam were now bound by habit, by convenience, by a sense of propriety and the usages of convention, but they lived separate lives and had fewer and fewer common interests. Close friends of Irene's noticed a change in her, at this time. She began to show a disposition to be dictatorial. She was sometimes irritable and she developed moods, baffling and unpredictable. They did not blame her. Adam Jory was a fine figure of a man and he had pushed his way high on the ladder, but these new political gyrations of his were enough to fret anybody. They were afraid, they whispered privately, that Adam was, after all, a trifle vulgar. So they made allowances for his wife. And she continued to hold her position as one of the leaders of "the upper crust" of the Southland.

On the surface it appeared that Jory was not paying too high a price for his investment in the good of Los Angeles, as he had called it to his city editor. He had broken boldly with the vested interests of business and Society and this had shocked his business associates and miffed Irene's friends. But he was now strong enough and important enough so that all these people had to overlook his lapse and make the best of the situation. Those who mattered to him and his future would forget and the rest he could ignore.

There was one group — small, compact, entrenched —

which he had overlooked but to whom he had given mortal offense. These were the half-dozen mighty moguls who controlled the sources of the city's bloodstream — cash and credit. They were silent, almost mysterious men, operating in the background and taking no active part in politics, in the Chamber of Commerce, in the Industrial Association or in the ballyhoo and conniving of the perennial boosters. But they did hold a veto power over every program, project and promotion and they did have what amounted to the power of life or death over the participants. Their names appeared seldom in the papers and then only as inconspicuous directors of the biggest banks and corporations. With perhaps two exceptions even their wives were well nigh anonymous, being mentioned only rarely and then as patronesses of good causes, charitable or cultural. But in fact these tycoons were virtually all-powerful; also they were reactionary, arbitrary and quite ruthless. Major Wellington Oddie was a member of this Camorra and the *Daily Sun* was its official organ.

Jory's crime was that he had gone over to their enemies, the crackpots of reform and the anarchists of organized labor. So they donned their black hoods and passed sentence.

Adam Jory was to be smashed.

In their own impersonal, secret, unhurried fashion they set on his trail their dogs of destruction.

As the time drew near for the opening of the trial of the two labor leaders for the dynamiting of the *Daily Sun* building, Los Angeles was split into two camps.

As employers' groups throughout the country had hastened to finance the conviction of the pair, Labor had replied with a bulging war chest for the defense. The District Attorney, a hard, driving, ambitious old-line politician, was provided with assistance by the best legal firms available, and a small army of detectives, spies, runners, gumshoe men and informers was recruited to help him investigate prospective jurors and gather evidence. Labor sent its best-known and ablest advocate

129

west from Chicago and several local attorneys of first rank
were retained to aid him. This staff engaged its own detectives
and, as the prosecution grew increasingly savage and confident,
added a force of informers, spies and snoopers to watch those
of the State. When one side found that its secrets were leaking it put agents inside the other camp, which compelled the
second to plant betrayers within the ranks of the first. Soon
spies were spying on spies and keyhole peepers on them and
this led to the bribing of the other party's investigators and,
Billy Wing asserted, to a situation where at least two or three
of this sordid clan were on the payroll of both sides. In such
waters peculiar fish, of course, swam, fed and were hooked, and
manufactured evidence, false reports and lying accusations
soon roiled and muddied the whole stream.

In a cause so completely covered by the newspapers and so
widely discussed and debated it was clear that difficulty would
be found in securing a jury. Hundreds of names were put on
tentative lists by the clerks responsible and the lawyers had
to provide elaborate machinery to investigate each man included. The well-informed knew that, with great sums of
money in each treasury, temptation to fix jurors would be
present — perhaps irresistible. And, as the day of the trial approached, this danger so absorbed the attorneys that several
of them on both sides gave it their whole attention. Vague
rumors flew about, veiled charges were made and heatedly
denied, and the tension increased. It was no atmosphere in
which to attempt to establish facts or determine strict justice
either way. Yet it was the atmosphere in which the case was
opened.

The trial was in its fourth week, with only five jurors accepted out of almost two hundred talesmen summoned, when
Billy Wing came to Jory's office.

"I've got bad news for you. The Kearns Agency has dug up
a union man and the District Attorney has screwed a confession out of him."

"That he dynamited the *Sun?*"

"That he bought the dynamite. He says that Walter Young gave him the money and told him where to go. When he brought the stuff back he turned it over to Jeff Carrigan and Carrigan blew the building."

Jory snorted. "Poppycock! Where did you pick up that yarn?"

Wing shrugged. "I get around. And it's straight, Jory."

"Do you mean that you think Young and Carrigan can be convicted on it?"

"Not only that; I think they're guilty."

Jory pushed away from his desk and walked the length of his big room. Finally he stopped — said in a quieter tone: "It's hard for me to believe. If it's true it means Walter Young may hang."

"There's only one thing that can save him from hanging, Jory. Make a deal with the District Attorney."

"What sort of a deal?"

"This isn't my scheme, understand. It comes from a magazine writer who's here covering the trial. He's always been for the underdog and he has a good head. I want you to talk to him."

"What good would that do? Why doesn't he go to the defense lawyers?"

"He thinks he ought to have an understanding with the business men who run this town, first. He says they're the ones who are out to hang Carrigan and Young."

"But the *Messenger* — oh, I guess I see. He wants me to break the ice for him — that it?"

"Yes. If he can convince you that the plan will work he feels that between you and the Band of Hope maybe even Major Oddie can be swung into line."

"All right. I'll see him."

The visitor was a small, wiry, intense, burning man, of swift gestures and passionate earnestness of speech.

"Los Angeles has a chance to do something pretty fine,

Mr. Jory — something that's never been tried before any-where. A chance to put Christianity to a practical test."

"Wait a minute, Stebbins. If you're going to preach — "

"Hell, man, that's the last thing I'm going to do. I'm trying to save the lives of two poor, misguided, blundering damn fools and at the same time give Los Angeles back its self-respect. But most of all I'm trying to end the labor war and bring industrial peace to America."

"A big order."

"Of course. I wouldn't bring you a little one."

Jory's pale smile crossed his face. "Go ahead, then."

"My friend Billy Wing has told you about the MacGonnigan confession. Yes. Well, Carrigan and Young haven't a chance to escape hanging, with that confession added to what your District Attorney already has. And I can assure you that he has plenty, and not all of it perjured testimony, either. If you hang those two boys Labor will have two more martyrs and the war between capital and labor will be murderous from this time on for twenty years.

"The business men here have got Carrigan and Young down. Labor is licked, as far as the dynamiting case goes. All right, suppose that you step in now — you and the other civic leaders and the industrialists and the I.A. and Major Oddie — and say: 'We want no more killing. We want no more revenge and hate. We want to make a settlement of this case by let-ting these two poor devils off with prison terms, then we'll sit down with Labor and lay out a plan to create here the best and happiest and most profitable city on earth for both sides — the boss and the worker.'

"You've got a Heaven on earth here, Jory — it says so in all your advertising. Make your boasts good."

They talked for two hours.

"It's good enough for me, Stebbins," Adam Jory said. "I'll get a meeting called. I haven't much hope that you can con-vince the rest of them, but you can try."

Stebbins laughed loudly. "You think you're the only

Christian in the town, eh? Won't you be surprised if you find that each of the others thinks he is, instead?"

No one believed this idealistic dream could come true.

But they agreed to give it a trial. It was even claimed that Major Wellington Oddie approved it.

Jeff Carrigan and Walter Young stood up in court a few days later and their lawyers changed their plea from Not Guilty to Guilty.

Carrigan, charged with the actual dynamiting, was given a life term. Walter Young, as an accomplice, got thirty years.

Adam Jory went to the County Jail to see Young again before the prisoners were taken north. No one could have looked less violent or dangerous than the mild, frail printer. He thanked Jory for coming.

"It's more than I deserve after all the trouble I've brought on you and the *Messenger*."

"Never mind that, Young. I came because I don't believe you're guilty. What's behind this damn foolishness?"

Walter Young studied his clasped fingers. "It was all damn foolishness, from the beginning, Mr. Jory. The boys — we know that now. None of us wanted to kill anybody. If we had it would have been a simple matter to get Major Oddie, or Zaar, or whoever happened to be president of the I.A. No, we wanted to throw a scare into the bosses." Young shook his head sadly. "We picked the one night in history when the *Sun* building was full of city gas."

"You keep saying 'we'. Do you mean that you were in this plot — that you were actually guilty?"

Young looked up into Adam's face with eyes steady, clear, untroubled. "I've told you before I was guilty of fighting the bosses. I'll tell you now that we'd been working for a year to organize the *Daily Sun* mechanical department. As president of our local, I was in charge of that job."

"Well, even in Los Angeles you can't be sent to the penitentiary for that," Jory said.

133

"No? Well, I'll tell you something else. I was in the *Sun* pressroom six hours before the explosion, talking to a few holdouts." He smiled shyly. "That's why I'm so sure about that gas." And, he added steadily, "That's why I told you they'd convict me. My alibi wouldn't have stood up in court two minutes."

Jory made an impatient gesture. "But you're not guilty. If you'll let me get a lawyer in — "

Young put a firm, arresting hand on his employer's knee. "Listen, Mr. Jory, I want it this way. I didn't plead guilty because I believed that writer fellow could bring us peace on earth. Partly I did it to keep from hanging. But mainly I did it to stop the District Attorney from putting his case into the records. Some of that case was made out of whole cloth, but too much of it was true."

"Then Labor is guilty."

"Labor would be found guilty."

"Don't bandy words! A lot of labor leaders would be dragged in and sent up. Is that it?"

"Perhaps. And, don't forget, I'd still stand a good chance of hanging."

"Not if you let us prove — not if you could show — "

Walter Young was smiling. "In Los Angeles, with a Los Angeles judge and jury and a Los Angeles prosecutor — and the *Daily Sun* trying the case in print day after day?"

Jory felt as though he were flailing at a stone wall. "Damnation, Young, you're as stubborn as a mule!"

"I guess I am, Mr. Jory. But here's another thing you have to remember: I was in the *Sun* plant that Tuesday afternoon talking up a pressmen's union."

They always came back to that and at last Adam gave up. "I'm not going to plague you about it, Young, but it seems quixotic to me."

"Likely. But a fellow has to do right the way he sees it, don't he? I'm grateful to you, though." Young looked down at his hands again and flushed. "Another thing. The

office has been sending a check to my wife every week since
— this hit me. She wanted — we both want you to know — "

Jory crossed to the barred door and rapped for the turnkey.
"Of course, Young. That's correct. Take care of yourself.
Good luck."

He hurried away, going by the *Messenger* business office.
The manager came to meet him at the desk.

"About that check to Walter Young's wife, Winston — has
it gone out this week?"

"I had them hold it up. I didn't know, after — "

"Get it in the mail. I want one to go to her every week,
till further notice. The same amount. See to it, will you?"

George Alexander, the tall, humorless, dull, entirely honest
old mayor whom the Good Government forces had elected two
years before was re-elected, by a majority increased because it
was cast within a few days of the sentencing of the two
"dynamiters" and Los Angeles wanted to feel safe and normal
again.

During that first term Jory had been told pointedly that
he could have almost anything of the administration that he
asked for. More bluntly than was necessary he had replied
that he wasn't interested. Now John Shelley approached him.

"Are you still out of politics, Mr. Jory?"

"Yes."

"Have you any objection to my asking for one appointment?"

"You? What in the hell — ?"

"Oh, not for myself. It's for Earl Tomblin, my lawyer
friend. I've consulted him on a lot of matters and he's never
taken a decent fee. He's a comer and he wants to get into
politics through the legal side."

"That's all right. What place is he aiming for?"

"City Prosecuting Attorney. It's a stepping-stone to election as District Attorney and that might lead anywhere."

"What do you want me to do?"

"Billy Wing has sounded out the Good Government crowd. I've had our City Hall man take it up with the Mayor's cabinet. The rails are greased. If you'll telephone the City Attorney he'll see the Mayor, and Tomblin will be named."

"I'll attend to it."

Late that afternoon the appointment was announced. Generally, public reaction was favorable and editorial comment approving. Only the *Daily Sun* blasted at it. Then it was remembered that young Tomblin had won a hard-fought civil case against Major Oddie a year or two earlier — a lawsuit involving a right-of-way to a ranch the publisher owned in the mountains up near Bakersfield.

"You'll have to watch your step, Tomblin," Billy Wing said to the new appointee.

"My skirts are clean, Billy. As long as I run my office properly — "

"My verdant young gosling," Billy broke in, wagging his head, "you're leaving the home pond today. Just pray God that when the *Daily Sun* has a pillow to stuff you're smart enough and strong enough to fly fast and roost high."

Adam Jory had another of those rare notes from Beulah Rountree.

> *Dear Ad*
> *They pray for you every night at the Young's — Amata and Steve. I almost feel like trying one of my own sometimes because of what you do for people that nobody knows anything about. Only I'm afraid my prayers might not do much good.*
> *We are fine and Judith is going to be beautiful.*
> *You remember I knew Walt Young at the old Sun shop and we've always been friends since. How my heart breaks when I think of him up there — because of spite and because he wanted to save other people.*
> *B*

CHAPTER SIX

A T DIAGONAL CORNERS of Los Angeles there were growing up in that period two amazing districts immediately
and heavily contributing to the fame and prosperity of Adam
Jory's city.

On the flats along the river to the southeast was Vernon,
hand-made into an industrial area where, along a network of
railroad spur-tracks, factories large and small were locating.
Some of them were old businesses moved to this more advantageous spot from their original locations; most of them had
been brought there, like the Carstairs Furniture Factory,
through the aggressive enterprise of the Band of Hope or the
less exclusive Chamber of Commerce. Between the ugly,
noisy, smoking plant structures and, stretching out all around,
were miles of cheaply built bungalows (the generic name,
in those days, for all Southland houses containing more than
one and less than seven rooms) where the hired hands lived,
and trading centers where shops and offices, a graceless public
school and a wretched little chapel or two, provided them with
the necessities of life, material and spiritual.

In the chaparral hills and the rolling barley fields at the
opposite northwestern corner was Hollywood, like grubby,
noisome Vernon an industrial district but one free of smoke
and grime, sidetracks and slag-dumps, throbbing engines and
the scream and clatter of machinery. Hollywood's manu-
facturing plants were sprawling and sufficiently tawdry but
they were fronted by palatial administration buildings, gener-

ally boasted lawns, flower beds and shady trees, and their confused and cluttered workshops were concealed from view by
vine-covered walls or high fences. Hollywood's workers lived
in substantial and inviting homes, their children went to
handsome modern schools and such of them as were wor-
shippers attended dignified and stately churches with stained-
glass windows and vested choirs. For "in pictures," even in
that early day, a showy façade was deemed as essential for
the individual as for the place where he worked, even though
in each case it was a false front.

The men who controlled things in Los Angeles had given
this budding enterprise the cold shoulder from the beginning,
with a strange perversity. They would spend money and effort
to bring in a glue factory, a company organized to process
women's hair nets, manufacturers of gopher traps or orange
squeezers, fabricators of sectional bookcases or bakers of
fig-newtons but they would have no truck with the movies.
This was partly because they could not conceive of entertainment as a merchantable commodity; partly because they
resented being treated patronizingly by the metamorphosed
pants cutters, carnival barkers and vaudeville performers who
were then the most active canners of drama out along Sunset
Boulevard. The fact remains that neither their money nor
their concern turned that way.

The generality of Angelenos also scorned Hollywood, but
for a different reason: the new activity was a form of thee-
ayter and was therefore *per se* immoral. These residents had
immigrated from the corn-and-pork belt of Iowa, Nebraska,
Kansas and Indiana where life, if drab, had been kept in-
violably Protestant and undepraved. Their forbears had rated
play-acting and play-going with card-playing and the public
use of tobacco and rum as cardinal sins and now they themselves
eyed with disapproval and even resentment the expanding
colony of mummers and coryphees on their very doorstep.

Unhappily the mistrust of such burghers proved presently
well-founded, not because they were right about theater but be-

cause this particular brash offshoot thereof was, in its beginnings, dominated by opportunists lacking both traditions and standards and peppered with noodles, doll-faces and rakehells lacking both standards and pride, and Hollywood engaged in more, and more shameless, Babylonian goings-on than had been forecast.

Meantime, however, Vernon and Hollywood grew up together as living testimonials to the virtue of Southland climate and the movie industry showed signs of becoming, for better or for worse, the overwhelmingly greatest advertisement Los Angeles had ever known.

John Shelley, the driving force behind the *Messenger*, had for some time been suggesting to Jory that it be made an evening paper.

He advanced many reasons, but three were persuasive. He pointed out that Los Angeles was a city where much was made of home life and where the long evenings of nine months in the year favored leisure in the latter part of the day. He thought that women and young people had more time for news then and everyone knew that this was the audience advertisers most wanted to reach. Secondly, he declared bluntly that the *Messenger* could never hope to compete with the *Daily Sun* in the morning field where, with plenty of money and a large staff, Major Oddie's journal could take time to get out a veritable encyclopedia of world affairs and so monopolize the attention of business men and of the leisure class. Shelley's third argument had to do with his own preference: he was hard-driving, quick-thinking, flashy; he liked spot news and knew how to get it fast and present it pungently. He was less interested in dull details of the life of the city, no matter how vital they might be, preferring those brief and punchy stories, moving or sentimental or startling, which gave a paper sparkle, variety and human interest.

The notion began to appeal to Adam Jory. He found that he could save money on his press-service and gain certain

139

advantages in the telegraphic news coverage because of the gain of three hours over eastern centers. Winston, his business manager, agreed with the city editor, citing other savings in payroll and a probable sharp increase in street sales. With three afternoon editions he believed that circulation could soon be doubled, and advertisers would listen to that sort of evidence, no matter what their personal views of *Messenger* policies.

The chance was made and the very first issues of the *Evening Messenger* carried enough more advertising to make a slight net gain even though the evening line-rate was lower than the morning charge. Circulation increased encouragingly. A few months later, for the first time, the manager's monthly report to the owner showed the paper's earnings on the credit side.

With a larger staff and a free hand, City Editor Shelley began to make news to augment the daily grist by conducting hard-hitting and swiftly-paced crusades — for decent hours for shop-girls, for pensions for the police and fire departments, for parks and playgrounds, for better schools and more of them. This policy made friends for the paper but most of the causes espoused involved the selfish interests of important men and firms, and toes were stepped on — the toes of employers, of big taxpayers, of lax city and county officials, of insurance companies, of the utility corporations. The friends acquired outnumbered the enemies made, but the latter were rich and powerful and the owner was their target. If Jory knew it, though, he gave no sign.

A human interest story Shelley developed at this time concerned a mild, colorless cashier in a downtown shop who had been arrested on a charge of embezzling small sums. The new police reporter telephoned in that Zander admitted the thefts but said that he had taken the money to finance his daughter's education at Polytechnic High School. The city editor sent Clare Shively out to follow up this lead.

It developed that timid, heartbroken Lucy Zander, who

140

was plain and not a brilliant student, had been trying to get through a business course so that she could help her father with the five motherless younger children. Shively brought in a drab and pitiful story and Shelley himself wrote it, not so much about the theft and the girl's tragedy as about the conditions that made such incidents too common in rich, proud, lucky Los Angeles.

The story touched many hearts; it made sober citizens think and it gave the humblest a feeling that the *Messenger* had an interest in their own griefs, sorrows and trials. Earl Tomblin, the City Prosecutor, persuaded the shop owner to withdraw the charge against Zander on the payment of the small sum taken. Zander was given work in the circulation department of the paper. And Lucy Zander was offered enough money by kindly readers to see her through her few remaining weeks of school.

She would not accept the money. She could not go back, she said, and face her fellow students. No employer would hire her anyway. She was frightened and depressed, though she defended her father valiantly. Tomblin, who talked with her, thought that she might do something rash if her obsession was not broken. If he had known Adam Jory better he should have turned to someone else; judging the owner of the *Messenger* by the policy of the paper, he went to him, urging that she be given a job in the busy Jory offices where she could be as obscure as she liked.

Adam, driven hard by a special stress of affairs, was short with him.

"I'm not running a charity center here, Tomblin. I'm not a philanthropist."

"This isn't a matter of charity, Mr. Jory."

"This girl's father is a thief, as I understand it, isn't he?"

"Not the way you mean it — only a desperate damned fool. And I'll warrant that you'd get your money's worth out of Lucy. The man who gives her a chance, after what she's been through, will get a sort of loyalty wages can't buy."

Unexpectedly Jory said, with that half-smile of his: "Can this girl spell?"

Tomblin laughed. "If she can't, she'll learn, if only out of gratitude."

"All right. You mentioned loyalty. That's a rare commodity. Send your waif to me and I'll take a chance on her spelling."

Lucy Zander was the most frightened human being Adam had ever seen. She was so shrinking and shaking that for once the big, blunt, dominating man was himself embarrassed.

"I hope you'll like it here well enough to help me out, Lucy," he said, in a gentle voice that was strange in his own ears. "Things have piled up on me and I need someone like you to straighten them out. If you could get my files so that we could find something in them once in a while it would mean a lot to me. Will you take that on first?"

Lucy, swallowing hard before she could speak, murmured that she would try. She looked at Adam Jory as though he were God.

The next morning there was a small vase of flowers on his desk. He was about to let out an outraged bellow when, remembering his new clerk, he checked himself.

"They're very nice, Lucy," he said. The girl blushed, stammered and burst into tears.

Soon she had made herself indispensable. She had a mania for order. She forgot nothing. She had to be fairly driven from the place at night. Herbert Kinney, eagle-eyed and jealous of his own prerogatives, accepted her presently when he was convinced she was harmless and when he found that he could put off on her some of his own detail work. She became as much a part of the machinery of the Jory offices as the typewriter she used, the files that she made miracles of efficiency and the water-cooler she made certain was regularly renewed. As much a part of the place, indeed, as the flowers that smiled and nodded, incongruous but ingratiating, on Adam's big desk, where she placed them every morning even when, in dead of winter, she had to buy them at a shop.

The great Aqueduct was completed, ahead of the scheduled date and well within the estimated cost. A great concourse of proud citizens stood in the sun of a warm fall day on the north rim of the San Fernando Valley and saw the first trickle of pure mountain water come down a cascade built to dramatize this terminus of its 250-mile journey over mountains and desert.

The chief engineer of the project, called on for a speech after the spellbinders had given their all, stood hesitantly on the staging set up for the occasion. A reporter had written an address for him; it was in his pocket. He did not take it out.

He faced the crowd, half turned, waved a hand toward the widening sheet of water sparkling down the rocky steep.

"There it is; take it," he said, and sat down.

Bill Mulholland's five-word oration became a Los Angeles legend.

John Shelley had a new reporter — a dry, sandy-haired, mild looking youth named Harry Noll — who held a roving commission and could be counted on to turn up important and unusual stories involving public officials, the utility corporations, big business and the county courts that made talk and helped sell the *Evening Messenger*.

Shortly after the opening of the Aqueduct the city editor sent Noll to the owner.

"Well, young man?"

"I noticed quite a while back that the Water Department had no plans for a line to bring our new water supply across the San Fernando Valley and into the city system. When I asked about it the City Hall sidestepped. So I shut up. But I went on digging."

"And found something, eh?"

"Yes, sir. Plenty."

"Why bother me about it? Why don't you turn it in?"

Noll looked at Adam quizzically. "Because I like working for you and I don't want to lose my job."

Adam Jory said, with that half-smile of his: "You won't lose your job for telling the truth in the *Evening Messenger,* Noll. Let's have this story of yours."

"Keno! Three or four years ago the engineers decided to sell the water to San Fernando Valley for irrigation and pick it up at the Narrows, under the Elysian Park hills. Somebody tipped off a number of moneyed men here."

"If you can prove that it would make a good story, Noll," Adam said, dryly.

"I can prove it."

Jory called a boy. "Ask Mr. Shelley to come in."

"Yes, sir."

Noll rolled a cigarette. He had a look of resignation oddly mixed with a rueful grin. Shelley entered.

"John, I think you can print Noll's information."

The reporter's cigarette fell from his fingers and he jumped up. "But Jesus, boss, the guts of my story is that land-grab." He laughed, with some embarrassment. "I mean — well, you must know what I mean."

Jory's stingy smile touched his face again. "I know what you mean, Noll. And, Shelley!"

"Yes, sir."

"Print the full list of the names of the land-grabbers, as Noll calls them. Lead off with mine. While we're doing this we'll do it right."

The editor nodded. "I sort of thought you'd see it that way, Mr. Jory. But it's only fair to tell you that it will raise hell for you in the Band of Hope."

"Shelley," Jory said, gravely, "if you don't look out you're going to be editing the *Messenger* by the *Sun's* 'sacred-cow and son-of-a-bitch-book' method some day soon. And if that day ever comes I'll either fire you or sell the paper. Get out, now, or you'll miss the early edition with Noll's scarehead."

The story created a sensation, of course — for a few days. A small evening paper that had been left out of the secret deal because of its antagonism to the ruling powers blazed forth with a noisy demand for the indictment of the land profiteers and impeachment of the city officials involved. But no crime had been committed and that squawk subsided. The *Daily Sun* indignantly denied that there was anything worse than a coincidence in the affair and Major Oddie tried to squirm out of the whole mess. Except that all the other papers immediately proved the *Sun* a liar, nothing came of its protestations of virtue — they were disbelieved even by Oddie's friends. A few citizens were sincerely and righteously indignant but the majority were only envious. All agreed that the irrigating of the big neighboring Valley, now part of the city, would provide rich little farms for thousands, add to the total productivity of the region and bring in new colonists and new money. What was so wrong about that?

Most of the lands were subdivided and the plots sold at great profit. Not only were farms established but several small towns were started, where the lots had a high speculative value, and a local boom began. The population of the Valley was multiplied by ten, twenty, fifty. Los Angeles could not long be peevish about such enterprise.

Generally, Adam Jory was praised for making the story of the grab public and taking his own share of the responsibility for it. Some thought that he was repentant; others that he had played a grim joke on his fellow-conspirators. The latter saw no humor in the business and agreed that Jory had again played traitor to his class. The local Camorra put another black mark against his name in their secret books. Otherwise the whole matter was soon forgotten in the rush of business and the growing prosperity of Los Angeles.

Jory had been one of the first businessmen in the city to see that the motion pictures had a future, not as art or entertainment, but as money-makers. He had had experience with

145

most of the enterprises that were contributing to the growth and
greatness of his city — a multi-million-dollar citrus industry,
the rich wine trade, the winter tourist crop, the real estate market, Vernon's factories and the production of oil; all of them
owed their existence and success to the single great Southland
asset, the sunny climate. Yes, even oil, for the learned said that
petroleum came from buried beds of antediluvian vegetable
growths, that must have been luxuriant. Picture-making, the
last of the children of the sun, was even more dependent
on its kindly rays than any of the others. Nothing could
prevent its flowering. As for the morals of Hollywood, he
gave them not a thought. He began to consider building a
theater exclusively for the films.

John Shelley had followed Jory's suggestion, made early,
that the *Messenger* pay some heed to the new activity, and
out of this had come a systematic coverage of the studios
that was soon including news and gossip concerning the people
engaged. The *Evening Messenger* had blossomed out with a
special movie column, written by a gushing young woman
whose vocabulary ran to superlative adjectives and who really
believed that The Drama came to its full stature only with
the invention of the gelatine film. She not only took Hollywood at its own high valuation but voluntarily raised the
ante. She was enormously popular in the colony. John Shelley
suspected that she was making more money than the paper
paid her but he kept his suspicions to himself. The advertising
department was beginning to carry a profitable linage of
movie-house announcements and Ella Robbins scooped the
other papers regularly with Hollywood tittle-tattle having a
considerable appeal to the customers.

This interest indicated to Adam Jory that, no matter what
the fathers of Los Angeles might think of the movies, the
children and probably the wives, too, were in rebellion. The
tinsel, glitter and romance of the world opening to them
blinded them to some of the older verities on which they
had been raised; it began to appear that Los Angeles contained

146

a population hungry for make-believe. But the prejudice and the Puritanism prevailing among the business men had prevented their trafficking in that shadow-world enterprise and the only places where motion pictures could be shown were remodelled store-rooms, dingy old auditoriums and one or two of the town's theaters, which were unsuited to this new entertainment.

When other matters gave him a little leisure Adam Jory concentrated on this phenomenon, reached a decision, set Dave Allison to work designing a building dedicated to movie presentation exclusively. A lucky coincidence blessed the opening of the Rialto in that autumn. Jory had leased the place even before it was completed to an experienced and adroit theater manager and Manny Richman signed up for his premier showing Hollywood's most discussed picture, "A New Star Rises."

Adam Jory, taking a new interest in the whole subject, was a regular reader of the Robbins column in the *Messenger* and therefore knew something about "A New Star Rises." It was to be the first "feature film" ever attempted, designed to provide a full evening's entertainment. The man who conceived and produced it was a new figure in Hollywood. He had a background of stage experience but unlike the other professionals who had drifted into motion pictures he realized that here was a different medium, requiring a new and different technique. Since (except for that device of wearing their caps hindside before) other Hollywood directors had merely adapted theater methods and conventions *in toto* he had to invent his own. What he came up with, including a simple story embellished and mounted with sets of unheard-of size and magnitude and a small cast surrounded by prodigious mobs of "extras," was a treatment almost completely new. His costs set a new record; several times in the long months of filming he had to stop work and skirmish up more money. Watching him sourly the established moguls of the business prophesied that the whole investment would be lost and that, after the film's first showing, the producer would never be heard of again.

147

The first showing was in Jory's Rialto. Both the theater and the picture made the opening propitious, but there was soon no doubt that "A New Star Rises" would be a sensation wherever exhibited. Eastern cities clamored for it, and repeated and even surpassed the Los Angeles success. It was hailed by critics as epoch-making and even soured gentlemen of the press, who had heretofore scorned the movies as beneath playgoers of any intelligence or taste, welcomed and praised it. Not only that. The producer's technical innovations, tricks and devices gave the camera new potentialities and the actors new opportunities; they had the effect of making earlier films seem amateurish and juvenile, especially to the more competent of the colony. As for the picture magnates who had snorted at the newcomer, they were soon madly scrambling to adopt his formulas. Many of them scrapped half-finished productions and sent unfilmed scenarios back to the writers for re-treatment. "A New Star Rises" had made most of their stock-in-hand obsolete and valueless overnight.

The picture ran for five solid weeks at the Rialto and established that Jory theater as a success.

Adam went to see the film one night, not to view it as entertainment but to learn something more about it and all motion pictures as merchantable commodities.

In the darkened auditorium he sat stolidly in an aisle seat at the rear from which he could escape easily. The place was almost filled and in a few minutes entirely so. Below the stage and at one side a glow of light revealed the organ console and its player; from hidden pipes hushed and solemn music rolled. On the screen a seemingly endless line of Civil War federal troops slogged along a country lane under blossoming trees. The camera turned to follow a single soldier, a thin-faced, weary nondescript, with nothing to set him apart from the others except this attention; the marching platoons disappeared and out of the screen leaped the head and shoulders of the tired boy, close enough to be touched, the frayed visor of his cap, the white dust on his coat, the almost unbearable ex-

haustion in his face striking the eye violently, pitilessly. Then
the plodding regiment again, another break — and the interior of a poor kitchen, steam rising thinly from the spout
of a teakettle, a cat sleeping beneath the stove and near-by a
cradle and just the foot of a woman who rocked it quietly.

Adam Jory forgot that he was looking at pictures of actors,
hired at so much a day to go through carefully planned pos-
turings, maneuvers, on some transformed barley-field west of
the city or in the shell of a house knocked together in a
few hours and propped up in the open, roofless and frontless,
to simulate reality. He was following their story, as it unwound
so slowly, with such wealth of homely detail and the cumu-
lative power and poignancy given it by the sheer weight of
background masses. He felt his heart stirring. His sympathies were entrapped by the fashion in which, without inter-
ruption of the greater movement, the creator continually carried him back to the three or four principals, so that all of the
rest of the epic was only the multiplied tragedy they lived.

There came a quiet moment in a garden where a Rebel
soldier, separated from his outfit, was hiding. He was a minor
character in the piece, presented with a light touch, for relief
from the somberness of the whole. Now he took off one shoe
and held it up to shake a pebble out of it.

Behind him a slim, dark girl came to a gate. Her appearance — she had not been seen before — caught every eye. It
caught Adam Jory's eye and he straightened in his chair and
his breath was checked.

It was a younger, more slender Beulah Rountree; Beulah as
she must have been at sixteen.

"A New Star Rises" became, for Adam, only the fragmentary
story and the infrequent and incidental reappearance of this
slender, gentle, laughing, heart-warming southern maid. She
was spoiled, swift, graceful, teasing; she danced and flirted and
refused to take even the horror of the ever-present war seriously; she hated damyankees more than she loved the Cause.
Under shrewd direction the actress revealed the hidden nature

149

of Leslie Blunt through actions and movements in themselves
trifling and commonplace.

At one point the audience around Adam Jory applauded. To
his surprise he discovered that he was clapping with them.

He had thought he would leave before the picture was finished. Instead he found himself blinking in a sudden glare
of light and sitting absorbed when the rest of the audience was
up and beginning to push toward the exits.

Two or three men nodded or greeted him by name before
he got clear of the crowd. He responded abstractedly. It had
ceased to matter whether people saw him in a gabbling mob
of movie fans.

He started walking, his mind busy with the sort of thoughts
he usually put away impatiently and abruptly. He was at once
exhilarated and depressed, immeasurably pleased and discon-
tented. It had been Beulah's daughter; he was in no doubt of
that. His daughter! He had to realize that fact by a deliber-
ate effort of will. He was proud of her — gratified by her success. But there was a sour note in his satisfaction. He had given
no thought to the picture people as people; he had gathered
from the *Evening Messenger* Hollywood column that they were
a casual, careless, light-headed crowd, without much stability
and probably of sketchy morals. He had been entirely in-
different to all that. Now it irked him. Judith, named for
his mother, should have everything Hollywood could possibly give her, but should have it without being involved —
with work, with odd Bohemian men and women, with the
inevitable competition, drive, pressure, rivalries, impositions of
any sort of business, even (perhaps especially!) the business
of this strange theater. By his own act he had lost the priv-
ilege of shielding her from these contacts and necessities.

But she had won her small triumph already and he guessed
that, in the make-believe world where she moved, even such
a victory was hardly won and only by the few. Yes, she had
talent and power as well as a blossoming beauty that would
become richer and fuller week by week. He had wondered, in

150

the past, what this unknown daughter of his had of himself.
She looked like Beulah. But had she got from him, perhaps,
some force or strength that was his? Beulah had written that,
even as a child, their daughter had been stubborn to get what
she wanted. His faint smile came and went. He had always
kept his eye on the main chance — and driven through every
difficulty to win it.

Before he knew it he had walked all the way home.

His wife was coming in from a formal dinner.

"How *could* you forget?" she stormed. "I told you this
party was one we had to attend together. Mrs. Hellman was
very upset."

"I'm sorry, Irene. I owe the Hellmans an apology. It slipped
my mind. I'll write and explain."

His wife threw off her coat petulantly. "What is it you do
with your evenings?" she asked, harshly. "I begin to wonder.
You used to make the *Messenger* your excuse. Tonight I had
Moffatt telephone your office to remind you. You had left
early, that mincing little secretary of yours said."

She went past him, up the wide stairs. He heard her close
her door with a violent slam.

He slept badly. But he was not thinking of Irene or her
social obligations and compulsions.

Lonely! Yes, that was it. In the midst of this surging, pushing, clamorous, exuberant, booming city, which his efforts
had been so exclusively devoted to building, he was lonely.

The discovery of his unknown daughter had made him so

There was war in Europe and this biggest of all big businesses was creating in America an era of easy money and plentiful jobs that spread its benefits to Los Angeles as everywhere
else and inevitably profited Adam Jory.

He had foreseen the automobile age and the wide use of oil
under steam boilers throughout transportation and industry.
As much as any of the local oil men he had kept up with the
quickening demands for petroleum products of all kinds and

151

he had surpassed most through Golconda Laboratories and young Wade's discoveries and developments. All of Golconda was, in effect, his affair, the railroad men interested being tied up with their regular work. But more and more Jory had turned the active management of the companies over to Herbert Kinney.

The plan to expand Golconda by gobbling up several small outfits and merging with Atlas and Pierce-Dakin, both strong concerns and heavy producers, had been worked out by Kinney in the preliminary stages; now the matter was turned over to Jory himself to close. The increase in demand caused by the European war and a growing feeling that the United States would be in the melee sooner or later prompted him to move swiftly to gather in Chambers Oil, the Whittier & Santa Ana crowd, Doolittle and the interests of the Strange family, all of which he had been working quietly for two years to get under his control. Of the two big companies he wanted to amalgamate with Golconda, Atlas was the first to sign. But two of the partners in the more important Pierce-Dakin Corporation hung back.

Johnson Pierce, heaviest owner in this organization, favored the combine and put pressure on his associates. Adam Jory, scheming to force the issue, gave it out that Golconda could not wait long for an answer. Pierce nudged his two partners — promised Adam to get action promptly.

It was at this stage of the affair that Pierce invited Adam to drop in with him on an informal afternoon at the home of two of the most famous stars in Hollywood. Adam had known that Pierce dabbled in many enterprises, mainly to keep himself amused and interested — mining, exploration, a weird (but profitable) salvaging expedition off the South American coast, an art gallery that, expertly managed by a shrewd dealer, made money with its three branch stores in the state and also gave its backer access to Bohemian circles where he enjoyed playing Santa Claus to struggling painters. Now Adam suspected that the capitalist had also put money into motion pictures. More to gratify Pierce than anything else, Jory went to the colony garden party.

He found the Hollywood world even more completely foreign to his own than he had supposed it to be. It was like going to a particularly lively Zoo, where strange and exotic animals dumfounded the visitor with their forms, their antics, their habits; with their squeals, snorts, grunts, roars, bayings, gibberish. The large crowd was made up mainly of sleek, good-looking men with vacant faces and of handsome and some beautiful girls and young women. Except for the common characteristic of being well-manicured, well-dressed and well-fed they were different in type, in nature and in intelligence. They were noticeably gay, with a sort of hard, studied gaiety and they were generally a trifle noisy. The few quiet and decorous individuals had to be sought out.

The host jumped to the back of a sofa, just after the two business men came in, leaped thence to a buffet table loaded with fine chinaware and plate, crowded with bottles and glasses and sparkling with silver, sprang from there to catch a big vine hanging from a tree above the lawn, set this swinging until he could leave it with a somersault to land lightly to the ground, amid squeaks, laughter and applause. A few guests turned bored faces away and Jory heard a demure girl say: "Doug is out again — and me here without my headguard!"

An enormous woman whose face Jory dimly recognized as that of a well-known picture "comic" carried a filled cocktail glass and a plate of little sandwiches to a chair and lowered herself into it with an audible sigh. Instantly then she threw the glass away, tossed the sandwiches into the air and shot up with a hoarse shriek, rubbing her great bottom and executing little grotesque dance-steps with rubbery knees. There was more laughter.

"The hot seat," Pierce explained to Jory, guffawing. "An electric plate in the chair cushion. There may be half a dozen of 'em scattered around, so watch out."

153

A liveried servant appeared, bearing high a trayful of drinks. Where the crowd was thickest he tripped over his own feet, and the tray and its contents spread havoc. An indolent, drawling guest stepped up to peer into the servant's face.

"Only Cosmo!" He pulled the man's bulbous nose, which came off, bringing with it the mustache. There was revealed a bland and unsmiling youth who took a bow to their applause and walked away to join three giggling young girls.

There were twosomes here and there making unashamed love. There were grave, solemn, worried-looking fat men, employing many gestures — occasionally penciling a memorandum in pocketbooks decorated with gold. "Ho-kay!" "See Nicky." "Fielding? Definitely he is a bum!" "Fomm such proposition is only one answer — oder that redhead makes by me a contrack or out she goes back to sellink notions." There was an argument, in unintelligible phrases, over the importance of a scene that they referred to as "the rat sequence." There were throaty voices, languorous voices, strident voices, studiedly male voices and unstudiedly tenor voices. There were people who seemed normal, who were quietly-behaved, who came without fanfare, paid their respects decently and left.

At Adam Jory's elbow Johnson Pierce said: "Adam, I want you to meet a little girl I discovered. This is Mr. Jory, Judith."

She was taller than he had supposed; she was poised and at ease; she was lovelier than her pictures. He made some sort of awkward talk with her. But he was taken by surprise and was at a loss. He was thinking: "Yes, she is Beulah. But she has my chin and mouth. She has more strength — and meaning — than either of us. Oh, Judith! Oh, my daughter! Come away from this with me. I want to know you. I want to know about you. What does life mean to you? Where are you going? Are you satisfied? Would you like something more, something real, solid, fixed? What *do* you want? What is there that I can get for you?

A passerby called: "Congratulations on the new part, Miss Wayne."

154

"Thanks, Mr. Woods."

"Your name is Wayne?" Jory asked, sharply.

The girl laughed. "The studio gave it to me. I guess if Martha Washington went into pictures they'd call her Elise Wigglesworth. Are you interested in pictures, Mr. Jory?"

"No. That is, I've got a few dollars in Picta-graph Films."

"What do you know about that? Then I guess I'd better make good. I've just signed up with Picta."

She was claimed by a tall, swarthy, lean-faced foreigner, immaculately dressed, with manners a little too perfect. She nodded brightly to Jory and went away with the tailored dandy.

"DeCosta," Johnson Pierce replied, when Adam located him. "Calls himself a Count. A bad egg. Well, have you had enough of this? Some people find the flash-point of Hollywood a little too low for them."

Adam Jory, thinking of Judith, recalled that oil refiner's figure of speech. A low flash-point — yes. Exploding like a gas requiring the minimum degree of heat to set it off. Hollywood!

And Judith of it, in it, a young girl exposed to its pressures, dangers, unpredictable sense of values — governed, inevitably, by its code, one alien to Adam Jory's world and incomprehensible to him.

What is it you want, Judith? Is there anything I can get for you — anything that, if it meant the last of my possessions, you would take from me — and leave all this behind you?

In a few hours he could find Beulah Rountree. Her note telling him of the gratitude of Walter Young's family had given him a clue he had lacked before. But he was cut off from her by his own choice — his own act. Unless she sent for him — appealed to him — he could not force himself on her, no matter what his motive. And how was he to know that Judith was not well placed, safe, happy? Who was he (except the father she did not even know) to set up standards for her or to interfere in her life?

His instructions to the city editor of the *Evening Messenger* were explicit.

"I've met this fellow deCosta — the one they call the Count out in Hollywood. Call it a hunch — but I don't like him. If you pick up any information on him, let me see it. We'll keep it handy . . . . No, I'm not barring his name. You can avoid playing it up, though, I suppose."

As time went on Adam's private file on the mysterious Count grew slowly. The man was a source of some gossip in Ella Robbins' gossipy Hollywood column, but Adam, breathing more easily, saw it only once coupled with the name of the rising young star, Judith Wayne, and then casually.

Golconda Corporation was perfected and chartered by the State of California. With a capitalization of $30,000,000 it had its own oil fields, its own refineries, its own pipe-lines, its own by-products laboratory and factory and its own fleet of tankers. Ground was broken for the erection of a company building, Golconda Towers, to cost $1,500,000, on a downtown corner formerly belonging to Adam Jory.

A subsidiary company, Golconda Service, was set up, with Herbert Kinney, secretary-treasurer of the parent concern, as general manager. Golconda Service, it soon developed, had options on strategic locations all over southern California for gasoline-supply stations so that Golconda could retail its own gasoline and lubricants, handle batteries and tires and cater to every need and want of the motorist.

Golconda stock began to climb. The word went out to the wise money that it was a good buy; this information percolated down through the lower strata of society and not only the "Oil Queen," Eliza Winter, and Johnson Pierce and Elbridge Brinton, of the Pacific Railroad, and Adam Jory were stockholders, but Mike Ruffo, bootblack, Jackson Washington, Pullman porter, Gus George, gardener, and scores like them. The West Coast Petroleum Recorder rated the new combine right up with the four biggest oil companies in the West and published an

156

article about the contributions of Adam Jory to the beginnings and the rise of the mighty industry. The editor tried to get a photograph of Jory to run with his story. Lucy Zander, the big man's confidential secretary, said that Mr. Jory had never had a picture taken.

To gain control of the new merger Jory had liquidated part of his real estate and other holdings. He had plenty left. And, on Lucy Zander's books, his total wealth was materially increased as the result of the transaction. She made a note of that total and laid it on her employer's desk. Adam glanced at it, grunted, and tore the slip into small bits.

"You said a while back that your father wasn't so well. They tell me at the *Messenger* office that he's been off this week."

"He oughtn't to try to work, Mr. Jory. He doesn't need to. Harry's got a good job now; we could take care of Dad. We want to get him a place in the country where he can putter around — raise a few chickens and a garden, maybe. And he could take the two youngsters with him."

"A good idea. Remember that deed I gave you to a little farm out in the San Fernando Valley?"

"The old Luke place — yes."

"Get it from the safe. I'm going to turn it over to you. Just the place for your folks. You can go back and forth, now that the carline has been extended . . . . Well, what are you waiting for? And don't cry! Damn it all, you know I can't stand women who cry! Blow your nose! Get out of here. I'm busy."

As president of Golconda, Adam was given a slightly warmer welcome at the Southwestern Club. He was too big now to be ignored and too powerful to be snubbed. He was necessary, too, to many of the schemes, projects, enterprises, promotions, that were continually coming up in this booming, bursting, prospering city in the sun, and the men who conceived and carried on those activities had to suppress their prejudices and personal feelings in many directions. Los Angeles must come first. It was almost a religion with them.

Only the Camorra of dim figures that moved silently and mysteriously behind them all — only its grim group remained unrelenting, implacable, fast in purpose. Adam Jory was a marked man on its books. And it was in no hurry; it had plenty of time.

Irene Jory was proud of Adam's Golconda merger. It was a subject of conversation among her friends, who quoted their husbands as admiring and envying the bold organizer. Irene was, in fact, a little hysterical about it. She seemed, at times, slightly irrational, though no one mentioned it above a whisper and within their charmed circle. She continued to be one of the leaders of Society — often a dictatorial leader and difficult to move. Mrs. Bridger, wife of the famous physician treating Mrs. Jory, quoted her husband as saying that Irene was going through a difficult period but would probably come through in a few months and be her old self again. One hoped so. Too bad that her husband, so handsome, so successful, so important, should kick over the traces in business, in that obstinate fashion of his. Yes, a big man, Jory of Los Angeles. But I'm afraid, my dear, a trifle common!

Indignation had driven Adam Jory into his first and only political activity, that had culminated in the Good Government victory. Like most businessmen he hated politics and be-grudged any time devoted to it. Having helped to elect the new regime he assumed that Los Angeles would thenceforward be honestly and decently governed, and that was all he wanted. But now he began to see signs, to his surprise and disgust, that the City Hall and the County Courthouse were filling up again with incompetents, rascals and the errand-boys of special interests and that the reform party was losing its grip.

That easy-going bystander and observer Billy Wing only chuckled at his wrathful complaint.

"What else did you expect, Jory? Eternal vigilance is the price of political power. You and a lot of other good citizens blew up eight years ago and the explosion you touched off lifted the old bosses right out of the plant. Then you dusted off your hands and went back to your own jobs. But the boys in the back-room didn't quit. They never do. They lie low for a while and wait for the breaks. Then they come out of their holes, a few at a time, and take over control again."

"Damn politics!" Jory cried. "A dirty business that no self-respecting citizen wants to get tangled in!"

"Of course not. So, in the end, you businessmen leave it to these boys in the back-room. All right — but don't squawk when you get caught in the door!"

The church element had played an important part in winning the Good Government party victory and this had given some of the brethren a taste of blood. They began to frequent the City Hall and to take a hand in running things. They were well meaning men, but their experience was limited and their vision was narrow. They continued to fret themselves over outlawed gambling, which still flourished, over the liquor business, which was dominated by the local breweries and arrogantly ruled, over the hydra-headed "social evil," with its complex problems no large community in history has ever been able to solve, and other ills having little or nothing to do with urgent needs of the growing city. Those business leaders who hated the Goo-goo movement because it had temporarily deposed them devoted their energies to weakening it by sheer weight of money and power. The professional politicians slyly egged the moral crusaders on, since fishing, for them, was always best in troubled waters. And both these elements watched and waited, knowing that the amateurs would sooner or later make a misstep and take a political header.

Exactly that happened.

The sordid murder of an erring wife and her paramour by the wronged husband set off the chain explosion. The pair were shot in a shabby midtown hotel which the police and the Headquarters reporters referred to callously as a house of assignation. The crusaders were not familiar with the term and it shocked them. They were much more shocked to learn

159

that the side-streets in the middle of the city were dotted with such places and that they did a substantial year-around business catering to the furtively amorous. In great indignation they stormed the City Council and demanded of the squirming legislators an ordinance outlawing all such resorts, providing round penalties for operators and visitors and directing the police to padlock the premises as punishment of the property owners.

Earl Tomblin, the conscientious and successful young City Prosecutor, tried to talk the outraged laymen out of their project, knowing full well that he would be called upon to enforce the law if it were passed. He urged that existing laws would take care of flagrant cases and that what they proposed would simply open the door to all sorts of abuses by the spiteful and the troublous and play into the hands of shyster lawyers, divorce detectives and petty blackmailers. Moreover he pointed out that such a law could not be worded so that it would not put in jeopardy the managers and owners of every respectable and high-class hostelry in Los Angeles, all of whom would be made personally responsible for the lawful marital status of guests, including those making up the huge tourist crop. What Tomblin got for his pains was a sniffy insinuation that he favored sin and, from the other camp, the doubtful honor of having the ordinance dubbed (first by the *Daily Sun*) "the Tomblin transom-peeping law."

His efforts failed and the law was passed.

Just what he had foretold transpired. Moreover, not content with prodding the police into a campaign to enforce the new statute, the crusaders organized a witch-hunt of their own and soon had the city in a turmoil and the hotel managers' association actually threatening to close down. The news went out over the press wires and gloating rival cities were soon picturing Los Angeles as a very Sodom of depravity. Vaudeville comedians bandied the rumors abroad and sophisticates sharpened their wits on them. A glib magazine writer crowned all these taunts with an article, soon widely quoted, under the

160

satiric title: "Los Angeles — Only Chemically Pure."

Humiliated Angelenos groaned and writhed. Generally they blamed the Good Government party; almost unanimously they damned its appointee, City Prosecutor Tomblin. Businessmen conferred grimly with the old-line political bosses who had been repudiated earlier. The Chamber of Commerce saw thirty years of expensive advertising in the strait-laced Middle West nullified overnight. When the ferment was at its height, a raid, made under pressure from the brethren by the police department's newly organized "morals squad," caught in its dragnet the black-sheep son of a prominent merchant. The news story went out before it could be caught and toned down. It was the last straw.

Late one wintry afternoon, after the courts were closed and most of the officers and attendants had left for the day, two city detectives and a lieutenant broke into the office of Prosecutor Earl Tomblin and found the bewildered lawyer staring at a young woman whose clothes were suddenly torn open and who burst into violent accusations against him. Tomblin was arrested on a "morals charge" and locked up in the cell downstairs. It was hours later before his bride of a few months and two or three friends were able to get together the $10,000 cash bail demanded for his release. Adam Jory furnished the last half of the amount, as soon as he was reached.

Tomblin telephoned Jory late that night.

"You shouldn't have done it, Mr. Jory. Mrs. Tomblin and I are almighty grateful to you. But I'd rather stay in jail than have a man in your position mixed up in this dirty business."

"Suppose you let me worry about that, Tomblin. I want you to understand that I don't believe a word of this charge against you."

Tomblin's voice broke. "Thank God for that, Mr. Jory. It's a frame-up of course. But it's a carefully planned job and they're out to get me."

"They can't hurt you if you're innocent, son."

161

"I'm afraid you don't know what I'm up against. I do. And I know that as far as my career as a reputable lawyer in Los Angeles is concerned I might as well be guilty."

"You're talking nonsense, Tomblin. The decent citizens will stand by you. Everybody must realize that this is only an attack on the Good Government administration."

"I hope you're right, Mr. Jory. But I can't see it that way."

He was right.

Except for the *Evening Messenger* the papers accepted the police version of the Downes woman's story that Tomblin had attacked her. Tomblin's statement that she had come to him asking protection from a brutal husband they printed as with raised eyebrows. Major Oddie let himself go in the *Daily Sun* and made a vicious attack on the prosecutor and, by extension, on all the remnants of the Good Government party still in office. The church element, dismayed and distracted, fell away from the accused man hastily. Some City League stalwarts defended him and a fund was raised to employ a lawyer for him. But the overwhelming majority in the city accepted the smug philosophy that where there was so much smoke there must be fire and prejudged him guilty.

Tomblin demanded an early trial but this did not suit the purposes of the forces behind the business. They wanted, as the young lawyer had foreseen, to try the case in the newspapers in order that the stigma might sink deep into the Googoo organization. One postponement followed another and it was well into spring before the nerve-wracked prosecutor was brought to bar.

Within a few days after the jury was sworn in it became apparent that the police could not hope for a conviction. Their whole case was the testimony of the woman, Vera Downes, although the detectives did their best to support it with statements as to sounds they said they had heard before breaking in the door.

Earl Tomblin's attorney tore this structure apart, largely with evidence that reporters for the *Messenger* had unearthed. Clare Shively had discovered that two morning paper reporters had been given advance notice of the raid on the office and had reported for work two or three hours early to be in at the kill. Billy Wing had remembered that Prosecutor Tomblin had caught one of the raiding detectives off-base in a bunco-ring investigation two or three years before and it was clearly proven that Officer Swing had threatened then to get even with the lawyer. Finally it developed that the Downes woman had moved from her shabby hotel room a few days before the arrest and had ensconced herself in a comfortable apartment which had been engaged for her by an underworld character known to be a police stool-pigeon. She would not admit that she was being paid for her part in the prosecution, but it was pretty clear that the jury had reached a frame of mind which made them unwilling to believe anything she said either way.

The five men and seven women making up the panel were out less than an hour — brought in a unanimous verdict of not guilty. Tomblin had few friends present. His wife was ill at home and his sister, two or three City League members and Adam Jory were surrounded by a motley crowd that was plainly disappointed at this anti-climax to early expectations. Some of them booed the judgment and Tomblin, haggard and worn, walked out of the courthouse through a lane of jeering and cat-calling hangers-on.

Adam Jory hurried to the office of the *Messenger* and sat there late while the staff turned out a monumental story of the verdict, the trial and the political activities and events that had preceded the raid and, the paper said editorially, led up to its staging. Jory was angry and in a fighting mood. He told John Shelley to take off the gloves and tell Los Angeles the truth. And the editorial Dr. Morehouse wrote and carefully polished, described Earl Tomblin as a scapegoat for the citizens who did not care enough for decent and honest and efficient city government to sustain the fight against evil, corruption and mal-administration. It was headed: Stand Up And Be Counted;

Adam Jory ordered it splashed across three columns of the first page.

It was midnight and Jory was about to leave when Billy Wing caught him.

"Mrs. Tomblin's doctor just called in, Jory. His patient is pretty sick and Tomblin hasn't shown up."

"You mean he didn't get home?"

"That's right. Shively thinks he may be drinking."

"I didn't suppose he was a drinking man."

"He isn't. That's what worries us. Shively is still here; we're going out on a still hunt."

"I'll go with you."

"We won't be looking at Rol King's or the Alexandria, you know."

"Humph! I'm over twenty-one, Wing. Come on."

They did not go to the best places, as Wing had hinted. They searched in dingy and obscure dumps and dens, all of them illegally open at that time of the night; they went into places that Adam Jory had not known existed in his city in the sun. Clare Shively, like a lanky dog on a dim scent, picked up the trail, lost it, found it again.

Earl Tomblin was run to earth in an oderiferous basement joint in the shadow of the County Courthouse. He was slumped in a chair and was in a stupor, his head cradled by his arms on a stained table. Shively awakened him with difficulty — went off for a pot of strong coffee.

"Brace up, Earl," Billy Wing said, half supporting the sodden, disheveled, bleary-eyed lawyer. "You're needed at home. Dr. Cash sent us to find you."

Tomblin stared into vacancy for a minute. His eyes focussed slowly.

"It's Billy Wing! An' Misser Jory. 'Lo, Misser Jory. Sup-suprise' see you here, 'sochiatin' with 'bandoned charac'er like me. Si down, ge'l'm'n. Mike, bring on drinks f'r frien's."

Adam said sternly: "We don't want anything to drink, Tomblin, and neither do you. I'm disappointed in you, young man. You don't belong in a hole like this."

Tomblin's befuddled brain struggled with the sense of the words. Suddenly he came reeling to his feet. Adam and Wing caught and steadied him or he would have fallen. He shook himself free.

"Hole like thish? Thish where I *do* belong! Any hole like thish. Know how I got here? Kicked here! No right 'n decent place. No right with decent people! Decent people are through with me. Shoved me into th' gutter. Tha's right!" A cunning look came over his smeared face. He lowered his voice. "Into th' gutter. An' wan' to know what I found in gutter?"

He fumbled for a pocket — pulled out a roll of money. He threw it on the table and Jory saw several large bills.

"Look a' that! Two thousan' there. An' plenty more where it c-came from. Where'd I get it? In th' gutter. Re-retainin' fee from a dirty, low, ou'cast pimp to 'fend him on panderin' charge I filed — me, City Pros'cutor." Tomblin grabbed at the money and scattered the greenbacks widely. "Yes, Misser J-Jory, 'S Angel's kicked me into gutter an' I fin' money there. T' hell with decent, 'spectable people. I'm kicked down in gutter — an' I'm goin' shtay there an' mu-muck f'r gold!"

Shively brought the coffee. They collected the strewn money and Jory entrusted it to Billy Wing.

"Will you boys see that he gets home?"

"Sure."

"Thanks. I don't think I can. To tell the truth I'm feeling a little sick."

It was true. Adam Jory was feeling sick.

As his big car rolled through the silent streets he looked at the Los Angeles he had helped to build — that he had loved and gloried in. The taste of its triumphs turned to ashes in his mouth. All this growth, achievement, unrivaled success, that he and others like him had believed in, worked for, been proud of — was it all futile and purposeless? Had they built

165

here a great city to the end that clean, ambitious, decent young men like Earl Tomblin should be sacrificed and their lives wrecked by unbridled forces of evil?

Spread out around him in the clear starlight he saw Los Angeles — beautiful, lusty, gracious — a place of comfort and a rich happiness that even the poor could have their part in. Mile after mile, from the mountains to the sea, its avenues ran on and on between the inviting homes, each set in its spread of lawn and garden bed, tree-sheltered, vine-covered. The scent of a million flowers was in the soft air; now and then the piercing sweetness of a mocking-bird's carol arose; off to the northeast the dark purple folds of the Sierra Madre mountains was a sheltering wall topped with the faint snow line of their heights, that looked down on the orange groves of the valleys — the vineyards and fields and orchards and pretty little towns scattered among rolling hills all about. Los Angeles, an Eden, a Paradise, a region to fulfill all man's dreams! Los Angeles, the end of the rainbow — the pot of gold! Los Angeles, the city in the sun!

Jory drew a deep breath. It was good to be here — good to be alive and a part of —

Then his mind flashed back to the half-lit, stinking, rat-hole on New High Street and to the drawn, dirty, defiant face of Earl Tomblin as he reeled up to throw before them his fistful of money — his first retainer taken from the gutter.

An old verse, learned when he was a boy and now remembered out of a long time of forgetting, came to Adam Jory: *For what is a man profited, if he shall gain the whole world and lose his own soul?*

A man — or a great, proud, rich city?

That autumn old Dad Kerner filed suit against Adam Jory for infringement of patents on a fuel-oil burner. The damages asked were in the sum of $1,500,000.

```
FOR SALE
At a sacrifice by
WM. A. ROWLAND & CO.


POPULATION OF L. A.
Now          577,000
1930       1,000,000
```

S AN FRANCISCANS TRIED a few jokes about the 1920 population prophecy of Will Rowland, the Los Angeles real
estate operator: his 1910 guess at the figure had been too
high by some 20,000.

But the jokes weren't very funny, even in the city by the
Golden Gate, for the federal census returns showed that Los
Angeles had passed her northern sister, by 70,000, and was the
largest community west of Chicago. Moreover the despised
pueblo was experiencing a fresh boom — expanding, spreading out, finding itself hard-pressed to keep up with its own
unbelievable development.

Bank deposits stood at half a billion dollars and clearings
exceeded four billions a year. The harbor San Francisco had

167

snorted at was handling cargoes totaling almost $200,000,000 in value annually and in the middle '20's that figure jumped to three-quarters of a billion. As an industrial and manufacturing center this despised village of sunshine, homes and retired farmers was confounding the statisticians with its output and it was one of the nation's leading producers of oil — crude, refined and processed. Its tourist crop was good for scores of millions more, in widely distributed hard cash. And this urban territory was surrounded by a county that stood first in the nation in value of farm, vineyard and orchard produce, topped by the multi-million-dollar citrus yield.

Postal receipts, building permits, street- and interurban-railway passenger miles, school attendance, church membership, assessed property valuations — choose what category you would and Los Angeles had staggering figures for you to roll on the tongue. If the population growth had disappointed Rowland slightly in the decade of the 'teens it made amends now. Chamber of Commerce figures showed the greatest influx of all in full flood in the early 1920's — a hundred thousand new residents a year. And the brash and blooming virgin city had no false modesty. She spoke exceedingly well of herself — and out loud!

Meantime, Will Rowland raised his sights again, upped his figures, incorporated his real estate business, grown too big to be sound as a private enterprise, and joined with the other civic leaders in mapping new campaigns for the aggrandizement of their city in the sun. They had been preoccupied thus far in laying the foundations for a prosperous commerce, a thriving industrial capital, a stable business structure and the continuous stepping-up of material progress. Now their attention was drawn to a novel and provocative program to give Los Angeles a more beautiful and bountiful life.

In the lush and turbulent earlier years the stridency of the boosters and boasters had drowned out the voices of those who advocated community investment in the finer things of living. Among the builders, promotors, grabbers, speculators, ex-

168

ploiters it had been difficult to hear the few artists, poets, musicians, educators and men and women of urbanity and taste. But these latter were infected as thoroughly as the former with a genuine love for their city. As much for her future as for their own satisfaction they had struggled along with the torch, keeping it alight as best they could. They brought in a few first-line road shows, a traveling opera troupe, a winter season of concerts, and they supported a poverty-ridden orchestra. They made it possible for one good bookstore to survive and, though they made no great inroads on the framed-picture business of the furniture emporiums, they did enable a handful of painters to keep soul and body together, however precariously. The local colleges and academies made hard going of it — began to emerge only by grace of such fortuities as one good football team, an appropriation from the legislature for a branch of the state university and a science teacher who won the Nobel Prize.

Certain aspects of this stubborn inner life in the city the business sachems managed to discern for themselves. Hollywood, attracting to its studios an increasing number of big-name actors, writers and musicians, proved that there was money in Art. Hollywood also was beginning to bring Los Angeles favorable nationwide publicity that no money could buy and it was drawing on a source of new population the Chamber of Commerce could not reach. Adam Jory, hiring the young chemist, Wade, to develop his petroleum by-product business, had not been the only capitalist to make a profitable investment in a graduate from a local college. And a local sports writer was selling pieces to the *Saturday Evening Post* and was reported to be making almost as much money from them as could be made by a first-rate bank teller.

When the apostles of culture became numerous enough and bold enough to propose that their causes deserved financial backing they got a hearing. As time went on they took some small orders. Business ventured timidly into the support of the symphony orchestra, into endowing a chair or two in college

169

faculties, into subsidizing an art gallery. The names of merchant princes appeared on boards of directors of these non-profit enterprises; they sponsored opera and tried the sensation of acting as patrons of art shows and a program of instrumental quartette music. The trend became a movement and the movement became fashionable. There was no money in it, but it did something for Los Angeles.

The significant fact is that this activity was launched at the right historic moment. Billy Wing's Band of Hope had given the city everything else — every material aid and advantage and opportunity required to make it grow big and strong and permanent. Here was a new outlet for the boundless enthusiasm and untiring energy of those civic leaders. They brought to the promotion of culture all the organizational skill and operating know-how that had hauled Los Angeles up by its own boot-straps since the days of the 1894 Fiesta. Scoffers told them that they couldn't buy the better way of life or make a contract for beauty and urbanity. They shrugged. They had in their files firm offers of the means to all the fine and gracious and precious things that the civilizations of history had created and they were closing the deals, one by one. Once those means were provided Los Angeles could help itself, to capacity. Here would be established a new capital of the arts, the sciences, of learning and the spiritual verities. If the better life could not be lived in such a setting and under such a sun, it could not be lived again on this globe.

Adam Jory had watched the beginnings of this shift of objectives with shrewd eyes and with his own reason for interest. He had been vexed and disillusioned by the outcome of the effort to give Los Angeles better municipal government and its ugly climax in the Tomblin case. Active enmity and public apathy had killed the Good Government movement, and the gradual return to power of the old railroad-public utility-underworld machine convinced him that the people didn't want their politics pasteurized. Billy Wing, puffing contentedly at his pipe, tried to console Jory with the observation that Los Angeles was no worse, and no worse off, than any American municipality. Dr. Morehouse blandly cited history to show that inefficiency, waste and graft were part of the price a democracy had to pay for its larger benefits. Jory glowered. His city ought to be different. But reluctantly he had to admit to himself that it wasn't.

The spreading cultural movement seemed to him to offer some hope. Perhaps this was the answer to the problem — the practical salvation of Los Angeles. Perhaps materialism was to blame for the low state of civic morality. If a people had every advantage lying at hand, with the necessities of life assured and the comforts and luxuries within reach of everyone who would make a little effort, surely then they would take a hand in keeping their blessings secure. At odd times, as the years went on, he had thought occasionally of what he could do with his own possessions to enrich the city he loved. Now he began to see doors opening that he had never known of or considered.

Irene, his wife, was already involved in some of the activities that were becoming matters of business enterprising. Now Adam put his name on subscription lists, accepted onerous chores on strange boards of directors, assumed profitless trusteeships, in support of projects entirely foreign to his own world. He who had not finished high school became a trustee of a university. He who could not identify one star helped raise the first million to bring to Los Angeles a telescope designed to penetrate the mysteries of uncharted stellar space. He who could not name a tune nor sit through a concerto was one of the half-dozen founders of the permanent Symphony Orchestra Association. He who had neither time nor taste for the theater was a generous contributor to a fund for building an out-of-door amphitheater where great music and drama would be offered to 30,000 spectators at a time, under the stars.

Secretly he hoped that all this strenuous and time-consuming participation in a field outside his own would bring him at least the glimmering of understanding and appreciation of

171

something new, pleasurable, rewarding to his starved spirit. But though he went more often to the programs, perform- ances, recitals, productions, demonstrations, ceremonies and ex- hibitions that he and his kind were offering the people of Los Angeles, he was disappointed. He had to conclude that he had no grasp of such things. Left out of him. Not his meat. And he felt cheated — a little sorry for himself.

He tried, with a strong man's impatience, to put such non- sensical, childish peevishness aside. Once he had been able to ignore or forget what was unpleasant, distasteful or even merely discomforting. He had always been the master of his longings, hungers, spiritual cravings. He had been Jory of Los Angeles, sure of himself and sufficient to himself. He had been content to keep his eye to the main chance and push on brusquely and ruthlessly toward his goals.

Now he faltered. Was he losing his grip? Was he getting old? What was wrong with him? He did not know.

Mark Valentine, Jory's attorney, was disturbed over the patent infringement suit old Dad Kerner had brought.

"If he had a good lawyer they'd give us a tussle, Jory. This fellow Wall is small-caliber but even so you never can tell what a jury will do, especially to a defendent they think has more money than he's entitled to. My advice is that you let me try to make a settlement out of court."

"No, thanks. Gus Kerner would never have got anywhere with his burners without me. I've protected his rights as well as my own and in twenty years I've paid him more than he could have made from all his notions together. You lawyers have ways to drag out a case like this."

"There are ways."

"Find 'em. Kerner will soon run out of money and this snide lawyer of his will give up. I propose to fight this suit to the Supreme Court and back again. That's final."

Valentine's office followed instructions and it was fourteen months before *Kerner vs. Jory* was called for trial. When it opened Mark Valentine was prepared with another demurrer; this resulted in an order throwing the complaint out of court and proceedings had to be started over again. Adam Jory paid a pretty heavy fee and a neat sum for contingent expenses — and grimly directed Valentine to keep up the fight.

Timid, devoted Lucy Zander was now Adam Jory's confidential secretary. Herbert Kinney was devoting his whole time to Golconda, of which he had been made secretary and "assistant to the President." Actually he was managing the big corporation and doing it successfully. There were times when Jory thought he detected symptoms of ambition and a love of power in the silent, sharp, industrious agent and on a few occasions he brought Kinney up short. His aide showed no resentment nor impatience. And there was no denying his ability. He had developed into a first-rate administrator, handling the complex affairs of the growing corporation shrewdly. As time went on, Jory left more and more of the details of its management to him. He was finding that his personal affairs, his civic responsibilities, and the *Evening Messenger* gave him enough to do, even though little Lucy Zander took all the details off his shoulders. She had become his right hand, though probably neither of them was conscious of the fact.

Miss Zander's father had died; the rest of the family were prospering, with one of the sisters married and another about to be. They took their notion of Adam Jory from Lucy and believed him to be a combination of King Midas, Sir Galahad and Santa Claus. After Zander's death they had returned to the city, one by one, except Lucy. She continued to go back and forth to the old Luke Farm, which she somehow contrived to keep going by hiring a man and his wife and driving them like slaves and herself like a third on Saturday afternoons and Sundays. Jory knew nothing of all this. He had forgotten the farm — knew only vaguely that his plain, tireless little clerk lived in the country. In one winter of torrential rains when she came in half drowned he ordered her peremptorily to get an apartment in a block he owned on South Olive Street.

"Mercy, Mr. Jory, I'm all right. I like rain."

"Nonsense. Do as I say."

She didn't. And the matter eventually slipped his mind, of course.

Among her other duties Lucy Zander had the task of attending to Jory's charitable contributions. It was the sort of responsibility he abhorred, not because he was mean but because he did not want to listen to the pleas of solicitors or the needy and because, above everything, he was made uncomfortable by any form of gratitude or thanks. When Lucy Zander had established herself as competent and responsible he had, in what he considered a moment of great inspiration, turned over the whole business to her.

"Take out ten per cent of our gross every year, Lucy, to start with," he had said. "Don't give to foreign missions or to schemes for reforming drunkards. Aside from that, use your own judgment. And remember, I don't want to hear anything about it."

As an afterthought he had instructed her to take over from Kinney the business of sending a cash sum monthly to Noll, of the Security (it was his old obligation to Beulah Rountree and their daughter) and to see to it that the *Messenger's* manager continued to mail a weekly check to the wife of Walter Young.

Twice Mrs. Young came to the offices to thank Jory. Lucy Zander talked to her both times — made her see, finally, that it would be better not to try to reach Jory. But she herself drew out the story of the printer's conviction and, moved by it and a liking for Mrs. Young, kept the acquaintanceship alive and, after a while, developed it into a warm friendship. Eventually she began to vist the home and to meet Walter's son, Stephen and later their friend Mrs. Rountree and her beautiful daughter, the movie star, Judith Wayne.

She didn't mention any of this in the office. But the new contact gave her inexpressible pleasure because the Youngs were never tired of talking about what a wonderful man Adam Jory was. And, as it developed, Mrs. Rountree, who said casually that she had worked, years ago, in the same shop with Walter Young and Jory, was equally interested in her employer and also had a great admiration for him, though it seemed to the jealous Lucy to be tinged too much with a sort of knowing amusement.

"She acts almost as though Mr. Jory were a small boy, full of tricks and up to mischief," the ruffled little wren observed once to Mrs. Young. "I don't know what to make of it."

"Oh, Beulah is that way, Miss Zander. I declare I never did know such an easy-going, jolly woman. Everything that happens seems to strike her funny-bone."

Sometimes the three women talked of Walter Young. Twice union workers had tried to get the prisoner paroled. But the big, powerful, ugly Industrial Association stood in the way, grim, unrelenting, unforgiving, implacable. Perhaps, some day, somehow —

Julius Nostrander died suddenly at his desk in the following spring, stricken while he was going over the papers in a real estate transaction.

The bond which unites many elderly couples had held the elderly Nostranders together so closely for over fifty years that Berthe Nostrander soon followed her husband. Her life had been built on and around that of her mate and she failed steadily, longing to leave a world that had ceased to have any meaning or comfort for her when he was gone.

Irene Jory was shocked and grieved by her father's death, but he was an old man and had not been well for some time She took the second loss harder. For a time Adam Jory feared for her health, particularly her mental health. She had long been highly nervous and often a little strange and now she went to pieces.

For once Adam let business go and devoted himself wholly to his wife. With a good deal of difficulty he persuaded her to take a trip to the Hawaiian Islands, believing with the doctors that this might divert her and bring her back to normal. But

175

after a few days of encouraging symptoms Irene relapsed into
a heavier melancholy — insisted on coming home.

A chance remark she made later gave Jory a welcome hint.

In a half-hysterical moment she cried: "It wasn't fair! It
was so sudden! Poor papa!"

"But his business was in good order, Irene. Are you fretting
because he didn't make a will?"

"Business!" she echoed. "Everybody remembers him for
that — for the Nostrander Block, the Nostrander Hotel, Nostrander Place in the new subdivision! He wanted to build a
home for old people — something fine and big. If he had
known he was going to die he would have arranged for that.
Now — !"

Jory recalled then that the old man had talked once or
twice about some such project. He had spoken vaguely of a
memorial to his wife, when she should pass away. It had
never occurred to him that she would outlive him.

Adam acted immediately. He arranged a meeting with Mrs.
Jory's attorney and an architect, a contractor and the rabbi of
the synagogue. Within a few days Rabbi Wolff went to call
on Irene Jory. At Adam's suggestion he told her that her
father had consulted him about an old people's home; he
brought with him an architect's rough sketch of a splendid institution where ninety or a hundred inmates could be housed
with every comfort and convenience — almost in luxury. Jory
had suggested as a site a large tract belonging to the estate in
the foothills southeast of Pasadena, where the rolling land was
dotted with fine old oak trees and from which one could look
across the city to the sea or north to the Sierra Madre mountains. The contractor had provided Rabbi Wolff with an esti-
mate of the cost of construction, including roads, pathways,
landscaping and the development of a water supply.

"You could call it 'The Julius Nostrander Home for the
Aged,'" the rabbi said. "There would be nothing finer in the
world."

Irene Jory was afire with enthusiasm.

176

"But for papa and mama — Julius and Berthe Nostrander Home. And twice as big. For two hundred. And they won't be called inmates. They'll be guests."

"Of course. But the cost, if you double the size, Mrs. Jory —"

"It's all settled. I'll send for the car and telephone Adam. I want to go out there. I want to see how it will look. Can you go with us?"

Within a month the first scrapers and steam shovels were on the property; within ninety days the steel skeleton of the main structure was rising.

Irene became absorbed in the project to the exclusion of everything else. She spent part of every day on the ground. For her birthday Adam, on a suggestion from Dave Allison, the architect, bought a cottage and had it moved to the building site. He had made an excuse to take her to Riverside to see a new wing of The Mission Inn that might give her some ideas for interior decorations, so that the contractor and the architect were able to get the little house in place and ready for occupancy before she saw it. She wept with delight. Now she could live some of the time right on the job. She transferred a maid to the cottage and set up housekeeping. Adam joined her occasionally. She was better than she had been for a long time — seemed wholly herself again.

The entire Nostrander estate was made over to the trustees who were to control and govern the Home. When it was completed, furnished and staffed there would be money enough remaining to endow it in perpetuity.

Adam Jory was not on the board. Irene had chosen it, with suggestions from Sussmann, the banker, Rabbi Wolff, Attorney Kahn and a few close friends. She herself had crossed off her husband's name, without explanation.

The jangling of his bedside telephone in the early hours of an autumn morning brought Adam Jory awake.

"This is Jory."

"Adam! It's Beulah!"

"Beulah? Oh, yes, Beulah."

"I've got to see you. I wouldn't phone, except — Ad, we're in bad trouble."

"Where are you?"

"I'm home." She gave him a Hollywood address.

"The girl — she's not sick?"

The woman's voice steadied.

"She's all right. But it's trouble for her, too."

"I'll be there in half an hour."

Jory dressed hurriedly. Damn Hollywood! he was thinking. This "bad trouble," whatever it was, had come somehow out of Judith's connection with the place — with its queer, unaccountable people. If only he had done something about it earlier! He hadn't thought enough about it. But he had felt uncomfortable and vaguely anxious. What, now, had transpired?

He let himself out of the house quietly and went to the stable, which had been transformed into a garage for the three or four automobiles. Lind, the chauffeur, lived upstairs with his wife, a maid in the house. The man come stumbling to the door.

"You'll have to take me out, Bob. And make it fast."

"Yes, Mr. Jory. Half a shake."

Adam waited only a few minutes, then they were hurtling through the silent, almost deserted streets. He had had few occasions to drive out in this direction and he was struck now by the development. The whole territory was solidly built up and the homes and the focal trading centers were modern, handsome, pleasing. He had known these areas as suburban subdivisions and, only a little earlier, as hayfields and dairies. Beyond Vermont, beyond Western and into Hollywood, with no break between and few vacant lots. The foothill village he had driven through on his way from the old Luke farm had become a sprawling city in itself, with a population probably four or five times greater than all of Los Angeles had had in those years. Adam had difficulty locating the lot he had bought thinking that one day he would build himself a country home on it. It was in the very heart of the motion picture capital. Probably worth twice what he had finally sold it for — a round sum, too — when he had liquidated some of his real estate holdings to get a larger share in Golconda Corporation. Will Howland had warned him. Well, a man couldn't have everything.

"This looks like the place, Mr. Jory," the driver was saying. "I don't see any lights, though."

"This is the right number. I don't know how long I'll be." Adam looked at his watch. "It's after two. Go to the Hollywood Hotel garage and wait there till I phone you."

"I'd just as lief stay here."

"Do as I say."

He turned in between the stucco gate-pillars and followed a walk that wound between lawns and flower beds. The house was a California bungalow of white plaster half-hidden by shrubs and vines. It stood well back and had a comfortable, cared-for, homelike look, without folderol or pretension. It was completely dark.

The front door opened as Jory's footsteps sounded on the steps of the wide porch.

"Adam?"

"Yes, Beulah."

Her hand, the fingers cold, caught his. She pulled him inside, closed the door and bolted it.

"The police came, but I played possum. I had to see you first." Her voice broke. "Thanks for coming, Ad."

She began to cry. He put out a hand awkwardly, in the darkness, to steady her and she threw her arms around him and kissed him hard on the mouth. He tasted the salt of her tears and felt her cheeks and lips wet against his.

"It's all right, Beulah," he said, his voice gentle.

She drew away and he heard her laugh, well-remembered, intimate, warming.

"I'm a big booby. I didn't think I'd carry on this way." He could imagine her straightening and lifting her fine shoulders. "I'm all right now. Come in here."

He heard another door open, then she switched on a subdued light. He followed her into a sort of sitting room, cosy and lived-in, with book shelves, a small piano, a fireplace and easy chairs. Beulah closed the door.

She had filled out and there was a touch of gray in her thick, beautiful hair. Otherwise she seemed little changed. She gestured toward a chair and pulled another closer.

"I don't know how to tell this, Ad. Yes, I do. I'll tell it right out. It's a murder."

What he had expected to hear he did not know, but it had not been that. Still he gave no sign.

"I don't care what it is, Beulah. I'll stand by you. Remember that."

She swallowed hard and her eyes filled. She was under a strain, but she had herself under control.

"I knew you would, Ad. Well, I'll need you. We'll both need you."

"Where's Judith? She's all right, you said."

"She's with some friends. You know them: Steve Young's folks. Steve's father is the printer — you recollect — "

"Yes. Is Judith in this thing?"

"Yes. If it hadn't been for her I wouldn't have called you. Or maybe I would." She smiled at him, looking game, strong, loyal. "I'm getting ahead of myself. I'll go back. Did you ever hear of a Hollywood rounder named deCosta?"

"Yes, I know of him. Called himself a Count."

"Amadeo deCosta. He's the man. He's dead."

"Killed?"

"Tonight, just after midnight. I was at his house. I went there after Judith."

He winced. But his voice was steady when he asked: "She was going around with him?"

"Let me tell you." Her voice sharpened and she spoke

180

angrily. "This man was rotten, Ad. He bragged about gold-bricking grown women, supposed to be respectable — and about ruining young girls. He had a cussed, mean streak in him, too — the silly fools who threw themselves at him, he just laughed at. He would insult them and walk out. The kind he really wanted were the ones he couldn't get without an effort."

"That's how Judith — ?"

"That's why we're in this. He has been stalking her for three years, like a slick, yellow cat."

Jory's lips twitched. "Why didn't you let me know?"

She inquired, simply: "How could I?"

This brought him out of his quick rage. She was, according to her lights and her nature, right. He had turned his back on her and married into a position that separated them. After that she had made her own life, dropping out of his completely and never trying to bridge that gulf. She had been scrupulous in cutting all the threads that might have bound them. Nothing but this crisis could have wrung an appeal from her — and in this crisis their daughter was involved. Yes, she was consistent and true, as she had always been.

"I'm sorry, Beulah," Adam said. "It was my fault. Go on and tell me."

"The man was fascinating — I'll give him that much. Sometimes, when he wanted to make the effort, he could almost fool me. And he made Judith like him. I could see that she tried not to — that she didn't want to. She had no chance when he cared enough to turn on that damned charm of his."

Yes, he thought, there were probably men like that. He knew little enough of the world of such men — and such women. He knew little enough of the whole field of personal relations and emotions — of love, courtship, sex — of temptations and devices and traps as between men and women. But he did know that there were those whose entire lives were largely made up of such enterprises, excursions, adventures, preoccupations.

181

Beulah Rountree's story went on into a world more than ever outside his own.

"For three or four years deCosta has been carrying on an affair with a famous star. With Ellen York, in fact. You must have heard of her."

"I know the name."

"DeCosta was supposed to belong to her. She thought he did, anyway; she was too conceited to believe the stories that went around — to believe what everybody else knew about him. He was always hunting. He hunted Judith."

Beulah took a deep breath and shifted in her chair. She went on quickly: "I watched him like a hawk. I was doing all right, too. But tonight he picked her up at the Broadmoor. Judith, I mean. She went there with the Douglass' — movie people, but real folks. They'd often taken her, when the party was going to be too high-toned for my style. Around midnight they missed her. After a while they got worried and telephoned me to know if she'd come home."

"And she hadn't."

"No. I didn't want to upset Greta Douglass, so I told Preston something — the first thing that popped into my head. Then I went back to my room and got out my gun — the one you gave me, remember, when we — when I was staying alone sometimes at the Santa Monica Canyon place. I put it in my bag and took my car and drove straight to deCosta's. I was that sure!"

She was speaking evenly now, without emotion. It was almost as though she were telling a story she had heard or read. She sat quietly, too, her hands in her lap, her eyes thoughtful.

"I know deCosta's house pretty well. We'd been there often — too often! The front door was unlocked and I walked in. DeCosta's servant Hand — a Canadian, I think he is, who's been with him a long time — was at the other end of the hall, but I didn't speak to him or give him a chance to stop me. There was a light in deCosta's library, as he calls it, and I went in. He was standing behind a desk and didn't look very well pleased with himself. Across the desk from him was Ellen York. She was having a tantrum."

"Judith wasn't —"

"I asked him. York laughed — a nasty, hard laugh. She said to me: 'You got here in time, Mrs. Rountree, if that's any comfort to you. Amadeo hadn't got around to her.' She put it another way. It doesn't matter. I wasn't there to pick a fight with that tramp!"

"And this man —"

"DeCosta was trying to make out that he was cool and calm. He lighted a cigarette. He made the mistake of laughing. It was that laugh of his — I don't know what there is about it, but it makes you feel dirty and ashamed and humiliated. I don't know just what happened, except that I had the pistol out of my bag and deCosta was on me, twisting my wrist. The gun fell and I ran out of the room. I went from door to door till I found Judith. She was dazed and sick, lying across a bed. She'd been doped with something. But she was beginning to come out of it.

"I got her downstairs as quick as I could and then I heard Ellen York squalling. And I heard a shot. I looked into the library and saw York on the floor holding deCosta's head in her lap. He was dead — I knew that when I thought back.

"Not then. I didn't think that far. I hurried toward the front door. I was taking Judith out when a man's voice spoke and I turned my head to see Hand, the servant, running into the hall from some door. He asked me a question, but I didn't understand. I got Judith into the car and drove away — drove here, first. Then I got panicky. The police would be hot on the case and of course they'd find I'd been there. I decided to take Judith to the Youngs'. They didn't ask any questions — they're the kind of friends who don't ask questions. They made some strong coffee — I suppose they thought Judith was drunk. She was still doped and kept going to sleep.

"After a while I came back here and telephoned you."

Without moving, Adam Jory, studying Beulah's face —
holding himself in — said: "What became of the gun?"

"I don't know. I forgot all about it. I forgot my handbag,
too. All I could think of was getting Judith away from that
place."

"This York woman works for the Silberberg outfit, doesn't
she?"

"She's Silberberg's top-liner. She's worth a fortune to him."

"So he wouldn't want her charged with a murder."

"She won't be, Ad. You don't know how Hollywood takes
care of its own. Or what sort of a drag Silberberg has in this
town."

"I know all about it." Adam thought a minute. He was
looking ahead, trying to see the business whole. It was not
unlike approaching a big deal of some sort, where a man
could make a fortune or lose his shirt. "Did anyone besides
this servant see you leaving the house?"

"A milk wagon driver came by. I did have sense enough
to know that he might recognize Judith — he was a kid who
would just love her pictures. So I looked twice and made out
the name of the dairy. It was a Sunnyside wagon. Number
sixty-seven."

Adam made a quick note. "Smart girl. And that was around
what time?"

"Around one o'clock somewhere."

They both heard a car in the street outside. It was pulling
up. Beulah started, putting a hand to her throat.

"It's the police."

"Probably. Listen to me."

"Yes, Ad."

"Are you all right now? Can you trust everything to me
and not get rattled?"

"Yes. Look!" She held out a hand and it was steady. Her
face was calm and her body relaxed. "I can go through anything I have to, with you behind me."

"I'll have to move fast, Beulah. But I wouldn't be much

good to you if the police found me here — tied me up with
the case. Is there a way out through the back of the house?"

"Yes. Into an alley. There's no light there till you get
over on to Virginia Street."

He took her hand. He leaned forward and kissed her.

"Keep your head and don't worry. Tell the police that
Judith went into the country from the hotel."

"What about that pistol, Ad?"

"You don't know anything about a pistol. You can just
say that your lawyer has instructed you not to talk. I'll take
care of everything if you can stall this business for a few hours."

Adam let himself out through a rear door as the front door
bell whirred in the kitchen.

Jory summoned his driver by telephone from the booth in
an all-night drugstore. As he hung up he had another thought
— found the number for Clare Shively's home and, after a short
delay, had the reporter on the line.

"There's been a shooting in Hollywood — a man named de-
Costa. I'd like to find out fast what the police know about
the case. Can you get anything by phone?"

"I can try."

"I'm on my way to my office. Jory Building. Give me a
ring there in about twenty minutes."

"Jake!"

Rolling townward Adam began calculating his next moves.
For several reasons he rejected the idea of bringing his own
attorney, Judge Valentine, into the business. He was not, in
fact, sure that what was required was a lawyer. A reputable
man would balk at subterfuges and a shyster would discredit
Beulah and Judith by the very fact of his connection with their
affairs. Recognized criminal lawyers were essential in court, but
in this instance a public trial was unthinkable — must be
avoided at all costs.

Then he remembered Earl Tomblin. The former city
prosecutor had renounced respectability that night in the New

185

High Street dive and Adam had heard that he had carried out his threat to go to the gutter for whatever money could be mined there. There might be a risk in confiding in Tomblin, but if money was what the embittered lawyer was after his services could be obtained. It was worth trying.

Dismissing the driver Adam hurried into his office building; he was delayed in getting an elevator, since the cages were operated during early morning hours by the night watchman and the fellow was making his rounds somewhere in the upper stories, but at last he came and Adam was at the door of his private suite. As he searched for his key, which he had seldom needed, he heard the telephone bell jangling.

When he reached it the instrument was dead. It was, he remembered, on an inter-office switchboard; he fumbled impatiently at the buttons, keys, plugged lines — finally got through to an operator.

"Sorry, sir, your party has hung up."

"Give me Information."

"Yes, sir."

A voice surprisingly alert and fresh, considering the hour, came on.

"I'm in my office and I don't know how to work this damned — this contraption of yours. So I want to stay right here until you get my party for me."

"Surely. The name please?"

"Earl Tomblin. He's a lawyer. If he can't be reached at his home, wherever that may be, I'd like somebody there to help me find him."

"We'll do what we can, sir. Just a moment."

Another voice came on the line presently. "This is the Supervisor speaking. Are you Mr. Jory?"

"I'm Jory." How did they know that? He hadn't intended to say.

"The operator isn't able to get your party at his residence, Mr. Jory. But we have another number here. You can hang up and we'll call you."

"I don't understand this telephone board. How will I know which phone to answer?"

"Leave the board as it is, then, Mr. Jory, and answer there. Do you want us to send an operator over to help you?"

"If you can send somebody to show me how — "

"Right away, Mr. Jory." There was a click, then the line opened again and the supervisor said: "Just a moment, sir. I have a call for you."

It came on — a woman's voice.

"Mr. Jory? This is Mrs. Shively. Clare asked me to phone you."

"Where is he?" Adam barked. "I told him — "

"I know. But you didn't answer when he called and he wanted to get to Central Station. He left me to tell you what he found out over the wire."

"All right. Go ahead, Mrs. Shively."

"A man named deCosta was shot and killed in his house." She gave the street address. "That was at a few minutes before one, they think. The only people in the house were a woman and deCosta's butler, or whatever he is — a servant. The woman got away."

"Did he find out the woman's name?"

"No. That's why he got dressed and went down to the Station. He'll telephone you from there."

"Did they arrest the man — that servant?"

"They didn't arrest him. The dicks — the plain-clothes men — are still questioning him."

"Thank you. And, Mrs. Shively!"

"Yes, sir."

"I wish you wouldn't mention any of this — I mean, that I telephoned, or that you — "

The woman on the line laughed. "I've been married to a reporter twenty years, Mr. Jory. Tell Clare not to talk, if you think you ought to, but don't tell me."

"Oh! I see. Well, I'm sorry I said that, then. Thank you."

This newspaper world! It was made up of people set apart

187

from all others, with different interests, objectives, ethics, points
of view. It continually surprised him — puzzled and pleased
him, at the same time. Now, for instance, he felt a sense of
relief — a steadying and heartening confidence in that lean,
narrow-faced, quiet, hard-bitten reporter. For the moment the
police end was covered. Shively had gone to Central Station;
Mrs. Shively needed no hints to be silent.

Then the telephone bell chattered somewhere in an inner
office and a light flashed on the switchboard. Adam picked up
the awkward headpiece and, twisting its bridle aside got the
receiver to his ear.

"We have your party, sir. Go ahead, Mr. Tomblin."

"Mr. Jory?"

"This is Jory, Tomblin. Where are you? How long will it
take you to get to my office?"

Tomblin's voice was heavy and perhaps thick. But he was
keen and alert enough.

"In the Jory Building? Ten minutes."

"There may be something you can do for me."

"I'll be there."

It was now just turning three o'clock. Jory, thinking hard,
reached for a telephone directory. As he thumbed it a knock
came. He crossed the room. Outside stood a stout, plainly-
dressed woman, wearing spectacles and with graying hair.

"I'm from the telephone company, Mr. Jory. My name is
Miss Albert. The supervisor said — "

"Come in!" Jory felt relieved again. In this emergency
everything seemed to come to his hand. "See here, Miss Albert, I have — er — something important in hand. Could you
take care of this telephone contrivance for me, for a couple
of hours?"

"Surely. Anything I can do, sir."

He blurted: "It's a confidential matter, you understand. I'll
pay well — but I must be able to trust you like I would one
of my own clerks."

The woman was taking off her hat and coat. She smiled

faintly. "I'm one of the night supervisors at the main exchange, Mr. Jory. Miss Grannis and I talked it over. We thought from what you said that you needed some help. So I came over. The Sunset Telephone and Telegraph Company is handling your board now, Mr. Jory, not Annie Albert."

She straightened the headpiece, put it on, began clearing the board, her fingers flying. A light flashed.

"A call for you, Mr. Jory. Where will you take it?"

"In my own office. Wait a minute."

At his desk phone he found that it was Clare Shively.

"Did my wife get you?"

"Yes. Thanks, Shively. What have you found out there?"

"Up to now the story is that a burglar walked in on deCosta and shot him. That's the version of deCosta's valet, a fellow named Hand. It's a phony, but the police are riding on it for the morning papers."

"All right. About the woman that Mrs. Shively mentioned — ?"

"Ellen York. A vamp on the Silberberg Studio lot. She was in the house when the police got there, on a call from some neighbors about gun shots they'd heard. The front office is giving out the story that she got away without being recognized. Nothing to that. The dicks didn't want to recognize her till they'd found out which way the case was going to break."

"Has any other — er — anybody else been mentioned? By name, I mean?"

"DeCosta was at the Broadmoor tonight — left there around midnight with a girl named Wayne — another actress. She hasn't been located yet."

Jory cleared his throat — forced himself to speak quietly. "Is this girl a suspect, do you know?"

"Of course the police suspect everybody who was with de-Costa last night. But they aren't going to do any guessing out loud in a Hollywood killing, Mr. Jory — you can bet on that."

"I appreciate you're getting down on this business, Shively," Adam said. "If it isn't asking too much, I'd like to have you stay there and pick up anything more that you can. I'll be here for at least another two hours."

"Would it be all right for me to come there?"

"Here? Certainly."

"I don't like telephoning. I'll nose around here a while longer, then I'll come up."

"Thank you."

Adam thought of calling Beulah's home, but decided against it. He was not very familiar with police methods; he had no idea how fast they worked or how thorough they were. Telephone wires could be tapped. Shively had been cautious, and he was at headquarters and completely acquainted with the techniques of "the law."

Meantime, heavy and somber behind his concentration on the urgency of this wretched affair, Adam Jory was conscious of grim fear for Beulah Rountree — and for Judith, who belonged to them both — who was a part of himself, now that trouble threatened her.

Earl Tomblin was greatly changed; he looked dissipated, flabby; he had lost his earlier alertness and gained instead a sort of ratty shrewdness; he wore expensive clothes carelessly and badly; on one finger a big, blue-white diamond flashed notice to the world that his guttersniping had been profitable. But Adam Jory, experienced in judging men, saw beneath these surface signs a hard, cunning, ruthless mental equipment — saw the very man he now needed. He did not hesitate.

"Thanks for coming, Tomblin. I find I need some help in an emergency."

"I've been under obligations to you for a long time, Mr. Jory. I'm glad you called me."

"We'll forget what you may consider obligations. In this case I may ask a good deal of you — and I mean to pay for what you do." He put up a hand. "No arguments. Is that clear?"

"Perfectly clear."

190

"Tonight a Hollywood character named Amadeo deCosta was shot and killed. You haven't heard about it?"

"No. I know deCosta, though. I'm not surprised that somebody has caught up with him at last."

"He was a worthless hound and is better off dead, Tomblin. A good many people must have felt that way about him. Men, and women, too."

"That's correct, Mr. Jory."

A faint smile touched Jory's lips — a mirthless smile. "We can agree, then, that killing the fellow wasn't a sin, though it was a crime."

Tomblin said, sharply: "We're not going too fast, are we? Do you know deCosta was killed?"

"If you're thinking of suicide, that's out."

"I see. I have to explore all the possibilities. Go on, Mr. Jory."

"I'll be frank with you, Tomblin. I am interested in a young actress in Hollywood whose name has already been brought into the case. She seems to have been one of the last to see deCosta before he was shot. Judith Rountree."

"Rountree? I don't know —"

Jory colored. "Her real name. In pictures she's Judith Wayne."

"Oh, yes. I know her slightly. One of the best of them all — a fine girl. She didn't kill deCosta. And I'll back that snap guess with everything I've got."

"I agree." Jory flattened his voice — spoke impersonally. "Her mother telephoned me about the shooting. I've known Mrs. Rountree almost ever since I've been in Los Angeles. I've just come from seeing her. I want to tell you the story she told me."

He sketched it baldly, with nothing omitted. Tomblin interrupted once or twice with his lawyer's questions. At the end he sat quiet a minute, turning the thing this way and that in his mind.

"Mrs. Rountree's account has holes in it that the police

191

can drive a truck through," he said then. "She had a motive.
It was her gun. The gun and her bag were left there, you say."

"She forgot them. She was thinking of Judith — of her
daughter. Nothing else. If you don't accept her story — "

"Hell, Jory, I'm not offering you my own doubts. Headquarters won't accept her story. But the man we have to figure
with is Morris Silberberg."

"The motion picture producer?"

"Sure. The other woman in the case is Ellen York. She's the
most valuable property the Silberberg Studio owns. And you
can take it for granted that Silberberg is in a huddle with his
stooges and his lawyers right now, somewhere out there in
Hollywood, working on an alibi. They can't just laugh off the
killing. They've got to have a goat. Somebody who could be
convicted — guilty or innocent. Anybody but York."

From the outer office the cool voice of Miss Albert called
Jory.

"Mr. Shively is here."

Adam had forgotten the reporter. He turned to the lawyer.
"It's one of my *Messenger* reporters. Clare Shively. He's been
checking the case at Central Station."

"Shively? Sure. Have him in."

The lean, dispassionate newsman entered.

"Hello, Clare," Tomblin said. He turned to Jory. "The
best gumshoe man in Los Angeles, Mr. Jory. A lucky break for
me, too."

Shively shrugged. "Save it, Earl. Wait till we see where
the breaks come." He addressed Adam Jory. "Captain Dorman
has had his orders, it looks like. He's turned Hand loose — de-
Costa's houseman. The detective who tipped me off that the
York woman was at the house at the time of the killing is
worried. He ran me down to tell me that he was mistaken. I
promised to protect him."

Jory said, angrily: "Protect, be damned. I'm interested in
protecting — "

"Wait a minute, Jory!" Tomblin interrupted. "It's all right.

You are as concerned with keeping the York woman out of this mess as anyone."

"I? I believe she killed deCosta."

"Between us three you do, yes. Not otherwise. Let me show you why."

"Go ahead," Jory said. He was at sea now. This business moved too fast for him.

"Remember that the Silberberg Studio has a million-dollar stake in the York woman. The whole motion picture business has a stake in keeping its skirts clean. Hollywood can't afford many more scandals, for business reasons, if for no others.

"Look at this straight — cold turkey. You're an old friend of Judith Wayne's mother. She's not in pictures — it's her daughter who is. Don't you see? I'm telling you how Silberberg's mind will work. He could get the unlimited backing of the whole picture industry to pin the murder of deCosta on — *anyone outside pictures.* Now, how does that leave us?"

Jory was shaken. The dissolute young lawyer's reasoning was bloodless, heartless, and it angered him. But he saw that that reasoning was logical. That was the way things stood. Here were the blunt, unspeakable, irrefutable facts in a dirty business — crime and its aftermath. He said, sullenly:

"Understand this, once and for all. On your showing this movie producer has a lot of power and will use it to save his star. All right, I've never had any reason to find out how much power I have — I and my money. We'll find out now." He struck his desk sharply. "I'll use everything I have to save Beulah Rountree."

Unperturbed, Tomblin nodded. "Good. And so you cancel each other out, you and Silberberg."

Shively said, drily: "But all the money and power on earth won't convince the police or the public that deCosta died of milk leg."

"No," Tomblin agreed. "We'll have to figure on a murder charge. So I come to my advice to you, as my client, Mr. Jory."

"And that is — ?"

"First, that you get together with Silberberg."

"I don't like that advice."

"You won't like the rest of it, either."

"Well?"

"Pin the killing on the servant, Hand."

"What? See here, Tomblin, I'll go pretty low in this case, but I'll be damned if I'll help to job an innocent man."

"Take it easy, Mr. Jory. To begin with, how do you know he's innocent?"

"He wasn't in the room. Mrs. Rountree said — "

"She said she saw him in the hallway after the shot was heard. But in her state of mind she might have been mistaken on time. The valet might have shot deCosta, then run out into the hall. Anything might have happened."

"But why should Hand have killed deCosta? You were talking of motive a while back?"

"Suppose that deCosta owed him back wages. Suppose the servant was secretly in love with Ellen York — or had a frustrated infatuation for, say, Judith Wayne. Or suppose that he agrees with you and me that deCosta needed killing."

"I don't believe — "

"Hell, Mr. Jory, I don't either. But you spoke of railroading an innocent man. And I want to tell you something else about that. Silberberg and his lawyers wouldn't hesitate one split second to charge the murder on Hand or Miss Wayne — *or on you* — if that would save the York woman."

Jory sat frowning. "I don't like it. If I can't afford to be squeamish, at least there must be some other way — "

"You're worrying about Hand. I haven't finished. I propose that we join with Silberberg in putting the finger on Hand. But not until it's too late."

"What do you mean now?"

"I think I can work with Morrie Silberberg's counsel to give the valet a number of excellent reasons why he should disappear — and not come back."

"Oh. So that's it?"

194

"That's precisely it. It may cost some money. But only pennies compared to the bank-roll it will take to pit you against Silberberg and Hollywood to see which of two motion picture stars goes to trial."

Jory took a sudden decision. There was an evil taste in his mouth; his mind was clouded with disgust. He didn't dare think this thing out; he could only act.

"I'm in your hands, Tomblin. How much of this can you handle?"

"If Shively will do some sleuthing for me I can handle most of it. For instance, locating that milk-wagon driver, Clare."

"The leg-work, yes," Shively said. "No fixing."

"Shelley will let you go for a few days," Jory said. "If you are willing."

"Sure, Mr. Jory."

"Tomblin, what about the newspapers? I'm more afraid of them than I am of the police."

"The papers will give the story a big play but they won't tell much. They know more about the libel laws than either of us do and this thing is as hot as a live wire."

Jory said: "I'll put some money to your credit in the Growers' Exchange tomorrow morning, Tomblin. And I don't want any accounting made. Now, what do I do?"

"You see Morrie Silberberg. I'll get him on the phone right now. What's more, I'll have him come here. We want him to do some of the worrying, and that's one way to turn the heat on."

The renegade lawyer reached for the telephone.

The Amadeo deCosta killing was splashed all over front pages that first day; it was needled into big displays on the second day; it was kept going on the third day. But it petered out, thereafter, like a rich pocket of gold in some barren desert gulch.

The police reporters and feature writers had leaped on it

195

greedily, licking their lips. But they were soon checked, slowed down, then stopped. The trouble was that there were no facts to go on. Every tip, lead, rumor, report, theory, clue failed. The dead man's flashy career as a Hollywood figure was soon shown to have been built on nothing more substantial than his own impudent claims to an importance he had never had. He had been an impudent and colorful liar. That has always been enough to go on in such fantastic realms of shoddy make-believe as New York's Broadway and Hollywood's Vine Street — to go on until the string is played out. Then it isn't enough to earn a brief obituary. You can do quite a bit with the prismatic airness of a soap bubble — until it bursts. So, in the deCosta killing, the papers found even the protagonist a very drab figment of the imaginations of a few sycophants, noodles and gossip-nurtured columnists and the truth behind his violent disintegration impossible to track down.

An unsolved mystery, the murder case faded gradually from the papers and so from the public mind.

Bennett Hand, the dead man's valet and house servant interrogated by the police on the early morning after the crime and temporarily released "under surveillance," disappeared. The authorities were glad of it, since they were able ever afterward to shrug their shoulders and say: all right, if he didn't kill deCosta, why didn't he stay here and make his claim stick? None of the case-hardened police reporters supposed him guilty. But that was only a negative conclusion of the matter — they had nothing positive except their strictly private guesses — all libelous.

A young man named Carl Green left his job as a driver for the Sunnyside Dairy and moved on to a farm near Chino that the neighbors understood had been bought with money left him by an aunt "back east some place." Silberberg Studio released a picture called "Bride of Dawn," featuring Ellen York, which grossed a million and a half and carried the sultry-eyed and luscious-lipped star to the pinnacle of movie fame. Two police detectives were sent back to patroling beats and a deputy county coroner, after turning over to a private detective a small, pearl-handled revolver, gave his wife the new home she wanted out in North Hollywood, complete with a barbecue pit and a small swimming pool. A three-day sensation was made of the news that Judith Wayne, beloved of young lovers and frustrated women of middle age, was retiring from pictures . . . . There were new, deep lines carved in the cold face of Adam Jory and his dark hair began to show traces of gray.

With appropriate fanfare Golconda Towers was occupied by the great Golconda Petroleum Corporation.

The edifice was spectacular, even for Los Angeles. Paulding, the eccentric young architect who had been eight years waiting for his first good commission, became the most sought-after designer in the Southland. He had hurled Golconda's twenty-two stories at the heavens in unbroken lines of gold and black onyx that carried the eye from sidewalk to flaming beacon-tip two hundred and ten feet above in a single breathless sweep. The structure was bizarre, it was vulgar, it was new-rich, it was preposterous and hideous; it was the pride and marvel and focus of interest of Los Angeles. It had cost two million dollars.

On the twentieth floor of this temple were the offices of the President, Adam Jory, who seldom entered them. They consisted of a suite occupying the whole floor, with cubicles for secretaries, auditors, messengers, telephone and teletype operators, and with an inconspicuous back-room for the Assistant to the President, Herbert Kinney, who seldom left them.

Adam Jory, visiting this throne-room for the first time, thought that his private office was pretty nearly as big as that Kramer Dancing Academy where he had gone to prepare himself for his first introduction to the social whirl of Los Angeles. Its floor was covered with thick carpets, its walls graced with fine, lush paintings by famous southern California artists, its furniture was black walnut and onyx, with gold fittings, ornaments and accessories. Into one wall was let a movable panel which, silently slid aside at the touch of a button, revealed a complete black-and-gold bar, amply stocked. Adjoining the office was a private library and den and off that a dressing room with shower and lavatory. Gold and black, of course. Adam Jory had never seen the plans for this luxurious establishment; they were Herbert Kinney's conception.

On one winter day Adam Jory went to the magnificent fane to sign some papers Kinney had prepared for him. While his pen ran rapidly on the indicated lines of one document after another Jory was thinking of this man of business who had served him so long. Kinney was still silent, still undistinguished, still intent, still invaluable at mastering details, attending to everything, keeping his own counsel, asking no questions — and answering as few as he could.

The papers disposed of, Adam Jory looked up at Kinney.

"Seems to me you mentioned a while back wanting another good name to go on the board."

"Yes. But it's got to be A-One."

"Would the name of Morris Silberberg scale high enough to suit you?"

Kinney, who was seldom surprised, was surprised now.

"The motion picture magnate? But he is only interested in pictures! There isn't a corporation in Los Angeles that wouldn't give its soul to have him."

Adam Jory's faint, rare smile, appeared. "The Los Angeles corporations I know anything about aren't blessed with a soul, Kinney — and it wouldn't fetch much of a price if one was found. But as for Silberberg, he's interested in Golconda. He suggested the idea himself, to me."

"I had no idea that you knew Morris Silberberg."

"No? There are a few things you don't know about me, Kinney — even you. Telephone the studio. Ask for a man named Ad Kline and mention my name. He'll make an appointment for you with this big fish you'd like to land."

CHAPTER EIGHT

A S THE FLOOD OF easy money rose higher and higher all over America in the roaring '20's Los Angeles bloomed and boomed and expanded and multiplied itself in every direction and in every way.

William Rowland was so busy with prodigious real estate deals he could not take time to have his signs and billboards re-lettered, though it was clear that his prophecy of a million population for 1930 was low.

The city's inner circle of enterprisers had made great strides in a few years in bringing about a cultural miracle. A copper king, permanently settled in this land of flowers and sunshine after several winters as a tourist, had taken over the symphony orchestra and made it a permanent asset of the young metropolis. Two struggling little museums became large and important, thanks to financial backing and able management. Art began to be recognized and painters, sculptors and architects patronized and encouraged. The new public library, one of the most beautiful in the world or by far the ugliest, depending on your school or tastes, crowned the downtown Normal Hill; it was so big and sprawling that the designer laid directional lines in the corridors, in color, so that you could almost always find the department or bureau you were looking for, with diligence. Eminent star-gazers had been attracted from many lands by the facilities of Mount Wilson and the very latest news of the farthest reaches of the firmament began to go out regularly under a Los Angeles date line.

199

Not the least of the cultural progress of what had so lately been a dusty, muddy pueblo of a hundred adobe huts strung out along a water ditch was due to the flowering of education thereabouts. Not one, but two universities, each with a student-body numbered in thousands, flourished and waxed great, at least on the football gridirons of the nation. The daughters of aristocratic families as far away as the Atlantic seaboard began to turn down Wellesley and Miss Goucher's to matriculate at Marlboro or Westlake. Savants and pedagogues were imported by dozens, signed to contracts such as they had read of on the sports pages just before the opening of major league baseball seasons but had never expected to be offered. And in its elementary and secondary school systems the whole Southland was soon leading the nation for attendance and for size and value of plant, the average high school gymnasium, for example, costing more than many districts in the land could spend for their entire layouts.

The sons and successors of the Los Angeles boosters who once brought their city through the doldrums with a fiesta had set out to exploit the better life and had made fools of those who said it couldn't be done that way.

Now, with that program completed and functioning, they turned their abundant energies and enthusiasms into still other channels.

They had long felt the need of a really metropolitan hotel; not a commercial hostelry or a big rooming house but an institution — a focal center of living and foregathering comparable to those as famous as the cities which they serve. Private capital was timid. Experts imported to offer counsel were dubious. Hotel chain owners held back. So the Band of Hope dug deep, spread the names of its members on a prospectus and sold stock, borrowed a lusty balance and built the hotel. Before its outer shell was up private capital became bolder, the experts changed their views, the hotel chain operators sent emissaries to the local believers and the hotel was leased at a fabulous rate and for a long term, with a dozen bidders disappointed. From the day it opened it was filled to overflowing.

Meantime the irrespressible optimists financed and built an interurban terminal the railways balked at financing; they raised more cash and erected a magnificent auditorium; they mortgaged their futures to construct the greatest sports amphitheater in the world, with a capacity of 100,000. As though this were not enough they bullied and badgered the transcontinental railroad companies serving the city into cooperating in the building of a Union Station, and when the corporations drew a poor mouth they over-subscribed a fund to make up the balance required.

Still in their stride, these ebullient boosters promoted a bond issue of staggering size and began the construction of a twenty-million-dollar municipal building in the Civic Center area at the moribund end of the downtown district. The pure and lovely spire of this sublime edifice rose sheer into the blue — but at its feet washed the moiled and odorous river of Main Street, a thoroughfare peopled by aliens, yeggs, degenerates, outcast men, abandoned women and lined with Cheapside shops, vile groggeries, poisonous gyp joints, verminous movie theaters, stinking flophouses and larcenous pawnshops — the logical debris of a section away from which honest business and decent customers had been growing swiftly for three generations, leaving behind them the ramshackle and ancient buildings in which the town's forefathers had made their humble commercial beginnings.

Los Angeles was the House that her Jacks Built. These were the maidens, all forlorn, as well as the men, all tattered and torn, as well as the men and women all be-diamonded and in mink and ermine, and all the heterogeneous multitude of people in between, and their sons and daughters and their strivings and aspirations, their sturdy religions and their metaphysical hocus-pocus, their greatness and pettiness, their urbanity and their country-village bigotry and vulgarity — these were those who lived in The House that the Jacks Built. There

201

was never anything like it seen on earth. Probably there never will be again.

This was the city in the sun of Jory of Los Angeles.

Jory was too important and influential to be left out of these civic enterprises. Though they were still angry at his repeated betrayals of his class, the inner circle respected him for his business shrewdness, needed him for his money and were chary of making open war on him because of his newspaper. They did exclude him from such deals as they could swing alone, and after the *Messenger* declared for better labor relations they were more circumspect about the devious plans of their Industrial Association. This amused Adam. Thanks to Billy Wing he usually knew what was going on in the I.A. And he soon learned that the local union heads also had a pipe-line into the enemy's G.H.Q., for their lively *Daily Worker* published a regular column of the doings of the "open shop" strategists and little seemed to escape it.

But the city's master minds counted Jory in on the Union Depot campaign and the City Hall project, the Hill Street terminal, the Public Library promotion and such enterprises, and most of them were cordial to him and tried to make him feel that he was one of them. He was offered places on the Library Board and the Executive Committee of the Union Depot scheme, but he refused both honors. It was plain that they were relieved. He saw this, but made no sign.

He was, in fact, too pressed by his own affairs to give much time to outside activities and he was also conscious of growing tired and, though he was not quite sixty, of feeling old. Even money-making was beginning to be distasteful to him, but he knew of no way to escape it — to quit. He had never had any interests outside of business — never played games, indulged himself, found a hobby. He hadn't read half a dozen books in his life, society struck him as silly and artificial, he was bored by the theater and what enjoyment anyone could get from music, except, possibly, a brass band, was beyond him.

202

Now and again he found himself trying to puzzle out just what it was that he did want. He couldn't tell. But his mind, canvassing the whole field of human activities, wandered to vague, unorganized thinking about quiet, rest and some simple companionship. Unbidden, pictures would return to him dimly from the past — a timid boy, kicking up hot dust on a country road winding beside a small, lazy river; the silence and peace of a graveyard in the shadow of a little church and the sound of an organ and singing voices — the weekly choir practice — coming to his ear; a wide, sandy beach, hot in the summer sun but cooled by a sea breeze that blew in with salty taste and smell, from out there beyond the big, slow, tireless rollers that swelled, gathered height, stood immobile for a breath, then crashed, throwing up spray and spume, and raced in and up the strand as though caressing the land . . . . Adam, relaxed, half-asleep, seemed conscious of a movement beside him — a hand touching his hair. He could almost hear a woman's long, deep sigh — of contentment, of fulfillment — and if he turned his head he knew he would see Beulah Rountree, smiling at him . . . .

He would come out of these rare trances sharply and feeling chagrined at his childishness.

Once it occurred to him that he had no friends — not a single friend. He examined this discovery curiously and without any particular emotion. Had he ever wanted a friend — sought one? No. He had never even felt the need of one. But, as he studied the matter, it seemed to him that everyone he knew had certain intimates, some few, some many.

He had been on that day at the Southwestern Club for a business luncheon. He recalled the hearty voices of the men all about him: their warm greetings to one another, their handshakes, back-slappings, noisy, affectionate salutes, many of them vulgar or even obscene: "Why, you old bastard!"; "Hello, you sweet sonofabitch!;" "Now here's the man that shagged O'Reilly's daughter!" And they would pound dice-boxes, match coins, buy one another drinks, in a closed circle of friendliness, tenderly abusive, wisecracking, yet advertising a sincere, deep, understanding satisfaction.

How had they saluted him? "Morning, Jory!" A nod. A rare offer of a drink — but he didn't drink at noontime. A moment's pause, in passing, and a question about the current price of Golconda common, or the offer of a piece of property or the solicitation of a contribution to some cause or other. The old tories, as always, merely snorting or cutting him. Well, he had never paid any more heed to that sort of incivility than he had to the few efforts men had made to get inside his shell, as Will Rowland called it. The real estate man had always been friendly; he would have become an intimate, perhaps, if Adam hadn't held him off.

A damned, crusty, self-sufficient piece of money-making machinery — that was his status.

And now there was creeping up on him a sort of fear that he stood in need of something more. But suppose that he were too late to find and win it? Suppose that the need should become a necessity! And time run out — the door shut!

After thirteen years of expensive delays, shifts, legal twistings, evasions, the patent-infringement suit of *Kerner vs. Jory* finally came to trial.

It dragged its tortuous length through ninety-four days of court sessions, then the jury disagreed.

"We can settle on a reasonable basis, Mr. Jory," Judge Valentine said, when the news came in.

"You can get a new trial, can't you?"

"Of course. But it seems to me — "

"Pitch into it, then," Jory interrupted.

So the case went back on the calendar again.

A great religious leader and evangelist had for some years been developing in Los Angeles an increasingly impressive following. She was a handsome, buxom, throaty woman, with a magnetic personality, the talents of a surpassing actress and a sound idea.

204

To a teeming and hungry multitude of Protestants who had been nurtured all their lives on a gospel of a Jehovah of wrath and a hell of fire and brimstone Sister Alice brought a God of Love, of Light, of Laughter, of Good Living — a jazz-age creed, properly entitled to publicize itself with the favorite adjective of the Coolidge-era advertising copywriters, streamlined. Flashing her radiant smile, preaching in her melodious contralto the apostle of Joy introduced to her congregations a Heavenly Father good-natured, easy-going, benevolent, who patted His children on the head and carried candy in His coat pockets for their delight. She was respectful to the Holy Ghost, portrayed as a sort of silent partner of the Trinity, but her Messiah was a jolly elder brother who enjoyed a good story, might have belonged to the Elks and batted .390 for the home team and who could be expected to drop into the kitchen after breakfast and cheer up a sister whom the sinkful of dishes was getting down.

For Los Angeles, overpopulated with middle-aged and elderly people who had fled rigorous winters, stifling summers and back-breaking toil, Sister Alice was the perfect spiritual guide. They had known little enough sweetness and light in their lives; now, relaxing in the balmy Southland sun where the necessities of life were easy to get, they hungered for some active pleasure. They had always been taught that happiness was suspect and indulgence was sinful. Sister Alice tossed all that puritanism out the window. Small wonder that the yearners flocked to her banner.

In their transports of delight they confused the preacher a little with the Deity she preached: they began to worship *her.* She fed their starved souls and minds and hearts and she filled their mouths with laughter and their eyes with tears of sentiment and emotion. When she asked for contributions they responded extravagantly. Most of the communicants were comfortably off; some were poor. But all gave. The few rich, Sister Alice worked on shrewdly. Offerings were strictly freewill, but she contrived to nudge their wills. Her take ran into tens of thousands weekly.

She claimed to be inspired by the Almighty and filled with The Holy Ghost and if the measure of her success were any criterion no one could dispute her claims. One of her inspirations was the founding of The Good-will Gospel, with its own creed of doctrine. Presently another was a vision of a suitable synagogue, and this the faithful hastened to provide for her in a huge, dramatic, towering temple complete with a fully-equipped stage, numerous small halls and meeting rooms, a baptistry for immersions, a costly pipe organ and an orchestra pit, a complete and complex lighting system, a radio broadcasting station and, adjoining, a pretty luxurious home for herself and her secretariat.

Big as it was the Good-will Temple turned worshipers away twice every Sunday and usually several times during the week. And whenever the elect gathered they filled the vaulted auditorium with their hosannahs of praise and thanksgiving to God — and to Sister Alice, His handmaiden.

Bessie Barrows, one of the Jory housemaids, was a spinster inclining to chronic melancholy when a sister-in-law took her to the Good-will Temple "just to hear Sister preach once." She was a natural vessel, empty and yearning, for filling with the new doctrine. The result was inevitable: Bessie was not only filled but she overflowed. She became an active proselyter and something of a nuisance to the other servants, although they rejoiced in the marked improvement in her spirits and (apparently) in the flow of her digestive juices.

The change in the maid was finally noticed by her mistress. Presently Irene Jory was listening to the convert, then questioning her, then becoming curious to see and hear for herself. Bessie was overjoyed. On one Sunday night that spring they went together to the Goodwill Temple, the maid exalted — "Just like Sister says, there's more joy over one lost lamb that's found than they is over the ninety an' nine!"— Irene emotional and already half-persuaded that some great new richness was coming into her life.

From the moment that, with organ pealing and robed choir in full voice, the drapes behind the pulpit parted and the single, shining, spot-lighted figure of the evangelist appeared, Mrs. Jory was a captive. The warm smile beamed on her alone. The strong, gentle arms encircled her. The full, deep, resonant voice spoke to her heart. She was moved to tears before the first prayer was ended; she was lifted up by the music; she was enraptured with the Scripture reading; when "The Message" was delivered she drank it in thirstily. Forgotten was her ancestral religion, lost all her doubts and fears, gone all her preoccupation with Society. When Sister Alice, over a background of tender singing, invited sinners to repent and join the Army of the God of Love, Life and Laughter, Irene Jory lifted a hand. She was one of scores, but she was not conscious of that. This was *her* Transfiguration! That radiant angel in white and silver and blue, emanating effulgent light in the half-darkened auditorium, was lifting her up to the very Throne Itself!

She had brought with her a small bill for the collection box. Now, hastily, she scrambled through her bag. Yes, there was a check-book. Bessie, breathing hard, borrowed a fountain pen from the fat man in front of them, whose red neck was damp with perspiration. Irene filled in the blanks. The maid, softly whispering, "Amen! Glory! Hallelujah!" peeked furtively — saw "Thousand" written in a shaky hand.

She began to cry.

Adam Jory became conscious of a change in his wife. She had been quieter and better through the long months of the building of the Julius and Berthe Nostrander Home for the Aged; then, when the place was opened, partly filled and operating smoothly, she had lapsed into another period of restlessness and instability. She complained that the professionals who conducted the Home were ignoring her suggestions and politely but firmly excluding her from any part in its management. Jory realized that he should have foreseen this development;

when it came to his attention it was too late. He began to be worried about Irene again.

But suddenly she had some new interest. He heard her singing, now and then, tunelessly but happily. He made out that the songs were hymns, vaguely familiar to him from his youth — all expressing happiness, hope, a loving Saviour, with all the gloom, blood, suffering, dread left out. Certainly these were not the anthems of Jewry; presently Adam found that she was not going to the Synagogue at all, but went out on Sunday mornings and regularly on Wednesday evenings.

"Did you drive Mrs. Jory out to the Home yesterday?" he asked Lind, one Monday morning, offhandedly.

"No, sir. She went to the Temple."

"I see. Don't mention that I asked, Lind."

The driver grinned. "To her? I ain't likely to, Mr. Jory. The Missus give orders not to tell you, neither, but I slipped."

A few more cautious inquiries told him the story: Irene had joined Sister Alice's church.

It was a relief to Jory to find his wife so improved, and certainly her religion was a matter of indifference to him, who had none of his own. Soon he had put the whole matter out of his mind.

Warren Gamaliel Harding had coined a word and ushered in an era; "normalcy" had put an end to want, unemployment, financial upsets for all time. The Ohio boys muddied their feet in the trough and tracked up the White House carpets considerably and the Prince of Good Fellows passed out of history's pages in the middle of a chapter that will never be finished, but by that time the country was on the Glory Road to stay. The thin-lipped, sparse, mirthless little country lawyer from Vermont had no need to do anything, so that is what he did, and The Millennium arrived.

Good times were like coals to Newcastle in Los Angeles, accustomed to such shenanigans, yet the Coolidge Boom struck there as elsewhere and the city in the sun went quickly and ecstatically mad. The stock- and real-estate markets soared, bigger business enterprises were launched right and left, newly annexed territories settled up, new subdivisions were platted farther and farther out, carlines were extended, the public utility companies tore up old streets to lay larger mains or erect higher poles and new streets to provide service for clamoring and always indignant subscribers and consumers, who wrote letters to the papers complaining of the tardiness. The city fathers met in protracted sessions, vainly trying to keep up with the crying demands of tens of thousands of in-coming families and industries and businesses but never managing to clear their desks, on to which clerks and attorneys and engineers and petitioners piled ever more and more urgent matters, ten pressing items appearing for each one that was frantically checked on and passed.

Adam Jory was in the thick of it all. His real estate hold-ings increased again, his paving firm was rushed, a dozen syndicates and pools clamored for attention and action. And these projects were all so big that they required the utmost concentration and the most mature judgment. He had by now put most of the load of Golconda on to the willing shoulders of Herbert Kinney, who appeared to be entirely capable of carrying it. The Kerner patent-infringement suit was coming up again and Lawyer Valentine's office was urgent for more ammunition with which to wage a battle Valentine was not entirely happy about fighting. Little Lucy Zander had complete charge of the big Jory offices — handled all details. Adam had provided her, at her own request, with an enlarged staff of auditors, accountants, file clerks, stenographers and messengers; they were so numerous that Jory had no track of them. A business analyst might have suggested at this period that his empire was over-extended; he himself suspected as much. But Los Angeles was moving so fast and money and opportunities were so plentiful that he could find no time to sit down coolly and dispasssionately to trim ship.

The one enterprise which gave him satisfaction and even

a certain pleasure was the *Evening Messenger*. But now he was being importuned to sell it to a nation-wide publisher, and the pressure of his other interests inclined him to yield. Always self-disciplined and suspicious of hobbies and avocations of all sorts, he began to wonder if he were not clinging to the paper principally because he enjoyed operating it.

The *Messenger* was paying, though Adam plowed back most of the limited profits. A new advertising manager, employing some tough talk and some high-pressure salesmanship, was beginning to bully the big local merchants into signing contracts; the increasing advertising budgets of national concerns brought in some of that gravy. City Editor Shelley's concern with the affairs and interests of human beings made the paper popular with the common multitude and the bright boys on his staff developed enough exclusive and startling news stories to keep circulation rising.

But the most potent factor in the growth of the sheet had been its fight for decent government and its support of union labor. The unions had never gotten a firm footing in the city, but most workingmen sympathized with the aims and both members and sympathizers read the *Messenger*. Jory forbade open warfare on the Industrial Association, the tight and powerful organization of the merchants and manufacturers, but he printed the news about its activities and in disputes could be counted on to lean to the employes' side.

The handful of devoted men in Los Angeles who kept the labor movement inching forward were the constant targets of attack, particularly by the *Daily Sun*. The dream of peace on earth which had motivated the writer, Stebbins, in the abrupt terminating of the *Sun* dynamiting cases had dissolved; even after Major Oddie's death his newspaper continued to fight the unions and to signal out its leaders for constant heckling. One of the latter was Steve Young, son of the man who had gone to the penitentiary. Steve was a tall, black-haired, courageous youth, with a Lincolnesque head and rough-hewn features; he had a magnetic personality and steadily acquired

210

skill and power as a speaker and an organizer. Adam Jory met him occasionally; he watched the younger man closely, remembering the father — observing, also, that Steve Young had, in his own way, some of the force, drive and singleness of purpose that had made Adam himself successful. The Young family, he knew, were friends of Beulah Rountree's, but he never mentioned the subject to Steve.

Yes, the *Messenger* had become a force for good in the community; it was a satisfactory property; it had heightened Jory's stature as a civic leader. But these were not reasons sufficient, he decided, for keeping the paper. The price being offered was excellent. He proposed one stipulation: that the entire staff, mechanical, business and editorial, should be kept by the new management or given three months in which to look for new places. This acceded to, he sold.

Herman Kahn, the elderly attorney who had for forty years handled the legal affairs of the Nostranders, came one day to Adam Jory's office. He was a dignified and gentle man — one of the leaders of the local bar and highly respected by all.

"I am much disturbed, Mr. Jory; I have called on you only because I see no alternative. The circumstances are, I must say, unsettling."

"Some trouble out at the Home, Mr. Kahn?"

"None whatever. But the Home is involved." He took off his glasses and began polishing them deliberately, with a fine handkerchief, rotating them in his long fingers — interrupting himself to breathe on the lenses, hold them up to the light. "Mrs. Jory has requested that I — er — break the Nostrander trust."

"That's nonsense, Kahn. You must have misunderstood her."

The attorney lifted his spectacles, gazed through them, breathed on the lenses, began polishing again. "I thought so myself, at first. I was finally convinced that I was not. I put her off — something I have seldom done with a client in a

lifetime of practice. She came back. Yesterday she warned me
that if I failed to act, she would retain another attorney."

"You say she wants to break the trust?"

"Yes."

"But that's impossible."

"Fortunately, yes." Lawyer Kahn put his glasses on, adjusted them. "Fortunately. Because Mrs. Jory wishes to turn
the Home and the trust over to this Goodwill Temple woman
— this Sister Alice."

Adam started, then sat back in his big chair. His body
sagged. He remembered that Irene had kept to her room for
several days past, when he was at home; he remembered, too,
that in recent weeks she had seemed nervous and unsettled. A
fear that he had felt before — that she was mentally ill —
clutched at his heart. He drew a long breath.

"Mrs. Jory has been interested in that church — religion —
whatever it is, for several months now. I'm afraid it — that it
isn't the best thing for her. But I don't see how I can interfere.
I'm grateful to you for coming, Mr. Kahn."

"I wish I could do something more helpful, Adam." The
old man took off his glasses, pocketed them, crossed the office.
"You have my deepest sympathy, I assure you. If I can be of
service, command me." He put a hand on Jory's shoulder,
gripped it, then went away, slowly and sadly.

As he had done once before, Adam put aside everything else
and gave all his thought and care to his wife.

It was a harrowing task. Physically Irene was well — better,
he thought, than she had been for some years. She was in good
spirits, too, much of the time, though her cheerfulness took the
form of religious exaltation — of songs, praises to God and
to Sister Alice, prayers of thanksgiving. She believed that she
had been reborn and that her life had been renewed by a
species of miracle about which she never tired of talking.
Abandoning all her old interests and affairs she was plunged
into multifarious Temple activities, that included several meetings a week, sacred concerts there, selected motion picture

shows in the Annex and Temple dinners. Seeing in her husband a possible convert she insisted on his going with her to the gatherings; to humor her, and not knowing what else to do, he went several times. But he could not stomach either the opportunist theology taught or the instant and concentrated attention given him by the zealous sisters and brethren. He tried to divert his wife from her obsession, but he failed.

Instead, Adam's efforts irritated her and she began to turn on him. She accused him of having blocked her efforts to take the Nostrander Home from its trustees and give it to the Goodwill Temple. She actually discharged Attorney Kahn and, as she told Adam triumphantly, retained two lawyers she had met at the Temple. With some difficulty he learned their names and went to see them. Their effrontery was colossal. Coolly they informed him that he was waging a futile campaign against Almighty God and warned him that, if he made any disturbance over the business they would go to the newspapers with Mrs. Jory's "case." Appalled, Adam was forced to truckle to them — to sue for peace. They settled for a fee and a round donation to "the Cause."

Meantime and afterward Mrs. Jory grew more and more hysterical, bitter against him, difficult to control. She called him anti-Christ and proposed to divorce him, giving everything she owned to the Temple and becoming herself a "Temple nun" — an order dreamed up by the Leader to receive women adherents with property and a yearning for a life of abstinence and service "removed from the world." Her hysteria led to a breakdown and Jory was compelled to send for a specialist, get her under the influence of opiates and put her in the hands of experienced nurses.

She was very ill.

For Adam, frustrated, distressed, blaming himself for having neglected her, yet baffled to know what else he could have done for her, that Spring was long and weary.

Although Adam Jory was recognized as organizer, head and

principal stockholder of Golconda Petroleum, the name of Herbert Kinney was beginning to appear more frequently in newspapers and trade magazines as spokesman for the corporation. Regarding its affairs Kinney was scrupulous to make it clear that Jory was the real power, the final authority; nevertheless the stature of this confidential agent grew rapidly and insiders accepted him as the real mainspring of the mighty machine, the man responsible, even more than Jory, for its spectacular success.

Almost imperceptibly Kinney was blossoming out in other directions, too. He was elected to a club which owned a golf course; presently it developed that he was a natural golfer and his name made the sporting editions. He became a patron of the arts and was seen at the theater, at movie premieres and at concerts. He was elected to a few lesser corporation directorates, including the board of a new and fast-growing bank. Quietly he had divorced his wife early in this period of expansion; soon he was being seen at night clubs, where he was welcomed as a distinguished businessman and a good spender. He acquired a yacht — or Golconda did — and on this sleek German-built boat entertained company directors, important stockholders, big customers, often with long-legged, sleek, highly varnished lovelies from Hollywood as "hostesses" to the visiting firemen. There was no criticism of Kinney; he was scrupulous, open, correct, untouched by gossip or scandal. And his extra-curricular activities never interfered with his devotion to the best interests of his companies nor with his acknowledged genius for upbuilding them. Especially Golconda!

Delighted directors, elected by gratified stockholders backed Kinney without question or hesitation, for Golconda Petroleum Corporation surpassed the highest hopes of all and grew rich, powerful and expansive. Golconda stock soared in a soaring market. Golconda drillers tapped new and ever richer fields; Golconda refineries increased in number and capacity; Golconda tankers carried company products into wider markets; Golconda Laboratories constantly perfected and marketed new and profitable by-products; Golconda service stations furnished the widely-advertised Golconda Red Eagle gasoline and lubricants the length and breadth of the state, then of the Pacific Coast, then of the five western states. Finally, Golconda surpassed all its competitors in the volume and boldness of its advertising campaigns, so that Golconda became a household word.

Behind all of this was the tireless energy, the shrewd brain, the daring enterprise and the ruthless drive of Herbert Kinney. Adam Jory, distracted by his own problems and especially by the shocking illness of his wife, watched his confidential man of affairs blossom out into a business giant first with surprise, then with puzzlement, finally with relief. Golconda was in good hands, at any rate. And Kinney's activities and success, of course, were enormously profitable to his chief. Not only did he increase the market value of Jory's stock but used that new American business device for expanding its big corporations, stock-splitting. Through this financial necromancy, share owners found themselves periodically beneficiaries of two-for-one, five-for-one, ten-for-one exchanges; on paper, at least, they reckoned their gains in staggering figures. Unanimously they hailed Herbert Kinney — and, of course, President Adam Jory — as modern Midases. At any rate, all agreed, their touch could turn engraved certificates into gold.

This was in the year 1928.

Lawyer Valentine, Jory's attorney in the Kerner case, had news.

"Judge Hanchett's firm has withdrawn as Kerner's counsel, Mr. Jory."

"So? What's behind that?"

"I presume that the old gentleman is out of funds. And Melvin, Wood and Hanchett don't take contingent fee causes."

"Likely that's the end of the business, then, Judge. No

responsible firm would take it on after Hanchett's office dropped out."

"Don't indulge any false hopes, Jory. I'm bound to tell you there are rumors that Kerner has found backers willing to advance money enough to prosecute the case against you."

"Nonsense! I don't believe it. Anyhow, we'll soon find out. Keep after it and we'll smoke them out."

The grave old lawyer rose. "You're paying the bills, of course, Jory. We'll press for a trial."

Obviously, this was good strategy in the circumstances. Valentine got *Kerner vs. Jory* on to the docket. Old Gus Kerner, worn thin, looking haggard and shabby, came into court with the sly lawyer who had first represented him, Brian Wall. Wall asked for a long continuance, pleading that the defense had staved the matter off for years and that he was not now prepared, on short notice, to try it. Valentine opposed the request vigorously and succeeded in paring the delay down to five weeks.

"At which time," the presiding judge said, tersely, "the case will go to trial. It has cluttered the calendar much too long. Next motion!"

A week later the newspapers noted that *Kerner vs. Jory* promised fireworks in its new hearing, since Melvin, Wood & Hanchett had been re-engaged by the plaintiff and especially since that dignified and eminent firm would be assisted by the trap-smart legal partnership of Ad and Joe Karpas. The *Daily Sun* added that the Karpas brothers were "well-known for their success in saving lost causes." In court circles this unusual association of law firms caused considerable comment. In Oscar Valentine's office junior members took off their coats and waded into preparation of Adam Jory's defense from a new point of view. Their chief, scrupulous and conservative, and regardful of his reputation for probity and ethical practice, sweated with them. He had never stood at bar in a case opposing the Karpas Brothers, but he knew their reputation.

216

A few days later Adam Jory met Billy Wing on the street.

"I understand, Jory," the lounging observer of men and events drawled, "that the Karpas boys are making a book against you in that patent lawsuit."

"Yes? What more did you hear?"

Billy Wing puffed at his pipe thoughtfully. "The gossip is that the underwriters are Rudolph Pullen's hatchet-men — Ezekial, Otis Russell and Old Man Warmeister. I've often wondered how long it would be before they moved in on you, after you kicked over the traces with the *Messenger*. That crowd neither forgives nor forgets, Jory."

Jory's faint smile played. "Your yarn is nonsense, in the first place, Wing. In the second place, you seen to think it ought to worry me."

"And it doesn't? Well, that's fine. Happy dreams, Jory."

Billy Wing lounged away. He left Adam trying to laugh off the matter. It was not easy.

Pullen's associates were the Camorra — the supreme masters of the enormous pool of money and credit that underwrote and underlay everything in southern California. Jory had never thought of them as concerned with the affairs of individuals.

Now, in this new light, he recalled many incidents in the past where a mysterious force had certainly operated to wreck promising careers, control intractable promoters, hamstring recalcitrant capitalists and curtail enterprisers who threatened to become too powerful. Yes, many of the pieces fitted together.

As applied to his own case, the most persuasive fact was that the recognized organ of this tight little group Billy Wing had called Pullen's hatchet-men was the *Daily Sun*.

Adam Jory told himself, firmly, that he would not let such fairy-tale fantasy disturb him. But it remained in his mind. And there it left its mark — its tiny sore spot that he could ignore but that would not heal.

He received a brief letter from Beulah Rountree, and as

217

always it gave him support in the midst of his difficulties.

> *Dear Adam:*
> *I knew you wouldn't want to be thanked for things so I haven't tried. But I wanted you to know we are all right and well. J simply wouldn't stay in pictures. She never liked it too much anyhow and what happened ended it.*
> *We have a quiet place in the country and maybe some day we might see you but not now. I'm sorry to read in the papers that your wife is sick and hope she gets better.*
> *I read all the time about you. It's fine how Golconda has done. I have put my little money into the stock. I always knew you would be one of the biggest men in Los Angeles and anything you are in will be a winner.*
> *You don't like to be thanked but thank you and thank you again and God bless you for what you did for J.*

This note was still fresh in his mind, fretted and confounded by many pressures and worries, when Lucy Zander came to him one day with a newspaper in her hand.

"A long time ago you mentioned something about being interested in the movie actress, Judith Wayne, Mr. Jory."

He was surprised; he did not know that he had referred to Judith to anyone except the lawyer, Tomblin. It didn't matter.

"Oh, yes. I — understand that she's out of pictures."

"That's right. And I thought you might not see this."

She handed him the paper and went out. Adam read:

> Judith Wayne, former ingenue star with Fashion and Pictagraph, was quietly married ten days ago in Wichenburg, Arizona. The story escaped the picture world because the marriage occurred under her real name, Judith Rountree.
>
> The groom is Stephen Young, the youthful fighting union labor leader.
>
> The happy couple refused to be interviewed except to say that they had been childhood friends.
>
> The bride stated positively that she will not go back into pictures, where she was beginning to achieve a sensational success three years ago at the time of her surprise retirement.

218

At the Central Labor Council headquarters it was stated that Mr. Young will continue his work as an organizer and official. At present he is a vice-president of the Council.

*   *   *   *

Headlines on the extras screamed:

SISTER ALICE SEA'S VICTIM

GOODWILL TEMPLE PASTOR THOUGHT
DROWNED AT BEACH

One edition after another poured from the presses — was soon sold out.

Los Angeles blazed with the sensational report.

For a time practically all business throughout the city was suspended.

Highways leading to the western beach towns were so jammed with traffic in an hour that motorcycle police gave up all attempts to control it. Electric trains were overloaded until the conductors gave up trying to get through to collect fares. Hundreds began walking beachward, most of them followers of the flaming-haired evangelist. By whatever means these swarmed toward the scene they wept, prayed, sang hymns.

Once on the shore they gathered for prayer, some of them crowded into the water. The tide had turned and guards and life-saving crews had the greatest difficulty in herding the fanatical back out of peril to their lives. The thousands who were not disciples gaped and pushed and stared, too awed to make the usual jokes at the expense of the faithful.

Meantime a swarm of reporters, men and women, mobbed the single person who could give them any first-hand statement as to what had happened. This was a severe spinster, Minerva Moore by name, who was one of the evangelist's secretaries and personal aides. She had told her story first to

a lifeguard earlier in the afternoon — the story that had been
flashed over police wires to break the sensational news. Now
she could only repeat it, which she did, as a few cynical
journalists observed at the time, with complete calm and with
carefully chosen and guarded words.

"Just before noon today Sister decided to come down here
from the Temple for a rest and a swim."

"Was she in the habit of doing that, Miss Moore?"

"Yes. We came down sometimes two or three times a week,
summers."

"Sister Alice went in swimming?"

"That's right."

"Where did she change — put on her bathing suit?"

"When we were coming for a dip she would get into her
swim suit at home and wear a dress over it. All she had to
do was to slip off the dress when we got here."

"Where did you leave the car?"

"At the end of the street up there." The secretary pointed.

"Then you walked down here?"

"Yes. We sat in the sun a while, then Sister went in for
a plunge. I was reading a book and didn't watch her all the
time."

"She was a good swimmer, wasn't she?"

"Yes. Sister was good at everything. She was a fine, strong
swimmer."

"Did you watch her at all? Do you know how far out she
went?"

"When I last noticed she was diving through the breakers.
It would have been far out, I suppose, for a timid person —
for one who couldn't swim well."

"Then what happened, Miss Moore?"

"I glanced up two or three times before I realized that I
couldn't locate her. But that had happened before. You
know how it is, when a good swimmer is out there rising and
falling with the swells."

"But you got anxious?"

220

"Not anxious. After a while I was curious. I stood up to look. I couldn't see her anywhere. I went down to the water and called. I walked along to where there were some other people in bathing. She wasn't there. I began to get frightened. Finally I ran for the guard."

They bombarded her with questions. Someone asked: "Where is the car you came down in?"

She replied casually: "I don't know. When I looked for it — this was later — it was gone. I suppose Mark went for help, or something. Mark is Sister's driver. I haven't seen him since."

Two or three reporters left the group, quietly. The questioning went on. But it developed nothing new.

Meantime life-saving crews were out in boats, a police power-launch was circling well off shore in ever-widening circles, and the near-by piers were black with eager scanners, some with binoculars.

While the search went on the prayer-meeting of the faithful continued, the crowd of suppliants steadily swelling. Some of the older women collapsed. One aged man dropped suddenly, was lifted and carried out, was examined by a doctor and pronounced dead of heart failure. The disciples paid no heed to these incidents; they concentrated on their heartbroken appeals to God to restore to them their Leader and Evangel. They were oblivious of the growing ring of spectators, gaping, hushed — a little awed.

The whole scene was dramatic — spectacular. Sister Alice, if she had devised it, could not have improved on it as a gigantic pageant, poignant, sensational, theatrical.

Adam Jory was in a conference with Lawyer Valentine and a group of engineers and experts retained to assist in defending the Kerner suit when Lucy Zander came in to whisper to him that he was wanted on the telephone by Lind, the chauffeur.

"Lind? I can't be interrupted — "

"I think you'd better talk to him, Mr. Jory."

Adam excused himself and went to a phone in an outer office.

"What's all this, Lind?"

"Sorry to call you, Mr. Jory. But I'm scared about Mrs. Jory."

"What about Mrs. Jory?"

"You heard the news? How this Sister Alice got drowned at the beach?"

"Something about it. Go on."

"The missis — she didn't hear it till a hour ago. She called me to drive her down here."

"Down where? Where are you?"

"At the beach. That's right. She's down with a mob o' the Goodwillers prayin' and carryin' on. She won't even listen to me. I ain't sure she hears me. She — she acks sort o' queer, Mr. Jory."

"I'll be right down. Don't bother Mrs. Jory but be there if she needs you."

Adam returned to his office. "I'm called away. I don't know when I'll be back."

"But, Jory, there are several points — "

"Take care of them. Good night."

Lucy Zander met him when he went out.

"I've ordered a Golconda car for you. It ought to be downstairs in five minutes."

"It's Mrs. Jory," Adam said, helplessly.

"I know. I'll stay here this evening so you can call if you want anything."

"Thanks, Lucy. I don't know what — "

He stumbled out. A heavy black car bearing on its door a small, red shield decorated with an eagle rolled to a stop and the uniformed driver touched his cap.

"Where to, Mr. Jory?"

"Ocean Park. And I'm in a hurry."

"Right-o!"

Darkness was falling when they reached the shore. Big bonfires had been built up and down the beach and their flames lighted the scene with a sanguinary glare. The crowd of idling spectators was thinning, for now the chances of some dramatic break in the case seemed slim. But the disciples of the Goodwill Temple were still coming in a steady stream until they numbered many hundreds. Experienced in handling their own fellows, the leaders of the Temple, early on the scene, had gathered in a huddle and quickly laid plans for a long vigil. Some went to buy food and coffee, others took on the duty of providing rugs, blankets and shawls for those who, at the first alarm, had dashed off to the beach in house dresses or wrappers in the middle of the warm day. Several rooms were engaged in an ocean-front hotel for emergencies and a patrol was organized to move about the assemblage, ready to give first aid to any whose age or weakness or hysteria made it necessary. Younger men and women were divided into patrols and assigned to walking the strand, in turn, watching for news from the offshore searching parties. Nothing was overlooked; everything was provided for, systematized. It was Sister Alice's way.

But the passing hours had weakened the hopes of even the most believing. Their faith in Sister Alice had led them at first to the conviction that her God of Love and Mercy would not let her die — that even if the sea had caught her some miracle would cause her to be restored to them. As this hope flagged they began to grieve. Many of them were emotional and even neurotic people, both men and women, and their sorrow began to be hysterical. Their cries and lamentations were carried inland by the cold night wind that blew off the gray and hungry sea.

It was then that Adam Jory reached the beach. Leaving the car where the traffic blocked its further progress he hurried down on to the sand. In the fitful light and with such a crowd he had great difficulty in locating his wife. When he finally saw her he realized at once that she was completely out of her mind. She wore neither coat nor hat; her hair had come undone and one thick braid hung down her back while the other, loosed by the wind, streamed over a shoulder and across her distorted face. She had a distraught and foolish look and there was a little foam on her lips. She prayed in a high, strained voice, her words unintelligible — kept lifting her hands, gesturing, flailing the air. Abruptly she knelt and bent her forehead to the sand.

Adam reached her side at last. In the center of the crying, singing, shouting, wailing crowd he was forced to shout, even when he knelt beside Irene and spoke in her ear.

"You can't do anything here, my dear. You'll make yourself sick. Come on home with me. Come, Irene!"

She looked up at him with staring eyes.

"Leave me, Lucifer!" she cried, shrilly, in a harsh, strained voice. "You are anti-Christ. You are accursed! Go away."

Adam took her arm and tried gently to get her up. She wrenched away — struck at him.

"I deny you! I don't know you! Praise God, I have a victory over you and all the works of hell!"

A burly man behind them, dressed in workman's clothes, caught Adam's elbow. "If the sister don't want you around, you better take the hint. Praise God!"

Others were turning to listen; Jory saw that it would not take much of a spark to set off this mob of half-crazed fanatics. He moved away, working his way out of the crowd. At its edge he found Lind, his chauffeur.

"I saw you talking to her, boss. It's tough. What d'you want me to do?"

"Have you had anything to eat?"

"No, sir. But I don't — "

"We may be here till late. You go and get a bite, then come back here. Where is the car?"

"In that alley." Lind pointed a thumb.

"All right. I'm going to find a telephone and get Dr. Jowett down. He's the only person I know who might help."

"O.K., Mr. Jory. I'll be back here in ten minutes. I can get a hamburger for you, too."

Adam located Dr. Jowett after some delay. He was at the Good Samaritan Hospital — could reach the beach, he thought, in half an hour.

"Perhaps you'd better bring a nurse, Doctor. Mrs. Jory — I'm afraid she may be — difficult."

"Don't worry, Jory. I think she'll be all right."

Adam left the amusement pier and started back up the walk. He saw the crowds were stirring, now — the curious spectators moving in — the Goodwill Temple members milling and churning about. The tight knot in the center had broken and several men were wading out into the surf, which had grown high and boisterous.

"Off to the right!" Adam heard someone shout.

"Farther out!"

"She's gone down again!"

As a great cry of pity and horror arose, Adam started running. He came to the fringe of the mob.

"Have they found the body?"

A woman turned a haggard face toward him.

"It ain't our Leader. It's one of the sisters. She waded out. Nobody saw her till it was too late." She began to cry and her voice was a wail. "She's gone to God! It was Sister Irene Jory. That rich woman that gave — What's the matter, mister? Say, Brother Thompson. Gracie. Come here, somebody, quick! This man's took bad."

Adam Jory, worn, haggard, gray, turned in his chair to greet Lawyer Valentine.

"The jury just came in, Mr. Jory. I left Mallard to make the necessary motions for a new trial — all that. Perfunctory. No use. No hope."

Jory's face did not change.

"We lost?"

"We lost. The jury was out less than an hour."

225

"And the verdict?"

"It's a crusher, Jory — unprecedented. A million, a hundred and twenty-five dollars."

"A hundred and twenty-five. You mean thousands?"

"No. A million, a hundred and twenty-five dollars. It was one of Abe Karpas' fancy touches. You remember — but, there; probably you didn't know about it. Abe picked up something Mrs. Kerner said, when she was on the stand, about a bill you refused to pay for painting the cottage your man Kinney gave them. It was probably one of the women on the jury who stuck out for adding that amount."

"Then Mrs. Kerner testified?"

"I told you at the time. You've forgotten. It was a typical Karpas move." The grave old attorney sighed. "They are a tricky pair, those Karpas boys."

Adam Jory was toying with a paper-knife on his desk. He spoke slowly, in a weary voice.

"You said something about an appeal — a new trial or something, Valentine."

"Of course. I supposed that you would want to — "

"I don't. Drop it, Judge. Do whatever is necessary to put an end to the whole business. Just tell me where and how to pay up — then send me your bill." He sat looking out from his big office windows over the city, his body sagging, his eyes sunken, his cheeks lined and ashen. "You told me once that somebody had put up the money to fight this case — a syndicate — a pool."

"There's no doubt about it, Mr. Jory. I can tell you now who they were — or come pretty close to it."

"It doesn't matter. How much of this judgment will Dad Kerner get? How much cash?"

"I can't answer that question. Between the lawyers and the backers, my guess is that it won't be much."

"That's what I'm afraid of. I'm asking you to stay on the case long enough to do one more thing for me."

"And that — ?"

226

"Find out as near as you can what the Kerners will have. Let me know." Adam's thin smile lightened his face for a moment. "I want to make sure they'll be all right. They're old now, with no kith or kin as far as I know, and they must be made comfortable for the rest of their days."

Judge Valentine drummed on the desk with a strong forefinger. "But, Jory, that seems to me — ah — quixotic. The jury —"

"That's it, Valentine — the jury. Twelve men and women have decided that I swindled Dad Kerner and his wife out of a million dollars worth of profits on the oil-burner patents. I'm beginning to wonder if the jury isn't right. And if it is I don't propose that those elderly people shall end up with nothing while Pullen and Elias Warmeister and the lawyers pocket the million."

Lucy Zander appeared in the doorway.

"Excuse me, Judge Valentine, but it's time Mr. Jory got over to the Athletic Club for his bath and massage."

"Now, Lucy —!"

"Don't Lucy me, Mr. Jory," the plucky little woman interrupted, valiantly. "I've got enough to do to keep this shebang solvent without having you go to pieces on my hands!"

CHAPTER NINE

> FOR THESE PROPERTIES
> SEE
> W. A. Rowland
> Rowland Bldg.
>
> ---
>
> Population of L. A.
> Now 1,238,000
> 1940 1,500,000

WHEN THE MARKET made liars of the millennium boys in 1928 the resounding crash affected Pacific Coast business for the moment but slightly. Los Angeles conditions, in fact, showed no immediate change whatever. Established enterprises continued to thrive, new projects were launched with confidence and real estate held steady — even rose here and there. Signs and portents of evil days ahead were observed by a few, but these "nervous Nellies" (The *Daily Sun's* characterization) were voices heard in the wilderness — their gloomy forecasts scouted. If they needed an answer it was provided by Will Rowland. His new population prognostication of a million and a half for 1940 was already gleaming from his widely distributed signboards; now he called the Band of Hope to-

228

gether and announced that he was bringing the Olympic Games to Los Angeles in 1932 and wanted backing to the tune of a million dollars. He got it, with cheers and a great banquet. It was the strategy of the 1894 *Fiesta de las Flores* over again: — a good stout tug at your own bootstraps. It was the unconquerable faith of the city in itself, its leaders, its future.

Adam Jory's name was on the list of underwriters and Lucy Zander sent his check for the amount of his assessment for the cause but Adam himself took no part in the planning or the dinner. He was not seen about town; was not to be found in either of his offices. It was reported that he was a sick man.

This was true, though the sickness was of the spirit only. He was suffering from the shock of Irene's death, and he was humiliated and abased by the public sensation it caused. From a shy boy, grown to a retiring man, he had always shunned publicity. Now he had found his private life and activities, his early struggles and his slow rise to power blazoned to the world, dragged forth because of his fortuitous connection with the sensational disappearance of Sister Alice, to him a mountebank, and directly responsible for the tragic end of his wife. And the echoes of that case had not died away when the climax of the Kerner patent infringement suit put him back on the front pages again.

For a while he tried to ride out the tidal wave of notoriety but, strong though he was, it engulfed him. He could not face it. For weeks he locked himself away in the big, empty, gloomy Figueroa Street home, attending to business by telephone or messenger and seeing only Lucy Zander or some manager or auditor she sent to him. Little Lucy, spunky and loyal, tried to shield him; she developed into a shrewd pint-sized vixen whom it was hazardous to cross and impossible to impose on. She ruled the Jory empire tyrannically and her spare time she devoted to worrying about her chief. He gave her a free hand

229

with the business, but he cut her off when it came to his own course.

"I'm all right. Just quit fretting about me. I'm not used to it and I don't like it."

She said sagely: "Maybe you'll have to learn that things happen to people whether they like it or not. The least you can do is take care of yourself. You'll make yourself sick at this rate."

"There's nothing wrong with me," he growled.

She wasn't so sure.

His first concern had been to pay the Kerner judgment and to pay it promptly and in full. One or two quick turns brought in half the amount needed; the balance he borrowed, with enough more to meet his lawyers' fees and costs. Coster, his auditor, informed him that, from first to last, the case had eaten up almost a million and a quarter dollars — as much as the burner enterprise had netted him in the twenty years it had been organized. He salvaged something a little later when Jim Jernigan came offering to buy the business, which Jernigan proposed to amalgamate with another company having its own plant. Jory was glad to be out of it — told Lucy Zander to have Rowland sell the Aliso Street factory building. And within a year, although at a sacrifice, he had liquidated enough other holdings, including his motion picture theater, to pay off the bank loan.

He went seldom to the black-and-gold temple of Golconda Petroleum Corporation and then only for a perfunctory board meeting or to sign papers that Herbert Kinney prepared for him. Sensitive to the mysterious fluctuations of the business barometer, in spite of his personal depression and distress of mind, Adam knew that the collapse of the Wall Street market was beginning to have its effect locally and he was surprised to observe that Golconda appeared immune — seemed as healthy and prosperous as ever. Kinney was a wonder — no two ways about that!

A diligent search had failed to turn up Irene Nostrander's

will. Attorney Kahn had drawn one for her, shortly after the death of her father, but she had taken it away with her.

In the end the old lawyer said: "We must presume that no will exists, Mr. Jory."

"Does that mean that the estate comes to me?"

"Yes. I can tell you that that was Mrs. Jory's wish at the time she gave me her instructions. And I recall that she wanted a thousand dollars paid to each of the servants."

"I'll see that they are taken care of. As for my wife's property, I want it to go to the Nostrander Home. All of it."

"That is very — a fine thing for you to do, Adam."

"It's what I believe Mrs. Jory would like done," Adam said, a little stiffly. He could never listen to thanks or praise. "Will you take care of the business for me?"

"Let me understand your wishes. The gifts to the servants and the costs of probate and so on — "

"I pay. With your fee. I want all of Mrs. Jory's estate to go to the Home."

Thus another story about the Jorys appeared in the papers. Adam winced when he saw them.

The sizable estate of Irene Nostrander Jory was to go, by order of the bereaved husband, to the Julius & Berthe Nostrander Home for the Aged, near San Gabriel. Mrs. Jory, it would be remembered, lost her life in the surf at the time of the disappearance off Ocean Park of the pastor of the Goodwill Temple . . . etc., etc. Incidentally, the mystery of that disappearance was still unsolved. Public officials were not entirely satisfied, although nothing tangible had developed to cast doubt on it, that the report of Sister Alice's drowning was to be credited . . . etc.

Adam threw the papers aside irritably. After a life of dignity, propriety, benevolence, was Irene to be remembered only as the tragic gull of that religious circus performer — her name forever associated only with the dubious melodrama on the beach? He wondered bitterly how long the travesty could go on. He could have taken any amount of obloquy or disgrace, he thought, if only he could shield her memory from the vulgar inter-connection with that drab event.

His cup was bitter, but he had yet to taste the dregs.

The headlines were thrown screaming across the front pages.

SISTER ALICE FOUND

GOODWILL TEMPLE PASTOR

KIDNAPPED — NOT DEAD!

Date lined from an obscure town on the Arizona-Mexican line the despatches reported that the red-haired evangelist had been picked up by an American cattleman and one of his Mexican *vaqueros* just across the border in an almost trackless desert of sand and cactus and brought into the little settlement of Las Bocas.

She was in blooming health and high spirits; with all her old verve and energy she told of having been snatched by three strangers, two men and a woman, and taken by automobile to a lonely adobe cabin in a remote spot many miles south of the point at which she had been discovered. Her captors had treated her kindly, she averred; she had never been frightened because she had had faith that her God would protect her and bring her safely back to her beloved mission. For a few days she would remain in Arizona, resting and giving thanks.

This was the first flash, pieced together and put on the wire by the local telegrapher who had never before sent out a newspaper story more involved than the border price of beef. Correspondents, hastily sent from nearer large towns, began feeding further details before midnight, but the heavy artillery was not moved up until El Paso, Phoenix and Los Angeles could rush their big-name reporters and photographers to the isolated village. As only one wire ran out of Las Bocas there were further delays; editors filled in with full-page layouts of

232

background, including detailed reviews of the Ocean Park dis-appearance, with all its lurid color and tragedy.

When the complete story did begin to trickle through, it was of a piece with the whole fabulous beginning. Although Sister Alice supplied a detailed description of the adobe where she had been held for several weeks and of the *peons* who had kept her there, searchers were unable to find any such cabin or any men, Mexican or otherwise, answering the de-scription. Although, from her account, the evangelist had walked across the barren waste and through dense tracts of cactus and undergrowth, the lynx-eyed city correspondents re-corded that her dress and stockings were whole, clean and fresh, and that her high-heeled shoes were unscuffed and trim. She claimed to have been most of two days and one whole night on the way, yet she had no coat and the desert night before her rescue had been bitter. There was no water along the route she had taken; she explained, as to that, that she had prayed and God had refreshed her by miraculous means — nothing less than a spring gushing from the sand, that had dried up when she had drunk. Her God, she cried, in a voice of exaltation, takes care of His own no matter where they are.

"From where I sit," a cynical paragrapher commented, to his editor, "I'd say that Alice's Heavenly Father certainly gets around."

It was later in that week that Adam Jory and a young broker from Will Rowland's offices went to the Aliso Street plant of the Jory Burner Company to appraise it so that it could be priced and sold.

Being driven back toward the business district, they found their progress blocked by a traffic jam of cars and by a great crowd of people, centering about the railroad depot.

"Some picture star in, probably," Austin said.

"It's no movie star!" the driver interrupted, over his shoul-der. "Give a listen!"

From the distant heart of the throng voices arose in song.
The singing spread and swelled higher.

> *There shall be showers of blessings;*
> *Send them upon us, we pray.*

Here and there they could see that women were sinking to
their knees. Men took off their hats. The hymn became a
prayer — and an anthem.

> *Showers of blessings;*
> *Showers of blessings we pray!*
> *Mercy-drops 'round us are falling,*
> *But for the showers we pray!*

A train came chugging slowly in. The crowd parted to let
it pass and closed in behind it. As the wheels ceased to roll
there was a dramatic pause — a hush.

Then a handsome woman in white, with a blue and gold
cape effectively draped over her shoulders, stepped to the railed
platform of the end car. She stood for a moment looking over
the field of upturned faces.

When she spoke, in that deep, resonant, throaty voice, her
words carried far.

"God bless you, beloved, for this welcome. Let's sing the
Doxology!"

The solemn words rose from five thousand throats, above
the clangor of the streets, the noise of the railroad yards, the
clatter of factory and mill.

It was Sister Alice, come home in triumph.

Eliza Winter was the young school teacher on whose lots
out Belmont Avenue way Adam Jory had brought in his
first well. Miss Winter, suddenly enriched with a comfortable
income, found teaching a pretty tedious chore and gave up her
school, to turn her whole attention to the oil business.

Being both shrewd and lucky she prospered; when she
was considerably older a newspaper reporter dubbed her "the

Oil Queen" in recognition of her achievements and her money. She affected to bridle, but actually she was gratified — began to live up to the sobriquet. That is, she became dictatorial and unreasonable and she quarreled with her help, her associates and her competitors. When one of the latter lost his patience and haled her into court she rallied her forces, hired a firm of smart young lawyers and beat him. This brush gave her a liking for the drama of the law and she was soon notorious as a perpetual and chronic litigant.

It was this rich, eccentric, contentious spinster who, in the fall of 1932, brought a stockholder's suit against Golconda Petroleum Corporation, alleging mismanagement, failure to make proper accounting, and the withholding of profits from share owners. She asked that the company's books be examined and an accounting be ordered. There was a large amount of verbiage but the plain implication of the whole complaint was a charge of fraud.

At about the same time, in spite of the efforts of the local boosters which included the successful holding of the Olympic Games, the Depression (already being spelled with a capital, as having become an historic milestone) had finally reached Los Angeles and business was trembling like an over-raced stake horse. Prices were falling, industry slackened off, the market heading downward. Smart money, taking the typical Los Angeles long view, snapped up every real bargain offered and this support prevented an actual panic. But the times were nervous and many Golconda stockholders ran for cover under the vague threat of the former school teacher's suit.

It was then that Herbert Kinney came out in his best form as a dynamic, aggressive, daring entrepreneur whom nothing could daunt. He demonstrated to the directors that the treasury could afford an extra dividend, and it was declared. He announced with a fanfare the discovery of a new oil field in Golconda territory. He reported an advantageous, long-term contract for crude oil with a Japanese syndicate. He bought additional newspaper space and he plunged heavily with a musical program and a news broadcast over a Coast radio network — at that time a bold and novel move.

Adam Jory, persuaded into approving all these activities, knew that he himself would have gone more slowly. He was visited by doubts and an instinct for caution. Not Kinney. And not the directors. They passed every measure the general manager proposed. They gave him a vote of confidence. When he explained the frequent need of quick decisions and instant action, in times as critical as business now faced, and asked for a freer hand, they adopted a resolution empowering him to spend up to $50,000 on any one item he deemed vital, without waiting for specific authority for each.

While Golconda was reacting to these shots-in-the-arm with a fresh outburst of vigorous health the local newspapers carried big stories of a cruise taken in the expensive company yacht, *Naulahka*, by a notable party made up of officials, big-name guests and a group of Hollywood top-rank stars. This was the last — the master's — touch. It was a bold defiance of hard times and pessimism. It was proof that Golconda stood four-square to any storm that might blow — that God was in His heaven and that all was right with the world — and with Los Angeles.

President Adam Jory was not on that cruise. But he noted the effect of Herbert Kinney's bold stroke — on Monday morning Gol. Pete rose two points in the market.

Still all this left the suit of the embattled Miss Eliza Winter to be faced. Adam could not forget that.

Lucy Zander reported to her chief that Attorney Kahn wanted to see him.

"About winding up the estate?"

"He didn't say, Mr. Jory. Just said it was important."

"All right."

In the afternoon Kahn came in, accompanied by a queer fish of a stranger.

"Mr. Jory, this is Mr. Izzard. He has brought me a docu-

236

ment that you'll have to see." The elderly lawyer took off his glasses — polished them.

"Who is Mr. Izzard?" Adam growled.

The queer fish replied. He was a spare, thin man, with a nervous tic in one cheek and a habit of clasping and unclasping his long, bony fingers, one hand in the other.

"I am an attorney, Mr. Jory. I represent Sister Alice, of Goodwill Temple."

Jory blurted: "I don't want any dealings with your client or her church. Kahn, I can't understand your bringing this fellow here."

"I believe you, Mr. Jory," the old man said, in a quiet tone. "It goes against the grain with me. But I had no choice."

Adam sat back, his body slumping. "I'm sorry I said that, Mr. Kahn. What's this about, you?"

The queer fish took a paper from his case and laid it before Adam without speaking. Adam glanced at it.

It was a will, signed by Irene Jory, leaving her entire estate, real and personal, to Sister Alice of the Goodwill Temple.

"Where did this come from?" Adam asked, sharply.

"It was in the possession of Sister Alice. She was the only living person who knew of its existence. After her — her recent trial in the wilderness — "

Adam Jory straightened and his heavy fist struck the desk. "None of your damned mumbo-jumbo here, do you understand? Your Sister Alice and her cant drove my poor wife out of her mind and brought about her death. If you've got to talk, leave out your Temple claptrap!"

Clutching his fingers the queer fish shrank back. He gulped nervously. But he tried to put on a bold face.

"No call to get violent, Mr. Jory. I was only explaining why the will didn't show up till — till yesterday. At least, that's the first time I heard of it. I went to the courthouse and found who was handling Sister — Mrs. Jory's affairs, then I went to Mr. Kahn. If you have any further questions — "

Jory was not listening. He looked from the document to

237

Attorney Kahn. "I suppose there is no doubt that this will
is entirely legal?"

"It is in correct legal form, certainly."

"That seems to be the end of the matter, then."

"Not necessarily, Adam. If it could be shown that undue
influence was used in —"

"I'm certain that my wife was not in her right mind when
she made this will, Kahn. She hadn't been well for a long
time and when this crew of fakers got hold of her she was
in no condition to oppose any wild scheme they suggested."

"Exactly, Jory. I suggest, then —"

"Excuse me, Mr. Kahn; let me finish. 1 am positive that what
I've said is the truth. But I'm just as positive that I am not
going to drag Mrs. Jory's name through the courts." He turned
on Izzard. "That's what you want to know, you shyster; now
you can take a long breath." Adam rose quickly, Izzard falling
back against one wall in fright. Adam did not look his way.
He crossed the room and threw the door open. "Now get
out. Get out before I break you in two!"

Izzard snatched up the will and ran, forgetting his brief
case. Jory hurled it after him down the hall and slammed the
door.

When he returned to his desk he stood there a moment with
his face working and his big fists knotted.

Then he relaxed. "You'll have to excuse me again, Kahn.
I've had a little more than I can stand of that oufit lately."

The grave old lawyer smiled. "No excuses, Adam — no
excuses. I'm only a little disappointed that you threw the case
instead of the counselor."

Adam's faint smile crossed his face as he sat down. He took
a long breath.

"Well, Mr. Kahn, that means that Mrs. Jory's estate won't
go to the Home."

"Yes. I'll inform the trustees at once."

"No, Kahn. Wait a minute. What was the appraisal on my
wife's property?"

238

The attorney breathed on his glasses, then polished them.

"In round figures it was around a hundred and eighty thousand dollars. That was in securities and real estate — a few hundred for jewelry and the like and some cash."

"Send me the total. I don't care what you tell the Board, but I am going to give you a check for the amount. I want it to go to the Fund in Mrs. Jory's name."

Attorney Kahn raised a hand. "Are you sure — "

"I'm usually sure, Kahn. And I don't like any fuss made."

The old man came to the desk. "At least I can thank you, Adam, for the Board." He hesitated, then said, gravely: "I have to remind you of something else — something you might be overlooking."

"Yes?"

"Yes. That will is inclusive. I mean that it covers all of Mrs. Jory's possessions."

"I understand that." Then Jory paused — frowned. "I see. You mean the home, too."

"You told me once that it was in Mrs. Jory's name."

"I put it in her name when we were married." Jory drew a long breath. "Thanks for reminding me. I had forgotten. I'll make my arrangements right away."

This last twist of the knife went deep.

The Figueroa Street mansion had never been dear to Adam, but it was home. Irene had furnished it, taken pride in it; there their life together had begun. Every corner of every room bore traces of her. If he had been more of a home-body or less absorbed in his single purpose of getting on, it would have meant more to him. But that was not Irene's fault; he had failed her. Now he did not miss the irony of events. He had owed Irene a debt of sympathy and affection that he had neglected to pay; now the debt was called and he was to be evicted like a delinquent tenant.

Once he would have been able to put such thoughts out of his mind, but it was not easy now.

A month later he moved his oddly few possessions to a

hotel. The Goodwill Temple presently offered the Jory mansion for sale.

Golconda was holding up well in the market when the Winter suit was called. Something of a stir was caused when it was announced that the spinster was to be represented by Gilman, Thrash, Morrison & Hankins, one of the strongest and certainly the highest-priced law firm in the Southland. And Julian Thrash himself, the big gun of the combination, took charge of the case for Miss Winter.

The news sent Gol. Pete down a fraction on that morning's board.

After three days of wrangling and technicalities Golconda's attorneys succeeded in getting their demurrer upheld and the complaint thrown out. But meanwhile Judge Thrash had gotten into the newspapers, as well as the court records, enough queries, innuendo, doubts and hints of dark doings within the company so that the victory was a doubtful one. Moreover he demanded and won permission to file a new complaint.

The net result was almost as damaging as a full trial would have been and Golconda began to be attacked on the market vigorously. Adam Jory watching closely, ordered his brokers to support the stock promptly and boldly. He was not doing this wholly in defense of his own interest, which was a large one, but because he knew that many people had gone into the company on account of his connection with it. For a while he stemmed the tide and the worst flurry of selling was stopped.

But the cost had been considerable. He liquidated other holdings but this was not enough and he was forced to borrow rather heavily. Presently the slow pressure on Golconda began to be exerted again.

While he was worrying and puzzling over this he met on the street one day that lounging and imperturbable observer of the local scene, Billy Wing.

"I've been meaning to look you up, Mr. Jory," Wing said. "But I sort of decided to mind my own business, for a change."

"That's either too much to say or not enough, Wing," Adam said, with his faint smile. "What are you attempting to tell me?"

"That the Philistines seem to be sharpening their knives to skin you and hang your pelt on the fence, Jory, if you really want to know."

"The Philistines, eh? I don't recognize the allusion."

"I'll put it another way — and avoid a slander charge. Did it strike you as odd that our addled Oil Queen brought Gilman, Thrash and Tom Hankins into that Golconda suit of hers?"

"I didn't think much about it, Wing."

"Do a little thinking, then. Who is the biggest client Martin Gilman and the Judge and the rest of that gilt-edged office have on their list? It's Elias Warmeister — with all his hundred or two big outfits, scattered all over the Southwest."

"Oh. Yes. Yes, I knew that. Then what?"

"Then Judge Thrash hasn't appeared in court for anybody except the old man himself for fifteen years — until he popped up to bolster Eliza Winter's feeble mandamus against your Golconda company. When that happened I did a little snooping. I found that Warmeister is a director of the Winter-El Monte Oil Company, which is Eliza's fat-cat producer."

Jory was thoughtful. "I suppose it's true that Elias Warmeister and Pullen and the rest of that crowd have never forgiven me for our *Messenger* campaigns. But if they wanted to strike at me there were other ways — "

"Yes? Any one better than using a half-cracked old lady to hide behind while they laid the groundwork for battering the be-Jesus out of your oil company? If you can think of one that's really better than that, Jory, let me know." Billy Wing took out a handkerchief and mopped his face. "Well, I got myself all heated up thinking about it, Jory. And if I made a mistake mentioning it, I'm sorry. I just can't seem to keep out of it when I see Earl Pullen and his gang of hatchet-men ganging up on a friend of mine. Adios! I've got a date to hunt ducks, and I'm late."

241

The encounter, the conversation, the implications of what Billy Wing guessed and suspected, left Adam Jory tired and, for the first time, seriously worried. He had to think it all over. He had to be convinced, first, that Wing was on the right track. Then, what, if anything, he could do about it.

Yes, he was tired. He hated to admit how tired. How tired every effort now left him! He stormed at little Lucy Zander for fretting over him, but he began to realize that all these difficulties, troubles, problems, trials, were taking toll.

One evening that winter Adam Jory, head bent to a torrential storm that was sweeping the city, was walking towards his hotel when he collided with a woman whose umbrella the wind buffeted.

"Beg your pardon," he mumbled, putting out a hand to steady her. "Hope I didn't hurt you."

The woman laughed and lifted the umbrella.

"Ad!" she cried. "Why, Ad!"

"Beulah! Well, this is a surprise."

They moved into the lee of a building. Beulah Rountree held the umbrella so that it sheltered both of them. They stood close, the wind and the rain sweeping around them — cutting them off, as it were, from the scurrying crowds. Her face was close to his; it seemed to him little changed — a welcome and warming sight.

He kissed her. He drew a deep breath. He was snatched out of his indrawn and moody solitude.

"See here, Beulah, I'm on my way to supper. Come with me."

She said at once: "Why not? Of course. But I'm a sight. I've been tracking around all day and — "

"I wasn't thinking of taking you to Levy's," he said, drily. "There's a little place a few doors along here where they won't care what sort of sights we are."

"I warn you, Ad — I'm starving."

He chuckled — a hoarse sound in his ears, unused to mirth.

"So am I — now. Let's get along."

The chophouse into which they turned was warm and snug. There were quiet alcoves in the rear; there were silent, deft waiters. Tableware and glasses sparkled and gleamed on snowy tablecloths, cozily lighted with shaded candles. The sharp smells of spices, lemon-peel and condiments cut through the tantalizing odors of grilling meats and toasted French bread, with a faint savor of garlic distilled through them. The pale amber of their cocktails made spots of color under the soft lights.

"Here's to just us, Ad!" Beulah said, lifting her glass.

"All right. Then we'll have another to Judith."

Beulah's olive-tinted face glowed into russet; her white teeth shone between her full lips.

"To Judith — and to Steve and little Timoteo," she said.

"Little — ?"

"Yes, Grampaw," Beulah answered. And her eyes filled, though she was still laughing.

"The boy's name," Adam asked, presently, "what did you call him?"

"Timoteo. Spanish. Steve's mother was Amata Borba. When she was little her family still owned a *rancho* down around Capistrano that ran from the ocean back into the San Jacinto mountains. Of course they lost it all. We *gringos* were too smart for those people."

"Steve Young — is he still in union labor work?"

"That's right. It's a hard life. I guess it's hardest on Judith. But she wouldn't have Steve any different. She's proud of him. She loves him."

Adam Jory was silent for a moment. "I guess that's all that really matters, isn't it, Beulah?"

Their waiter, a bent little Italian with bushy white hair and shaggy eyebrows, brought on a fragrant, steaming bowl of *minnestrone*, then a salad, crisp and pungent. Warmth, odors, their drinks, the food relaxed Adam — loosened Beulah's tongue. She chattered, gossiped, laughed; she made him laugh.

243

She told him little about herself or her life, but she was full of Judith and the child. He was not a husky child, but he was smart and he was lovable beyond belief.

She broke off to ask, abruptly: "That awful preacher — that Alice woman! Do you suppose she really was up there in the mountains all the time?"

"What are you talking about?"

"You mean you haven't read tonight's paper? O, Ad, I forgot! I'm sorry."

"You're talking about Sister Alice?"

"Yes. A reporter found that a red-haired woman just like her was living up at Grizzly Lodge with a Temple organist — a fellow named Gladstone — Girdlestone — something. All the time that she was supposed to have been locked up there in the desert by the kidnapers. And her big Buick was there, in the garage that the man rented. The car she went to the beach in that day — anyway — well, it was Sister Alice, all right."

"I haven't been reading the papers much lately." Adam frowned, musing. "Beulah, I despise that woman. I have reason to. But somehow, all at once, she doesn't seem to mean anything to me any more, one way or the other. Nothing that usually bothers me seems important now. Maybe it's being with you. I can't just make it out."

She put a strong hand on his across the small table. Tears filled her eyes.

"Then I'm glad I'm here." She sniffled, snuffed, laughed. "Don't mind me, Ad. And you eat! Don't sit there letting your food get cold."

That was how she had talked to him in the old days — the days so long gone. He almost grinned. He began to eat, and the food tasted good.

Presently he said: "You don't tell me anything about yourself. I want to know."

"Oh, me? I'm all right. I'm just fine. I've got my own little place. It's not very stylish or fancy, but it's homey. And it's near enough so that I can see my darlings every day."

"You say you're all right. Have you enough — ?"

"Mercy, yes. I've got some shares in Golconda. And my house and lot — paid for. I work, too. I keep books for two neighborhood stores out our way and that gives me everything I want."

"See here, Beulah. Give that up. I want you to. I'll have my office put more each month to your credit in the bank. I'm sorry — I should have thought of it myself long ago."

She looked blank. "Are you talking about the hundred you used to send to the bank after Judith came?"

"Yes. I'll have that doubled — "

"But, Ad! Why, I told the bank long ago that I didn't need that money any more. They were supposed to tell you. Do you mean they didn't?"

"No. Then you haven't drawn it lately?"

"Not since Judith went into pictures. Not for several years."

"Then it must be there waiting for you. Draw it. I'll see that there is plenty more when it's gone."

"Thanks, Ad. But you see, I don't want it. I don't need it. I like to work. You're good — but I won't touch that money."

He remembered — how well! — that it did no good to argue with her. He dropped the subject.

It suddenly struck him that he was eating like a farmhand — as he had used to eat in the old days at Dad Kerner's or down at the beach when Beulah was planning and cooking the meals.

He realized, too, that he was quiet, rested, at peace.

His heavy weariness and deep absorption in business, money, his difficulties, his perils, were forgotten.

She did not mention the deCosta business; he did not mention the Kerner patent suit and its outcome. He thought of both matters; he thought she avoided them deliberately — and he thought, too, that it was better so.

"Running into you was the best thing that's happened to

me in years, Beulah," he said, when they were rising to go. "Can we do this again sometime soon?"

She stood looking at him soberly.

"I'll have to think it over, Ad. Don't let's worry about it now. This has been wonderful — for me, too. Maybe we'd better leave it there. We might spoil it."

That was the only answer she would give him.

When they went out they found that the rain had ceased and that the stars shone brilliantly, except as big, tumbled clouds sailed swift across the sky to the north. Beulah refused to be taken home in his car, or to take a taxicab.

"I'm a street-car rider, Adam," she laughed. "I like it better that way, anyhow. See my own kind of folks. *Adios!*"

For the first time in months Adam slept that night without tossing, turning, starting up out of nightmares.

Unbidden, his mind, singularly quiet, at peace, was making a vague picture — of an end to tumults, struggle, strain, complexities and of the beginning of a different existence, in a different setting, where nothing must be done, fretted over, rushed at, wrestled with, but where were plain duties, simple needs, homely pleasures, contentment, satisfaction, friendliness — days in the sun — in the open — on the good, warm earth. And in and out of that picture he seemed to see, still vaguely, a child — a little, dark-eyed, boy, "not husky, but smart — and *lovable* — "

In the next few days he found himself conjuring up that picture again and again. Once this unsettling time was past it would be possible to drop out, slough off responsibilities, liquidate, ease off, slow up — presently step down. Soon, perhaps. Yes, soon!

District Attorney Paul Kemp was a smart and ambitious young politician. A Los Angeles product, he was well aware that his future depended not only on prosecuting rascals but on picking his rascals to prosecute.

When the full effects of the market crash finally hit the

West Coast and the great horde of shoestring speculators
saw their paper profits swept away in a few weeks there
arose a great outcry for vengeance. The District Attorney's
office was overrun with angry investors shouting fraud. Most
of the local newspapers, quick to line up with the mob, supported them; public opinion ran against promoters, organizers,
company officials; the pressure of this widespread feeling was
felt even by the courts. It became fashionable to send corporation officers, overconfident brokers and over-zealous stock
salesmen to jail.

Paul Kemp displayed great industry, but he moved cau-
tiously and warily. He held more than one conference, over
matters properly in the province of the grand jury, with the
civic leaders who had selected him for his place and who
would determine how far he was to rise from it in the future.
The day came when he had to sound them out on the gravest
problem that had ever come into his office.

They heard him with amazement — a few with incredulity.
But he told them that some weeks of delicate investigation
had given him the facts.

"I know it seems impossible, gentlemen. But I am able
to say now that, if you decide to have me go ahead, we can
get a conviction."

"Well?" the banker said, turning to the others. "What's
to be done?"

A successful promoter growled: "Looks like the time has
come to clip some wings, Joel."

"I've waited a long time for it, myself," someone else
added. "I'm for going ahead."

But some were thinking deeper.

"If his company goes down it may take everything with it,"
Grant Paynter warned.

"It would be a black eye for Los Angeles. Can we stand
another black eye right now?"

The banker turned to Paul Kemp. "What started you on
this trail to begin with?"

247

"I had a complaint months back from Eliza Winter. The 'Oil Queen,' you know. She's been beefing about bad management — you've seen it in the papers."

Sussman laughed. "Nobody pays any attention to Eliza. Bringing lawsuits is a disease with her."

"Wait a minute. You were going to say something more, Kemp."

"I was going to tell you that Miss Winter came back to see me a few weeks ago. She had been sent back."

"Sent?"

"By Elias Warmeister."

Grant Paynter exploded. "Why in hell didn't you say so?"

A few days later the district attorney had a telephone call from Isaac Sussman.

After listening for a moment Kemp said: "Then I'm to go ahead, Mr. Sussman?"

"You're to go the limit, my boy. And if you still want to be mayor you'd better handle this thing yourself — and you'd better get that conviction you were talking about."

"A man named Adams was here to see you today, Mr. Jory," Lucy Zander said. "He wouldn't say what he wanted. And I didn't like his looks."

Jory answered carelessly: "Some solicitor, likely."

"He's no solicitor. You remember that I was a witness three or four years ago in that case against a man who forged your name to some papers."

"Vaguely."

"This Adams was a detective in that case. I don't forget faces, Mr. Jory."

"That's true. Well, I haven't been forging papers, nor even robbing fruit stands. I'll see this detective of yours."

The caller seemed harmless enough, when he returned.

"Just making a routine check-up, Mr. Jory. A sailor by the name of Swingle has come to the d.a.'s office with a beef about his wages."

"A sailor. I don't hire any sailors. If he was on a company tanker — "

"No. Seems he's a hand — or was — on that yacht of yours, the *Naulahka*."

"You've got the wrong pig by the ear, young man. Wait a minute. Isn't that the boat that belongs to Golconda?"

"It's the one Mr. Kinney and the other officials use, Mr. Jory. But it's registered in your name."

Jory thought a moment. "All right. I'd forgotten about it. Then what?"

"Well, to tell you the truth, that's about all. I just wanted to be sure that you owned the boat."

"If it's registered in my name I must own it."

"Of course. Sure. Sorry to have bothered you." The unabashed visitor rose to go. "By the way," he said, casually, "were you out on the *Naulahka* on the trip when Golconda Distributors was organized?"

"Was that the day this sailor of yours didn't get his wages?"

Adams laughed, not quite so sure of himself. "It may have been. My instructions don't cover that point."

"Better get it covered. Good day."

Lucy Zander came in. "I had the door open a crack. Mr. Jory, I still don't like the looks of Adams."

Jory's rare, faint smile touched his lips. "You're so particular, Lucy. If you weren't, some man might take you off my hands."

Lucy didn't smile. "You must be better. That's the first time you've sprung your favorite joke in months. But what I want to know is why the district attorney is interested in the Golconda yacht."

"Maybe he's thinking of buying it. Or maybe there is a sailor whose wages haven't been paid. I certainly am not going to worry my head about it."

Lucy worried a little, but she was always too busy to waste much time on that woman's luxury. She had forgotten the incident when young Mr. Adams returned once more.

He was accompanied by another, bigger, less prepossessing individual and, without a word to her, they crossed directly to Adam Jory's door, rapped sharply — then pushed in.

"Sorry, Mr. Jory," she heard Adams say, "but we've got a warrant here for your arrest. It's on a grand jury indictment. If you want to telephone your lawyer — any little thing like that — we ain't in any hurry, you understand. But we'll wait here, if it's all the same to you, while you're attending to it."

Golconda Petroleum Corporation, that mighty structure, came tumbling down.

On the morning after Adam Jory's arrest Golconda stocks and the securities (Oh, word of superlative irony!) of its dozen subsidiaries were falling on a hundred blackboards faster than attendants could write. The market had opened on a snowslide of offerings that became an avalanche. The debacle was complete and awful. In every broker's office in the West telephone exchanges were clogged, tickers ran behind, frantic customers mobbed the clerks, principals stormed their banks. Gol. Pete dropped from 186 to 90 — to 76 — to 60 and Golconda-controlled companies were virtually wiped out.

To add to the confusion and to complete the wreck, it soon appeared that insiders, mysteriously forewarned of the smash, had been shorting the stocks for several days and the crisis therefore caught a large number of houses and their clients who might otherwise have ridden out the storm.

The wise talk on the street was that Adam Jory was bankrupt. He had been supporting the market for months. His fortune — and the measure of it, as the catastrophic news ran abroad, reached fabulous figures before night — was swallowed up. He was defiant. He was penitent. He was sick. He had given bail and disappeared. He was dead. But no one said: "Jory? He's all right. He'll come back stronger than ever!" No one, except little Lucy Zander, her head on her chief's desk, her eyes red from crying, but her faith still strong. Only Lucy Zander, and she didn't count.

Late that afternoon Adam Jory returned to his offices with Attorney Valentine. There had been some delay in raising bail; finally the lawyer had cut through the difficulty by dealing with a bonding company.

"Now, Mr. Jory, as to your defense, I would suggest that you authorize me to retain competent counsel to direct the case. I am not — that is — "

"You're not a criminal lawyer, you mean."

Valentine cleared his throat. "I'm sorry to — that you put it that way, but — "

"Don't be, Judge. It is a criminal case and if I planned to make a fight I'd need the best criminal lawyer in town."

"I'm afraid I don't follow you."

"Judge, you've read those indictments. They charge me with embezzling, swindling, issuing false financial statements, selling stock that didn't exist, falsifying payrolls and overdrawing my personal credit account." Adam's faint smile appeared fleetingly and wanly. "About my worst crime was buy- a two hundred thousand dollar yacht — that I never saw or heard of till lately and that I never aspired to own. The little people who have gone to smash with Golconda might forgive me the big crimes. They'd never forgive me the yacht."

"But you're not guilty, man!"

"Is that going to matter, Valentine, in a case it's taken my business enemies five or six years to work up?"

"I am aware of the difficulties in our way, Jory. But you have to make a fight — "

"Wait a minute, Judge. The truth is that I am guilty."

"You trusted this fellow Kinney — a first-rate scoundrel. That was your only offense."

"It was enough. And there's no defense against it."

"Then you mean to say that you will let your enemies send you to jail because you were — well, because you left matters to a rascal who was evidently in their pay throughout?"

"There was my crime. It was a crime against thousands of people who trusted me — my name. I'm guilty."

"Then, in God's name, what do you mean to do?"

"I mean, Valentine, to take my medicine."

Two weeks later Adam Jory rose in court as Mark Valentine pleaded him guilty to three of the nine counts in the grand jury indictment.

His voice uncertain, Judge Stover pronounced sentence: a term of from two to five years in the state penitentiary.

Late the next afternoon Jory of Los Angeles became a number in San Quentin prison.

Herbert Kinney faced the bond-holders' committee that had taken over temporary management of the mighty Golconda Petroleum Corporation, now an insolvent wreck.

He was still presenting a bold front, but he was badly shaken.

"But, gentlemen, when you put Mr. Selden and Mr. Twist on the board three years ago my understanding was that I was to be kept on as general manager and later made a vice-president. There must be some mistake."

The hard-eyed old man at the head of the table snorted.

"Your mistake, Kinney — your mistake. You've done what you were told to do and paid to do. Now you're through. Get out. Clear your desk and get out. With what you've managed to pick off, you'll do well enough, I reckon."

252

CHAPTER TEN

T HERE WAS A LAST formality at the outer gate and Adam Jory's tired heart beat fast until the trusties swung the barred barriers back and the driver of the rented car began to pick up speed outside. They followed the bayshore for a mile or so, then swung west, ran out of the hills behind the prison, then left it behind them.

Jory took a long breath. He tried his voice self-consciously. To his ears it sounded harsh and metallic, as though it had become as rusted as iron gratings and as hard as the clack of a turning lock-bolt.

"Seems to me I remember this suit you brought up, Lucy. One of my old ones?"

"The one I thought you liked best, yes. I'm afraid you can still smell moth balls, but it'll soon air."

With his thin hands he pulled at the coat. "I wouldn't have thought I'd lost this much. Looks like a bag on a beanpole, as they used to say when I was a boy."

"You'll put on weight fast enough," she said, cheerfully. "It won't take you long, once you're home."

He said, in a low tone: "Home!"

The car turned into a busy highway and Jory shrank back as the traffic stream caught them up. He was actually frightened and he braced himself tautly and shut his eyes. Trucks, buses, darting and gliding and rattling cars streamed against them or overtook and passed, twisting in and out. When he looked again the faces of the passengers were vague white blobs. He

253

got himself in hand with an effort.

"Eh? What was that, Lucy? I guess I wasn't listening."

"I was telling you about the farm. The old Luke place. Where you lived when you first came to California."

He turned his head. "You mean — I'm going there?"

"I thought maybe you'd like to. It's in good shape, now. Matt Trent has had it for the last four or five years and he's a first-rate farmer."

"Now it comes back to me. You live there, don't you? You stayed on there?"

"I did. I've moved back to the city. And I didn't renew Trent's lease. I thought you'd want to be sort of by yourself for a while. That's what I thought, anyway."

He had forgotten the traffic and his timidity — fear. The sun shone warmly down out of a sky clear except for tumbling masses of fog that spilled over the high double crown of Tamalpais to the west. He took another deep breath and the clean air, smelling of the sea, went deep into his lungs.

"I'd like that better than any place you could have found, Lucy. I'd like it. Is the old fig tree still there — the one beside the house where the grass used to get so high?"

"The grass still gets high, Mr. Jory. And the fig is still there. It's a big tree now. You wouldn't know it."

"I'll like it all. I can't get there soon enough."

For weeks that remained uncounted Adam Jory sat in the hot autumn sunshine of the San Fernando Valley, his thin body relaxed and his tired mind almost completely idle. After the first few uneasy nights he began to sleep more soundly and through long hours; occasionally he dreamed, either about people or happenings confusedly brought back from his youth, or about prison days. On waking he had difficulty in finding himself; he looked about for bare, white-washed walls, or for barred doors and windows, or he lay, still torpid, expecting momentarily to hear bells harshly rung, their echoes metallic and insistent, and the ugly, growling murmurs of a thousand caged men. These dreams and these memories slowly faded.

But no brighter dreams came to take their places. He had no interest in the future — no plans for anything. The past he was glad to forget. He lived only in the present, from hour to hour and from day to day. He sat in the sun, inert, idle, shambling, listless.

He had served nineteen months of his five-year term, then had been pardoned. This action by the prison board and the governor surprised him. He had wondered a little who or what had been behind it, judging from inmate gossip that it was not a usual thing. But he asked for no information; he had had almost no contact with the other prisoners from the first, for he had been given some light office work to do and had lived apart from the rest except at meals, where talking was banned.

Prison life worked a great change in him physically. His hair turned white and became thin though it still had that tendency toward a wave that had once given him an attractive crown. He had lost weight and had gained an habitual stoop — the tired stoop of an old, old man. His full face had shrunk and lost its color; now it was heavily lined and the jowls sagged. His eyes had become dull. His spirit had been broken; he had let himself go under the load of degradation that he felt, caged and guarded and anonymous among four thousand caged, guarded, anonymous, lost men.

He had forbidden Lucy Zander coming north to visit him, turning over all his affairs to her, with a blanket power-of-attorney to act for him. Beulah had written, but he had replied almost shortly, asking her not to try to see him, as she had proposed. Attorney Valentine went once, when in San Francisco on business, but Jory had told them to send him away. He had had no other visitors.

He had thought he would ask permission, later, to see Walter Young, still here somewhere serving out his long sentence for complicity in the *Daily Sun* disaster, but the notion faded. That they did meet resulted in Jory's contracting a

255

heavy cold and being hurried to the prison hospital in an
early stage of pneumonia.

For a few days he was too sick to notice much that went
on around him, but the fever and delirium passed and he
became conscious of one quiet-voiced nurse who had tended
him, night and day.

"Aren't you Walter Young?"

The thin, wiry wisp of a man in the white uniform laughed
delightedly. "That's me. I told Dr. Stanley you were my old
boss — you belonged to me."

"You've been with me all the time. You haven't even
slept."

"Don't you worry about me, Mr. Jory. The main thing is
to get you well. Here, drink this broth and then go to sleep
yourself."

Sitting up in the sun later Adam tried to thank the old
printer.

"It's the other way 'round, Mr. Jory. After what you did
for me and what you've done for my wife and the boy, seeing
you through was the least I could do."

Even when Adam felt quite well again they kept him on
in the infirmary for a week. He commented on this to the
prison doctor.

"That's Walter Young's doing, Jory." The brisk, capable
physician dropped the ear-piece of his stethoscope to his neck.
"Walter's been head inmate nurse here for fifteen years and
we give him a pretty free hand. You're his patient, you see."

"He doesn't look strong to me, Doctor Stanley."

"There's a heart condition there. We've recommended him
for parole but there seems to be too much pressure from your
home town, Jory. All I can do is see that he doesn't work too
hard."

"For other people?"

"Oh certainly. He doesn't do much for himself."

"He hasn't changed. That's been his whole life."

The doctor nodded. "I know. I know the whole story."

He moved away and Jory heard him muttering profanely and angrily as he went.

When the old pressroom foreman appeared again, neat, efficient, cheerful, Adam thanked him, quoting Dr. Stanley. And he went on: "I've been watching you, Walter. You don't seem bitter or soured."

The thin, gray convict looked off through the barred windows of the ward to where the sun sparkled on the broad blue bay waters and warmed the wooded hills of the peninsula beyond. "I have my bad hours, Mr. Jory. Then I remember that I went into the fight of my own free will, mind you — against the old order — against the big fellows who could only stay big by keeping things as they were. They put me away.

"But times are changing now. The damned fools who want things *as they ought to be* are coming up too fast for them. They can't knock heads off at that rate. And so the old order is passing."

Jory growled: "I'm thinking about *you*. Here, in this place — put away, as you said." He touched the white-painted bars of the open window. From a sentry box on a nearby wall a hulking guard looked their way, shifted his heavy rifle on his knees and spat down into the Yard. "You're here because you made a fight for something you believed in. That's all."

"Yes, that's all. But I keep thinking that maybe my coming here will help bring the day nearer when men can't be jailed, ever again, just for believing."

In the following spring, still in the prison, Walter Young died suddenly, in his sleep.

At the old Luke farm the hot days of the fall passed and a light rain fell, harbinger of southern California's winter. But the sun filled the days still and Adam Jory lolled in it, refusing to look backward, having no desire to look forward. But he did begin to take a faint, almost mechanical interest in the present — in what went on around him.

Lucy Zander had engaged a silent, strong, plodding neighbor to attend to the chores and keep the place up; Joe Pettit's stout wife, more of a talker than Joe, came over to wait on Jory, get his meals, keep the rambling old Luke house neat and well-ordered, and to see that no one and nothing disturbed him. Ida Pettit moved quickly, for a woman of her size; it tired Adam to watch her. But Joe would never tire anyone, not even himself. He lumbered, ploughed, loafed along through his various jobs, unhurried, unsweated, methodical — as slow, his wife said, good-humoredly, as molasses in January. Adam could watch Joe. And he did.

He came unconsciously to some knowledge of the man's routine: the chickens to be fed and watered, setting hens to be taken off their nests for a short run and some gobbled food and gulped water, a penned turkey to be tended and the big, clumsy old horse to be brought out to drink. Ida set out part of a bottle of milk and Joe lumbered to the house for it and went back to the barn, followed by a dingy yellow cat and her four definitely miscellaneous kittens, Ida being dead set against any feeding of critters around the rear porch. Once a week Joe got out a box, put it in the shade of the big fig-tree, set the wash-tub on it, carried buckets of steaming water from the kitchen, then took an old cloth from a cupboard on the screened porch and wiped the braided-wire clothesline. This was on Tuesdays; Ida did her own wash at home Mondays. On Wednesdays Joe started the motor and pumped the farm tank full, keeping half an eye on the wooden gauge-bob that moved up and down in a grooved guide on the side of the tank. If he forgot and the tank overflowed Ida would come storming from the house, cats and barnyard fowls fleeing every which way, and shut off the switch. Thursdays Joe raked the yard . . . . Fridays he pruned. . . . . Saturdays he drove their old Ford into town with Ida to do the shopping . . . . and on Sundays, when Joe only watered and fed, he went home to change into his church clothes . . . .

The weeks went by and Adam found himself looking forward to meal times, to the arrival of the rural-route mail carrier, to the thump on the graveled driveway of the rolled evening paper, hurled from a chattering and rusty jalopy by a whistling boy. He began to anticipate the visits of Lucy Zander, with her budget of news — to listen to that news and to care what it was. Then, one winter day, the old plow-horse got out of the barn and strayed away and Joe, hunting him, was late in returning. Adam looked at his watch two or three times, clucked to himself: tsk! tsk! got the basket and went out to gather the eggs. Back at the house he found the stub of a pencil, after a search, and set down the day's lay: 11 . . . . After that he took over that duty — presently added responsibility for the night feeding of the two dozen chickens.

For thirty years Jory had not handled more than a few dollars at a time in cash. In a bill-fold he had always carried a few twenties and tens; in his pockets perhaps two or three dollars in silver. Dealing in hundreds of thousands, he seldom saw any money at all — only entries of sums on a statement, a check, a balance sheet. At that time the name, Jory, scrawled on a chit or a bill had been sufficient to command any service or to buy any object in Los Angeles. In a tin box in his private desk Lucy Zander had always kept some bills and currency for his use; whatever he took out she replaced immediately. Over a long period it was a surprisingly small amount.

Now the little tin box was in a table drawer in the farmhouse sitting room, where Lucy had put it on her first visit after Adam's return. He hadn't touched it — hadn't so much as opened it. He had almost forgotten it.

Joe Pettit came to the porch one day to say, in his slow drawl, that the old horse had to be shod.

"All right, Joe."

"Asa Woollem allus gets cash money."

"Well, pay him cash."

"Yes, sir. But I run out o' cash."

"I see now. Well, the shoeing will have to wait till Miss Zander comes out, then."

The farmer looked at him a moment, then shrugged. "Suit yourself," he said, and started away.

Adam called him back. "Wait a minute, Joe. I don't carry any money — haven't needed to. I'd forgotten that there was some here. I'll get it."

There was a hundred dollars in currency and ten in silver in the tin box and Pettit took a five-dollar bill without comment and went on his way.

Jory, smiling a little, realized that the man thought he was close — had tried to get out of advancing the small sum needed. If he knew Joe, that impression would persist; likely Adam would never live it down. It amused him.

But while he sat drowsing there in the midday sun, warm and healing even in early December, his mind began to follow this thought — this thought of money, the first he had had for many months. Lucy Zander had left that little stock of cash for him. The old farm was being operated, taxes paid, bills met, the Pettits hired, the chickens fed, the old horse shod —

He had assumed that Joe Pettit thought him stingy.

Suppose Joe thought that he was Miss Zander's pensioner.

Jory sat up with a start. His face flushed and his heart slowed its beat.

Suppose Joe were right!

He slept badly that night. The next day Ida Pettit observed that he was off his feed and remonstrated with him.

On the second day Lucy Zander came out for her regular biweekly visit. Jory, awaiting her impatiently, sat at a table that was strewn with papers covered with figures. He had in front of him a sheet bearing a long series of notations.

He looked tired — and grim.

Adam's first burst was almost unintelligible. He was irascible, stormy, explosive. He fired questions and would not listen to the answers. He pounded the table and upset a bottle of ink, whereupon he swore mightily — something Lucy Zander had never heard him do before. She burst into tears.

Jory sat back staring at her. He threw down his papers.
He jumped up, overturning his chair. He went around the
table and patted her clumsily on the shoulder.

"What on earth are you crying about? Don't do that!
Here, take my handkerchief. I'm sorry I swore. I'm sorry I
yelled! For pity's sake, tell me what's wrong?"

The thin, plain, graying little woman looked up at him. He
had snatched up the ink bottle, smeared his hand, then drawn
it across his face with a helpless gesture at her outburst. She
broke out laughing — with a catch in her voice.

"That's what I don't know — what's wrong! You need
your handkerchief yourself; you've got ink all over you. No,
not that way! Give me the handkerchief! Sit down."

She scrubbed him like a schoolboy.

"Ouch! You hurt!"

"It serves you good and right, Adam Jory! There!" She
threw the ink-stained handkerchief into the fireplace. "Now,
go back to the beginning and let's see what this is all about.
Who is it you say is paying your bills? Start there, for goodness sake!"

Adam gulped. "Aren't you, Lucy?"

"*Me?* Whoever — what — where — ?" Then she laughed
again and took a long, free breath. "Oh, my goodness, is *that*
it? Why, no, you're paying your own bills. Wait! Let me
see that sheet there."

He handed it over, with a sort of abashed meekness.

"I've been trying to figure things out, Lucy. All of a
sudden, just the other day, I remembered that I'd lost about
everything. Bankrupt, wasn't I?"

She was laughing again, but again her eyes were wet.

"Not bankrupt, Mr. Jory. Pretty close to it. But there was
enough to pay every cent off — every cent. I knew that's
what you'd want done first."

"Of course. Thanks Lucy. And I'm sorry for — "

"Fiddlesticks! Where was I? O, yes. Everything was paid
up, in full. You've got left two old houses — the one on

261

South Hope and that barn of a place out near Vernon — and two good lots on Western. I had to mortgage all of them, but you've still got quite a little equity there. And there's almost four thousand dollars in the bank." She sat back, looking at him primly. "This list of yours is out of date. It shows you owing a couple of hundred thousand. You can throw it away."

He gathered up the whole litter of papers and tossed them into the fireplace. He glanced up at the old clock ticking on the mantel.

"Four o'clock already — and I haven't fed the chickens or gathered the eggs. Want to help me?"

"I wouldn't be much help. And I've got to start back. When I come out again I'll bring you a check-book so you can pay the farm bills yourself." She flushed. "I've only kept on tending to things so you wouldn't have to worry about them. And I'll bring you a fresh bottle of ink, too."

Jory's faint smile appeared. "I hope the Pettits won't think you hit me with the old one."

"Humph!" Lucy snorted. "I won't say that I didn't feel almost like it when you went off into that tantrum of yours."

That evening Mrs. Pettit had no complaint about Jory's appetite.

Walking out to the mail box on the country road became another item in the routine of Adam Jory's days.

There was little mail for him. Lucy Zander wrote many brief notes about unimportant details of business, coupled with sage advice as to his care of himself. Now and then there was a short, kindly letter from Lawyer Valentine. Once John Shelley typed a missive, on cheap copy-paper and in almost unintelligible journalese, with an ancient machine from the type-bars of which the letter "s" was missing — the "o", "a" and "g" solid blurs of packed lint and old ink. Will Rowland sent him a friendly hail, every few weeks, on his business letter-head, that carried the realtor's population guess for 1940 in

red ink. Adam, never a correspondent, put off answering these
salutations for weeks; when he did reply it was briefly and, he
thought, stiffly. But he did not know how to better them. He
could only say that he was doing fine, thanks.

Sometimes, hearing the rural mailman's customary horn
signal he went out half-hoping that there would be a letter
from Beulah Rountree. But no.

Likely she didn't know where he was. He hadn't wanted
her to visit him in the prison. And there was the taint of prison about him still, so that he didn't want her to come now.
He had long grown used to feeling lonesome and he was impatient with himself for feeling more so now than ever. He
thought often of Judith — wondered about her, her family,
her situation, her happiness. But he was cut off from her forever. Bad enough that her little boy's other grandfather had
died a felon; she need never know, thank God, that there had
been two of them. What a coincidence! What a cruel irony
of the Fates!

No, there were no letters from Beulah.

Mail continued to come for the Trents, who had leased the
little farm for so long. That winter there arrived quite a
number of catalogues from seedsmen; with his stub of a
pencil Adam would mark them for forwarding. One day the
wrapper came off a fat bulletin and Adam's eye was caught
by the four-color cover — a riot of petunias, roses and stocks
and, on the back, an array of almost unbelievable vegetables.
Adam thumbed through the pages — at the back found an
order blank.

The next day he despatched it, half filled. And in the next
week Joe Pettit had plowed and harrowed for him a plot of
black soil and he was laying out a garden bed, coached by
Ida Pettit, self-constituted critic, counselor and prophet of
failure.

Rains and bright, crisp days alternated; the packet arrived
from the east. Adam had got circulars and pamphlets on vegetable growing from the state university in Los Angeles, had

263

clipped articles from the papers, had subscribed for a farm
journal, had had Lucy bring out books from the county library.
Ida Pettit criticised all of these dourly, but this was simple
jealousy. Cornered, she admitted there might be something
in some of it.

There were a few brilliant days in late January that set
the prepared plot to steaming and soon Adam could work it
and plant. Joe Pettit hauled manure from the old barn — the
barn, pretty dilapidated now, where Adam, the consumptive
youth, had been used to hitch up the team and set off with
his load of fruit and vegetables for the city beyond the hills.
Now the lean, white-haired old man spaded and forked and
raked and hoed until his hands blistered, his neck got a crick
and his back was all aches and twinges. Mrs. Pettit couldn't
seem to keep ahead of his appetite. He rose at dawn, going to
the window the first thing to see if it would be a bright day;
he fell into bed soon after dark and slept like a fed cat. When
the first green shoots of his onions pushed up through the
dark, mellow, fragrant soil he sent Joe to the Boulevard store
to telephone the news to Miss Zander. Towards the last of
February he ate his first home-grown salad.

"There ought to be money in growing lettuce and onions
like mine, Joe," he said thoughtfully, the next morning.

"You gettin' idears, Mr. Jory?" Joe inquired, chuckling.

In a late catalogue from a local nursery Adam happened on
a supplement advertising a sale of day-old chicks from a big
Inglewood hatchery. The picture showed round balls of down
bustling and foraging on a peat-moss carpet under a circular
sheet-iron brooder. The text was eloquent on the subject of
poultry profits. The prices seemed ridiculously low: — healthy
chicks, only ten cents each; special chicks from the eggs of
tested breeding flocks, fifteen cents; chicks from trap-nested
hens with records of better than 210 eggs per year, 25 cents.
In lots of 500, at appropriate reductions.

Adam went out to the long laying houses some earlier ten-

ant had built in his time on the farm. They were in bad repair, but Joe Pettit "allowed as how they could be tinkered
up."

"Do you know anything about raising chickens, Joe?"

"No, praise God. But the missis' got a aunt that runs a
egg farm over to Tropico."

Mrs. Pettit drove Adam to her relative's the next day. Mrs.
Jacks had three thousand hens, in modern houses. Adam
watched her gathering eggs. She had two cases set on a
rubber-tired wheelbarrow; she filled them from part of the
nests in one building.

"How much are eggs bringing now, Mrs. Jacks?"

"They're down this week some. Twenty-nine cents today."

"How much does it cost you to produce a dozen eggs?"

"I figure around nineteen cents, the way feed is right now.
But we manage to average eight to ten cents over costs."

On the way home Jory was doing mental arithmetic.

He asked Mrs. Pettit to stop at the Boulevard store and he
telephoned from there to Lucy Zander, asking her when she
could come out.

"Right away. Is anything wrong?"

"No. Everything's fine. I'm just having an idea."

On the fourth of April Adam and Mrs Pettit were lifting
chirping, comical, downy little chicks from the ventilated
cardboard flats in which the express company had delivered
them. Adam squatted on his heels — watched them stretch,
gape, start running about. They tested the water in the spot-
less earthenware drinking vessels; they crowded and cheeped
and dribbled but they lifted their heads, like parodies of the
old farmflock hens, to let the drops run down their throats.
They discovered the long shallow feeding trays with excite-
ment, falling over each other — scratching and pecking away
industriously, then bustling off again. They soon found the
area of warmed air under the big electric brooder; they squatted
or stretched out there on the peat-moss, falling asleep at once.

"Six hundred and fifty-four, Mr. Jory," Ida Pettit counted,

pushing aside the last crate. "How many did you make out?"

"Three-fifty-eight. That's over a thousand."

"Sure. The hatchery people put in a dozen extra, most always, just for good measure."

"That's a nice thing to do," Adam Jory commented. He thought they must be a fine outfit to do business with.

"You certainly got a strong, healthy lot, Mr. Jory. I don't believe the's more'n three or four yanty ones in the batch."

Adam set an alarm clock and every three hours of the night he got up, put an overcoat over his pajamas and went out to the brooder house.

Under the electric hovers the yellow chicks sprawled in a ring, a few cheeping sleepily. They stirred when he walked in and some of those on the outside of the circle scrambled over the rest and sank down farther in, arousing protests. If he turned his flashlight on them a dozen or so would get up, stretch, scurry to the feed trays or for water. When he clicked the flash off the adventurers twittered and ran back toward the dim light that glowed under the brooder.

Adam sat on his heels, contemplating them happily. He dozed off, once, lulled by the sleepy peeping of the brood, the pleasant warmth of the room and the faint strange odor of the fledgelings. He nodded. Herbert Kinney appeared, carrying a sheaf of papers. Adam's head came up with a jerk. It took him a minute to find himself.

Then he laughed quietly. "Not me!" he said. "Never again!"

He went back to bed.

By that summer he had more than four hundred fine, trim, handsome pullets and the old laying-house repaired, reroofed, sprayed, and equipped with new roosts and batteries of nests. Meantime Joe Pettit had gone shopping and had come back with two young Holsteins, with their first calves. Adam hadn't liked the smell of the buttermilk he had been getting from a neighboring dairy. So Joe had built a cow shed and in a corner of the shored-up barn had put a room for a separator and a motor-driven churn.

266

The cockerels Adam had raised and sold for friers paid for the equipment and his butter was soon meeting part of the little farm's feed bill.

In a disreputable old car that wheezed and banged and clattered and promised to fall apart, but somehow didn't quite keep its promise, a man drove into the Luke Farm lane one day in late summer. Adam wakened from a lazy *siesta* in the half shade of the vine-covered porch and looked out to see a shabby stranger alight, lift a cloth-wrapped package from the seat and start up the walk.

"Brought you a mess of trout, Jory," Billy Wing said.

"Wing! How did you—? Come in. Come on up. Where did you drop from? And what's that you brought?"

"I've been up on the Sespe for a week. I've eaten fish till I breathe through gills. There's a mess here."

He unwrapped the damp cloth and displayed, in a bed of cool-looking leaves, half a dozen speckled rainbows.

"Caught them this morning. Got some cool place where you can put them?"

Ida, summoned, received the donation and disappeared with it. Billy Wing yawned, stretched, pulled out his pipe and pouch and slouched into a low chair.

"Nice little farm you've got here, Jory. Old man Luke's wasn't it?"

"You know everything—and everybody, Billy."

"Used to hunt out this way, when there were doves and quail running thick all over this end of the Valley. Yes, I knew Deacon Luke. Hm-m! You're looking tip-top."

"I never was better, Wing. This—suits me. How did you find me—know I was here?"

"Heard it somewhere. I don't know." Billy Wing scratched a match on a boot-heel and began puffing. "Seems to me you got your start here, Jory, didn't you? I read something about it once, when they were writing you up."

"Yes. I had a letter to a doctor over in Glendale when I

came west. I had bad lungs. Dr. Mathis sent me to old Mr. Luke. After a bit I got the idea of peddling fruit and vegetables in Los Angeles . . . "

He was surprised to find himself telling the whole story.

The two sat looking off from the porch as he talked. Spread before them was the shallow basin of the San Fernando, cross-hatched with highways that were black with cars and trucks. Above the sprawling plant at Burbank, airplanes hummed and chattered. Under the mountains to the south they could see the alien minarets, spires, towers and false-front structures of the two giant motion picture studios. Off to the north the scar made on the tawny folds of the hills by the aqueduct line ran ruler-straight down to its last reservoir. Like the voice of the surf the distant roar of the city beyond the southern hills came to them.

"I got into things, little by little. I had a hand in things. You know, Wing. I had quite a hand in things — in making Los Angeles. It's hard to believe, sometimes. Hard to believe, now."

Wing took his pipe from his teeth.

"You did a good job, Jory — you and the rest of the Band of Hope. I poked fun at you — I cussed you, too, plenty of times. But take it all around you did a good job." He paused, then added, as though to himself: "Finished."

"What's finished?"

"The job. Los Angeles."

"Nonsense! It's just well started."

"In one particular, Jory — size. Of course it will have more people, more factories, more schools. Yes, more and bigger and taller and longer and higher and richer and all the other comparative degrees and a few superlative ones. But the plan is finished. The pattern is set. That was the job the Band of Hope did — that you had a hand in. It was your job and you did it well — and now you're through."

The slouching philosopher chuckled. "Look at her, Jory — at Los Angeles!" he went on. "She's a great, big, bustling, healthy, buxom country girl — and she'll never grow up. We know now what she'll look like, how she'll dress, what she'll say and do when company drops in, what her tastes and capacities are — she won't change. She'll always be a little overdressed, with her shoes worn down a little at the heels, and she'll use some bad grammar and laugh too loudly at your jokes, and she'll embarrass the family pretty often. But man, oh, man, she'll always be handsome and she'll always be generous and friendly and she'll always be fun to take out and one hell of a lively baggage to sleep with!"

Billy Wing pulled himself up from his chair. "There, now, you turned on the faucet and look what gushed out. I came here on an errand, Jory, and it damn' near slipped my mind."

Adam was smiling faintly. "Then it wasn't just to slander the city, Wing?"

"No. It was to tell you about a few friends of mine who have organized a fish-reduction business down at the Harbor. They're going to extract shark-liver-oil and grind fertilizer — I don't know much about the details. But it's going to be a big concern."

Jory said somewhat stiffly: "I haven't any money to invest. And I never was a speculator."

"I'm not talking about speculations. The boys have all the backing they can use. What they are looking for is a high-grade executive to head the shebang. And you're their candidate — and name your own salary."

"Me?" Adam was nonplussed. "After what happened — "

"Hell, Jory, most people know you were railroaded because of your union labor attitude and the Good Government fight. The men who are organizing this fish business are hardheads and they want you on a hardheaded business basis."

"I see." Adam wanted to say that he was glad to know that he was not an outcast, but he couldn't. "Well, thanks, Billy. Right now I'm pretty well satisfied with things as they are. And I've got another idea I'm mulling over."

"There's no hurry. But just remember they want you, most

any time, if you change your mind. Adam Jory is still a big
name in Los Angeles. I'll be getting along. *Adios!"*

Occasionally in the weeks that passed Adam remembered, as
Billy Wing had told him to, that he was wanted. But meantime the Luke Farm was paying part of its way. And there was
that idea he had been mulling over. He had got it from a magazine article. It was a plan for marketing farm produce by
and for a whole community. "It would be a boss scheme for
the Valley," Adam said to himself. He began to work on it.

Those San Fernando Valley residents in the neighborhood
of the old Luke farm were oddly-assorted — retired oldsters,
suburbanites, commuters, Hollywood characters with elaborate
layouts, and practical truck gardeners, orchardists, poultrymen
and operators of small dairies — with one thing in common:
they loved the land and had an urge to live close to it and to
use it. The first group were not dependent on their farms, most
of which were really show places, so they gave away or wasted
a great amount of fine produce. The little-farm owners grew
high-grade specialties but in quantities so small that marketing
them was uneconomical. The overall picture Adam Jory had
seen was reawakening his old instincts as entrepreneur.

His city clothes had long since been hung away. In his
new dress — denim pants, blue work shirt, flopping straw hat,
he came to be known around the countryside as the tall, thin
old gentleman who'd had that trouble a while back but who
had a good idea for a Co-op to sell Valley produce. When they
came to him and asked him to get them started Jory had a
plan all mapped out. Colin Campbell, the writer, furnished
his big truck, Luigi Rigiero drove it, a dozen of them con-
tributed to the first load that went over the Pass into the
city and at the Farmers' Market Luigi sold out clean before
eleven o'clock that morning. Two weeks later there were three
truckloads and two commission men were out trying to buy
John Fetzer's squabs, Gorman's capons and the out-size straw-
berries that were the pride of Fritzi Amananti, the dancer,

who had the old Needham place and wore real pearls (they said) while she irrigated. All three called up Adam Jory and he advised against dealing with Kahn & Sons.

"I'll have somebody in town find out who they are buying for," he said. "Then we'll see if we can't deal direct."

It was Lucy Zander he put on that trail, of course. She not only learned about Kahn & Sons but a good deal about the commission business. She found the Valley growers a couple of big hotels and a club where stewards were willing to pay for quality produce; that's how she began working for the Co-op. Soon she was living in a cabin she fixed up on the old Luke place and practically running the whole concern, with Adam as the unpaid president and business strategist.

No matter what he said Adam Jory could never prevent the tidy Ida Pettit from cleaning up after him, which meant that he could never find anything. He complained to Lucy Zander about it.

She sniffed. "I don't wonder Mrs. Pettit cleans up after you. Look at this room!"

She waved a hand and Adam looked. He had papers, statements, farm journals, market reports, government bulletins all over the big sitting room table, two chairs and the lumpy old sofa that had been in the house since the time of the Lukes. The fireplace was gorged with discarded materials, for Jory still made it a practice to destroy business and personal papers when they had served their purpose, instead of consigning them to a wastebasket. Yes, the room was cluttered.

Lucy solved the problem, as usual.

"I'll have Luigi Rigiero come through town on his next trip and bring you out a desk and a filing cabinet. You can't expect any woman to keep house in such a junk-yard as this!"

That week the desk, the filing cabinet and an ancient swivel chair were delivered and Adam spent all his odd hours organizing himself and his business effects. He was so absorbed in this agreeable operation that it was several days before he

271

realized that the three old-fashioned pieces of office furniture
were the ones with which he had started his career. The
clumsy, sturdy roll top desk, the cumbersome swivel chair and
the oak cabinet had been in the little cubbyhole he had rented
after leaving Major Oddie and the *Daily Sun*. He had bought
them from the former tenant; no telling how long they had
been in use even then.

He challenged Lucy Zander with this discovery.

"That's right," she said, curtly. Adam thought that she
waited for him to say something more; when he didn't she
went on, in her brisk fashion: "I never did believe in throwing
good furniture away."

"But I understood everything was auctioned off. And I don't
remember seeing this desk and chair after we left the Nostrander Block."

"No?" she countered. "Well, there it is, anyway."

He thought of it after she had left. He realized that she had
seemed to expect further questions — that she had hesitated
and looked almost frightened. She had hurried away, as
though relieved. He understood, now. Of course; she had bid
these pieces in at the sale of the Jory Building office fixtures,
with her own money. Sentiment, of course! But a kind of sentiment that had in it something fierce, dominating, protective.

That young lawyer, Earl Tomblin, had told him that if he
would hire the schoolgirl, daugher of Zander, the petty thief,
he would get loyalty, whether she could spell or not.

Loyalty. Yes — and a good deal more. Adam Jory ran
a hand down the slow curve of the old desk gently. His throat
felt dry and his eyes stung. He was glad he was alone. For
there were tears in his eyes.

A mile or so north of the Luke farm stood an abandoned
house, behind a crumbling field-stone wall, surrounded by the
sere bleakness of a dead lawn and backed by several out-
buildings, a neglected orchard and a fenced enclosure that had
been once an elaborate layout of kennels where blooded Ker-

ry terriers had been reared. It was known as the Waltheim
Place. The builder had been a hack writer back in Kansas City
who had blundered into radio writing, had been given a whopp-
ing contract, had rushed to Hollywood and into an extravagant
life which had seemed to call for a blue-and-silver convertible
coupe, custom-built, and the Valley "studio."

It was an old story in the region. Oscar Waltheim had found
his wife dowdy, old-fashioned and countrified and his two
small children subject to measles, whooping coughs, a dislike
for Hollywood moppets and a yen to go barefoot all summer.
He had also found a platinum blonde who painted her nails a
deep magenta. Presently he sent the dowdy family back to
Missouri, on a generous allowance, and brought the exotic
blonde to the Valley studio. It turned out that she was a
dipsomaniac, and other unpleasant things. The writer tried
to match her drink for drink, became fumbling and quarrel-
some and lost his radio contract. Within the hour his frail
Lilith had retained a lawyer and tied up everything he owned,
most of which, as it proved, was in partnership with a bank and
three finance companies. Waltheim and she between them
managed to get the little farm into a tight knot of litigation —
and for four years the seasons, the elements, stray tramps and
mischievous boys played hell with the costly 10-acre property.

Adam Jory had heard vaguely of all this; when he began
to come and go he appraised the place, judging that it would
be a first-rate speculation, once it was pried loose from en-
tanglements. But he was through with speculations.

Lucy Zander had been watching it, too; one day she drove
Adam by and they inspected it. Yes, a nice little farm. The
house was well built, there was a considerable investment in
fencing, rock-work and water-piping; there was a fine, deep
well and a big tank house. The lawns and garden beds
could be brought back and a year of care would restore the
orchard. Lucy agreed that it was a shame he didn't have the
money to snap it up, the minute it was offered for sale, which
of course it would be some day.

To Jory's amazement, a week or so later, Lucy, half-timidly, half-defiantly, announced that she had bought it herself.

"You bought it?" Jory was about to ask: "What with?" But he stopped himself in time. "What can you do with it? It's too big for you. And it will cost a couple of thousand to put it into shape."

"I'll manage it somehow," Lucy said. She was nervous and queer about the business, Jory thought. "What I want to know is, will you tend to getting it fixed up? I'm no hand at that sort of thing." Lucy went on, hurriedly: "I've already found a renter for it."

Adam smiled. "Oh, that's it. I hope your renter can use four extra bedrooms and that big studio room."

"They'll make out. It's a big family."

"Of course I'll tend to it. Fact is, I'd like to do it."

Lucy fidgeted, toyed with her shabby handbag, looked like she was guilty of some crime. "They're sort of anxious to get settled. Do you suppose you could — well, hurry it along a little?"

Adam frowned, trying to make out what ailed the dried up little spinster. A suspicion crossed his mind. Good lord, Lucy wasn't planning to get married?

That was too ridiculous.

"I'll do the best I can, Lucy," he said. "I'll get right at it Monday."

All the time the work of repair and restoration was going on Miss Zander's aberration persisted. She was busier than ever she had been, which was saying a good deal. She went to the city more often. She seemed to avoid Adam and she showed no interest in what was being done to the Waltheim place. She had that timid, guilty air and Adam imagined that she wasn't eating regularly and was getting, if possible, thinner.

Meantime, though, he was having a grand time with the rejuvenation job.

Matt Trent, who had rented the Luke place for so many

years and now had a lease farther up the Valley, was putting the abandoned orchard into shape. When the last of the painters was out of the house and Adam was having the driveway re-graveled and rolled, Trent reported that his work was finished, too.

"It's better than new, Mr. Jory," the practical young farmer said. "And if Miss Zander's renters don't show up, my wife would like to take it off her hands."

Adam reported the offer.

"All right," Lucy Zander said, abstractedly. "If there's any hitch I'll let the Trents know."

There was certainly something queer about the whole enterprise. Adam couldn't make it out. After all, people Lucy Zander's age *did* get married. In her case, hard to imagine it. But why?

He gave it up.

"Well, your renters can move in any time now, Lucy. Zeb Callendar's painters got out today and there's only that light fixture to install — the one that was delayed."

"That's fine." Miss Zander was leaving for the city and was hurried and almost curt. "Don't forget that there's a Co-op directors' meeting this afternoon."

She scurried away.

For a little sparrow of a woman, Adam thought, she was a miracle of energy. She went from morning till night, tireless and indefatigable. In the years she had developed into a sort of wispy and kindhearted slave driver. She seemed to cherish an illusion that they were all afraid of her — the Pettits, the Co-op employes and even Adam himself. Occasionally one of her scoldings, proddings, grillings would leave him chuckling — for he had learned to chuckle.

"No. I guess Lucy isn't in love," he thought, now.

He was never to guess that she had been in love — ever since the day she had put the first little nosegay on his desk.

On that Sunday morning Adam was working on his farm

275

accounts. The old roll-top desk stood beside a wide window through which he could see the sun-warmed Valley, half-country, half-city, and wholly Los Angeles. Yes, he had had a hand in bringing the Aqueduct from the Sierras to this rabbit-ridden waste and in annexing the whole region to the city in order to make legitimate a dubious secret deal between a dozen of the insiders. His *Messenger* had published the scandal of that slick enterprise; it had been his first offense against his fellows that had led on and on to his place in a courtroom dock. They had never forgiven him. Well, the Aqueduct deal, the other boosters' projects, his own trouble — they had turned out for the best. Good and bad, right and wrong — who could tell? The years would. Billy Wing, slouching, casual, cynical, caustic — the observant Wing had said that those boosters and boot-strap tuggers had done a good job. Yes, they had built Los Angeles.

Adam brought his mind back to the accounts.

The totals said that, in the past month, he had made $94.80, net. There would be a small member's check from the Co-op on the first of the month — call it a hundred dollars. Something like $1200 a year and the little farm improving every day. The income-tax phrase came to his mind — *"earned income."* What had he *earned* in the old days when he had been at the top of his success — when Lucy Zander had banked tens of thousands from the Jory enterprises?

There was a letter on the roll-top desk from the Pacific Fisheries & Reduction Company, the outfit of which Billy Wing had told him. Had he changed his mind? Would he consider $35,000 a year and a ten-percent interest in the booming young industry?

Adam leaned back in his old swivel chair, shaking his head. No, thanks, gentlemen. No, he had had to live to be seventy to find out what it was that he wanted to do, but he knew, now.

Outside, little Lucy Zander drove into the yard in her dented old car. She sat in it for a while, straight and absorbed.

When she got out she started up the walk briskly, at her usual gait. Then she hesitated, stopped, turned back. Adam wondered if something was wrong with her. He was about to go to the door when she seemed to make a decision. He heard her come in by the front door, letting the screen bang.

"You in, Mr. Jory?"

"Sure, Lucy. Come in."

She entered, her lips pressed into a straight line and her face tense.

"Is something the matter, Lucy?"

She gulped. Then she said, in a strange, harsh voice: "Yes, there is something the matter. Adam Jory, you're the stubbornest, blindest, troublesomest human God ever made and somebody had to do something about it. So I did. And now I'm glad of it!"

Jory was nonplussed. He tried to think what errand he could have forgotten — what blunder he had been guilty of to drive Lucy Zander to this unprecedented outburst. "If it's about those eggs, Lucy — ," he began, mildly.

Miss Zander sniffed. "Eggs! Fiddlesticks! It's little Timmy Young. It's Judith's boy."

It was the last thing he could have expected. "You mean Judith Rountree?"

"Judith Young, yes. Her boy never was strong. Some old fool of a doctor told them he'd outgrow it. A few weeks back they took him to Dr. Gerson and found it was the boy's lungs."

"Good God!"

It was like a blow in the face for Adam Jory. In all his thought of Judith, all his loneliness for her, all his helpless concern, he had never thought of this. He should have thought first of it. His own frail mother had inherited the "lung fever" that had killed her mother, the Civil War-time bride. It had burned in him — sent him to California — to this very Luke farm. And now, unaccountably dormant through a generation, it had struck Judith's son!

Adam settled back, his hands gripping the arms of the

old office chair. "It isn't too late, Lucy? A child—he can be cured, surely."

"Yes. But let me tell it my own way, or I'll get flustered and leave something out."

"Go ahead. How did you come to know Judith and the boy?"

"She married Walter Young's son, Steve. And I got acquainted with them through the checks you sent every week, after Mr. Young's trouble." Lucy colored and stumbled over her words. "That's how I — it was then I met Judith's mother."

Adam said, quietly: "I see now. I guess Mrs. Rountree told you that she and I—"

"She didn't tell me anything, Adam Jory. How can you think such a thing?" Lucy fidgeted. "I do wish you wouldn't interrupt or put words into my mouth. You get me all flustered."

"I'm sorry, Lucy. Don't mind me."

"Where was I? Oh, about little Timoteo, Judith's boy. I made friends with him right away, from the first. I loved him, from the day I saw him, when he was three weeks old. And when I saw how puny he was I tried to get Steve and Judith to let me do something for him. I wanted to get him out here, into the country, where he could have milk and eggs and play in the sunshine. They were nice about it, but they're proud, Adam. It wasn't till Dr. Gerson told them what was the matter that they would listen to me. And so—"

Adam Jory looked up quickly. "And so — you bought the Waltheim place!"

"I bought it. But not with my money, because I didn't have enough." Lucy Zander's confusion overcame her again. "Adam, I guess you've forgotten. That secret drawer in your old desk there."

"Secret drawer? Oh! Yes, I'd forgotten it." He swung around in his chair. For a minute he could not recall how the mechanism worked, then he pulled out the little hidden compartment.

278

He had not opened it for thirty years, but now memories
came sharply back to him, as though it had been only yesterday. There was a crumpled orange-colored ribbon bearing the
legend: *"La Fiesta de las Flores* — 1895 Official."* His marriage license. The check he had given for the Aliso Street
property when the Jory Burner Company had been started
— his first major venture. The stub of a railroad ticket —
souvenir of an outing he and Beulah had taken on the Bal-
loon Route in the days when that swing through the orange
belt was popular. A clipping about the organization of his
first oil company, from which Golconda had grown. Another
describing what the *Daily Sun* had described as "the Jory-
Nostrander nuptials." . . . Three notes in Beulah Rountree's
schoolgirl handwriting. Phrases from one of them jumped to
his eyes: " . . . . a baby girl;" . . . . "I've named her Judith."
And, about money: " . . . Mr. Noll will always know where
we are."

Lucy's face was crimson but she confronted him stoutly.
"Before I sent the desk and things out here to you I cleaned it
out — and I opened that drawer by accident. I couldn't help
seeing — I mean, I read enough, without meaning to. You've
got to believe me, Adam. I never *snooped* in my whole life!"

Adam smiled. "Of course I believe you, Lucy. After all
these years I'm glad you know the only real secret I ever had."

"Anyway, that's how I came to remember about the hundred
dollar bill you had given Herbert Kinney orders to send to
the bank every month. For twelve years or more it had been
lying there. Mr. Noll had told me that — that it wasn't being
drawn out any more."

"I remember, now. Yes. I had been told that, too, but
then my trouble came along and I never thought of it again."

"When I knew — when I guessed, from what I saw in the
drawer, what that money was for I wasn't sure what to do. I
didn't want you to know I'd poked into your affairs. There
was no one to talk to about it, don't you see?"

He nodded. "I see. Not even Mrs. Rountree."

"How could I talk to *her* about it? Well, I — I just plunged right ahead. I used my power-of-attorney and drew out that money. You can blame everything on me. And I won't care. There."

Jory saw now. The pieces fitted together. He stood up and crossed the room. He lifted Lucy Zander and faced her, his big hands resting on her thin, narrow shoulders.

"My dear," he said, in a husky voice, "I've made a lot of investments in my life but only one is still paying dividends. That's the investment I made in you, when you were nineteen and put flowers on my desk."

He bent and kissed her.

Lucy gasped and turned a more fiery red than before. She laughed weakly and the laugh choked her. She turned her head away, fumbling with the big handkerchief he lent her.

Adam shook her gently.

"And now," he said, in a changed tone, briskly, "how soon can we get little Timmy and the rest of them out to the new place?"

She stopped in the middle of a sniff.

"Get them out? Didn't I tell you? They *are* out. Last night. Furniture and all. And if you'll get your hat we'll go over there. They're all waiting for us — all five of them."

"Five?"

"Of course. Beulah Rountree and Steve and Judith and little Timoteo — and Amata Young, Steve's mother. I *told* you it was a big family."

*   *   *   *

A tall, thin old man and a wiry, healthy, olive-skinned boy of twelve stood on the roadside watching the painters put the finishing touches to a big sign in the open field across Santa Susannah Road.

THIS PROPERTY FOR SALE
Ideal For Subdivision

THE W. A. ROWLAND CO.

Population of L. A.

Now   1,504,277
1950   2,500,000

The boy pointed to the bold prophecy.

"Two million and a half! Do you think she'll make it, Uncle Adam?"

The old man chuckled.

"She always has, Timoteo. She always has."

www.ingramcontent.com/pod-product-compliance
Lightning Source LLC
Chambersburg PA
CBHW020606260626
47157CB00003B/887